I0770865

SAFE WITH US

ETTA LANE

To the girls who can never have just one.
Go ahead.
Indulge.

Dear Reader

This book contains some darker themes with depictions of PTSD, parental drug abuse (off page), and character death (on page). There is stalking and kidnapping that occurs on page. There are mentions of attempted sexual assault. While these scenes were written to create a more vivid, in-depth story, they may be triggering to some readers. Mental health is something that I highly value, which is why I let it play out throughout the book. Your mental health is important and if you cannot read through others facing PTSD, stalking, and nightmares, then this may not be the book for you. Please know your triggers and read with that in mind.

Love, Etta

PROLOGUE
BRIAN - AGE 24

My parents have always loved to host parties, and my baby brother graduating high school was as good as any to throw a huge one. I made sure to fly up for a few days to watch him walk across the stage and celebrate this milestone with him. Of course, his partner in crime was there with him. I'm honestly not sure if Danny would have even graduated without Kelli. He's not dumb, quite the opposite, but the whole classroom setting has never been his thing. He and Kelli graduated yesterday, and today is their party. Kelli's mom didn't plan anything for her, so my parents added her to this party, making her feel special like always.

"Can you sneak me one of those?" Danny leans against the deck railing next to me, pointing to my beer.

I eye him over the beer in my hand. "Nope."

"So much for being the cool, big brother." He rolls his eyes, looking over the yard and the people milling about, talking.

"Where'd Kelli go?" I ask, trying to keep my voice even and disinterested.

"Hiding under the tree. Her mom decided to work at the last minute and didn't even show."

My face twists up in anger. That girl has never asked for anything, and to have her mother ditch her, yet again, it wasn't fair to Kelli. "I'll go talk to her," I say before heading around the yard, avoiding all my parent's friends. I hate the awkward small talk they make and the 'thank you for your service' comments that I constantly get. I push some of the low-hanging willow branches to the side, and sure enough, Kelli is leaning back against the trunk, hiding under here, away from the world.

"Hey, Kel." I sit down next to her bumping my shoulder into hers.

Her quiet voice wraps around me, "Hey, B."

"Wanna tell me why you're hiding under here when there's a party in your honor happening just a few feet away?"

She adjusts the straps of her sundress. "It's not really for me and we both know it, not that I don't love and appreciate your parents for adding me into the mix. I'm just taking a moment to myself."

Emotion wells up in my throat. Kelli has been around my family ever since she was six when Danny declared her his best friend. My parents have tried to show up for her when her mother didn't and I have tried to look out for and protect her in the way a big brother should. But sitting here under the tree, seeing her in person for the first time in two years, she didn't look like a little sister to me. She had a beautiful, light pink sundress with painted nails to match. Her blonde hair was curled beautifully around her head, but her blue eyes held a look beyond her eighteen years. They were sad and tired, yet were still the most striking thing I had ever seen.

I wanted to take away her pain, and while we were

younger, I would have had no problem scooping her into my arms for a hug. Now, though, I felt like I couldn't. Like it would be different. So, I tried to distract her instead, "Are you still thinking of going to nursing school? That's what you mentioned the last time we talked."

Her whole face lights up as she responds, "Yeah, I'm going to Boston College with Danny and doing the nursing program there. I've known for a long time that I wanted to be in a career field where I can help people, and nursing just feels right."

"I am so proud of you. You've come so far from the little girl chasing Danny and I around the house, holding the snake you found in the garden." Her abrupt laugh is husky and rolls through me.

"I forgot all about that!" She shrieks, burying her head in her hands.

"My mom was not happy," I chuckle with her, "But look at you now. A beautiful and strong woman who is about to take the world by storm." My fingers gravitate to her hair of their own accord, twirling a curl around my finger and tugging on it. "College is going to be so good for you. You'll get to experience new things, meet new people, and find yourself outside of this town. I may not be around as much anymore, but I am still here, rooting for you every step of the way."

She's quiet for a moment, her piercing blue eyes locked on mine. "You know, we had a similar conversation about six years ago in this same spot when you were leaving for basic training. I'm proud of you, too, B. I know being away from home is hard, but you are making a difference every day you put that uniform on. You inspire me; I hope I can do the same every time I put on scrubs. I'm excited for college, I just feel like it's missing something."

I understood that statement. Looking into her eyes, seeing her as an adult and not a child, I suddenly get the feeling of something missing as well. My words feel small leaving my mouth, "Maybe someday you'll find what it is."

She leans in closer, her delicate hand sliding into mine. "I hope so." With that, she stands up, pulling me up with her, and leads us out of the tangle of branches hanging low to the ground. We re-enter the party, all while her hand stays wrapped in mine.

1

KELLI

love my job, I love my job, I love my job. If I keep that mantra on repeat in my head, I may just make it through this day. While I truly love being a trauma nurse most days, today is not one of them. I have already been here for seven hours, dealt with a foreign body removal, stab wound, heart attack, and we just received the call for three car crash victims incoming. Dr. McNeil mentioned that it sounds like one will need to be pronounced on arrival, and one is a small child. These are the hard cases that make for hard days. The growing sirens outside the ambulance bay have my feet in motion to prepare.

The ambulance doors fly open as the EMTs unload the first patient with a paramedic performing CPR. The gurney holds a woman who couldn't be older than twenty-five. Dr. McNeil sent the new resident and his team to take over compressions, rushing to bay one with her to see if they could revive her. As the next ambulance comes to a stop, sirens still blaring, Dr. McNeil takes the next gurney with a screaming little girl strapped on it and rushes her into bay three with two nurses. That leaves the senior nurse, Natalie, and I to handle the last patient who just happens to be a very belligerent man. We could hear him yelling at the EMTs before they even had the ambulance doors open. He is aggressive with all of us, arms flailing, as the paramedics try to do the hand off to us. Natalie made eye contact with me over the gurney; yeah, it was going to be a long rest of the day. "Sir, my name is Kelli, can you calm down so we can get you into a bed and do our assessment? It looks like you have one nasty gash on your head." We grab fresh gloves as we help wheel him into the room.

"That bitch pulled out in front of me," he slurs and stumbles into me as we transfer him from the gurney to the bed in bay forty. "It's her own fault I hit her. Swear I'm going to sue her for this." Natalie and I keep our mouths shut as she moves to one side to get him hooked up to the monitors and I start a central line on the other for a blood draw. Natalie presses some gauze to the cut on his forehead and he rears back screaming. "OW! You can't just put your hands on me like that. I want a new nurse!"

"I'm sorry, sir, I need to get your cut cleaned to see how bad it is. You may need stitches. I am the Nurse Manager on staff and the only nurse currently available. If you can't be compliant for me, you can wait, but it may be quite a while before someone else can come in. You're bleeding pretty badly. I would hate for you to have to sit here bleeding for a few hours," Natalie grits out through a tight smile. I can see his glassy eyes narrow, his fist clenching as he rears his arm back starting to swing. My reflexes kick in and before I fully realize what I'm doing I shove Natalie out of the way as the punch lands on my chin. I stumble back as Natalie screams and runs out to get security. The patient stands from the bed and lunges in my direction. Adrenaline is coursing through me as he reaches for my scrub top. I cock my hand back, punching him in the stomach without thinking, then run toward the nurse's station before he can try to strike me again.

Everything from there happens in a blur. Security rushes into the room and subdues the man before I even make it to the nurse's station, clutching my jaw. The cops arrive and take our statements, my jaw still aching fiercely. The only positive is that the patient was severely overweight with a large gut, so besides an ache, my wrist and knuckles were fine from the punch to his stomach.

Two hours later, with an ice pack still held to my face, I find myself in the head of PR's office with the Chief Nursing Officer (CNO) and Dr. McNeil. For being in a hospital, it was ridiculously nice in here. He has a couch with big throw pillows along one wall, a wall of windows overlooking the city on another, and a huge mahogany desk. Dr. McNeil sits on the couch, but the CNO sits in one of the two chairs in front of the PR man with me. "How are you feeling, Kelli?" Ms. Quinn, the CNO asks.

"All things considered, pretty good. The officers said I wouldn't be in any legal trouble because I hit him out of self-defense. I wasn't trying to be combative, but I am not about to catch slack from the hospital for this. I would do it again in a heartbeat." I stare with my best no-nonsense look. I was not going to lose my job over being assaulted.

"Absolutely not!" the PR man assures me while leaning over his desk. I really should have paid attention when he said his name. "We called you in here because another patient happened to catch the altercation on their phone. The door and curtain of the bay were still open, which again you are not in trouble for, but it was all caught very clearly. Unfortu-nately, that patient immediately posted it to social media and it got picked up by our local news channel." He winces. "They reached out to us already and would like an interview with you. I think it is the best move for the hospital to smooth this out. We'd like to paint you as the hero versus a volatile staff member, if you catch my drift."

You have got to be kidding me. "I didn't get into this profession to be a hero. Taking a punch for Natalie hardly would classify as a hero, and honestly, hurts like hell. Can we just let them run the video and you can put out a statement or something? That's kind of your job, isn't it?" I liked my privacy; I kind of relished it in fact. No part of this sounded like a good idea to me.

Dr. McNeil clears his throat from behind us. "I have to agree with Craig here, Kelli. A statement is not enough, they will search and find your name. This information will get out either way. Getting ahead of it would benefit you and the hospital. Plus, it's the Monday night news, who is really going to be watching? Ms. Quinn and I have talked as well and she will move staff around so you can have the next week off. Paid, of course, if you agree to this. We think it would be best to let things cool off around the altercation."

I roll my eyes at his smirk. There's a reason he is the nurse's favorite doctor, a whole week off is unheard of. "This week off better be worth it, and can I have a hair brush first?"

The news crew sent over a cameraman and anchor to interview me within an hour. As I waited for them to set up, I met with more of the PR team as they prepped me on appropriate things to say and HR came down to have a talk with me, as well. My shit-tastic day felt like it was never going to end.

When I was finally able to leave work, I texted Danny and told him to meet me at my house with wine when he got off work. What were childhood best friends for, if not to vent about the hard days, and also get drunk with while watching yourself on the news? My jaw was still throbbing as I poured my second shot of tequila when I heard my front door open. "Honey, I'm home," Danny called out in a sing-song voice. "Now what was so important that I had to rush he-" his voice cuts off as he gets into the kitchen and sees me. "What the hell happened to your face?"

"Funny story, I had an unruly patient today and my interaction with him landed me a bruised jaw, a week off of work, and apparently the highlight reel in the news tonight." I blew out an exhausted breath.

"I guess that's as good of a reason as any to get drunk on a Monday." He pours us wine while I put the TV on and explain how bizarre my day had gone. We cuddled up on the couch as I overdramatized the incident, which had us both in hysterics. We were both on our second glass when the news finally ran the story.

Local Mercy Hospital nurse, Kelli Winters, gave us an exclusive interview after a video of her protecting a fellow nurse earlier today has gone viral. While she says she was just doing her job, I have to commend her for being a hero. I don't think many people would take a hit to protect a fellow employee and handle the situation as well as she did. The following clip is the viral video> Warning: it is a little graphic.

"Hells bells babe, he really clonked you. Impressive reflexes though, those kickboxing classes are clearly paying off." Danny laughs to himself clinking our glasses together.

"I'm so glad that my pain is entertaining you, jerk." I push his shoulder "Ooh, here's my interview, time to chug!"

"I really appreciate the kind things being said, but I was just acting on instinct. No one should be unsafe in their workplace, but unfortunately sometimes that happens in the Emer-

gency Room, despite the incredible security at Mercy. I would have pushed any of my co-workers out of the way and want to thank security for getting there so fast and keeping us all safe."

"Would you like to make a comment about that punch to the gut at the end?"

"Not only will I protect my co-workers but I will also protect myself. We are taught to do no harm in school and I take that very seriously, violence is not something that I take lightly. That's all I have to say about that, thank you."

"You heard it here first folks, humble heroes at the hospital. Back to you, Alice."

I grabbed the remote and clicked off the television. I had officially had my fifteen seconds of fame and I hated it. "I better not get anyone trying to talk to me or recognizing me from this," I mumble into my wine glass, definitely past tipsy, as Danny pulls his phone out of his pocket. Brian's name flashes on the screen before he answers it on speaker. Brian's angry voice cuts through before Danny can even say a word. "What the hell Danny, is Kelli okay?"

"I'm fine, Brian, you can cool the protective big brother act. It was one hit and nothing is broken," I cut in. He lost the right to worry about me a long time ago. The fact that he bothered to check in on me, without actually talking to me, really pisses me off too.

"You should see the bruise forming. It's going to be one ugly mother for a while," Danny adds in unhelpfully.

"Why wasn't he already restrained before that? He was clearly drunk and volatile! You should be safe there. Are you sure you're okay? Do you need anything?" Brian is Danny's older brother and had always been a fierce protector of Danny and I. He is six years older than us, but from the first time I went to their house in first grade and he found out I had no siblings, he took on that role of big brother for me. I spent a lot of time at their house growing up. It was just my mom and me, and she worked long hours to support us. I looked up to him, he never treated me as a nuisance as I followed him around constantly asking him to play with us.

When I was 16, their family had a Christmas party where Brian surprised the family and showed up on leave from the Army. He had been somewhere in the Middle East, but wasn't able to disclose more than that. That visit was the first time my little school girl crush started feeling like more. I would never tell Danny, but Brian was no longer a pseudo big brother in my eyes after that. The older we have gotten, the more my attraction to him has grown.

Four years ago, he had a week of leave from another deployment that he spent with his family. I was invited to family dinner with them a few times over that week. That's when I realized things might finally be changing for him as well. He made sure to sit by me at the table, his knee often bumping into mine. His eyes traveled to my lips during a few conversations; that didn't go unnoticed. The last night before he had to head back to his deployment, we went out for dinner and drinks with Danny and his husband Alex. The two of them headed home right after dinner, but Brian asked me to stay. We stayed at that table for hours, talking and laughing and getting to know the people we had grown into. When it got late, I got bold and asked him if he wanted to come back to my place.

I'd had a crush on him for most of my life. I was going to take the chance, now that he might finally feel it too. We sat on my couch talking about what we saw for our future. We were surprised to find we both wanted the same things. I told him how I felt and he told me he has felt that same draw to me since day one. As time went on that draw has turned into attraction and pride for who I had become. We talked until the sun came up, and when he left, he kissed me and told me that this would be his last deployment. He was coming for me when he got discharged. We emailed daily for weeks after that until one day the emails just stopped coming. It's been four years and he has yet to come for me and my heart has yet to fully recover.

"Kelli?" Brian's voice comes from the phone again.

"Sorry, I was spacing out. I am fine, promise. I don't need anything. Thanks for checking on me though, B."

Danny rolls his eyes. "I will keep an eye on her, and I'll call you later this week. I have a friend who wants to upgrade their security system and I want to put them in contact with you. Talk soon bro." He ended the call and slid his phone back in his pocket. "Are you sure you don't need anything? I hate leaving you alone all the time."

"I'll be fine. It was one punch to the jaw. At least this happened when the weather was nice so I can work on the house some more this week. It's the perfect excuse to spend some time in the yard. Might even take a bubble bath one of these nights."

He pins me with a deadpan stare, "or you could relax like a normal person who gets a week off after working 60-hour weeks for months on end. Seriously, Kel, you deserve to have down time sometimes, you know? You are always pushing yourself so hard. I wish you would give yourself the time to rest and recharge."

My shoulder nudges his as I sip some more of my wine. "Gardening is relaxing to me. I promise I will take some time to myself this week."

Danny didn't stay much longer, eager to get home to Alex, and he had to work in the morning. I bought this home three years ago and while I loved it, it was starting to feel lonely and empty. I didn't have the time or energy to date, but I suppose I needed to start putting in the effort. Twenty-six wasn't exactly old, but it seemed everyone around me was settling down and I wanted someone to share my life with, especially on nights like tonight.

2

KELLI

y week of vacation was flying by. Thankfully, the weather stayed nice so I was able to deep clean the house and get a bunch of yard-work done. My flower beds and hydrangea bushes haven't looked this nice since I moved in. My walls and baseboards were scrubbed clean, and I even cleaned behind my fridge, which hasn't been moved since I moved in. Brian sent me a grocery delivery Tuesday despite my protests of being fine. It included a candle, bubble bath, and bath salts, which was sweet but weird since Danny swore he didn't tell him I mentioned taking some baths. His text said it was to help me relax so I could stay home and avoid the looks I would inevitably get at the grocery store, courtesy of my purple chin. For not being around each other much the last ten years, he clearly still knows me and my recluse tendencies well.

Working as a nurse meant I was either working or sleeping, and I thrived on that lifestyle. Having too much down time meant too much thinking time, and that always led to me thinking about Brian. This week, especially with his delivery, meant I spent most of my time with him on my mind. Four years, and my heart still longed for him, despite him treating me like an afterthought. Or a thought at all.

Four days of cleaning and gardening and I was itching to get back to work. As the Friday evening sun was setting, I decided to enjoy a beer on my porch. My little wicker chairs weren't much, but the green cushions and white pillows were adorable and comfy. The orange and yellow sky shone through my neighbor's homes, streaks of color shining over my small porch, making me long for a clear view to enjoy the full sunset. As the sun continued to set, I nursed my beer, scrolling through my Instagram when a direct message came through.

It was from someone I wasn't following. Their username was 'xMr.Wintersx'. The hairs on my neck stood up as I read the message.

I like a woman who fights back. Makes things more exciting. Would you fight me, Kelli? – Mr. W

What. The. Hell. This is why I didn't want to do that stupid interview. I clicked on the profile which had no followers and no posts. Their profile photo was a screenshot of me from the news. I immediately reported and blocked the profile after taking a screenshot of the message and sent it to Danny.

Danny: Bet you're really regretting that interview now, make sure you block his creepy ass.

Kelli: Reported him too.

Danny: Good, let me know if he tries to reach out again, I have guys for that. *winky face*

I'm not sure what that means, but his husband is a police

officer so I'm sure he knows all sorts of people. The bright side is that, so far, besides a few texts from coworkers, this was the only person who seemed to have paid attention to or seen that little news segment.

The weekend was filled with binge watching trash TV, reading romance books and dinner with Danny and Alex. Monday came all too soon, and thankfully, things were totally normal at work. No one mentioned the incident or the interview, and no one died on my watch. Ten hours on my feet after a week off exhausted me, but it felt nice to be back. Pulling up to my home that evening, I sat in my car for a few minutes trying to muster up the energy to get my trashcan and mail from the curb before heading inside. Trudging on tired legs, I walked to the mailbox first, and then carted the trash can to the side of the house. Once inside, I dropped my purse and keys on the entry console, then flipped through the mail as I headed to the kitchen. It was mostly junk except for a plain envelope with only my name on the front. Standing at the island, I flipped it over and ripped it open, pulling out the little card inside. Written in neat black handwriting was another creepy note from Mr. W.

YOUR BLUE SCRUBS MAKE YOUR EYES SHINE. MY HAND AROUND YOUR THROAT WOULD MAKE THEM GLITTER.

—MR. W

Hands shaking, I slowly stepped back from the counter

trying to keep my breathing under control. I grabbed my phone from my pocket and ran down the hall to lock myself in my room as I called Danny. He answered on the third ring, "Hey babe, how was your first day back?"

My voice cracked as I tried to swallow the lump in my throat. Sinking back against my bedroom door, I let myself slide down to the floor. "I think I need Alex's help. I think I might have a stalker."

He was quiet a moment and I could picture his jaw working back and forth. "What do you mean you think you have a stalker?"

"I got a note in my mailbox signed from what I think is the same Mr. W that messaged me on Friday. He mentioned my blue scrubs that I wore today." I could hear his sharp inhale on the other end.

"Where are you now?"

"I'm locked in my bedroom. This is stupid, I am stronger than this, but he knows where I live. He's watching me." I wiped at the errant tear that escaped.

"Do not move or leave that room. Alex and I will be there in 10. I'll use my key to get in, so don't be alarmed. When I hang up, I want you to call Brian immediately and tell him you need an updated security system with cameras." The worry in his voice was evident.

"Okay, see you guys soon."

By the time Alex and Danny yelled that they were here, Brian had set up a plan and told me he would have my new system delivered by Wednesday evening and a crew out on Thursday to install it. I was impressed with how quickly he set it up, but he simply replied that owning the company meant he could create the schedules however he saw fit. I lied and told him everything was fine and that I just wanted an upgrade. He sounded worried, but I could take care of myself. I had been doing it for years. I didn't want him to see me as the little sister he needed to protect anymore.

I stood up, unlocking my door and met Danny and Alex in the kitchen. They both turned to me as I walked in, their eyes showing a mix of worry and pity. Danny sat up and came over, wrapping me in a tight hug. I showed them the envelope and note and explained to Alex the previous message I had as well. Alex used a tissue to grab it and stuffed it in a sandwich bag from under the sink. "I really think we need to call the police on this, Kel," Alex said as he looked at me with troubled eyes.

"I did. I called you." Alex has been working with the police department for seven years, making detective last year, which was exactly why I had called him and Danny.

"I'm not here in an official capacity, so I can't make a case and can't run this for prints. If this person escalates the situation, it would be best for you, and for legal reasons, to have a case open and ready to nail them with," he pleaded.

"I am getting my new security system delivered Wednesday and I will make sure the cameras cover the mailbox. If he reaches out again, I promise I will call the police. I will even keep that note in the bag just in case, okay?" I didn't see the point in opening a case now. I didn't have much to go on, really just one note since I couldn't say for sure the message was from the same person. I'm sure my new cameras will deter them anyway.

Danny sighed, "Fine, but you are staying with us until they're delivered on Wednesday. Go pack a bag; I'm not budging on this."

On the drive home from work Wednesday, my bone deep exhaustion was really hitting. Even though I knew I was safe with Danny and Alex, sleep didn't really come easy. Even with my anxiety, I am looking forward to crawling into my own bed tonight. Things at the hospital kept my brain distracted during the day, but at night is where everything comes crashing down around me. I haven't told any of my co-workers about the note; Alex and Danny are blowing things out of proportion. Yes, the note and the message were creepy, if not vaguely threatening, but I haven't heard anything else from this person. It freaks me out that he knows where I live. I am sure it was not all that hard to find though. With my new security system being installed tomorrow, he would have to be an idiot to come back by. I will be fine, and everything will go back to normal.

I haven't heard from Brian yet today so I'm not sure if my system has already been delivered. As I turned down my road, a black truck was parked on the street in front of my house. Maybe I take it all back, my system isn't installed yet and that could be him now. I slowed a little, making the snap decision to drive past my house and back to Danny's. As my car passed the back of the truck though, I saw the triple S logo on the truck door. It was Brian's company, Stirling Security Systems, and there was a man leaning against the front bumper talking on his phone.

He must be the one delivering the system, so I pull into my driveway. As I put the car in park, I reached into my purse and wrapped my hand around the switchblade just in case. Stepping out of my SUV, I turned to the man that was still on the phone and slowly walking up my driveway toward me when my breath caught in my throat.

There are men and then there are MEN. This guy was

ALL MAN. He looked to be about 6 foot tall with dark hair, cut short at the sides, a little combed over on top with broad shoulders that stretched his black t-shirt over his equally broad chest. He was fit but it is clear his body was hard earned and not just 'show muscles,' as I liked to refer to them. Tight cargo pants fit over his equally massive thighs before meeting his black work boots. As my gaze reached his face my eyes latched onto his bright emerald green ones surrounded by thick dark lashes and dropped down to his full lips that were slightly tilted in a smirk. Yeah, I had definitely been caught ogling him.

He stopped about five feet away from me, free hand in his pocket, but was still on his phone uttering a couple 'mmh-mms' and 'yups' while not breaking eye contact with me. His unwavering green-eyed gaze was unnerving, like he was assessing me, but he kept his face void of emotion so I couldn't tell what he was thinking. He finally let out a heavy sigh, "Do you want to just talk to her so I can get started on the install? I really would like to be home before midnight." He was silent a moment longer, then held his phone out to me, still careful not to come any closer. "It's Brian. While he talks your ear off, I am going to take a quick look around your house.I will need to get in at some point to install the access panel."

I slowly lowered my knife back into my purse and reached out to grab his phone. "Hello?" I heard B start talking immediately, but didn't fully pay attention as the mystery man started walking toward my porch. "I'm Kelli, by the way," I yelled after him, "and you are?"

"Josh," he replied without slowing or turning around. Okay then. Josh was not a big talker.

I focused back on the phone as I leaned against my car.

"Ignore Josh's attitude," Brian was saying. "He's my business partner, the one who actually created the systems and will know exactly where the best places to install the cameras are to keep you safe. In all his big brains, though, he still hasn't figured out how to talk to people. I'm sorry I couldn't make it out to do the install myself. I didn't want just any employee out there for you. That's why he's a day earlier than planned. He had some free time, so I sent him to ensure it gets done the way I would want it done."

"Brian, you didn't have to do all of this. Also, you never emailed me the bill like you said you would. I don't need anything crazy, just maybe one or two cameras, and a flood light would be great." I stayed leaning against my car as Josh hauled boxes out of the back of his truck up to the porch. "Seriously B, what is he doing? It looks like a lot of equipment?"

I could hear the smile in his voice, "Weird about the bill, I'm sure it will come through eventually. I told him your house size and left it up to his discretion. Josh was in the Army with me and knows what good protection looks like, so he will do what he sees fit and you won't complain. I have a business call I have to hop on, so just go inside and let him do his thing. Call if you need anything else okay, Kel?" There was a slight pause before his voice lowered. "I miss you."

"I miss you too B. Thank you for this, truly." I hung up and walked to the porch handing Josh his phone. "So Josh, I am exhausted and ordering in. You like Chinese? I'm assuming you'll be at this for a bit?"

He looked up from the box he was pulling wires from, staring deep into my eyes again for a few beats. "Chinese sounds great, thank you. I'll knock when I need to get inside for the access panel."

With that, I unlocked my door and slipped inside, immediately re-locking the door. I needed food and a shower. Why is it I only see hot men when my hair is a tangle on top of my head and I smell like antiseptic? I'm sure my mascara is smudged in with my dark eye circles. Whatever, I have more important things to focus on right now, like food.

3

JOSH

I am going to kill Brian when I get home. When he said a small favor, I didn't realize he meant driving three hours to install and wire a whole home system. It is nice to finally meet the infamous Kelli though. I have been hearing about her for years, knowing way more about her than she would probably like. Shit, he had photos of her in his room and our office that were old but sweet. I was absolutely going to give him hell for making me do this. I picked my phone up off the porch and sent a text off to him before I got started.

Josh: Damn man, you forgot to mention that she is my walking wet dream.

As much as I just wanted to piss him off a little, the text wasn't a lie. Kelli was stunning from her short stature to her curly blond hair and big blue eyes that were filled with an odd mix of fear and bravery. The scrubs she wore did their best to hide her body, but I knew from Brian's photos she had curves that could bring a man to his knees. Pictures did not do her justice though. I was stunned when she stepped out of her car looking like a hot mess and yet effortlessly beautiful. Brian and I may have shared women in the past, but I knew this one was off limits. It didn't mean I couldn't look though, and enjoy the look in her eyes when she took me in. My phone buzzed in my pocket as I was installing the porch camera and floodlight.

Brian: If you touch her I will take an ax to your computers. Does she seem okay? She said this was just a precaution but something about it doesn't sit right with me, she's had that house for three years. Why now?

Josh: Don't know, we exchanged three sentences. She seemed fine? She will be more than secure with these cameras and I am putting the alarm system and floodlights in too. Seems like it's a quiet neighborhood.

Brian: Okay. Seriously though, don't even hit on her.

Josh: Yeah yeah, she's your wet dream too I know. I'll let you know when I'm done here. You owe me for this shit.

Brian: I owe nothing, being in her presence is payment enough.

Josh: I'll be in her alright.

Brian: Fuck you.

I couldn't help but chuckle. He knew I wouldn't do shit and would only talk to her when it was necessary. I didn't really seek out women all that often. Ruffling his feathers was just too easy when it came to Kelli, and he deserved it for sending me all the way out here.

I was walking along the side of the house to determine where movement would set off the flood light I just installed when a little car pulled in behind Kelli's. A scrawny kid got out carrying a brown paper bag with the Chinese she must have ordered. I pulled out my wallet and tipped the kid before grabbing the food and made my way back to knock on her door. Footsteps echoed, followed by the lock clicking before the door opened revealing a fresh-faced Kelli. My eyes immediately dropped to her pajamas of matching shorts and a shirt with little frogs on them. They hugged her body tight, showing her ample cleavage and hips that were a perfect handful. It took a minute for me to drag my eyes back to her face. Thank god Brian wasn't here to punch me in the chest but he probably should. "Nice pajamas."

My eyes tracked the flush that crept up her neck. "Thanks. I thought you were my delivery driver, I didn't get to tip him." She stepped back to let me through. "Come on in, I ordered a variety since I don't know what you like." She looked me over again avoiding eye contact before turning to walk toward her kitchen. She seemed a little flustered, not something I expected from a trauma nurse. I shouldn't be assessing her, but it was a habit. Years in the military meant I was constantly on alert and assessing everyone around me.

"I tipped him." I muttered back trying not to stare at her ass that was filling out every inch of her little shorts while following her through the house. The house looked nice, clean with muted shades of blues, pinks and greens, giving it a homey feel. I didn't look too hard, still too distracted by the sway of her hips as she walked to the kitchen.

"Thank you, you didn't have to do that," she said as she pulled out plates and forks before putting them on the island, then grabbed the bag from me to unload the various boxes of noodles, veggies, chicken, pork and shrimp. "I got plenty, so please don't be shy. Have a seat and get whatever you would like. Can I get you anything to drink?"

Kelli was clearly just as chatty as Brian. "Water is fine, thanks." I put a little of everything on my plate and started eating. I know it was rude to not wait for her, but I still had to install a camera out back, the access panel at her doorway and set up the alarm system which would take the longest and it was already 7pm. Maybe I would get a hotel for the night and not make the long drive back home.

"So how long have you and Brian known each other? You guys started the company two years ago right?" she asked, sitting in a stool next to me as she set water in front of both of us.

"Almost three now. We have known each other for 10 years." I have never been one for small talk and definitely not one to talk about my time overseas.

"You've known him since childhood, right?" I didn't want to keep the conversation going, but a distraction was best before she asked more about our time serving. I didn't want to be rude again, but I still had so much to do. Although, I did want to hear more about her side of things with Brian. He was still pining for her, and I was curious if she still felt the same.

"Yeah, his brother Danny and I have been best friends for most of our lives. His family has kind of taken me in as one of their own. B and I were close growing up, but started talking only a few times a month once he joined the Army. The last few years we haven't been in touch as much though." She looked at her plate as her face flushed again. I knew all about the circumstances that changed things between them and led to them no longer talking. Four years ago, he came back from a visit home telling the whole unit about her and how she was going to be his when he got out, but that all changed soon after.

She took a huge bite of orange chicken, the sauce spilling down her chin. "Do you have much more to do? Brian said originally that he would have someone do the install tomorrow. I feel bad you are here so late doing this."

"I just have the back camera and inside stuff left to do, two to three hours at most." I noticed when Kelli got us water from the fridge, she pulled a pocket knife from a drawer and set it on the counter closest to her. It was an odd thing, and showed how leery she was, even with someone her best friend trusted. Brian's gut instincts have saved my life before and him thinking she wasn't safe hasn't left my mind. "Is there a reason you decided to get a security system?"

Kelli stiffened next to me. "Nope. I just figured it was time to make some updates around here and this was the first step." She was still looking down at her plate, refusing to meet my eye, and it was clear she was lying through her teeth. That didn't sit well with me, I was not one to walk away from a woman that needed help.

"Seems like a nice neighborhood but added protection is never a bad thing. I'll try and finish quickly and get out of your hair." Mostly I just needed to step away from the sweet floral scent that had been surrounding me for our entire dinner. I'm pretty sure it is coming from her wet hair because I get a waft of it every time she turns her head. Brian has been hung up on this girl for years so I know there has to be something special about her. I had to admit that she was sweet and beautiful but that isn't really my type. I prefer a woman that doesn't take shit from others, and has more of an edge than the wholesomeness that was radiating from Kelli. Someone that doesn't care that I come off as brash and can handle being dominated in the bedroom. That look of fear in her eyes as she watches my movements has me wanting to make sure she is safe though.

My sisters had that same look as Kelli throughout our childhood and I hated it. I couldn't always protect them then, but I can help Brian protect Kelli now. He has saved my life enough times that this is the least I can do for him. My dad left when I was young and my mom turned to drugs to cope. My sisters came soon after that, both from random men my mother had slept with to get her next fix. They were lucky enough that she kept mostly clean throughout her pregnancies, but it never took long for her to relapse. Our home became a revolving door for sketchy men our mom would date until they discovered how bad her little habits were, or they realized my sisters and I were a permanent fixture. I was ten, my sisters seven and five, when a few of the men started trying to be a little overly involved with them. That continued on until I was big enough to make it clear they were not to be looked at or touched. From then on, I have had a hyper awareness for the wellbeing and safety of women that is ingrained in me at this point.

Kelli tensed up as I got up and rinsed my plate in the sink before putting it in her dishwasher. Her blue eyes stayed wide and trained on me as I passed where she left the knife on the counter. "Thanks for dinner. I'll be out back for about twenty minutes then I will be back inside for the rest. I'll need to cut a small hole in the wall in your entryway for the panel, but I'll clean up the mess."

I looked down at my watch to ensure the new system had the right time and date. I lost track of time since it was almost ten and I don't think I've heard Kelli for at least an hour. She was last making noise in the living room, so I headed there and found her asleep on the couch. She had a blanket draped over her, a book open in her lap and her head lulled to the side. In the gentle light of the lamp beside her, I can easily see the dark circles under her eyes. Her body is still tense even in sleep, her shoulders not slumped into the couch. There is definitely something she is afraid of if she looks this uptight while sleeping. I knelt down in front of her and nudged her knee, hoping not to scare her. "Hey Kelli, I'm done."

Her eyes shot open as she abruptly sat up and yanked her hand from under the blanket pointing a pocket knife right at my throat. Her eyes went wide as she took in her surroundings, blinking as she scanned my face. After getting oriented, she looked down at the knife handle she was holding right below my face. I slowly and gently reached up, taking the knife from her. "Kelli, before I show you how to use your new system, I am going to need you to tell me what's going on. Don't even think of lying to me again." I spoke quietly but firmly, still kneeling before her. The girl was clearly afraid of something, and if someone was harassing her, I was damn sure going to make sure Brian and I took care of it.

She moved the book from her lap, setting it on the small table next to the couch and held her hand out for her knife back. "It's not a big deal, but you can't tell Brian. I don't need him seeing me as the kid sister needing protection anymore."

I snorted, moving my hand up to rub my thumb over her knee in what I was hoping was a comforting gesture. "I don't think that's a problem, but sure. This will stay between us. Why did you need the cameras?"

"My little news interaction has brought me some unwanted attention. It's not a big deal, just someone left a note in my mailbox. It only happened once, I'm sure it won't happen again." Was she trying to convince me or herself? I felt like there is more to this story still and I didn't like it. My need to protect never left after my time in the Army; in fact, it may have gotten worse. Being raised in a home where protection was needed but not provided had messed with my head. The mandated military therapist said I was projecting, but who the hell cares if it was a good thing. I made a promise to my sisters I wouldn't let a woman in my life be abused or threatened again. It was a major reason why I built this business with Brian. Kelli was special to him, but if I couldn't tell him, then she was now mine to help protect. Looking at her uneasy expression, untamed curls and her frog pajama shirt pulled down low, I was enamored with her and needed to ensure her safety.

"If this person contacts you again in any way or you feel unsafe at all, you need to call Brian, Danny or me immediately." She rolled her eyes despite her shoulders still being bunched up tight. I leaned back on my heels pulling out my phone while still rubbing her knee with my other hand. "I mean it, I don't play around with safety. Give me your number."

Her blue eyes bore into mine for a moment before she recited her number for me. I sent her a text so she would have my number as well. I grabbed her hand, pulling her up from the couch. "Okay let me show you how to set and disarm the alarm and how to view the cameras on your phone, then I will get out of your hair." Her beautiful curly blonde hair that smelled so sweet.

By the time I got back in my truck it was almost eleven and I was beat. There was no way in hell I was driving home but I didn't want to get a hotel and leave Kelli. That look of fear in her eyes was still haunting me. Her system was all set up for her, but I needed my computer to get it set up for me as well. I wanted to set it up so I could monitor her cameras and get notifications when the alarm was set and disarmed as well. It may not have been standard protocol, or even legal, but I didn't care. I needed to know she was safe and no one was creeping around her house. I sent off a quick text to my sisters to check in on them. Situations like this always brought on my guilt over them. I moved my truck a few houses down and stayed through the night, watching Kelli's place until she left for work again the next morning.

4

KELLI

Waking up Thursday morning wasn't as rough as the previous few days. Despite staying up later than normal, I slept with ease. I'm not sure if it was due to the comfort of the cameras and added security or if it was the emerald green eyes that met me again in my dreams. I replayed our interaction on the couch, except in my dream when he stroked my knee, his hands slowly moved their way up until he hooked his hands around my shorts and peeled them down. I need to get laid. I was grateful it wasn't the familiar brown eyes that have been haunting my dreams for the last few years, though. As it was, I still needed a cold shower before work.

My schedule at Mercy Hospital varied, but most weeks I ended up doing six, ten hour shifts due to understaffing. This week was one of those weeks and although I had already worked Monday, Tuesday and Wednesday, I had to work today, tomorrow and Sunday as well.

My drive into work was a little distracted by thoughts of Josh. I wanted to text him and thank him again and ask if he got home safe, but I don't even know where he lives. I hope it's around Boston since he stayed so late last night, but it would make more sense if he lived in Winthrop near Brian since they are business partners.

He honestly didn't show any interest last night aside from the hand on my knee and only gave me his number in case I was in trouble or my stalker came around again. I had my every few months booty call Tyler to keep the cobwebs clear, but other than that, I haven't really dated since I started at Mercy five years ago. My schedule was too crazy for it, and now I realized I was seriously out of practice. Something about the way Josh carried himself had me believing he would do a much better job than Tyler, so maybe it was time to get back on that dating train.

As I pulled into the employee lot, I pulled out my phone to let Danny know I got to work safe. He was like a mother hen these last few days, constantly checking in. The halls from the employee entrance were mostly clear, but Natalie's signature high ponytail popped out of the locker room in front of me. She waited as I dropped off my purse and we made our way to the break room together to fill up on coffee. Our shoes squeaked on the newly polished floors throughout our shift, which normally annoyed me, but working with Natalie always made for a good day. There were no losses on our watch and things remained surprisingly quiet which gave us a lot of down time to chat.

"What do you think, do I text him?" I spun my chair in slow circles at the nursing station. I decided to tell her about the direct message and note in my mailbox, and of course, Josh.

"I mean, he did give you his number. Even if he said safety was the reasoning." She took a slow sip of her coffee leaning back in her chair. "If he truly showed no interest then maybe that was the reason, but I feel like you should give it a day or so and see if he texts you. I would be surprised if he didn't. You're a total catch."

"Ugh, you're probably right. This whole situation is just really making me realize that I don't want to be alone anymore, you know?" I love my mother dearly but I was starting to see similarities in how we prioritize a steady income and career to be able to rely on ourselves instead of relationships. I don't want to look back ten years from now with the money to travel the world, but no one to travel with. Money wasn't all that life was about. "I will wait and if he doesn't text by Saturday then he really isn't interested and I will work on setting up a dating profile. Just the thought makes my skin crawl with all the superficial men and small talk I am going to have to go through."

Natalie's laugh echoed around us. "Welcome to dating in the 21st century, it's a dog-eat-dog world out there. If you're lucky, it will be a dog eat cat world though." She winked at me and continued laughing as she got up to check on a patient.

A little after five, purse and phone in hand, I sauntered out to the employee parking lot. Maybe I would pick up dinner on the way home and eat it on my porch while watching the sunset. I pulled up some local restaurants, scrolling through their menus as I walked to my car. I felt lighter than I have all week, and Danny only texted me five times today to check on me which was an improvement. I promised him we could go out for drinks tomorrow after work so he can see with his own two eyes I am still alive and well even though he just saw me yesterday morning when I left his house. My car beeped as I unlocked it and I threw my purse into the passenger seat. A familiar white envelope tucked under my windshield wiper caught my attention as I climbed in. Snatching it off the windshield, I slammed and locked my door. My hands trembled trying to tear open the envelope. A photo slid out, falling into my lap. On the front was me walking into the hospital that morning smiling down at my phone, taken from entirely too close. I flipped it over to see the note written on the back.

YOU LOOKED BEAUTIFUL TODAY.
- MR.W

My eyes scoured the parking lot to see if anyone else was around while the hairs on my neck rose. There were a few other staff members walking to their cars but no one stuck out or was looking in my direction. My chest heaved with slow deep breaths as I tried to stay calm and get my trembling hands under control. This note wasn't threatening like the others, but he was watching me and that thought alone was terrifying. The keys turned in the ignition and I slowly pulled out heading for home. I was no longer in the mood to stop for food, my anxiety at an all-time high as I checked my mirrors every thrity seconds the whole way home. I know I promised Danny and Alex that I would call the cops the next time but this note wasn't threatening and women were not often taken seriously. I also wasn't going to call Josh, I wasn't any more unsafe then I had been before, and realistically there was nothing he could do.

I have been protected by Danny and Brian for most of my life. Brian fought my battles when I got bullied in school, and Danny confronted my high school boyfriend when he cheated on me. Both had made it clear to everyone in my life that I was not to be messed with. I was tired of constantly relying on others, I wanted to be my own protector. From here on out, I would be aware of my surroundings, have security walk me to my car in the evenings, only go out in groups when possible and ensure the alarm was set at home. This man was not going to intimidate me any longer. He wasn't threatening me, and I would bet he liked initiating fear. Mr. W would not get that satisfaction from me anymore.

The rest of that week I stuck to my resolve and did everything I could to keep myself safe. I didn't tell Danny about the new note I got yesterday when we went out for dinner and drinks after my shift on Friday. Josh never reached out and I took that as my sign to start putting myself out there.

With the decision made, I set up a dating profile like I had promised Natalie. The prospects weren't great, but I was putting in the effort and I was proud of myself for that. I found another envelope on my car on Tuesday, this one with just a note.

I SAW THE NEW CAMERAS, TRYING TO WATCH ME LIKE I WATCH YOU?
- MR. W.

This note wasn't exactly threatening either. It also made me feel a sense of pride and security. The fact there was no photo meant that he must have noticed me always looking around and couldn't get close enough to take one. Him knowing about the cameras meant he had driven by my house again, but the fact that they kept him far enough away to not put the note in my mailbox was good enough for me.

The following Friday, I had set up a date from my dating

app. While I was nervous, I was also kind of excited. I put on a pretty blue sundress with some wedge heels and left my curly hair down. Carter, my date, had picked a new restaurant downtown for us to meet at. I arrived a few minutes early and saw him already standing outside the large wooden door of the restaurant waiting for me. He was good looking, average height with some muscle tone and a clean-shaven face, but he was wearing khakis and a polo, which is unfortunately a strike in my book. It didn't look bad per se, I just have always preferred a more rugged look. He looked up from his phone and caught my eye walking up. His gaze traveled slowly down my body, his lips tugging up in a smirk as they came back up and met my eyes again. "Kelli? Wow, you are even more beautiful than in your pictures."

My lips pulled up in a small smile. "Thank you, it's nice to meet you."

He took a second to give me another quick once over, stalling on my exposed legs then pulled open the door. "Shall we head in?" At least he was a gentleman. The host seated us right away at a small table near the corner of the restaurant. Sitting down, I picked up the menu immediately so I could do something with my hands. Why did first dates feel so uncomfortable? The waiter came over to grab our drink order, but Carter rudely cut him off before he could finish going over the happy hour specials. "We will have a bottle of cabernet with two glasses, and the spinach artichoke dip to start." The waiter looked over at me, but I was a little too stunned to disagree. I hadn't even had a chance to go through the drink menu.

"That sounds fine, can I just get a water with that as well?" He nodded giving me a small smile then moved to the next table.

Carter still perused the menu without asking if what he

ordered for us was fine with me. I was going to write it off as first date nerves. "So," I cleared my throat, "are you Boston born and bred?"

"Yep, I have lived in Wellesley all my life. I can't see myself living anywhere else. I went to Boston College even though I had offers from Ivy Leagues. My parents bought me a place in their neighborhood so it was worth it for me to stay local." He had barely looked up at me and was still flipping through the menu. "I think we should get the steak, it would pair best with the wine."

It was becoming clear this wasn't first date nerves, but red flags and narcissistic behavior. Lucky for him, I happened to love a good steak and would absolutely suffer through dealing with him for it. I was also looking at it as good practice for getting back into the dating game. When the waiter brought over our wine and appetizer, Carter ordered the steaks for us. Thankfully, the waiter asked me how I liked mine cooked and what sides I would like.

The rest of the dinner was spent with me asking Carter questions of which he answered and hardly asked any back. As the meal came to a close, he picked up the check which I had no qualms about. I felt like that was deserved after having to listen to him drone on about himself for almost two hours. I thanked him for the meal, politely declined his offer to go grab a drink and drove myself home. While that date sucked, I was proud of myself for going anyway. I couldn't help but think about Brian on the drive home. My one night with him four years ago had set the bar entirely too high, and it wasn't even a date. The conversation, the connection that felt soul deep, and the feel of his lips on mine at the end of it all. It was still haunting me. It was only my first date, though, and next time I would spend a little more time getting to know the person through the app before I agreed to a date.

5

My coffee maker beeps at me from across the kitchen at the same time as my front door opens. My alarm starts chirping as Danny's cursing floats down the hall to me as he tries to disarm it. I pour two cups of coffee, setting one on the island for him when he finally gets the alarm off and saunters into the kitchen. "I hate that stupid alarm. Brian sent someone to install one at our place last week despite my protests that it was unnecessary. Alex has gotten shit at work because I couldn't get it turned off fast enough on Thursday and the cops called to check if it was a real emergency and it got around his department." A loud laugh bursts from me. Danny was helpless with technology. He adds creamer to his coffee, standing across the island from where I'm sitting. "So, tell me about your date last night, everything you hoped and dreamed of?"

I groan and put my head down on the counter. "It was so bad. Like beyond so bad. He ordered all our food and drinks without asking me what I wanted, he talked about how amazing he was the whole time, and he wore a polo shirt."

"Not a polo! God, straight guys have no class. Well, we can't all be your prince." His lips lift into a smirk. "Let me set you up on a blind date! Alex has a guy at the department that he thinks would be great for you."

"I'm not opposed to it, but you are putting together two careers who tend to have terrible schedules. We would never see each other."

"You're right, that kind of defeats the purpose of having a guy to protect you. Speaking of, any new notes show up since the one in your mailbox?" His eyes narrow, his lips turning flat like he already knew the truth.

I don't love that he still sees me as someone that needs protecting. "I can protect myself. I don't need a man to do that. I want a man so I don't have to be so lonely."

"You can't avoid my question. I grabbed your mail on the way in, Kelli." He looks pissed as he stomps around my kitchen pulling out an envelope from his back pocket and hands it to me. I look down at the familiar scrawl of my name written on the front. Sliding my finger under the seal flap, I dump its contents onto the counter. Two photos fall out this time. I grab them both first looking at the front. One was of me and Carter outside the restaurant before our date where he had one hand holding the door and one hand on my lower back as I walked in. The other was dark, but I could make out Carter splayed out on the ground with a split lip and blood leaking from his nose. "What the fuck," Danny mumbles from next to me. I turned them over and read what was on the backs. The first one said, *No one touches what is mine -Mr. W.* The second one said, *You're mine, Kelli - Mr. W.*

We both sat there in stunned silence staring at the photos, while a million thoughts ran through my head. I shouldn't have gone out with anyone while I had a stalker. It was extremely irresponsible and now Carter got hurt because of it. I let my guard down and failed to check my surroundings while walking into the restaurant.

Stupid. I was so stupid. I hadn't even felt Carter's hand on my back either but clearly, he had put it there for a brief moment. I think I need to call the police this time. I look over to Danny, but he is already on his phone, eyes roving from the photos to me and back.

Before I could even get my mouth open all the way, he interrupts. "I don't want to hear it, Kelli. I'm calling Alex to get over here then we are calling the police. You are not allowing this to go on any longer." I wasn't going to argue. Instead, I moved on shaky legs to my room to grab the other notes that I had been collecting in the bag with the first one. When I come back out to the kitchen, Danny was pacing around the island, his brown eyes locked on mine as soon as I entered. "Alex is on his way. He said he was calling in some guys he trusts that are on duty and they will meet him here."

"Okay." My eyes turn downcast because he's about to find out I have been lying about there not being other notes. Instead of facing his angry glare, I scroll through my phone to pull up the security app Josh had downloaded. I knew how to watch it live, which I only did when I got a notification that something had triggered the motion sensors. It had only happened so far when my car was pulling into the driveway or when a package was delivered to my porch. I wasn't sure how to watch previous activity though to see if I could spot someone putting the envelope in my mailbox. "Have you and Alex ever watched back previous feeds from your security system? I can't figure it out."

He scrubs a hand down his face. "I haven't and I don't think Alex has either. Call Josh or Brian before the police get here. See if they can walk you through it and how to make a copy of it so we can have extra evidence."

My feet pad down the hallway back to my bedroom as I debate who to call. I know Danny won't keep this from Brian anymore after all this, but I'm not ready to deal with the anger I knew he would have towards me for lying to him. Plus, Josh told me to call if I needed help with the system. His deep voice answers on the second ring. "Hello?"

"Hey Josh, it's Kelli Winters. I'm hoping you can help me out with the security system."

"Yeah, of course, are you having problems with it?"

"No, I just need help with the app. I only know how to view the live feed from the cameras, but was hoping you could explain how to review previous footage. That is a possibility, right?" God, I hope it is. If I can catch a video of this guy, this nightmare can be over.

"The app keeps the feed from the previous 72 hours, so if it is in that time frame it should be no problem. What is the time range you are looking for and which camera? Is there something specific you need?" His tone lowers practically growling as he puts everything together. "Did something happen with your stalker?"

A heavy sigh slips past my lips, "I just need to see if any cameras caught someone putting something in my mailbox. It would have been sometime between ten last night and nine a.m. this morning. I need to get a copy of it, too, if there is something."

"Kelli, you need to tell me if something is going on. Are you safe?"

His rough voice is demanding and sure with a hint of worry. I bite my lower lip to stop it from quivering. "Yes, I'm fine, just another little note. The police are coming to take my statement and the notes. Can you help me with the cameras or not?" I was irritated when I had no reason to be, but I'm overwhelmed and fear was starting to creep in again.

"I will go through it and send you anything I find. And Kelli? I'm telling Brian." With that he hung up. Well, I guess it's better he hears it from him and not Danny who could tell him just how many notes I have received by this point. I walk back to the kitchen to find Danny and Alex both stone faced and staring at me.

"Hey Alex, I didn't even hear you get here. Thanks for being here for this and helping." I supply with a small smile.

"My colleagues should be here in about two minutes and when they get here, you are going to explain to all of us about how, when and where this whole bag of notes and photos came from." That would explain the expressions. Nodding, I take a seat at the island with my head in my hands. What a cluster this was all ending up to be. I was forever going to curse that damn patient who took the video that set this all off.

Two hours later, I was locking my door and setting the alarm. The cops took my statement while I went into detail about when and where each note had shown up over the last few weeks. They had taken the bag with all the evidence, as well as an email copy of the screenshot of the first DM and the short clip Josh had sent me. One camera angle caught someone dressed head to toe in black putting the note in my mailbox around 3 AM. They looked to be wearing a hat, hood and gloves, but they couldn't be seen getting into a car, just walking away down the street. They had also taken the info I had about Carter and were going to try to get in touch with him in case he caught a glimpse of who attacked him.

Danny and Alex stayed about an hour after the cops did to

make sure I was okay. That would have been sweet, except they spent the first twenty minutes yelling about how reckless I have been not telling anyone about the notes sooner. They tried to get me to stay with them again, but I don't want to. While I am scared, I don't want to put anyone else in danger. Plus, this person knows where I work and has had no problem following me around, so I don't feel like their house is any safer than my own. I spent the rest of the day in my pajamas on my couch eating every comfort food I owned and binge-watching rom-coms on Netflix to make me feel better.

My body jolted awake from the spot on the couch where I fell asleep to the loud sounds of crashing coming from the back of my house. On instinct, I reached for the knife on the side table and scrambled to find my phone. My hands shook as I searched through the cushions until my hand wrapped around it. The jarring sounds of glass shattering were still coming from different directions in my home. I immediately dialed 9-1-1 while running toward the hall bathroom that had no windows. Slamming the door shut and locking it, I sunk back against it. "9-1-1 what is your emergency?" a lady answered me.

"I think someone is breaking into my house, it sounds like they are breaking my windows. Please hurry!" I rush out in a whisper-yell.

"Ma'am are you somewhere safe? If you can, get to a locked room. Are you at 138 Maple Drive?" she responded calmly.

"Yes, that's my address and I am locked in the hall bath. I don't hear footsteps but I think another window just broke." My strangled voice broke at the end. Danny was right, I have been so reckless and stupid. I should have stayed with him. I should have called the cops sooner.

"I have officers on the way, they are less than a minute out. I am going to stay on the phone with you until they get there. Is there anyone else at the home with you or any animals to be aware of?" she asked in the same calm, even tone, making me feel like she was in complete control of the situation.

"I think I hear the sirens now. It's just me. Do I need to let them in?" Despite her calm manner, I was freaking the hell out. It sounded like the crashing was getting closer and closer.

"They will search the perimeter then make their way in. They are aware you are locked in the bathroom, and will knock and let you know when it is safe and clear to come out."

Car doors slammed and voices rang out sounding in different directions. Knowing help has arrived didn't seem to be making a difference on the panic coursing through my veins. My vision blurred as I tried to hold in the tears, my body still trembling. I clutched my phone to my ear like a lifeline as I waited to get the all clear.

The loud slam of my front door crashing open hit me like a jolt of lightning. The voices continued to yell out as they searched through the inside of my home. "I can hear them in the house now. Thank you for your help. I am going to hang up now." There was a soft rap on the door then.

"Ma'am? The home has been cleared, you can come out now." It hit me all at once how close I had just come to serious harm and my adrenaline started to fade. My whole body was shaking like a leaf as I slowly unlocked the door trying to drag in breaths to keep from passing out. I couldn't get enough breaths in; my throat felt too tight like I was breathing through a straw. I saw an officer crouch down in front of me, but my ears were ringing and the edges of my vision were turning black. His lips moved as he turned slightly to someone behind him while reaching for my hand as everything went dark.

6

BRIAN

Logan holds up a bottle of water to get my attention as he walks over. As much as I am not in the mood to talk, I could really use the water. I have been out here chopping wood for over two hours already and I can still feel the hot rage pulsing under my skin. Kelli has been in danger for weeks and didn't tell me, and I wasn't sure if it was her betrayal or my brothers that hurt worse. They should have told me what was going on. To add to my anger, Josh had known as well and has not said a word to me. When he told me this morning what has been going on with Kelli and that she was just now getting the police involved, it took everything in me not to hit him.

He knows why I let Kelli go despite my feelings toward her. He knows exactly how I feel about her safety. That burning beneath my skin was getting worse again. It felt an awful lot like shame and fear, but I wasn't going to acknowledge that. It is better being felt as anger and rage, and I'm going to continue working it out until I can get a clear head. Every part of me wanted to get in the car and go to her and ensure her safety, but that clearly isn't my place anymore. She called Josh, not me. I don't even have the right to be angry over it since I'm the one who pushed her away.

I put my ax down as Logan tosses the water bottle to me. "You going to spend the whole evening out here? Pretty sure you already put a month's worth of time in on that heavy bag this morning."

I grunted, swallowing down the whole bottle. "I need to clear my head so I don't do something stupid. You know physical exhaustion has always been my go-to."

"Okay, but I think you should talk about what's going on in your head. If not to me or Josh, then talk to Kelli. It's been four years man and you still feel the same way. Don't you think it's time you have a real conversation with her?" He crossed his arms and fixed me with his stare. Logan has always been the more sensible and emotionally intelligent one between him, Josh and I. I couldn't talk to Kelli though, I needed to move on. How could I explain to her that I don't trust myself to keep her protected and to be everything she needs, so I stayed away so she could find someone that could be that for her? I was not the man that I was four years ago. Now she was in danger despite all that and the shame of not being able to save my whole team in Iraq was right back, front and center in my head again. I couldn't talk about it to her or the guys, I just needed some time.

"Did you come out here for a reason, or just to lecture me?" Logan wasn't the one I was angry at, but he was in the line of fire right now.

"Don't be a dick. You need to come inside, it's dark and you've punished yourself enough for one day. Cool off, go to bed, and we can talk in the morning." He turned and stalked back toward the house knowing I would follow. Despite me being the leader of our unit, he has always had an air of authority people respect and follow, including myself. He was the fun one, the light one, but when he got serious, everyone listened. Josh, Logan and I served in the Army together for eight years. Josh joined the year after me, and Logan joined the year after him. We were lucky enough to spend almost our entire careers together before getting out around the same time and moving in here.

As we walked up the steps on the back porch, Josh came running out of the sliding doors looking pissed and worried. "I've been yelling for you! Something is going down at Kelli's house. You need to call Danny and get your ass in the car right now!"

My heart started pounding in my chest, fear and anxiety spiking through me. "What do you mean? What's happening? Is she okay?"

Josh stomped back in the house towards the office as Logan and I followed. "I told you I had notifications set up on her system to alert me and two minutes ago they went off. Someone spray painted over the two cameras at the back of her house. I have the front two pulled up and you can hear glass shattering through them." In the office he sat in his chair showing us her feed pulled up on his monitors so we could see what was going on. Through her front porch camera we could see two police cars pulling up now, guns drawn. My feet were on the move running toward the mud room to grab my wallet and keys before I could even process it all.

"Call Danny! I'll keep you updated on anything I see or find out." Josh yelled from the office.

"Take my Charger, it's faster!" Logan shouted from behind me.

I was in the car and on the road in minutes. The drive to Boston was about three hours, but I was determined to get there as soon as possible. I called Danny as soon as I was on the main road through the speaker system. Before he could get his hello in, I was talking over him. "You need to get over to Kelli's house right now. I'm on my way, but I will take too long. The police are there and someone covered her cameras, but that's all I know."

"Shit," he said as rustling sounded in the background and then a muffled, 'Alex get dressed'. "Okay we are on our way. I'll have Alex see what information he can get on the way over and I'll give you a call back as soon as I know anything. Drive safe and talk soon." I appreciated the love Danny had for Kelli. He may not know that my feelings for her go beyond that of a close friend or big brother but he knows I put the role of protector onto his shoulders when I left home at 18.

Once on the highway, I stayed a steady thrity mph above the speed limit. It was late enough in the evening and there was no traffic, so I could cruise around the scattered cars that were there. I got a call from Josh informing me that she was taken away by ambulance but looked to be okay. Danny's call came not long after letting me know she was at Mercy Hospital being monitored because she blacked out from a panic attack. They would release her as soon as her vitals were stable and her blood pressure was back down to normal. He and Alex were going to stay with her until I could get there, then they would go back to her house and pack some bags for her.

We agreed that she would not be alone in her home until her stalker was caught. I honestly didn't love the idea of her staying with Danny either, but until I knew exactly what happened tonight, I would agree to it. Kelli was going to fight us over it but I would not accept her being in danger any longer. As I'm driving, I can't help but think over the last couple times I spent with Kelli.

BRIAN - AGE 18

"So, you are really going to join?" Kelli asks, sitting down under the willow tree next to me. It has been our thing for years when she slept over. I spent a lot of evenings sitting under this tree in our backyard and Kelli always found a way to come join me.

"Yeah, I am. I leave in three weeks." She looked down at where she was pulling up grass and spreading it over her feet.

"I'm going to miss you."

"I know, Kel. I'll miss you, too. This is my next move in life, though. I have a chance to make a difference. A chance to help people in the way that I know how." Even though Kelli was only twelve, she was always understanding and wise beyond her years. I have thought of her as one of my best friends for a long time. It may seem strange to most, but her and my family were the most important people in my life. Joining the Army had been a goal of mine for years. I had a shot to make something of myself and of my life while protecting the people I loved.

"I have had you looking out for me for the last 6 years of my life, I guess it's only fair I share you and let you look out for others now, too." She sniffled and put her head down on her knees. "You are going to be amazing B. I'm really proud of you."

My chest felt tight, a knot building in my throat. How this little girl knew just what to say to hit me in the feels, I would never know. I made a vow that night to watch her from afar, and ensure Danny knew it was his job to keep her safe and loved while I couldn't.

That day played over in my head as I drove. I spent a lot of time away from her and she was safe that whole time.

Somehow now that I am back, just a few hours away, she isn't safe anymore and that tore a hole in my heart. Another memory flashed behind my eyes.

BRIAN - AGE 28

"You know, things have always felt deeper with you, Kel. Even when we were kids, you were my best friend. You have always seen me for who I truly am and I don't know if I ever fully appreciated it or saw how rare that is until now. You are incredible, and I hope that you know that." God, she was amazing. Sitting on the other end of her couch, cheeks flushed from her drinks and us laughing for the last few hours, curly hair spilling all around her. She certainly isn't the little girl I left back home all those years ago. *"I am so proud of you for getting your nursing license, I always knew you would end up in a career helping others. Is it everything you hoped it would be?"*

"It is, and it isn't. I mean, I am still pretty new in the field. The ER is filled with a lot of hard days, hard situations and hard outcomes, but I wouldn't trade it for anything. Being able to save a life will always be worth it, even if some days I have to hold a hand as a life slips away."

That was why Kelli was a cut above everyone else. Selfless to a fault, just truly wanting to make a difference in the world around her. My career has been so fulfilling, but I was tired of the deployments, of the nights alone. I was ready to settle down into a quieter life, and I wanted to settle down with someone like Kelli. No, not someone like her. Her. Kelli with her quiet strength, alarming beauty, ridiculous pajamas, independent and driven, kind and giving. Even after years apart, she felt like home. I was ready to come home.

"This is my last deployment. I am ready to build a life

outside of the military. Have a family. I want that life with you, Kelli. I've known you most your life, my soul knows yours. I want to know your heart. I want to earn your heart. Could you want that with me too?"

Her blinding smile set my soul on fire. "Yes, B. A thousand times yes."

The whole car ride I thought on all our times together. My pseudo little sister, my best friend, the girl I adored turned into the woman that I fell in love with. The last few years I have spent focusing on building the business with Josh, and trying to get back to the man that I was before everything happened. All I wanted was to be the man that Kelli knew. The one she wanted, needed, and deserved. I did all that work going to therapy, building a life I was proud of where I could be home with her every night and it wasn't enough to protect Kelli and keep her safe and loved. What did I have to offer? I have run out of time, and I either need to step up, get over my fears and make her mine, or I needed to find her stalker and then really let her go for good. Being a prisoner in my own mind of loving Kelli from afar is slowly killing me. No woman would ever measure up, it was her or no one.

I pulled into the hospital lot a little over two hours after I had left home and rushed into the emergency room. Alex was standing near the entrance on his phone, waiving me over as soon as he saw me. As I approached, he nodded toward a hallway that I followed him down as he finished up his phone call. "Kelli is fine and I will take you to her in a minute, but I wanted to talk to you without Danny before you went in there."

I flexed and clenched my fists at my side preparing for what he was going to say next. "Her stalker snuck through a neighbor's backyard and spray painted her back cameras. I have already gotten the footage from Josh. There were glimpses of the man on there, but he had a full mask and gloves, hiding anything defining. He then threw six bricks through different windows. It's still not clear if his intention was to threaten and scare her or to take her, but Brian, the notes attached to those bricks are bad." He ran a hand through his short beard as he pulled up something on his phone. "I am not supposed to have these because I'm not on her case, but a buddy sent them to me."

He handed me the phone with a text thread of photos pulled up. I clicked on the first one, a brick with a note taped to it surrounded by shattered glass. The note said *Snitches get stitches Kelli.* The rest of the photos looked similar as I scrolled through, but the notes got more and more threatening and violent.

They can't keep you from me.
You won't be safe until you're in my arms.
I always get what is mine.
You made a mistake Kelli, your punishment is coming.
My girl needs to be taught a lesson.

I looked up at Alex at a loss for words. I needed to see her with my own eyes, to hold her in my arms and ensure she was okay. "I need to see her. Right now."

He put a hand on my chest holding me back. "Hold on, Brian. She doesn't know about all of this yet, and I don't want to tell her until she is cleared to go home. And on the subject of home, I think she should go home with you. I can't guarantee her safety while I'm at work, and if this guy is watching her house, then he has seen our cars there. It wouldn't surprise me if our place was the next target."

It wasn't even a question in my head. "I agree, she is coming home with me. I'll need your help with a few things though." I shot off a text to the guys to let them know.

> Me: Kelli is coming home with me. She'll be staying for a while.

Josh: Is she okay?

Logan: I'll make sure the guest room is ready.

> Me: She will be, she may not be thrilled about staying with us though.

Josh: She doesn't know?

Logan: What does she like to eat? Do you think she'll bake with me? I'll make sure she feels welcome.

> Me: Hands off. She doesn't know yet, but she will. It's on us to keep her safe. I'll fill you in on everything in the morning, won't be home until late.

Josh: You know we will. Drive safe.

Logan: We are here for you both. Love you brother.

By the time Alex and I had come up with a game plan, he took off to get a head start on his part while I finally went to see Kelli. I have only seen her twice in the last few years. I wasn't avoiding her, I was just cautious of which family events I went to depending on if she would be there or not. I wasn't prepared for how hard it would hit me seeing her in that hospital bed, even knowing she was okay.

Her honey blonde hair was in a big mop on top of her head, dressed in a hospital gown with manatee pajama pants sticking out the bottom. Her face was make-up free and just as beautiful as always. She was laughing with a nurse standing beside her bed, but Danny got up from her other side having seen me walk in. "Good to see you," he wrapped me in a quick tight hug. "Thank you for calling me and for coming. Alex texted me a recap of the plan so I am going to head out to pack up some bags for her. Give me your keys and I will put them in your car." He said in a hushed whisper for only me to hear. Raising his voice for Kelli to hear, he made an excuse to slip from the room. "I'm going to run to the bathroom and find Alex, I'll be back in a bit."

Kelli looked up then, and her whole body stiffened. Those beautiful blue eyes slowly softened as she took me in. I made my way to her bed as she continued to stare at me unblinking. My heart was racing under her unyielding stare, not knowing what she was thinking. I don't even know if she wanted me here, let alone if she knew that I was coming. She certainly isn't going to be happy with me in about twenty minutes when I tell her that she is moving in with me for the foreseeable future. Yet, my mind and soul felt more at peace than they had in years. The effect from just being near her was overwhelming.

I got to her side, reaching out to squeeze her hand when she pulled me in for a hug, still not saying a word to me. "I'm here dove," I whisper into her neck as her whole body relaxes into mine. "I've got you now." I hold on to her for longer than is necessary, rubbing up and down her back before reluctantly letting her go. I pulled Danny's chair closer to her so I could still hold her hand. "How are you doing?" I don't miss the watery look in her eyes as she took a deep breath, looking up to the ceiling.

"I'm okay, despite everyone making a big deal." She side

eyes the nurse who chuckles while she removes a cuff from her arm.

"Your blood pressure and heart rate are back within a normal range. I'll let Dr. Pham know and I'm sure he will let you get out of here," the nurse says before exiting the room. Kelli removes her hand from mine and pulls her knees up to her chest, resting her head on them. Her head is facing me as she looks at me warily.

"Why are you here, Brian? And how'd you get here so fast?"

I snicker and grab her hand back again, rubbing circles into the inside of her wrist. "I sped the whole way. Wouldn't be surprised if I have a warrant out for me now," I joke.

"That doesn't answer the first question." She looks down at our connected hands but doesn't pull away this time. Her eyes drop down to my outfit again. "What were you doing before you came here? Your shirt and pants are filthy." I look down, and sure enough, I am a mess. My jeans are covered in dirt, my flannel is fully open and the once white T shirt beneath it has brown smudges and sweat lines on it. Yeah, not my best appearance I suppose.

"I was chopping wood, and then I heard you were in trouble and just got in the car. You know I will always come for you, Kel," I sigh as she looks away again. I know she is thinking about the night I promised I was coming back to be with her, and never did. "So, we need to talk about what happened tonight." I say, ready to change the heavy mood that has settled over us. The subject change doesn't help at all as she bristles and pulls her hand back.

"The police haven't told me anything yet and I don't know where Alex went." She sounds defeated, and it makes me hate this whole situation even more.

"I spoke with him in the hall before I came in here. That

man threw six bricks through your windows, all with threatening notes on them. As pissed as I am right now that you have been lying to me about all this, I just want to make sure you're safe. Danny, Alex and I agreed that the safest place for you to be right now is with me." Her eyes shoot to me, but I cut her off before she can argue. "There is no way in hell you are going back to your house, and Danny and Alex have been to your house so frequently, there's no way your stalker wouldn't go over there to find you. Alex is already talking to HR to get you some time off, and Danny is packing up some of your stuff. When you're ready to get out of here, we are leaving out of the employee entrance and going straight back to my place where you will stay until this man is caught."

There is no way I will allow Kelli to fight me on this. My house is the safest place for her, and more importantly, I want her there. I have missed everything about her and to be able to have her in my home, close to me at all times, was something I craved on a visceral level.

She crossed her arms over her chest, bunching up the big hospital gown. "So because you three decided, I just have to go along with it. You're not responsible for me, Brian. I'm not yours, I would hardly say we are even close anymore. You're off the hook. I'll get a hotel or rental or something for the time being. I can't just leave work." Her arguments were weak and she knew it. Alex had informed me that she was also being watched while going to and from work. "Thank you for your concern, but I am a big girl and I can take care of myself."

This version of Kelli was different from the girl I had left behind. I used to be the person she looked to in order to fight her battles and say out loud what she couldn't. There was always a little fire in her, but she used to keep it well hidden. I wonder what has changed to bring that fire to the surface? I clenched my hands and leaned forward to put my face in hers. "You are mine, little dove, and you will absolutely be coming with me. I know you can take care of yourself, but I will be damned if I let another man get his hands on you. I will carry you out of here kicking and screaming if I have to. Don't think you want that in front of your co-workers but so help me, I will do it."

Her face turns red as she shifts her legs in the bed. "If you really wanted me around, you would have come back for me four years ago. You didn't. So, this little caveman act is because you feel you have to, not because you want to and that's bullshit, Brian. I am not your responsibility and I refuse to be your burden."

A doctor walked into the bay right then before I could explain to her that she was my responsibility, but she was never and would never be a burden. That being able to have her in my home and the ability to look out for her was all I wanted out of life. There was so much I could say, probably should say, but now we would have time to have those conversations.

The doctor told Kelli her paperwork was ready and she was good to go home, followed by the nurse that was in here earlier informing her she was off the schedule for the next week, and that HR was going to be in touch with her. Kelli had a death glare aimed at me the whole time and I tried to keep the smirk off my face, but I saw the subtle relief in her posture underneath it all. I knew this was the right move, and despite her stubbornness she knew it as well. I shot off another quick text to the guys letting them know we were heading home now.

I helped Kelli find her slippers she had come in with, and couldn't help but chuckle at the manatees on her tank top that matched her pajama pants. She had always been adamant about her pajamas having animals on them, and I loved that she never grew out of that. She didn't have a jacket with her, and I wanted to give her my shirt, but it was filthy and smelled like sweat. I'm sure Logan has a sweater in his car she can wear so she doesn't get cold.

"I can carry you out, it will keep your slippers clean." I offer knowing she will hate the idea.

"I am perfectly fine walking." Her hands rubbed over her arms to keep them warm.

As we leave the hospital, I wrap my arm tight around her shoulder to help cover her as best as I can in case there is a chance her stalker is around and to give her some of my warmth. We met Danny at the car that he had parked by the doors of the employee lot. "They wouldn't let me in the house so Alex was in charge of packing some things for you, I hope he got everything you will need. Don't worry about anything here, we will take care of the house and the damage. Alex and I will keep you updated on the investigation, but you WILL stay with Brian until this man is caught." Kelli crosses her arms again. "Don't even give me that look, Kelli. You didn't see the damage he did. Your life is not worth you proving something to us. I love you, and be safe." As my baby brother holds her close and kisses her head, I feel my chest squeeze tight. It has been so long since I have seen them together, and it reminds me of everything I thought I had in my future and everything that I lost.

7

KELLI

The silence in the car was deafening as I leaned toward the side window and tried to sleep. Of course I couldn't, between my frustration, my overactive brain and the heated looks I could feel Brian giving me, I was very painfully awake. I wasn't sure if he was upset at the fact he was kept out of the loop, or that he was now stuck with me for the foreseeable future. That, however, is all on his shoulders. I didn't choose this. I still wasn't really sure how to feel about it all. There was no denying that Brian has always felt safe to me. Even though he crushed me, my stupid heart longed for the feeling of safety that his words brought me.

To make matters worse, he looks even better than when I saw him last. When he walked into my hospital room earlier, my brain short circuited. He towered over me at 6'2" and even with his dirty jeans and open flannel, his body looked larger and harder than ever. God, those thick powerful thighs that filled out every inch of his jeans were going to haunt my dreams. The sexy scruff that clung to his sharp chin and deep brown eyes that always could see straight to my soul. I don't want to have to stay in the same house as him, with his devastatingly rugged good looks. He crushed me without an ounce of remorse and I can't easily hide the pain of that from him. Hopefully his house is big enough that I can avoid him as much as possible.

That's when I remembered what Danny had mentioned a few years back. I sat up, looking over at him, "Do you still have roommates?"

He glanced over at me as he merged toward an off ramp from the highway. "Yeah, Josh, Logan and I live together. Don't worry, they don't mind you staying and are good guys."

He had to be kidding. Not only was I being forced to invade his space, but now I was also thrust upon two others as well? I'm sure they don't want me there, and Josh was not super high on my list of people I wanted to see. I was still a little embarrassed about the fact that I never heard from him again, but he was kind when we met and when he answered my calls. I know Logan also served with them, but that was as much as I knew about him. I huffed out a breath. "I don't want to put anyone out, you can just bring me to a hotel now. I'm nowhere near Boston, and I'll use cash." Being forced to rely on even more men was starting to really piss me off. To make matters worse, I really could use a good cry and a tub of ice cream again, and I don't need that humiliation to be witnessed.

"Not happening, Kel. Logan already won't shut up about having someone new to bake for," his jaw ticked like he was annoyed by that, "and you met Josh. He makes a habit of being a loner and is just happy you'll be safe. We have a guest room ready, but you'll have to share a bathroom with Josh. You'll be safe with us and that is all I care about."

I wasn't too sure on how to respond to that, so I just let it be. I was too tired to argue, it was after 2 AM now, and my body was ready to crash. We drove on back roads surrounded by massive trees, and every once in a while, there was enough of a gap that I caught glimpses of a lake. It looked like a beautiful area, and I couldn't wait to see it in the daytime. I could no longer see any homes, just long driveways that were well spaced out. Eventually, Brian flipped on his blinker and we turned right into a driveway with a large automated gate that opened as we drove up. The trees were just as dense along the driveway as I stared into the inky black woods. When pale light appeared ahead of us, my mouth dropped open.

The massive cabin, if you can even call it that, in front of us was breathtaking. It had elements of a traditional log cabin, like the beautiful cedar logs making up most of the two stories surrounded by massive stones at the base. The front porch was large and covered, with the most incredible set of double doors in the center. Brian pulled into a three-car garage to the left of the home, turning off the car with a heavy sigh. I looked over as he dragged his hands down his face looking utterly exhausted.

His head rolled toward me as he took me in. His brown eyed gaze stayed on my face for a minute before slowly making its way down to my feet and back up. I should have been embarrassed about the fact that I'm in a big sweatshirt he had handed me from the car, my manatee pajama pants and my Ugg slippers, but I wasn't. Brian looked at me with such a softness, and a hint of longing, or maybe that was just wishful thinking on my part. It had been so long since anyone looked at me that way, probably since he looked at me last all those years ago. I was waiting on him to say something, anything, but he didn't. He just stepped out of the car, moving around back to the trunk to grab my bags. As I stepped out to follow, my eyes traveled around the garage. I noticed Josh's truck and a blue Jeep along the back wall with stacks of organized storage shelves and tool boxes. I walked back to the trunk to help, pleasantly surprised to see him pulling out a large suitcase and two large bags. Hopefully this means that Alex had gotten and packed everything that I would need.

I grab one of the bags and hold a hand out in an "after you" motion for Brian who has the other two bags. "Lead the way."

We step through a large mud room where Brian ditches his wallet, keys and shoes into a cubby, so I do the same with my slippers into an empty spot. I follow him quickly through the rest of the dark house, getting a glimpse of a large kitchen and spacious living room as we start ascending a staircase near the front of the home. The top landing of the stairs is open to the home below, with a hall to the left and right. "You and Josh are on this side, Logan and I are on the other." He strides down the right hallway where there is a door on either side and one at the end. He points to the right, "that's Josh's room, the bathroom is the door at the end, and this will be your room." He pushes open the door to the left, flipping on the light.

The room is large with a matching oak dresser, bed and nightstands. The walls are a pale gray that match the soft and fluffy looking comforter. I let my fingers trace over it as I walk further into the room. The curtains, throw pillows and chair in the corner are all a beautiful sage green. Besides a lamp on the nightstand and a picture of a hazy forest on one wall, it is a plain room, but still looks elegant and cozy. Brian sets my bags down outside the closet and looks around the room as if he is inspecting it.

"There are extra towels in the linen closet in the bathroom

if you want to take a shower. The sheets and everything are fresh. Is there anything else you need before the morning?"

"No, thank you. This is really nice." I just wanted to crawl into the bed and sleep for days until this whole nightmare was over. "Really, Brian, I know I have been acting ungrateful, but thank you."

He pulls me into a hug, pressing my face into his chest with one hand while stroking down my back with the other. I slowly feel my body relax and melt into him. He smells like sandalwood, the earth, and a hint of sweat. The more my body relaxes, the more my pent-up emotions from the day struggle to break free. The knot in my throat feels thick, my lower lip quivering as I try to take even breaths. Brian bends down, cradling my body in his arms, and carries me over to the bed. He pulls the blankets back with one hand and gently lowers me into the soft bed. Covering me back up with the comforter, his fingers push my wayward hair from my face before he leans down to place an achingly soft kiss to my forehead. "Get some rest, Kelli. I'll see you in the morning." With that, he walks out, turning off the light and closing the door behind him. I take in another slow breath, waiting for the tears to come. Before they can, sleep takes me.

Waking up the next morning, I feel sweaty and disoriented. I blink up at an unfamiliar ceiling a few times before sitting up and looking around, remembering the cozy room I am in at Brian's house. The subtle smell of cinnamon and juniper trees hits my nose. Looking down, I realize I still have the sweatshirt on and am under the thick comforter, too. I slept so soundly, I don't think I moved once last night. There's no clock that I can see, so I slip my legs from under the covers and trudge over to my purse at the bottom of the bed, pulling my phone out. Of course it's dead. *Why?!* I open the bag I carried in, looking for a charger, but instead find my make-up, shower and bathroom supplies. It looks like Alex just opened all my bathroom drawers and shoved everything he found in here, as well as everything in my shower. I can't complain though, at least he was thorough with packing.

I move to the next bag and find shoes, my laptop, my Kindle, and my chargers. *Win!* I pull out my phone charger and plug in my phone, setting it on the nightstand. Moving back to the first bag, I pull out everything I need for a shower and meander my way to the bathroom. Thankfully, no one is in the hall because one look in the bathroom mirror when I close the door has me cringing. My face is puffy, my eyes lined in dark circles, and my hair is a frizzy nest on top of my head. I take a good look around the bathroom and let out a small squeal of delight. The floors and shower tiles are stunning black slate tiles. There is a mahogany double vanity and a large window over a large free-standing tub that overlooks the woods outside. It is all moody tones with crisp lines. It's hard to believe that someone uses this bathroom at all. I open a few drawers and sure enough, there are men's supplies below one of the sinks, but nothing lined up on the counter.

The glass paneling in front of the shower is clear, the wall adjacent to the shower head filled with buttons to control the jets and temperature. I mess around with them until I have the hot water going. Stripping out of my pajamas, I grab my shower supplies and step in. The heat and the water pressure feel amazing on my tight muscles. If I can just spend my time here between this shower and the comfy bed, I would be happy. As I lather my hair, my stomach lets out a grumble that echoes into the room. Okay, maybe I would also need to spend some time in the kitchen.

Feeling like a whole new woman, I step out of the shower realizing I forgot to grab a towel and the linen closet is on the other side of the bathroom. Looking around, I make the executive decision to use Josh's towel and just grab a new one for him. I wrap his oversized blue towel around my body and walk across the tiles to the closet to grab a new towel to replace his and grab one for my hair. A quick glance in the closet proves this is the only blue towel and all the ones in the closet are white. *Shit*. I grab two white ones and put one on his hook anyway, using the other to wrap around my hair. After brushing my teeth, I grab my pile of clothes and try to slip back into my room to get dressed. Right as I step out of the bathroom, Josh steps out of his room and our eyes lock. I freeze as his gaze slowly trails down my body, his nostrils flaring when he sees the blue towel wrapped around me.

"Logan made coffee and breakfast," is all he says as he turns and practically runs downstairs, while I slink back into my room embarrassed. I throw on some leggings and a sweater, put my hair into a bun on my head and make my way downstairs. This is going to be painful and awkward no matter when I do it, and I could really use a cup of coffee so it might as well be now.

I can hear the guys talking downstairs as soon as I am in the hallway. I slow my steps, trying to make out what they are saying, but when I get to the balcony, my feet stall. There is a beautiful wood railing open to the large living room below, but that isn't what stopped me. Beyond the room is a two-story wall of windows looking over their large expanse of a yard all the way down to the lake. It has to be mid-morning based on the sun glittering over the water. From here, it looks like they might have a small plot of beach at the edge of their yard with a few trees scattered throughout. Both sides of the yard are surrounded by dense woods and large trees. It is private, but yet, it has an open feel and is absolutely breathtaking.

I am standing there staring so long, I don't realize the

voices below have stopped talking. I look down to see Brian and Josh sitting at a dining table to the left and a man that must be Logan leaning against a large opening that leads to the kitchen with all three staring up at me. I give a small awkward wave and turn, heading the rest of the way downstairs.

Logan's warm smile greets me first. "Good morning, Kelli, it's nice to officially meet you. I'm Logan, you hungry?"

I smile back, avoiding the other two sets of eyes I can feel on me. "Nice to meet you, too. I'm starving, and I would kill for a cup of coffee."

He lets out a soft laugh, putting his hand on my arm leading me into the kitchen. "Let's get you some food then. I made all the fixings for breakfast burritos. There's bacon, eggs, potatoes, and peppers on the stove, and tortillas, cheese, and sauce options on the island. What would you like?"

The kitchen is beautiful with gray cabinets, marble counters and an oversized butcher block island. My eyes travel around, spotting the coffee pot, my feet immediately heading to it to pour myself a cup. Logan huffs a laugh, moving around me to open the fridge. "A woman after my own heart. We have some creamers, half and half, and milk in here if you need it. Want me to make your burrito while you do that?"

"Please, that sounds great. I will take a little of everything in it." I grab some vanilla creamer and pour it into my cup. I put the creamer back in the fridge, then turn and lean against the cabinets next to it, taking a sip. A small moan escapes as the first sip hits my tongue, heavenly after my day yesterday. Logan is standing at the stove making my plate and I can't help but let my eyes wander down him. He is taller than Josh and Brian, probably around 6'4", but he isn't as big as the other two. Where Josh and Brian are all bulging muscles,

Logan is more lean muscle, but definitely still cut. He is wearing a white t-shirt that shows off the swirling colors of his tattoos on his biceps and clings to the muscles of his back every time he shifts around. He also has on black sweatpants with no socks. I can't tell if my mouth is watering from this divine coffee or the man in front of me. "Thank you for making breakfast. And letting me stay here."

He turns to the island to add cheese and salsa, but pauses to make eye contact. "It wasn't even a question. We are happy to have you here and the three of us will ensure you are safe. With that being said, those assholes aren't always the greatest with words, or actions for that matter, so don't take anything personally and let me know if I can get you anything." Logan hands me my plate nodding to the table in the next room. "Go ahead, I'm going to make myself one and I'll be right in."

Josh and Brian are sitting across from each other at the table. I wasn't sure I wanted to sit by either of them at the moment. Despite him putting me to bed, I was still mad at how dismissive Brian was to my feelings yesterday. Even if his demands did make me a little hot. Every action still made me feel like a burden and there was no communication from him that said otherwise. I grab the chair next to Josh and sit down. "Sorry for taking your towel," I quietly mumble to him. "I forgot to grab one. I will wash it and put it back." I can feel my face heat with mortification, so I hide it behind a sip of my coffee.

"It's fine." He mutters back before taking a bite of his burrito. I glance up at Brian who is glaring between Josh and me. They both have plates in front of them, but it looks like they waited to start eating until I got here. It was an oddly sweet sentiment, especially coming from these two grumpy men.

Logan sits down across from me. "How did you sleep, Kelli?" he asks, digging into his burrito. Sitting across from me, I get a better view of him, and damn is it a nice view. His light brown hair is a little unruly with a sexy mussed up look above dark blue eyes on a classically handsome face. Straight white teeth, golden brown skin, and panty dropping dimples when he grins at me. It's becoming clear that while I might be safe in this house, my panties certainly aren't.

"I slept great. That bed, and honestly, even that shower, might be the best things I've ever encountered."

I can feel Brian's gaze boring into me from across the table. "If you need anything, just ask. Logan has a grocery list on the pantry door. Add anything to it you want and we will get it for you. I'll show you around the house after breakfast. We have cameras around the property, so you're free to spend time outside whenever." I roll my eyes at that. Like I would be asking permission to go outside. "Don't roll your eyes at me. If you would like to go anywhere, you can ask one of us to take you but it's probably best if we avoid that. If you want to walk the property, one of us can accompany you. Josh and I work from home most of the time, and Logan is in and out all week for work, but we will ensure you are never left here alone." Brian's protectiveness of me clearly hasn't waned over time.

"So, you forced me to come stay here and then essentially put me on house arrest with babysitters? I am not the little girl you used to know, Brian. I won't be treated like a child, I will happily go back home and relieve the burden of your self-imposed babysitting duties."

"Damn it, Kelli! If you want to behave like a child, I will treat you like one!" He rakes his hands through his hair, tugging a little on the ends. "Why is it so hard for you to accept help? This home with the three of us is the safest place for you right now. That's all I want." He looks down and drags his hands down his face. "I just need to make sure you are safe." He sounds defeated and I feel a little bad for that. Logan leans over and squeezes his shoulder while pinning him with a meaningful stare.

"I'm sorry. I don't mean to sound ungrateful." My voice is as small as I feel. I grab my plate and head toward the kitchen. There are whispers behind me as the first tear falls. I put my dishes into the dishwasher and head back for the stairs to hide in my room.

8

LOGAN

Well, we were off to a great start there. As soon as Kelli gets in the kitchen, I turn and punch Brian in the shoulder. "You need to cool it. She woke up yesterday thinking everything was fine and in the span of 24 hours, everything has changed. We know she is safest here, but we need her to be able to feel that. She is still a person with feelings, and to that point, a very strong independent person based on her career and your stories. You have stripped her of all of that." I level him with a glare and move it to Josh. "And you need to make an effort to be kind to her. Both of you need to do better."

I hop up in search of Kelli, catching her halfway up the stairs. "Kelli, wait," I state as she stops and turns to me, and I immediately feel like an asshole seeing the tears in her eyes. "I'm sorry about that. I meant it when I said we want you here. How about I show you around so you can see it's not too shabby of a place to be on house arrest," I joke.

She wipes her eyes and chuckles. My distraction techniques have always been a strong suit of mine. "Alright come on, we can start upstairs." I step around her and walk up the steps to her and Josh's side. "You already saw your room and the bathroom. Obviously, this is Josh's command central."

I push Josh's bedroom door open. His room is all dark woods, blacks and grays just like his bathroom. On one wall he has a large desk with three monitors and all his tech he has designed on shelves around it. "We all have offices down-stairs, but he prefers to do most of his geeky stuff up here. Don't tell people, but we are all a little geeky in this house." She makes a hum sound as she looks around, but doesn't enter the room so I move on. "Brian and I have rooms on this side. We both have private bathrooms that you are welcome to use if you ever need to." I take her to Brian's bedroom first. His bed is a mess of sheets and blankets, which is not at all like him, so I know he is on the way to spiraling into a dark place again.

Kelli actually walks into his room and lets her fingers trail on his dresser, looking at all the photos lined up above it. I'm doing my best not to watch her too closely, but damn, it's hard. I've seen photos of her, in fact one is hanging in front of her right now, but they do nothing to capture her beauty. Her tight black leggings are hugging her long muscular legs and accentuating her perky round ass. She has a cropped baggy sweater on that shows off her toned stomach, but hides the rest of her. A small button nose and pouty pink lips. What really gets me, though, is her light blue eyes and the secrets they hold. She holds so much depth and emotion in one look and it tugs at something in me.

"Has he had these photos up long?" She asks, looking at one on the end of her asleep on Brian's chest he had taken. It is the same photo he had printed and hung by his bed in our barracks when he came back from his leave at home.

"Since the day he moved in." She looks up at it one last time before walking back towards the door. We go to my room next, and I feel a little bout of anxiety. I haven't had a woman in this room yet and I suddenly feel aware of the clothes sitting on the floor next to the hamper. My bed is also a mess, but that is par for the course with me. "Here is my home sweet home." I watch her walk around my room, taking it all in. I have forest green walls with white furniture and a comforter. She looks at the few photos I have on my walls of my family, then peeks into my bathroom, which I know has stuff all over the counter.

"I don't know why I expected this place to be a mess, but you guys are surprisingly clean and organized." She walks back toward the hall. "Well, the other two are at least," she says, smirking over her shoulder. She's got me there. I keep the house clean, but my room is the one place just for me, and the mess makes me feel more human.

"It's that military training that has been ingrained in us. I probably do the most cleaning of the three of us, but we all pitch in."

She slows as we walk back down the stairs. "That's surprising. I can help with that while I'm here, I find cleaning relaxing. I'm also a pretty decent cook, so I am happy to help with meals, too. Do you guys normally eat together?"

"I'm never going to turn down help, but know you don't have to do anything. We eat most dinners together when we can, but fend for ourselves the rest of the time. Sometimes on the weekends, we do breakfast together like this morning." Dishes clang from one of the guys still cleaning up in the kitchen, so I head to the stairs leading down to the basement.

"Oh, okay. What are your guys' schedules like? Do you work with Josh and Brian for their security company?"

With a hand to her lower back, I angle her toward the movie room first. "I actually am a detective for the county, working as a computer forensic investigator. I can work from home a bit, but travel to any of the precincts in the county to help with any cases they need worked on in person. Josh and Brian don't necessarily hold typical business hours. Josh is always working on upgrading and reworking the tech, and Brian focuses more on the business aspect of it. They travel sometimes for client meetings and such, but are pretty flexible in their schedules. But continuing on with the tour, this is what we call the movie room. Feel free to use it and anything in it whenever."

When designing the remodel for this place, this room was my favorite. Along one side wall is built in shelves with books, knick-knacks and games. In the center of the room is a large U-shaped couch that could easily seat 10 but mostly we use it for sprawling out to watch movies or play video games when the mood strikes. On the main wall is a large projection screen that rolls up when we aren't using it. The other side wall has a small poker table and two leather chairs that only Josh uses when he can't sleep and sneaks down here to read. Kelli smiles to herself as she reads over the titles of some of the books. When she turns back to me, I wave my hand for her toward the gym on the other side of the basement.

I push open the heavy door, "This is our gym. It is sound proof, so if you want to blast your music, go ahead." She walks further in taking in all the equipment and space. We have a row of free weights, a squat rack, treadmills, rower, and bike. We also have a large mat we use for sparring, a punching bag, and an area with yoga mats, bands and mobility sticks for our cool down. As three men that had to stay physically fit for so many years, this was necessary but it also has become our safe space to work out our lingering frustrations.

"This is really nice. I don't think I can come down here though, I would only embarrass myself around you guys."

Her eyes drift to my arms and linger before moving back up to my face.

I try to hold my grin back, but fail. "There is never any judgment here. Plus, it could be fun to train with us, I bet you could even convince Josh to spar with you. He could really teach you a lot." Her eyebrow raises in question. "He may be a big guy, but he is surprisingly nimble and quick. Brian and I have yet to get him pinned without him allowing it."

She laughs at that as we move back upstairs. It's a beautiful and carefree sound that I want to hear again. "Whose house is this, by the way, or do you guys own it together?"

I figured that question was coming. My family's money has always made me a little uncomfortable. I'm not into materialistic things or shows of wealth like them. This 3,700 square foot home has been my only splurge, and it would be considered a modest home by the rest of my family's standards. It's also caused problems with women in the past when they found out how much my family is worth.

"Technically it's in my name, but it is all of ours. I bought it before I joined the Army after falling in love with the location, but it was just a small run-down cabin. When we all started talking about getting out of the military, I had it remodeled and extended to make it perfect for us."

A sweet smile graces her lips, and damn it if I don't love her smile. "That's pretty amazing of you. To not only share your home with friends, but to also build it to specifically fit them. I can see why you love it, though." She absentmindedly stares out the wall of windows overlooking the water in the living room.

"They're family. It's what you do for your family. Let's continue this, shall we? Josh helped to design this living room. He wanted the large stone fireplace and wall of windows. These four actually all slide together into the far wall to make it almost completely open to the deck." In front of the fireplace is a brown leather couch, loveseat and two chairs arranged around a round coffee table. We have a few odd blankets and décor items thrown around the room, but it's glaringly obvious this home is inhabited by three men. The dining room is open to the living room and has a long live edge table. "You have already seen the kitchen, and laundry room, so that just leaves this hall."

With a gentle hand on her back, I steer her down the hall. Her warm skin below the sweater is smooth against my fingers as I hold back from gripping her further. "Half bath is on the right here, and then these two doors are offices. Mine is on the end, and this one, Josh and Brian share." The door is cracked, so I push it open to a glaring Brian. His eyes soften as soon as they land on Kelli, but go right back to glaring at me when he sees my hand at her back.

"Hey, Kel, what do you think of the house so far?" Brian moves his gaze back to her and roams down her body. Her body goes rigid in front of me the longer she stays in front of him.

"There are worse places to be on house arrest" she quips. I can't help my smirk at her snarky repeated phrase.

"I'm sorry, Kel, I didn't mean to make you upset. What can I do?" He looks pained, eye brows pinched together. I know how much love he has for this girl, he just doesn't know how to show it anymore. I want to help him, but I also want Kelli to feel comfortable in this house and her body language right now is showing anything but.

"Let me finish my tour in peace." With that she walks out and heads for my office.

I just shrug at him hoping time between them both will help. "Give her time, man." With a rap of my knuckles on the door frame, I turn to follow Kelli.

I find her in my office looking at all the photos on the shelves behind my desk. "Is this your family?" She asks, pointing at a photo of my brothers, parents and I at a New Year's party my parents hosted a few years back.

"Yeah, Luke and Caden are both older than me. They followed in my parent's footsteps; Luke is a surgeon like my mother and Caden is a corporate lawyer like my father." It is clear, even from that photo, how different I am from my family. They were all dressed in brand names, not a wrinkle between them, whereas I was in jeans and a button down, much to my parent's dismay. They still don't understand why I decided to join the Army, and while they certainly aren't disappointed in me, my accomplishments will always pale in comparison to my brothers.

"You all look so happy," her quiet voice sounds sad.

"What about your family?" I ask. I know she has no siblings from Brian, but that's about it.

"It's always just been my mom and me. It was lonely growing up. She is a great mom and she did her best with me, but she worked a lot and I was put on the back burner pretty frequently. That's why it was so great when I met Danny and his whole family took me in." She smiles up at me. "Brian and Danny fought with me like I was their long-lost sister, and their parents showed up at my soccer games when my mom couldn't. Their mom took me prom dress shopping, she even bought me my first bra." I chuckle with her at that, as that sounds exactly like the Stirling family I have come to know and love. "They let me feel what it was like to be part of a family. Set the standards for what I want when the time comes for me to have one."

She turns back to the shelves and continues looking at the photos. It made my chest feel heavy that she felt she had to be part of someone else's family and not her own. My parents hired nannies to help with us boys because of their wild schedules, but when they were home, they tried to be all in with us. Sitting at the table helping us with homework when they could, showing up to major events, taking us on trips without outside distractions. Every kid should have parents that put them first.

"Look at you all," she squeals, pointing at a photo of our squad on our last tour. "Wow, you guys look hot in your uniforms." My blood heats in a way I won't be telling Brian about. "Do you guys still keep in touch with everyone?"

A knot wells up in my throat like it always does thinking about that last tour. Brian never steps foot in my office, and I know this photo is the reason. While I like it as a reminder of the incredible team we had and in honor of the life we lost, he feels it's a reminder of his failures. No matter how many times we have told him it was not his fault, he held onto that guilt. There were nine of us that worked as a team for most of that deployment. We all were really close, spending the majority of our down time together as well. We had two women, Kayla and Ashley, on the team. Ashley and another member, Caleb, fell in love while overseas and started talking about getting married once they got home. We all watched it happen and should have said something and gotten them separated, but seeing a love like theirs had us letting them quietly break the unspoken rules.

Six weeks before our deployment ended, we were sent on a mission to gather further intel on a tip that had been handed down to us. We were in a two-car motorcade traveling toward a small town to get surveillance and drone photos to verify if the tip was good or not when we were ambushed. Our route was blocked with a car on fire, and before we could get turned around, gunshots were ringing out. We took on heavy fire and were vastly outnumbered. Josh took shrapnel in the thigh when the IED exploded next to us, and Henry, another member, was shot in the shoulder. While most of the rest of us escaped with only cuts and bruises, Ashley took a hit to the neck that ended her life immediately. Brian was the officer in charge of that mission and the one who planned out the route that we took. Because of that, Caleb still hasn't forgiven Brian, and Brian has never forgiven himself.

"Mostly," is all that I offer her. I put my hand on her back again, encouraging her to move toward the door, wanting to be done with the conversation.

"Can we walk down to the water?" Kelli asks, looking so full of excitement and thankfully not picking up on my mood shift. Seeing a true smile on her face helps brighten my mood as we head out the sliding doors to the back porch. The center of the porch houses an outdoor sofa with a small fire pit in the center and an outdoor table and chairs. Both sides have a covered section, one housing our small outdoor kitchen, the other housing our hot tub. As we walk through the yard, I tell her about our security measures out here which include scattered cameras along the property line and the yard line that are triggered by movement.

When we get to the small pebbly beach, Kelli immediately toes off her sandals and dips her feet in the water. A loud laugh bursts from me at the surprised scream she lets loose. "Oh, come on, it can't be that cold," I taunt knowing full well that water is cold year round. She slowly turns around with a glint in her eyes and I know I'm in trouble.

"Oh yeah?" She kicks her leg at me, sending water spraying over my sweats. I can't believe the boys are inside sulking and pissing off this woman. Her whole world is crashing around her and yet here she is trying to make the most of the situation and not letting it wreck her. When her whole face lights up and she lets out a lighthearted and carefree laugh, I feel the radiance of it down to my bones. There are people that you cross paths with in life that you just know are going to stamp themselves on your soul, and you get to keep a piece of them forever. I've always considered it a passport of sorts, where I collect these little moments and pieces of others to carry with me always. Watching Kelli splash around in the cold water, face turned up to the sun, a look of absolute reverence on her face… yeah, she was officially stamped.

"You're going to get it now!" I grab her around the waist, hiking her over my shoulder and walk further into the water. Squeals and giggles erupt from behind me as she tries to grab onto my shoulders and pinch my lower back, yelling at me to put her down. "Put you down, eh?" I'm up to my knees now in the water, but hold Kelli up high enough her toes are barely touching the water. I gently slide her down my body, lowering her into the water while she kicks her legs, soaking both of us even more.

We both race back to the shore laughing. She plops down on the beach, not a care in the world that her leggings are soaked and the ground is dirty. I sit down next to her, enjoying the companionable silence for a while. This small beach and private lake is a big reason for me originally buying this land, yet I couldn't think of the last time I had come out here to just sit and enjoy it. Eventually, she broke the silence. "Thank you, Logan. I really needed this today."

I let my head roll to the side, taking her in. Her bun is coming undone, strands of her hair sticking out all over, her face flushed, and yet, she's by far the most striking woman I have met. I cross my arms over my bent knees so I won't be tempted to push her hair behind her ear. "You can talk to me, you know?" I watch her shoulders hunch as she starts closing herself off immediately, her whole body seizing up. "But if you just need someone to hang out with and clear that mind of yours, I'm your guy for that, too."

I want her to open up to me. I want to know more about her than what Brian has shared over the years. I have always been the one that my friends come to with problems. The level- headed, think it through with an outside perspective type. I know I could help Kelli with how she was feeling, but I needed her to open up to me. We stayed out on the beach for another two hours, talking and joking with each other before eventually making our way back inside. As Kelli headed upstairs to shower and nap, I decided to head to the local precinct to see what I could find out about her case and see if I could help.

9

KELLI

After spending the morning with Logan, I took a quick rinse to shower off the lake. I told Logan I was going to nap, but I just needed an hour to myself to unpack my things and clear my head. I was surprised to find my closet filled with empty hangers for my clothes. By the time everything was unpacked and neatly put away, my stomach was growling again. Venturing out of my room, I went in search of the boys to see if they had eaten lunch yet. I still don't love the idea of being stuck here, but I'm still grateful for them taking me in and keeping me safe. Since Josh was right across the hall, I decide to start there. His door is cracked open, so I knock, then slowly push it open. He turns around in his desk chair when I peek in.

"Hey, Kelli, are you okay?" Taking that as an invitation, I walk a little further in his room. His computer setup looks totally different with all the monitors on lighting up the wires and parts spread out over his desk. The slight scent of cedar and vanilla surrounds me as I walk towards him.

"Yeah, I just wanted to see if you have had lunch yet? I

was going to make a sandwich and can make one for you if you would like."

His eyebrows hike up, a little surprised before they soften and his lip quirks up, but he quickly shuts it down returning to a blank face. "I would love one, thanks. I just need to finish this and I will be right down."

"Perfect, do you know where Logan and Brian are? Figured I would ask them, too."

"Logan went into work, but Brian is probably in his office." His back turns to me as he starts tinkering with the parts on his desk again, so I exit his room and mosey downstairs to find Brian. Josh's brash attitude shouldn't surprise me after he set up my cameras, but the brush off still stung a little. The office door downstairs is wide open, showing Brian slumped behind his desk blankly staring at his computer.

"I work the same way with patients; if I stare at them long enough, they just fix themselves," I quip from the doorway, trying to gauge his mood. His brown eyes meet mine with a smile on his lips, but it doesn't reach his eyes. Apparently everyone but Logan is going to act a little standoffish with me here. Logan said they want me here, but with these reactions, I can't help but feel like I'm a burden.

"Please tell me you need something I can help with because this client contract is frying my brain." His long legs eat up the distance between us easily until he is hovering over me, pushing a piece of my wild hair behind my ear. His fingers trace down the side of my face stopping to hold my neck possessively. "I'm sorry I was harsh. I just need to know that you're okay. I know I overstepped."

I cover his hand on the side of my neck with my own before letting it trail down his arm and fall back to my side, giving him a small nod. "I was going to make sandwiches for Josh and me, and wanted to see if you would like one, too?"

He pulls on that strand of my hair he just pushed back like he used to when we were kids, dropping a chaste kiss on my head before walking past me heading for the kitchen. I stare after him a little dumbfounded.

"Let's go, I'm not making these by myself," he calls over his shoulder as I follow him, shaking my head. I guess he's getting over his attitude from this morning. As frustrated as I am with him, he holds a large part of my heart and I miss being able to joke and talk with him. He and Danny have always been my best friends, and it really hurt losing him in that capacity.

I pull out ingredients from the fridge while he gets what we need from the pantry. We work in companionable silence, him handing me plates with the bread ready while I cut up tomato and lettuce slices. I put the meat and cheese on while he spreads on the condiments. I forgot how well we worked as a team and how easy it could be between us. When we were kids, we could have conversations with just our eyes. It used to drive Danny crazy. Our age gap has never inhibited our connection and ability to just be real with each other. When I got frustrated with my mom missing another soccer game, or not coming home until way after dinner without telling me, Brian was always the one I went to. It wasn't until I was in my teens that I felt that connection change for me. Danny joked once that he saw my 'crush' on his brother, but it was so much more than a crush to me.

Josh came down and we all grabbed a plate and went outside to sit on the patio to eat. We talked about their company and how things were going with it. I had no idea that they were so successful. Danny has mentioned it randomly throughout the years that things were going well, but I didn't realize the extent of that. They had contracts with businesses all throughout Maine, Massachusetts and New

Hampshire, along with those bought for personal use spread throughout the United States. As it turns out, they only have employees to install the systems in businesses and homes within that three-state radius. Even with that, most who bought for their homes installed everything themselves. It made more sense now why Josh came out to install mine and not a random employee.

I told them about the best, worst, and funniest cases that I have worked on in the emergency room. The assumption that we don't see funny scenarios is widely inaccurate. At least twice a month we get the 'fell and accidentally impaled themselves in the ass' people. Drunk men coming in with injuries due to a dare or bet was pretty common as well. I loved a good break from work, but I expressed to them the guilt I felt about leaving work without notice. Despite the circumstances, I knew I was leaving the hospital even more short staffed and sitting around has never been a strong suit of mine.

With a lull in the conversation, I turn to Josh. "Logan mentioned that you would be a good sparring partner and could teach me how to get out of some dicey situations. Would you have time to do that this week?" His green eyes widened with excitement but were quickly replaced by a look of unease. After a glance to Brian, his eyes soften and he nods.

"Can you be up and in the gym by 6:30 every morning?"

"Absolutely! Can we start tomorrow?" I was really looking forward to it. Being able to better defend myself would help my confidence, plus I wasn't going to complain about rolling around on a mat with him. Today he's wearing a shirt that hugs every muscle in his body from his defined pecs down to the v leading into his tight jeans. I take in the warm summer day around us to stop myself from drooling and blatantly staring more than I already have been.

"You know, I could teach you, too." Brian nudges my knee with his. Refusing to meet my eye, he keeps his gaze solely fixed on his plate, but I can see the hurt there.

"I know, but Logan said sparring was Josh's specialty. Would you want to take evening walks with me, or maybe we can tinker around in your flower garden? I really can't sit around here for however long this takes." A muscle in Brian's jaw twitches as he grinds his teeth.

"Yeah, that's fine. You can hang out in my office whenever you would like. Josh and I have talked about handing over some of our responsibility to others and decided we can start that now in order to be available to you these next few weeks." I felt a punch in the walls around my heart that they have already talked about spending more time with me. While I don't want to be a responsibility to them, the thought that they're doing this for me feels really good. Or, it did until I realized what he said.

"Weeks?!" I practically screamed at him. "You think they won't catch this guy for weeks?" I can't stay here for weeks. I need to get back to work, and they would definitely fire me for being gone that long. Plus, what would I do for weeks on end while here? My heart cannot handle being this close to Brian for that long. I have spent years telling myself that he doesn't want me and I have to move on. Being in his house for the last not even 24 hours has been hard enough. My soul called to his. My body was calling to all three of the guys and that is a recipe for disaster if I have to spend weeks here.

"Catching a stalker is not easy. Most cases go unsolved, and most of the solved cases only happen when the stalker gets bold and does something risky like attempting to kidnap or approach the person." Brian doesn't even look sorry about it. Josh at least looks at me with pity, but that doesn't feel much better. "You aren't leaving here until he is caught. Alex and Logan have been in contact, and Alex informed him that HR at the hospital has put you on leave indefinitely until it is safe for you again. They are being really understanding. Logan can show you the emails when he gets home, but ideally, we don't want you emailing them without an encrypted computer so your IP can't be traced."

I stare at him in absolute shock. How dare they do this behind my back. I have worked my ass off for the career that I have, and I love working in the emergency room at Mercy . I push my chair back and walk back into the house, letting the slider slam shut on my way in. As if taking away my freedoms here isn't bad enough, now they are messing with my career. I head back to my room, but the thought of Brian coming to talk to me before I calm down has me grabbing my Kindle and heading to Logan's room, crawling into his big bed to read. His pillows smell like a mix of cinnamon and my favorite Juniper tree, a heady and intoxicating scent.

I don't remember falling asleep, but I wake to Logan gently rubbing my shoulder. "Hey, Kelli, I made dinner if you want some?" He smiles but it doesn't reach his eyes like earlier. Either he doesn't like me in his room, or he talked to the guys about my little outburst earlier. I sit up to follow him downstairs when he pauses at the doorway. "I'm sorry that we talked to the hospital on your behalf. Alex was assured this would not impact your job security, and that your job would be waiting for you when you get back. For what it's worth, they spoke very highly of you and said they would do whatever it took to get you back to them safely, but understood the severity and extenuating circumstances of the situation."

This is exactly why I went to Logan's room. In 24 hours he has been more understanding and in tune to my emotions and thoughts than even Danny who has been my best friend for twenty years. I have never met a man who is so willing to apologize and eager to make me feel seen. It calls to something in me, because the only other person who I have ever felt truly seen by is Brian. While here though, he has been bulldozing me with his words and actions and not making any effort to make sure I am okay with any of it. "Thanks, but I still don't appreciate being treated like this isn't my life. If you guys would have talked to me, then I could have relayed that to my job."

Downstairs in the kitchen, I make a plate then head to the dining room, choosing the seat next to Josh. I keep my head down and don't get involved in the conversation. I decided I will make an effort to talk with Josh and Brian and clear things up tomorrow, but I need the space for today. If I have to stay here for the foreseeable future, then I need them all to be honest with me about what is going on. As Logan and I loaded the dishwasher and wiped the counters, he invited me downstairs to watch a movie with the three of them.

After only one day here, I was already exhausted despite my nap. My head was a mess. Reading my Kindle in that bathtub upstairs, being able to work through all my thoughts and feelings was too enticing, so I declined. After a solid soak in the tub, I set my alarm for 6 AM and tossed and turned until finally falling asleep.

10

JOSH

Sleep has never come easy for me, and deep sleep plays an evasive game with me in which I always lose. It started in my childhood with always being hyper aware of my sisters' bedroom doors being opened at night. I became attuned to all of our house's noises and waking up easily if needed, which has stuck with me ever since. Last night, I laid in bed staring at the ceiling for hours. After Kelli was kind enough to make me lunch, I let her run off upset with Brian without even checking on her.

Communication was always what broke down every situationship I had been in. Even the low maintenance women I was with eventually demanded I talk about how I felt and open up with them. It never happened. It was never really a relationship so I didn't see the point. My sisters swear that I am great at being open and honest with them, and that my problem is simply that I haven't met the right woman that I am willing to be open for. Not sure that I agree with them on that, but only time will tell.

When Logan came home and found her asleep on his bed, he came back downstairs and laid into us. There was no doubt, we knew we had messed up, but neither Brian nor I were sure how to fix it. Or more so, I didn't know how to fix it and Brian was too busy stewing in his feelings to make the effort. I've never been the best with getting my thoughts and feelings out to others though, so Logan was the best choice for her to talk to about it. He was all too happy to volunteer to spend more time with her, only pissing Brian off further.

Something pulled me out of my fitful sleep, and I laid there once again staring at the ceiling, trying to figure out what I had heard when the noise started again. The sounds of muffled voices drifted into my room, making me jump out of bed and rush to the hall. Kelli's soft cries could be heard out here, and I winced knowing I was not innocent in upsetting her. A better man would knock on her door and check on her, but I wasn't sure how to be that man. I turned back toward my room when a whimper sounded through the door and a quiet 'help, please help me' followed. Instinct took over as I rushed into her room only to see her wrapped up in her blankets with her hands covering her ears. In the moonlight, the glistening of tears on her face was visible as she kept muttering to herself to get help.

Nightmares and night terrors were nothing new to me. They had plagued me for months after our ambush, but I had yet to see someone else suffer from them. Sitting on the edge of her bed I gently pulled her hands down from her ears.

"Kelli, wake up." My voice was soft trying to slowly wake her from the dream, which only seemed to scare her more as she started to scream. "Kelli," I shook her hands with a little more force, "wake up, it's Josh. You're safe, it's okay, you're safe." Her screams stopped, but her whimpers remained as her lashes fluttered open, taking in her surroundings before landing on me. Wide eyes filled with fear bounced between my face and where my hands were still holding hers. Blinking a few times as the realization of where she is and who I am kicks in. Her body slowly started to relax back into the bed until her eyes trailed down me and her hands clasped in mine. It's then that I followed her line of sight realizing I'm sitting awfully close to her, dressed only in tight boxers while still holding her hands in my lap.

"Josh? What are you doing in here?" her whisper sounds a little breathless. Quickly letting go of her hands in my lap as my cock twitches at the sound, I curse it immediately, willing it to stay down.

"You were having a nightmare. I just wanted to make sure you were okay." Standing from her bed and taking a few steps away, I look back down at her. Despite the tear tracks and wild hair, she looks beautiful. My eyes can't help but fall from her face and trace down to the silk wrapped tight around her breasts where her nipples are pebbled and hard. I immediately look back up at her face, a little disgusted with myself for even going there. I know what she is feeling right now. The fear that seizes your body and slithers down your spine trying to shake the panic when waking from a nightmare. "Are you going to be okay?"

"Eventually," she mumbles, wrapping herself back up into the blankets. Nodding, I start back toward her door. Her sweet flowery scent was all over this room, it reminds me of the honeysuckle flowers my sisters used to pick as kids. Her soft voice stops me at the doorway, "Thank you, Josh. For checking on me."

With nothing to say to that, I slip from the room, closing her door and lean against the wall next to it. Her sleep-soaked voice is causing the blood to rush south again, despite knowing I should not be turned on in this situation. She was having a nightmare for God's sake, probably about the man that was threatening her, and here I am, lusting after her in the hall. But between her sweet smell, and her hard nipples poking through her silk camisole, my cock does not have the same idea.

I make my way back to my room, putting on some shorts and a t-shirt before heading down to the gym. It wasn't like I would be able to go back to sleep at this point anyway. I did an hour on the treadmill before moving to the weights. Punishing myself in this way is nothing new, and I need to get rid of these feelings sizzling through my veins before Kelli comes down here and I have to roll around on the mats with her. At 6:30 on the dot, the door opens and Kelli pops in, looking a little overwhelmed and embarrassed. I try not to stare at her too long, but damn she looks incredible and my dick still hasn't forgotten her breathy voice and hard nipples pointed at me two hours ago.

She's wearing little black shorts that cling to her like a second skin and a pink loose crop top showing off a slice of her tan stomach. Her hair is up in a tight knot on her head, and damn if I'm not getting hard again just thinking about getting on the mat with her. I should have taken care of myself earlier, but I wasn't convinced that would have made any difference anyway. Putting my weights down, I stride over to her, still just standing in the doorway.

Keeping my head on straight around her is going to be necessary, so I will just stick to what I do best: avoid talking about feelings and getting real with her. "Do you want to do a couple minutes on the treadmill to warm up, or do you want to just jump right into it?"

A pink flush spreads down her chest as her ocean blue eyes meet mine. "Thank you for last night. I'm sorry, I've never had a nightmare like that." Is that why she looks embarrassed? If Logan were here, he would tell me to talk to her about my nightmares so she feels more at ease. If this was going to be her home for a while, and she wanted to train with me, her embarrassment around me would not be conducive. I was about to tell her that she was not the only one in this house that suffered from them and she shouldn't let it bother her, but she kept talking before I could. "I think I would like to get right to it. I have some anxious energy I need to get out and beating your ass sounds like a great way to do it."

A bark of a laugh breaks out of me. "Alright crazy, I would like to see you try." Her flush spreads up to her cheeks, a small smile gracing her lips. "Don't get shy on me now. Let's get you taped up so I can see what you got." I appreciate that she uses humor to deflect. Most people may not consider me a funny guy, but I was much more comfortable dealing with humor than pain. The last time I found a woman's humor truly funny was before my accident. Logan and Brian are constantly ragging on me to lighten up, so maybe being around Kelli would be good for that. Her slender fingers are soft and look fragile as I tape up her hands. Goosebumps travel her arms when I grab her wrists to slip them into the smallest set of gloves that we have, which are still quite a bit too large for her. I make a mental note to order some that will fit her better.

We start off with proper punching technique, which she seems aware of already, so I pick up some mitts and have her do some punching sequences with that. I am pleasantly surprised at the strength she has and the knowledge of how to use her legs to put power in the punches. We move to the heavy bag after a bit, and I hold it in place so she can show me her full strength and form.

With every punch, her shoulders loosen, and her eyes harden, determination and anger leaving her body in waves. I should have her move to the mat again to go over some self-defense and attack techniques before she tires herself out, but I can't make myself tell her to stop. She is working through some things, and it's a beautiful thing to watch. Sweat is dripping down her face and neck, and yet she hasn't let up once. Completely lost to witnessing not only her powerful body at work, but watching as exhaustion hits, yet she pushes through, giving it every last ounce of strength she has. Before she can push herself to the point of passing out, I stop her and help her stretch and cool down.

We are sitting across from each other on the mat while I un-tape her hands and she takes small sips from a water bottle. Trying to focus on her hands and not the way her lips wrap around the rim of the bottle, I clear my throat. She is certainly more than the wholesome girl I met a few weeks ago. There is such a fire in her, and while I still think she is too damn sweet, I see so much more. "You said you've done some self-defense classes before, right?" I ask to try and assess where to start training from here.

"Yeah, but the majority were just teaching how to punch correctly, where to put your weight, and where to aim." She pulls her shirt over her head so now she's in just a sports bra and little shorts, and looks at me, smiling slowly, all while using that shirt to wipe the sweat from her face and neck. "I want to learn how to take you down."

Her spark brings a chuckle to my lips. "I can certainly teach you to try, but you aren't taking me down if I have anything to say about it. Your distractions, while welcome, won't work on me." I trail my gaze down her chest as she blushes again, and damn if I don't like it a whole lot. We spend the next hour going over a few ways to break a hold from the front and behind, as well as how she can get an attacker on the ground.

She has a lot to learn, but there is no denying that below

her sweet exterior is a hard and badass center. That thought alone is a total turn on. Her sweaty and lithe body slides against mine as we maneuver take downs and I hold her close as she works to break loose and I know I'm done for. We set up for me to attack her from the front one more time and she dropped her shoulder, tackling me down on the mat. Kelli immediately jumps on me to rain down punches when I grab her wrists and use my hips to flip our positions. Her chest is heaving, wide eyes on mine before they drop to my lips. *Fuck.* I can't do this with her. Even if Brian says he can't be with her, I don't think he would be fine with me filling that role.

I quickly let go and climbed off her, walking to the mini fridge in the corner to grab us more cold waters. I use this time to my advantage to adjust myself in my shorts while my back is to her. "You did great today, little flame. Want to take some time to stretch out?" I say as I hand her a bottle.

"Little flame?" she asks, staring straight at my dick, which despite my efforts, is still visibly hard.

I sit down so I can hide it a little better even though it is probably pointless now. "Yeah, you're small and underestimated, but you have the power inside of you to wreak total havoc. I'm guessing on the underestimated, because I sure didn't think you had that power in you before today." A slow, sad smile coasts over her face before she looks me in the eyes a beat longer than comfortable, forcing me to look away. I feel bad for underestimating her; I want to make it up to her. Maybe tell her about my nightmares in the past so she feels safe to talk about hers. It's not fair to put all her emotional traumas on Logan to deal with, especially when I can personally understand this one.

11

KELLI

"Better be ready for the havoc you're crafting." I joke back, throwing my shirt off to the side so I have room to spread out. My body is wrecked, my arms feel like they're made of Jell-o and yet, my mind is clear and all my lingering anxiety is gone. I need to cool down and give myself some time to psych myself up for the two sets of stairs between myself and a shower. I stretch my legs out in front of me, reaching for my toes. As Josh follows suit, I notice his shorts ride up revealing a jagged scar leading up his thigh. The muscle below the scar is a little disfigured, but still well defined and large.

He shifts uncomfortably, pulling his shorts back down to cover it. Back in nursing school, I did some volunteer work with the local military hospital. I learned quickly that most of those men and women who sustained injuries hated the amount of pity they received. I have no pity for Josh though, just empathy and maybe a little medical intrigue. Treading carefully is going to be the key here.

"Can I ask about the scar?"

"What about it?"

"When did you get it? It's really impressive that you have no limp or altered gait. You must have had a great physical therapy team." I spread my legs wide leaning down to one side as he follows again.

His gruff voice sends chills down my spine. "Four years ago on deployment. It was rough there for a while, but Brian really pulled me through it all." We switch to the other leg, continuing to stretch.

"Do you want to talk about it? I don't want to pry."

He sits up and runs a hand through his sweaty hair, pinning me with a pained look. "Yeah, I think it would be good for you to hear about this." I'm not sure what he means, so I stay quiet, waiting for him to talk when he's ready. His voice is low but strong as he continues. "There was an incident toward the end of our last deployment. An IED exploded near me, causing a large piece of shrapnel to get embedded in my leg. Logan and Brian were with me at the time, but thankfully, they didn't sustain any major injuries. They got the bleeding under control the best they could, but we were still under fire so it took a bit to get us all back to base."

His eyes had a faraway look, like he was back there, living the moment again in his mind. "I lost a lot of blood, but I was alive. The docs there rushed me into surgery and called it a success, but the wound had been exposed to a lot of bacteria and shit. They had a plan to fly me to the nearest military treatment facility as soon as I was stable. Not even 24 hours after surgery though, my leg was turning purple and I had a fever around 104."

"Sepsis," I whispered.

"Yeah. Brian had stayed with me that whole time and was freaking out. He was yelling at everyone, trying to get me flown out ASAP. When they got a helicopter ready to take me, he refused to leave my side. He got threatened with an

Article 92 for it, but he went with me anyway. When we got to the hospital, they rushed me back into surgery. I had flesh-eating bacteria, so they had to remove the infected muscle and tissue."

He leans back, lifting his shorts all the way up to his groin, showing me the entire thing. The scar is about ten inches long, wrapping from his inner to outer thigh. It's not a clean, smooth line, likely from the amount of muscle and tissue that was removed. I lean forward a little, my fingers itching to touch the muscles around it, but not daring to ruin this moment. He watches my every movement, then lifts his other side up as well so I can see the comparison.

"I lost a lot of my muscle. Despite all the work in physical therapy and since, my thighs are still different sizes, but the pain is minimal and movement and mobility is at about ninety-five percent of where it was before. I wish that was the end of the story. After the second surgery, the infection spread to my foot. They said that it can travel through the bloodstream, and although they removed all the infected tissue, it can still happen. They wanted to amputate."

My breath hitches. I have seen a number of cases where the patient seems to be the exception and one bad thing after another seems to happen to them. It's hard to watch and to even understand why one person's outcome can be so different from another's, despite similar injuries and treatment plans.

"Brian fought for me though. He refused to accept that as the only option. There was the option for high dose antibiotics to stop the spread, but they wanted to take the safe option of amputation. I was hopped up on so many painkillers, I probably would have allowed it had Brian not been there advocating for me. My life would have been a lot different without him. He bulldozes sometimes." My head cocks to the side giving him a pointed stare. "Okay, he bull-dozes a lot," he chuckles, "but he does it with the best of intentions. When he loves, he loves with his entire being and there is nothing, and I mean absolutely nothing, he wouldn't do for those he loves."

"I get that. I've seen it most my life. I'm sorry you went through all of that, but I'm glad you had him by your side." His green gaze is fixed on mine, so I let a smirk free. "Scars on guys are hot though. Gives you a mysterious bad boy vibe."

His laugh is loud and hearty, his head thrown back as his chest bounces. "Did I really need the scar to be seen that way?"

"No." I answer honestly with a smile. We stare at each other in silence for a moment, his eyes roaming over my face before they soften and he looks down.

"About last night…" he starts.

"We don't need to talk about it," I cut in quickly. It's the first time I have ever had a nightmare that felt that real. I wasn't able to go back to sleep after Josh left, and I was a little embarrassed that I woke him up from it.

"I had them, too. They started a few weeks after that second surgery. I would see myself lying on the side of the road bleeding out. Sometimes I would picture myself waking up, realizing my leg was gone. Logan and Brian took turns waking me up because I would wake them up with my screams." His eyes stayed glued to the water bottle he was holding, his fingers playing with the label. The silence stretched between us as I tried to find the right thing to say. Finally, his green eyes traveled up my body, landing on mine. "It's okay to get them. It's okay to feel however you feel. You don't need to be embarrassed about anything here with us. We just want to help, and I just wanted you to know that I understand. If you ever want to talk about it, you can."

He looks uncomfortable with this conversation, and yet he's opening up for me. To help me. My eyes burn, tears forming on the lower lashes trying to break free. I didn't expect this from Josh, especially with the minimal talking he has done so far. I don't feel like a burden to him. One rogue tear breaks free, sliding down my cheek before I can brush it away. He's giving me a glimpse into who he is, and even a little insight into the man Brian has become. He is just doing his best to protect me. It seems like they all are, and after only one day here, they are making me feel more cared for and seen than I have in years. Maybe this house arrest won't be so bad.

Josh lets me sit in my feelings, giving me the option to talk about it now. I'm not ready, though. I don't want to relive it yet. He must sense that I'm not ready to open up about it, so he gathers his water and sweat towel, heading for the door. "Thank you Josh. For everything." His hand stalls on the door for a moment as he looks at me with care. He nods once, then lets the heavy door slam behind him, leaving me to let my tears free in peace.

When I finally make my way upstairs, the water in our shared bath is running so I grab some clothes and sneak into Logan's bathroom to take a shower. His bed is messy as I walk past, and it brings a smile to my lips. The rest of this house is so clean. Even in his bathroom, there's no toothpaste in the sink, no stains in the shower, but his things thrown around his bedroom makes him a little endearing. I don't forget to grab a towel from his shelf before getting in the shower so I don't have a repeat of the other day. I do steal his shower gel, though, to wash off all the sweat as his cinnamon scent clings to my skin. I like it more than I want to admit, knowing if he were to wrap me in a hug, this is what he would smell like.

After getting dressed, I make my way downstairs to find Logan rummaging around in the pantry. "What are you doing in there?"

His head pops around the door with a wide smile. "Hey you. I was thinking of doing some baking, would you like to help?"

"Absolutely! What are we going to make?"

"I was thinking maybe some muffins. There are blueberry bushes out back that need picking that we can put in the muffins."

"I love blueberries! I've never made muffins from scratch, but I am great at following instructions." He starts pulling jars from the pantry, handing them to me as I line them up on the island.

As he hands me the sugar, his fingers brush against mine. His eyes meet mine for a moment as he leans closer, breathing me in. "You smell like me."

My cheeks heat with embarrassment. "Yeah, sorry. Josh was in our shower and you said I could use yours. I didn't have my shower stuff, so I borrowed yours."

"Don't apologize, baby girl. I like it. You can use my stuff whenever you need." He grabs two bowls from a cabinet, handing one to me. "Shall we go get some blueberries?"

We make our way out to the side of the house where there is a cluster of blueberry bushes bursting with blues and purples. "Wow, you weren't kidding. We will have way more than just for the muffins."

He starts picking the ones toward the top, so I start on the bottom. "Yeah, Josh eats these things like candy. He planted these bushes right after he moved in. Whatever we don't use, he will demolish in a day." I love that they are hands on with their food like this.

"Do you guys have a vegetable garden?" I ask plopping some more blueberries into the bowl.

"No, it's been talked about, but none of us have an exceptionally green thumb. Brian tends to the flowers around the house for the most part, but he has been so focused on growing the business that a garden has been pushed to the backburner."

"That doesn't surprise me. His mom loved to garden, she taught me everything I know about it. We used to spend hours helping her weed and prune in her garden when we were kids. I still love it to this day. I like that you guys do everything around here. I thought for sure when I saw the size of this place, you would have a lawn service and cleaners."

He looks at me with mock horror. "What?! No way, we do it all. Josh mows, I cook and clean, and Brian does the flowers and most of the wood chopping, but we all pitch in and help each other out wherever it's needed. I've been taking on the mowing this month since Josh is deep in research for his new camera, and even though he would never ask for the help, I know he needs it."

I love that. I love the clear love and respect that they all have for each other. With full bowls, we head back inside to start on the muffins. I wash all the blueberries while Logan starts to measure out the ingredients seemingly from memory. "Don't you need a cookbook or something?"

He whips his head around to me. "That's twice you've offended me this morning now, Kelli. Take a man out at the knees, why don't you."

Giggling, I grab the towel on the counter and whip it at him, striking him in the back of the leg. "Shut it. I just didn't expect you to have exact measurements memorized."

His eyes narrow, a mischievous smile gracing his lips. "You've done it now, pretty girl." With a quick flick of his wrist into the bowl he's holding, I am covered in a dusting of flour. I squeal, whipping the towel at him again before trying to make a break for it around the island. Logan's long legs leap up and over the island in pursuit. He attempts to leap down in front of me, the bowl of measured out flour still in his hands. My feet are moving too fast and I slam right into his chest with an audible thud, taking us both out. As he falls back, he lets go of the bowl to grab my arms, angling me to fall onto him instead of backwards.

I lay there for a moment, trying to figure out what the hell just happened, and marveling at how quickly Logan saved me from cracking my head open when he starts sputtering beneath me. Sitting up, I look at him flat on his back below me covered in flour as he tries to spit it out of his mouth. Laughter bubbles out of me as I try to wipe it from his face. "Are you okay?" I manage to wheeze out between my laughter that just won't stop now.

His hands reach around, tickling into my sides. "Oh this is funny, huh? Just wait until you see your hair, Cruella." I squirm in his lap trying to get out of his grasp, gasping for air between my laughter.

"Okay, okay! I concede!" He lets go of my hips as I try to slide off his body while attempting to ignore his growing dick below me. His dimples pop as he smiles and winks at me, helping us both stand up. Clumps of flour fall from my hair as I shake my head. "Damn, you weren't kidding. I'm covered in it."

"Guess we don't need aprons at this point." His hands wipe down my back and over my ass in the guise of helping clean me off, so I take advantage as well letting my hands trail through his soft hair and down the hard planes of his abs.

He steps around the island to start measuring out the flour into a new bowl when we are semi cleaned off. I mix the wet ingredients together as he pours some protein powder into the dry mix.

"Do you guys go through a lot of that stuff?" I ask putting muffin liners in the tin pan.

"Sometimes. We try to get our protein through lean meats and such, but it definitely gets used. Josh uses it the most. He often makes a protein shake instead of lunch or for a snack."

"Do you think he would like it if I made him some protein rich snacks?"

Logan pauses to look at me, his blue eyes bright as he takes me in. "Yeah, I think he would love that." Once we have all the mix scooped into the liners, Logan puts it into the oven and starts cleaning up the mess and washing the dishes. I help with the dishes, then raid the pantry for the ingredients I need. Unsurprising with Logan's baking habits, they have everything I need. Logan sits at the island as I combine ingredients for blueberry protein balls for Josh.

"It's really nice of you to do that for him," he says, snacking on the leftover blueberries.

"He really helped me out this morning." I almost want to tell him that he opened up to me about his nightmares, but it felt like a private moment, and even though Logan already knew about them, I felt like saying it would break Josh's trust. "I just want to do something to show him that I'm grateful."

"Hmmm," he says with a mouth full. "Is this where you saw yourself at twenty-six?"

"Hiding out with three guys, two of whom I barely know? No, I can't say it is."

He chucks a blueberry at my head as I continue rolling the ingredients into little balls. "You know what I mean."

"Yeah, for the most part, it is. I thought I would be in a steady relationship by this point. Maybe married. But that's my own fault for working so much. I had goals of owning a home and having a thriving career, and I have both of those, so that's good. Is this where you saw yourself at thirty? Are you thirty?"

He chuckles, "Yes, I'm thirty. Josh is thirty-one, and I'm sure you know B is thirty-two. At eighteen, when I joined the Army, I thought for sure I would do the full twenty years of service, but the deployments and being unsettled all the time was hard. I never saw myself living in the woods with my two best friends but I wouldn't change it. I also thought I would be married by now."

"Why aren't you?"

"I haven't found the right woman. I've dated around some, had a girlfriend I could have loved, but she didn't understand me living with the guys. She thought it was weird, and wanted to get our own place. I didn't like that, I want a wife who loves the guys as much as I do. We have talked about raising our kids together, our wives being best friends. She clearly wasn't the one since she didn't even try to get to know them. I'm ready though, for marriage and kids. I have my life put together, everything settled, and now, I'm just waiting for the right one to come along."

"I can understand that. There was an anesthesiologist at work I was flirting with for a while. We had similar sched-ules, similar interests, and he seemed well put together. One day, Danny brought me lunch and we ran into the guy in the hall. Turns out he has a problem with 'the gays,' as he so eloquently put it. I shut that down so fast. It's important to find someone who not only fits with those in your life, but who also wants to fit with them." I stack up the protein balls into little storage containers and put them into the fridge as Logan pulls the muffins from the oven.

When I turn around, Logan is there, blocking me with his body. His hand skates down my face before gripping the side of my neck. He leans forward, placing a chaste kiss on my forehead. "Thank you for your help," he whispers against my skin. Pulling away, his soft eyes linger on mine. "I'm going to shower all this flour off. If you want to smell like me again later, just let me know." With that, he's gone, but the feel of his hands possessively on my neck stays behind.

12

KELLI

The next morning, I get up early to train with Josh again. I'm already sore from our first day of training, so he focuses on takedowns and escape techniques. When my arms completely give up on me, he makes me run on the treadmill for thirty minutes. I don't know that I feel as giddy about these workouts anymore because I really hate running. When we meander upstairs, I use Logan's shower again, reveling in his scent. As I'm about to step out of the shower, I hear Brian holler in the room that he is running a quick errand and will be back soon. I'm not sure if that was meant for me or Logan, so I don't answer and keep drying off.

Logan is downstairs making bacon and eggs when I make my way back down, grabbing myself a cup of coffee. "Brian is running an errand this morning. He yelled it into your room, but I was in your shower so I think he thought it was you in the shower."

"He found me on his way out. He should be back within the hour, I think he has something planned for you guys today." He says flipping the bacon in the pan.

"Is it bad if I'm scared to ask what this plan is?" I pour some creamer in my coffee before sitting at the island.

"I think it's an apology plan. I know he feels bad about being a little overbearing with you." Hmm, well I do like apologies. I sip on my coffee, watching Logan move around the kitchen with ease. I never thought a man cooking could be such a turn on, but he makes it look good. He's shirtless this morning, honestly a bold choice while frying bacon, but I'm not going to ask him to put a shirt on. His muscles are delicious, my mouth is watering. I'm not sure if it's from the smells or the view.

When everything is done, he plates up some for both of us and joins me at the island, leaving a plate to the side for Josh, as well. He buries his nose in my hair taking a deep breath. "You smell like me again. As much as I like it, I think I miss your pretty scent."

"I need to stop showering at the same time as Josh. All my stuff is in our bathroom."

"Hmm, maybe. I have another possible solution, too." He hums around bites of bacon. Before I can ask what his other solution is, the door to the garage opens. Brian comes in with a small grocery bag, setting it on the counter.

"Can I get your help when you're done, Logan? And Kel, can you change into something you don't mind getting a little dirty?" He asks, taking out a new pair of purple gardening gloves.

"I'll take care of the dishes then get changed. Are we gardening, B?" The excitement is radiating from me.

"Yeah, if you are up for it. It's overdue. I got some new things for us to plant." His grin is sheepish and adorable. I can't believe he did this for me. I love to dig around in the dirt.

I fill the dishwasher and wash the pans before heading

upstairs to throw on a black tank and some running shorts. On my way back down, I grab the purple gloves off the counter and slip them in my pocket before heading outside.

I step out to the back deck as Logan steps around the side of the house, carrying a flat of beautiful flowers in a range of colors. When he sees me standing there, he smiles and sets the flowers down, nodding to the ground, "this is some apology." It's then I notice the four other flats overflowing with little flowers. Logan's already walking back around to the front before I can ask how many more there are.

I walk down to the yard, bending to get a better look at all the flowers when Brian comes over, pushing a wheelbarrow with four rhododendron bushes in them. "How many flowers did you get for us to plant?" I ask, standing to help him unload them.

"You like flowers, so I got a mix of ones that will look good in the garden now and ones we can plant so you'll have fresh flowers in the fall, too. You know, in case you're here or want to visit or something." He rubs the back of his neck uncomfortably.

"That's really sweet, thanks, B. I can't wait to get started. Do you have a place in mind for all of these, or are we winging it as we go?"

"I figured we would wing it. I still have another load to get from the truck if you want to start looking around at the flower beds back here and get an idea. We have a few flower beds by the front porch, too, that could use some color." He pulls the last bush from the wheelbarrow before making his way around the front again. My heart beats faster watching his forearms flex as he shifts it over the grass. We never got more than a tiny taste of each other, and with his kind gesture and popping muscles, I am really wishing we could try for more.

When the truck is finally empty, Logan heads back inside while Brian and I plan out the flower placement. "I think I like the little flowers in front, maybe mix some pinks and oranges. Then the rhododendron bushes spread out in the back so they have space to grow and the rest of the flowers spread out so there is a little color everywhere. What do you think?"

"I think you have the better eye, so what you say goes." Brian grabs the pink and orange flowers and brings them to the front yard, where we start spreading them out and planting them. "Remind me to take a picture when we are done to send to my mom. She will be so proud of us."

"Does she know I'm here?" I ask, placing a little flower into the hole I dug.

"Yeah, Danny told her yesterday. We don't want anything about you being here said over the phone so he and Alex went to dinner there last night. She's worried about you, but is glad you're here." His large hands are so careful when planting the dainty flowers. It reminds me so much of when we were kids. It feels full circle, seeing him as this built, battle-hardened man being cautious to not squish any petals.

We work side by side, finishing up the rest of the front flowers before moving to the back of the house. "Are you comfortable here?" Brian blurts out as we set out where the rest of the flowers will go.

"Yeah, it's a beautiful place and the guys are really nice. I miss my home, but it has lost a little of its appeal with every-thing going on. I feel comfortable here. Why do you ask?"

He pauses, sitting back on his heels to look over at me. "It's just important to me. Your safety is my biggest priority, but I want you to be happy here, too."

"I'm happy, B. Are you happy? With your life, where you're at?"

"I'm happy enough. I love this little slice of paradise we have built for ourselves." He doesn't look at me, still just digging little holes to put the flowers in. I want to ask about our past, about where things are with us, but I don't want to ruin this little bubble we are in right now.

"Are any of you guys dating anyone?" I pull the last flower from my flat and put it in the ground.

"No." Okay then, I guess that's all I'm getting on that conversation. There's a dying rose bush next to where I'm planting, so I start snapping off the dead growth.

"Do you have pruning shears for this?" I look over to him to ask right as a thorn pokes through my gloves, making me wince.

Brian is off his knees and next to me in an instant, gently pulling my glove off. "Are you okay? You know you shouldn't prune roses without the leather gloves." There are a few drops of blood dripping from my finger and before I can pull my hand from him to wipe it on my shorts, Brian sucks my finger into his mouth. I sit stunned and a little breathless as he keeps my finger in his mouth, sucking the blood from it. It's a hot and possessive move, giving my body all sorts of ideas of where else his mouth might feel good. He plucks it back out of his mouth, licking his lips. "All better. Let's take a break and get a band-aid. I picked up a surprise while I was in town."

Without dropping my hand, he helps me up and walks me into the house. My feet follow, but my brain is still a pile of mush on the ground. He has been so hot and cold since I got here, but damn when he is hot, he is on fire. When we get into the kitchen, he lifts me up, placing me on the counter. "Don't move."

He comes back in a moment with an antibiotic ointment and band-aid that he carefully puts onto my finger like it is some huge injury and not a tiny prick that has already stopped bleeding. I finally find my voice, "You do know that I'm a nurse, right? I can handle a cut finger."

He drops a kiss to the top of the band-aid when he is done. "I know, I just don't care. I took care of it for you." When he turns around to throw away the trash, I hop off the counter only to have his hand land on my hip squeezing it in place. "I didn't say to move, Kel. Get your ass back up there."

A shiver runs down my spine at his words. I think I like this version of his overbearing. "Yes sir," I mumble under my breath, as his spine straightens at the words. He opens the fridge, pulling out a large glass jug of lemonade. It's what his mom used to have for us every time we helped her. "You made us lemonade?"

"Nah, I don't have that skill. But there is a lady in town that makes juices and pies for some of the local restaurants, so I picked up a jug from her." He says like it's no big deal as he pours both of us a glass. But it is a big deal to me. He's a nurturer at heart, a protector, too; it's just been a while since I've seen this side of him. He hands me a glass then takes a big sip of his own.

"Thank you, this is amazing." We drink in silence, then he places our empty cups in the sink. He grabs me by the hips to take me off the counter and sets me on the ground. I roll my eyes at the possessive move, but really, I am relishing in his touch. He takes my hand and leads me back out to the yard where we plant the rest of the bushes and prune the roses together. When the last rose bush is done, I lie back in the grass, enjoying the cool breeze over my sweat-slicked skin. Brian lays down next to me, picking up my hand.

"How's your finger?" He asks inspecting my hand like it's at risk of falling off.

I pull my hand away and slap his chest. "It's fine, ya brute. It was a tiny prick."

"I worry about you, Kel. Even the little things like a few drops of blood. You have to know that," he says as his eyes find mine, full of honesty.

"I know, you just sometimes have a funny way of showing it." I tell him honestly. "Any chance you can show me how to use your riding lawn mower?" I ask, changing the subject.

"Why?"

"I'm already sweaty, and I've always wanted to ride on one. Might as well mow the lawn while I mark it off my bucket list." I shoot him a genuine smile. I do really want to drive one around, but mostly, I want to help Josh out.

Brian pulls my hands, helping me to my feet. "Alright, I guess. I'm bringing you out the rest of the lemonade, though."

"And a snack, too?" I flutter my lashes at him.

He drops a kiss to my curls, "Yeah, I'll get you a snack, too."

13

The next few days all start the same way with Kelli and I training every morning. I find myself leaving my room more often than normal, working down in the office with Brian just to see where Kelli is and if she's doing okay. Her resilience shines through in our training, but I see the pain in her eyes. Some days she is better at hiding it than others, but behind her easy smiles and lighthearted jokes, I see the battle she is trying to fight alone. I didn't realize how much I had isolated myself until Brian mentioned how nice it was to spend time together again, even if it was just working in the same space. While it wasn't the reason for being down here more, I have to agree with him.

Kelli spends some time reading on the porch after breakfast when the weather is nice, then spends most of her time with Logan. They hang down by the beach, cook and bake together, and even clean together. Yesterday, I walked into my room to find my laundry folded in nice piles on my bed. Logan has never done my laundry before, so I know that it was her. I wanted to say thank you, but like the coward I am, I never brought it up. I haven't had someone do nice things for me just because. The guys and I all help each other out, but we don't go out of our way to do things like that.

I'm the only one who has done my laundry since I was 10 until her. She's constantly doing nice shit like that for me, making me lunch and leaving it on my desk when I'm busy or wiping down the mats and equipment when we are done training when she noticed I stayed back to do it every time. This week she mowed the lawn, which is my chore and she made protein snacks for me. She told me about them when I came down to snag a fresh muffin. I thought they were for everyone until Logan told me she made them special with blueberries just for me. There has also been a bowl of fresh picked berries in the fridge every day with a sticky note with my name on it that I know is from her. Part of me hates all that she's doing because my thoughts are constantly being overrun by her and my body feels alive when she's around.

Logan's deep laughter mixed with her light and sunny laugh makes its way through the house. I have to admit, it brightens the place up a lot. Having her here has made me realize how long the three of us have been in survival mode. Since moving in here together, we really haven't done anything but focus on our careers. Logan has dated a little here and there, but never gotten to the point that they have come to the house or we have met them. Brian and I have gone to the bar to find someone to scratch the itch a few times, but that's it. It makes me want her to stick around. Every morning, I feel myself being pulled further into Kelli's orbit. She has this inner fire that comes out more and more every day that I didn't see at first but am wildly attracted to. Every time she joins us for movie night, I see the looks from Brian and Logan, filled with hope that she will sit by them, and I know I have that same look. Even knowing they are both attracted to her, too, I can't stop myself from thinking what it might be like to be with her.

She doesn't take any shit from us, and yet, she has this sweet nurturing side where she quietly does these acts of service for us. She organized Brian's filing cabinet yesterday while he was in town for a meeting after hearing him gripe about it. He thinks it was me. While I should have told him it wasn't, I feel like that's something they need to work out on their own.

I'm not sure Brian feels the same as me, though. I can see him tense up every time her laughter floats into the office. They had their day in the garden and they talk at meals. Yet, they still are avoiding spending too much alone time together. Brian refuses to tell her why he walked away from her all those years ago. The glances she sends his way when he isn't looking are full of longing. The pain between them is so evident, it's almost tangible. All it would take is an honest conversation between them to alleviate so much of it. I brought it up to Logan since that is more his area, but he thinks they need to make that leap on their own when they are ready. Until they decide to have that honest conversation, we will continue to tiptoe around their weird relationship, and all three of us will continue falling for her a little more every day.

Logan comes into the office Thursday afternoon, shutting the door behind him looking frustrated. Last Sunday morning before Kelli came downstairs, we had a discussion about ways to keep her protected here. Brian insisted that the best way forward was to clone her phone, his insistence on ensuring her safety and wellbeing understandable. He felt that was the best way to keep an eye on any messages she may be getting from her stalker. Logan and I didn't love the idea of it, and I fought hard against it. Brian is sure that if we ask her, she'll say no. His pained expression as he explained how he had his heart walking around outside of his chest with her ultimately got Logan to side with him. I didn't agree that it needed to be behind her back. I was outnumbered though, so Logan cloned her phone that afternoon while she was asleep in his room. So far, she has only gotten one message on her Instagram from someone named Mr. Winter that said *You can run, but can you hide?* Logan made sure to delete it from her phone, but has been working with his department on trying to track down the IP of who created the account.

Despite voicing my opinion, they decided we should keep it from her. While I understand their desire to protect her, she deserves to know the truth when this is her life. They don't even know about her nightmares and if I tell them, I fear they will just push harder to keep all this from her. She asked us for honesty, though, and I have seen her strength. I know she can handle this. It's just one more message so far and certainly not the worst he has sent her. She is so much stronger than they give her credit for, even in this fucked up situation.

"Have you been able to find anything on this guy?" Brian asks when Logan sits on the couch between our desks.

"No, not yet. This guy isn't your average Joe. He clearly has a background in tech and knows what he's doing. I talked to Alex today and none of the notes have any fingerprints or DNA on them, and no cameras around the hospital or her home have caught anything or they have been wiped." He sits forward putting his elbow on his knees and hangs his head. "I am waging this internal war of wanting to find this jackass and making him pay, yet hoping we don't so she can stay with us. I like her here."

I look to Brian and see his jaw tighten. I have been waiting for the fall out between them, because while I feel I have kept my feelings toward Kelli pretty hidden, Logan has not. He flirts with her all day, and is constantly finding excuses to touch her that don't go unnoticed. I don't feel any jealousy toward it, but I see the heated looks Brian gives him. His jealousy is wavering just below the surface and I don't think it will take much for it to bubble over. Finding this guy is a top priority for all of us, but it's easy to see we all have a similar internal war going on.

"We will just keep doing what we can to keep her safe and happy here, and you keep working with Alex and your department to do what you can to find him. If he tries to message her again, though, we need to come clean about the cloning and we need to tell her he hasn't disappeared," I level them both with a glare. I don't want her to leave, and maybe knowing he is still trying to find her will ensure she wants to stay with us as long as possible.

14

KELLI

Glass is shattering around me as I try to get up and run from it, but I can't get my legs to work. They feel like they are stuck in quicksand, refusing to move. He has come for me again. I just need to get somewhere safe until help arrives. I try to pull myself down the hall using my arms. A scream rips from my throat, begging for help, but my voice is blocked out by the breaking windows. I pull my hands over my head to block out the manic laughter as more glass begins shattering over my head.

Strong hands grip my shoulders as my eyes flutter open. "Kelli, it's okay, you're okay." Josh's comforting scent hits me first, and I immediately feel at ease. Latching onto his arm, I try to steady my breaths, breathing in his signature scent, focusing on the warmth of his skin under my fingers. This is the fourth time he has had to wake me up from a nightmare, and every time, he just wakes me and leaves. I think it's because I have yet to take him up on his offer to talk about them. I have yet to be able to fall back asleep after he leaves, and despite trying to hide it from the guys, I'm exhausted and it's taking its toll. I squeeze his wrist as he goes to stand, "Please stay." I can't look him in the eye if he rejects me, but to my surprise, he doesn't.

He doesn't get under the blankets, instead lying over top of them on his back while he folds his arms across his stomach. I look over at him in just his boxers, looking stiff as a board, and let out a snort. "You can get under the blankets, I don't bite. Or there's a blanket on the chair in the corner." He gets up to grab the throw blanket then climbs back on next to me, this time facing me. I reach out and grab hold of his hand that is folded under his head. "Thank you."

"Go back to sleep, little flame, I've got you." I close my eyes and feel his hands trail over my face, tucking my hair back and continuing lightly down my shoulder. Aside from our workouts, this is the closest we've been. I've caught a few lingering glances from him, but this is the first time I have felt like there might be something more there. I feel safe here at his side, and in no time at all, sleep takes me away.

Josh is gone when my alarm wakes me up, but the bed is still warm next to me, so he must have stayed most of the night. Training with him in the morning has been a good motivation to drag my butt out of bed. His personality is starting to slowly poke through as he gets comfortable with me, and honestly, I don't hate it. There were some light jokes passed between us yesterday, bringing out the most genuine laughs I have heard from him yet. My original thought of him being moody and mysterious was wrong. I'm discovering he is just closed off and needs someone to help open him up and let him be comfortable enough to be vulnerable.

Putting on a pair of skimpy shorts and a tight sports bra, I make my way down to the gym. The fact that he stayed with me last night means something to me, so I figured I should pay him back by giving him something nice to look at. Every morning, it's just been Josh and me, but when I open the door today, there's music blasting. In the center of the mat, Josh and Logan are sparring. I gently let the door close behind me so I can watch them before they notice me. My eyes track over both of their shirtless bodies, slick with sweat. Josh's arms, pecs and back are covered in tattoos, which only seem to accentuate his large size. Despite being the shortest of the three, he is definitely the most muscular. He has thick thighs, strong arms, a broad chest and back muscles that ripple with every movement.

He gets a good hit into Logan's side, flipping him down on the mat easily, making my mouth water. Logan's shoulders, biceps and chest are tattooed, as well, and where he doesn't have the bulging muscles that Josh does, he makes up for in the definition of his muscles and abs. A clear and cut six-pack leads down to that delicious v dipping down into his shorts. As they wrestle for control on the mat, his shorts slide down a little more, and now I'm positive there is drool hanging down my chin. If I ever need material to get off to, this will be the exact scene I will play in my head.

Logan taps when Josh gets him into an arm bar, and they both get up chuckling when Logan finally notices me standing here. "See something you like, baby girl?" He smiles wide, his dimples popping out. He started calling me that yesterday, and I have to admit I don't hate it. I joked I was going to call him Daddy, but he insisted that if someone in the house should have that name, it should be Josh because he has the 'daddy dom' vibes. As if I wasn't attracted to them all enough, that definitely added to it. I have yet to really be thrown around and dominated in the bedroom, and I certainly don't hate the idea of Josh doing it.

"I saw Daddy kick your ass, and I definitely like that," I quip. Logan snorts as Josh chokes on his water, but his eyes flare. It doesn't go unnoticed that he looks away and discreetly adjusts himself. Turns out Logan was right and it seems he likes the term. I would be filing that little tidbit away for later.

"It's you and me today," Logan says, striding over to me. "I've been wanting to see what your sensei is teaching you down here, so now's your chance to kick my ass." I smile sweetly and move to walk past him when he grabs my elbow to put his lips to my ear, "plus, I want to see what has Josh jerking off every morning in his shower after he gets done down here with you."

My face flushes immediately at that. It's no secret I was wet most mornings leaving here, but knowing I was having the same effect on him made me feel good. I have yet to do anything about my feelings, though. Knowing Josh hears my nightmares has me cautious of what else he might be able to hear. Now I'm thinking it might not be the worst thing if he does hear me come. I have never been shy about sex. I shouldn't be embarrassed about taking care of a need.

"You tired of teaching me already?" I ask Josh as he grabs his shirt, flinging it over his shoulder.

"Josh and Brian have a meeting in Boston this morning, and they likely won't be home until late. If you need anything from your house while they're out, they can get it," Logan answers for him.

"I'll be back to training with you tomorrow. Don't take it easy on him. He's terrible at protecting his left side, so use that," Josh calls out as he heads past me for the door. "Be good today, Kelli. Daddy will get a full report when he gets home." With that he walks out the door and my jaw hits the floor as Logan's loud laugh erupts from behind me.

"Damn, didn't expect that from him. He likes you. I haven't seen that side of him in years." He had a quiet reverence to his voice. I knew last night when he agreed to stay with me that something between us was changing. I wasn't really sure how to feel about it. I like Josh and I am wildly attracted to him, but he still wasn't going out of his way to open up to me minus that first day. Logan on the other hand is so easy to talk to. Spending so much time with him this week has been great, and things have slowly been changing with us as well. His teasing and flirting are becoming more apparent, and I am certainly not mad at it. I am just as attracted to him, but can I live with these guys if something happened between one of us? What if I want something to happen between more than one of us?

On top of that, I don't want to do anything to upset Brian. My heart still belongs to him, but we have been keeping things very surface level. I need to grow some balls and talk to him. I just want to know why he never came back for me and what changed. Does he still feel anything for me, or would he be fine with me being with one of his friends? It was a conversation I was going to make sure happened this weekend, because being in this house with these men for another week with nothing happening is looking like a slim chance.

Logan and I did a two mile run on the treadmill then sparred for an hour. Josh was right about his left side, which helped me take him down twice, but he spent most of the time kicking my ass. Every move he made also seemed way more sexual than it needed to be. I swear he was rocking his hips into mine, and grabbing my ass way more than necessary. My hands couldn't stop themselves from trailing down his abs a few times as well, every dip in between them was as soft as it looked. Every ounce of my body begging me to let them trail down further.

As we start to tire out, sweat pouring down our bodies, we decide to do one last round. He promises to go easy on me, which is a total ploy. I get him into a headlock with my legs around his waist from behind when he taps. Instead of tapping my arm, he taps out on my leg, letting his fingers slowly graze up to my hip. As soon as I release him he flips around and has me pinned with his hips laying flat between mine lining his very hard dick with my center. I watch as his blue eyes darken, his pupils blown wide. His eyes trail down my neck to my sports bra, following the path of a bead of sweat. Leaning down, he traces his nose up my neck to my ear, sending a shiver down my spine. He nips at my ear, whispering, "You smell so fucking good after rolling around with me."

Before I can even think of what to say, he is up and helping me stand, not one bit embarrassed about his hard on pointing at me through his shorts. He smacks me on the ass as he walks past me, not bothering to turn around when he says, "Go shower and we can make some breakfast together." He's out the door before I can move, leaving my jaw hanging open for the second time this morning.

I head upstairs to mine and Josh's bathroom with the intent to take care of the ache between my thighs in the shower. If I have to potentially stay here for weeks still, something is going to have to give. The hot water soothes my sore muscles as I wash off the sweat from my workout. My hands drift down my body, rinsing off my body wash, but all I can think of is Logan's hands in their place. I let my fingers pluck at my nipples before gliding down to the apex of my thighs. Picturing his strong fingers splaying over me before taking one finger to circle my clit. My body is so keyed up, I know it isn't going to take me long.

Moving my thumb to my clit, I let my middle finger move further down before pushing it into me. I'm dripping from the thought of his body back on mine, his solid and impressive erection pressing into me. I ride my finger before adding a second trying to satisfy the ache. Logan's blue eyes never leave my fantasy, the way he looked at me like he wanted to devour me. My thumb rubs faster, my fingers picking up their pace. With the thought of his hard body above mine, writhing against me, I moan out his name as I come. It's a quick orgasm, satisfying the need, but it does nothing overall to tamp down the feelings inside of me. I take my time with the rest of my shower, washing my hair and doing a full body shave.

By the time I get downstairs, Logan is already making us pancakes. His hair is still wet and messy on his head, which just adds to his sexy disheveled look. He grins over his shoulder at me, continuing to flip the pancakes. After getting out some plates and the syrup, I cut up some strawberries and add them to a bowl with some sugar. Hopping on the island, I let my eyes explore his body as he continues to cook, in which he returns my eye fucking over his shoulder every chance he gets.

Logan finishes the pancakes, turns off the stove, then turns to face me while leaning against the counter on the other side. "You look refreshed," he smirks.

Oh god, can he tell that I just got myself off in the shower? My face must be turning as red as it feels because he laughs, walking over placing his hands on the counter around me. Gently nudging my legs apart with his hips, he stands in between them. "The one downside of that large bathroom you love so much is that the sound in there tends to echo. It's how I know about Josh every morning."

He watches my face with rapt attention as realization dawns that he just heard exactly what I was doing. I pray to every god I can imagine that he at least missed out on the part where I moaned his name when I came. I have been using

Logan's bathroom to shower every morning when I finish working out because Josh always goes to the one I share with him. Evidently, I have been missing out.

I try to hide my embarrassment by making a show of slowly skimming my eyes down to his crotch. "I see your earlier problem has been taken care of as well."

That doesn't seem to do the trick, because he just pulls my hips closer to the edge of the counter against him. "Do you like that thought, baby girl? That I fucked my fist to thoughts of you while you fingered that pretty little pussy to thoughts of me? It took me no time at all to finish, never does with you on my mind." I can't hold back the moan that slips out, his hips grinding into me as he starts to harden again. My hips move forward on their own rubbing against his length drawing a moan from him this time. He takes a step back, chest heaving, but puts his forehead against mine just taking a minute to breathe. "We should eat before it gets cold." He steps back so I can hop down, feeling a mix of disappointment and relief as I follow him with our plates to the other side of the island.

We decided to spend the rest of the day cleaning the house and the deck together. It is really nice to get out of the house for a bit, and doing these mundane things with Logan gives me a sense of normalcy despite everything going on. Spending most of the last week with him has taught me so much about him. He taught me how to make the perfect loaf of sourdough bread and the most incredible fluffy muffins. We spent so much time at their little beach, talking about anything and everything, that we brought two of their Adirondack chairs down there. Conversation with him comes easy and the silence is comfortable. He has the best sense of humor and we laugh so easily together. Yet, there is this whole other side to him, too, full of emotional maturity and a deep understanding of my feelings even when I don't voice them.

The weather has been perfect today, so we decided to grill chicken for dinner while waiting for the guys to come back. He has avoided talking about what happened between us this morning, making my nerves buzz throughout my body. The chemistry between us is palpable, but I don't know what he wants to happen between us, if anything at all. Before that conversation can happen, I want to take advantage of the fact that Brian isn't around. I still have no idea what transpired to make him all but remove himself from my life and I'm tired of waiting to find out. Watching Logan man the grill with his back turned to me gives me the courage to finally ask. "Has Brian ever told you about what happened between us four years ago?"

He lowers the grill lid, striding over to sit across from me. "Yeah, baby girl, he has." He looks almost sad, the pity written all over his face.

"What happened? What changed for him that he just cut me out of his life?" My eyes move down to my hands in my lap, unable to look him in the eye for this next question. "Was it me?"

Logan immediately moves to his knees in front of me, gently grabbing my chin so I have to look into his beautiful blue eyes. "Absolutely not. Don't for one second think that he stopped caring for you. Even now." His sigh is deep and filled with frustration as he seems to ponder what to say next. "Something happened to him that changed his perspective on his future. I don't agree with it, but it's his choice. Just like it's his story to share with you when he is ready." I pull back at that. He has had four years to tell me and still hasn't. If it weren't for my stalker, I'm not entirely sure he would even be talking to me now. "He is getting there," Logan promises as he moves my chin to force us into eye contact again.

I just nod my head at that. Not sure if forcing Brian will be the right way to get him ready, but at this point, I'm willing to try. "I know that you have feelings for him. It's clear there is hurt there, but I can see the looks you give him when you think no one is watching." He clears his throat and looks out at the water. "He still has feelings for you, he never stopped and I am not sure he will ever stop wanting you. He loves you in his own way, but until he heals a part of himself and comes to terms with things, he won't be able to love you the right way and he knows that." He looks back at me, a look of adoration mixed with shame covering his beautiful face. "He's my best friend, and I would do absolutely anything for him. Including not pursuing you, despite how I feel about you. That's if you still want him, too. I need you to really hear me, Kelli. You are the most beautiful woman, inside and out. You make me feel at home in a way no one ever has, and I want you so damn bad. But if it's Brian you want, I will keep my distance."

A million things run through my head. I love spending time with him, flirting with him, watching his confidence shine in everything he does. If I'm honest with myself, I can see myself being happy with Logan. He felt like an instant best friend and comfort to me from my first morning here. But, he said Brian loves me so he can't love me. What the hell does that even mean? Do I want to wait for him for another four or more years to see if he changes his mind? I don't want to be alone anymore. Before I can try to articulate any of that, Logan plants a kiss on my head before walking back to the grill. "Really think about your feelings. You have options here. Chicken is almost done. Want to grab us some plates and the sides, and we can eat out here?" *Options? What options?* I guess that conversation can wait until after dinner.

It's my first time eating dinner out on the deck, and I immediately hope it isn't the last. There's something so magical about it that makes me feel at peace. The early evening sun rays beaming off the water gives everything a golden hue, the breeze through the trees around us keeps it a cool and comfortable temperature, and even the chatter of the birds and little critters relaxes me. "I think I feel more at home here than I ever have anywhere else," I confess.

Logan looks over at me, silently taking me in for a long moment. "That's exactly what Josh said the first time I brought him and Brian here. I have always felt that way here, too. On our last deployment, Brian brought up that he was considering buying the property next-door, which got Josh and him throwing hands. Apparently, he also was looking at the property." The smile that graces his lips is full of mirth. Looking out over the water again, he takes a sip of his beer, shaking his head at the memory. "When I showed them my ideas for the remodel and told them I wanted them to move here with me, they agreed instantly. It just felt right. They ended up buying the property next door together, so it extends the land we have around us. My parents thought for sure that the three of us were together romantically. Most people probably did," he chuckles, shaking his head.

"You three have never..." I ask, unsure how to finish that. He laughs again, warming my insides with the sound.

"Nah, I mean Josh and Brian have shared a girl a time or two, but have never been together in that sense." That was news to me. I had trouble picturing them together with a girl, but what do I know? I've never had a threesome. The more I thought about it, though, the more the idea intrigued me. I could picture one of them kissing their way up my thigh while the other slid their dick into my mouth… and now I'm back to needing new panties again. I might have to add that to my list of things to ask them about at some point. "Have you ever?" he asks. I'm not sure if he means have I been with someone of the same sex or have I been shared, but the answer is the same for both.

"No, but I won't lie and say it's not at the forefront of my mind now. Both of them sharing me, working me over." I suck in a deep breath as my cheeks heat. "Hell, add you in there and I don't think I would ever leave this house again." He groans a deep and pained sound that travels straight down to my pussy.

"Fuck, I can't sit here thinking about that." Logan starts cleaning up plates and carries them inside, me trailing him with my own. As we load the dishwasher, he looks over at me with a sly grin on his face. "You know what I think it's the perfect night for?" He raises an eyebrow at me, making me realize I am going to agree to whatever comes out of his mouth. "Hot tub."

After a week of training with Josh every morning, a soak in the hot tub sounds amazing. We finish cleaning up the rest of dinner before going upstairs to get changed. The only bikini that Alex packed is my skimpiest red one, and now after being here for a week, I can't help feeling he did that on purpose. The guys are supposed to be grabbing me my other two, as well as some more of my clothes since it is looking like I will be here a while longer. Maybe they will be home in time to join us. I have a sneaking suspicion that Logan is doing this to either torture me, or torture them when they get here. After the pictures that floated through my mind at dinner, I sure wouldn't hate being half dressed in a small space with the three of them.

When I step out onto the porch, Logan is bending over the

side, messing with the hot tub settings. He has on bright pink trunks that fit his personality so well that I can't help but laugh. As soon as his eyes slide over to me, he goes still. He makes no effort to hide his slow perusal of my body as a sexy grin crosses his face. "Hot damn, baby girl, you look absolutely incredible. Spin for me?" He makes a little twirling motion with his finger.

I can't help but oblige, slowly spinning with my arms out. I smile to myself when I hear his low groan at seeing the back. This is the suit I mostly wear at home while working on my tan so the bottoms are barely covering at best. By the time I turn all the way around, he is zeroed in on my ass, his eyes hooded, lust written all over his face. I walk the rest of the way over and slowly step in, trying and failing to hold in the moan at the feel of the hot water on my sore muscles.

"You are going to be the death of me," Logan mutters under his breath as he readjusts himself while stepping into the tub on the side opposite of me. We settle in and enjoy the peaceful silence for a bit until that sly grin crosses his face again. "You up for a little game?"

15

I normally don't mind making a trip to Boston, but this one sucks. Josh and I had a 10:30 AM meeting with a potential new client who wanted our security system installed in their six business locations. The meeting went well, and I think we will have them signed by the middle of next week. That was about where the good of the trip stopped, though. We met with Alex and Danny for lunch after the meeting to catch up and get an update on everything going on with Kelli's case.

"There is nothing else to do from our end. Despite my pushing, the case is at a stand-still. No one is actively working on it. Unless he keeps contacting her and Logan and his team can trace it or he finds Kelli and goes after her again, there is nothing else to do right now," Alex says around a bite of his burger.

I know all of this already, but I still don't know how to feel about it. All week, my head has been a mess and I have been struggling to sleep. Having Kelli so close has been everything I have been missing for the last four years, but I still won't let myself truly have her and it's killing me. To make it all worse, I can see Logan falling for her and even Josh is softening to her. I want her safe and free to live her life, however that looks. I know I need to push to find another way to catch this guy, but that also means she would come back here and I'm not ready to see her go. Hearing her laughter ring throughout the house this week has been the sweetest form of torture.

"How's Kelli doing up there? You guys better be treating her well," Danny states as he levels Josh and me with a glare. We warned Kelli not to reach out to people on her phone and specifically not to text anything about where she is or who she's with. Without knowing just how far this guy's tech skills go, we don't want her to risk anything. I know it's hard on her and Danny to not talk every day.

"She's been having some nightmares, but other than that, she seems to be handling things okay," Josh answers before I get a chance to. I look over at him, but he refuses to look at me. She's been having nightmares? Why didn't I know this? She never said anything. Neither had Josh. It's just one more reminder that I have done a shit job protecting her. She's in my home and I don't even know what's going on with her.

We finish up lunch and make promises to keep each other updated before we make our way over to Kelli's house to check on it and grab some more of her things. The boarded-up windows on the side are the first thing to stand out as we drive up. Danny mentioned at lunch that they had ordered her new windows and they should be installed by the middle of next week. Parking the car, Josh and I walk around the house to examine the back windows, which are boarded up as well. Hot anger rolls through me all over again as I picture Kelli hiding in her bathroom, fearing for her life. Josh and I replace the defaced cameras, and we ensure the rest of the house is closed and boarded up and hasn't been messed with.

Once inside, Josh hands me a list of items Kelli asked us to grab for her. I make my way into her bedroom to get her clothes. I can't help but take a moment to look around at her space. Her honeysuckle scent is still lingering, reminding me of having her wrapped in my arms. The big bed in the middle of the room is made up with way too many throw pillows, drawing a smile from me. She has always been a sucker for cozy things. Moving to the closet, I grab the items on the list, then move to her dresser. I grab the few things in there she needs, pausing when I open her underwear drawer. I feel like a pervert, but if this is the closest I can get to seeing her in them, I'm going to take it. I don't mean to poke through, but red lace catches my eye and I pull out a sexy lace and silk thong with a small heart cutout on the back.

I decide to add that to the bag of clothes just so I can picture her wearing them around the house. I'm about to close the drawer when I notice the edge of a photo sticking out on the side. Reaching back in, I pull out the photo and am immediately taken aback. It's a photo of us in my mom's living room taken that last trip home before everything happened. I'm leaning against the wall with Kelli in front of me, wrapped in my arms. She's smiling sweetly at the camera, but I am too busy staring down at her to notice. I don't even remember this being taken, but I remember the moment and how good it felt to have her in my arms.

I hear Josh call me from down the hall, so I tuck the photo into my back pocket and head back out. "Everything with her security looks good, all windows locked and it doesn't look like anyone has been in here. We should head out, though. If her stalker is still watching her house, we really don't want him to see us here and try to follow us back. Also, Logan called while you were packing to say she got another message from him, this one a lot more threatening. He sent it to us both." My jaw worked as I tried to tamp down my fear and rage.

As we climb back into my Jeep, I tuck the photo in the visor after throwing her bag into the back seat. Josh notices, but thankfully, he doesn't say anything about it. I'm grateful that it's him with me; it's rare he talks about feelings, unlike Logan. Apparently, that isn't the case today though. We make it on the highway before he starts his inquisition. "You going to tell me about that photo?"

"No." I don't even know what to say about it. I shouldn't have taken it, but I felt something crack in my chest when I saw it there. Does she still look at it and think of how we felt together? Does she still think of me, because damn it, I have not stopped thinking of her.

"Logan's into her, you know. Not just in his overly flirty friendly way either. He wants to pursue her and unless you tell him otherwise and soon, something is going to happen between them." That cuts deep, but I already figured that out. Logan's never been one to hide his feelings and from what I can tell, she feels something for him as well. I know I should just let it happen. It's the whole reason I let her go. It will kill a part of my soul to see them together. She was meant to be mine. "You have nothing to say to that, man," Josh laughs but it lacks humor, "you really are being a pussy, aren't you?"

"What the fuck is that supposed to mean? And why the hell didn't you say anything about her having nightmares?" I tighten my hands on the steering wheel, trying to stay calm while Josh glares at me. "Everything I have done is wrong when it comes to her."

"No shit, jackass. Have you sat and talked to her once since she got here?" I went to say yes but he continued, cutting me off, "I mean talked to her, not at her. You need to shut your mouth and listen to her. And while you're at it, you need to tell her why you walked away from her and continue to push her away."

He's right, I have been avoiding having a real conversation with Kelli. There is no doubt in my mind that she will ask me about why I never came back for her, and I'm not ready to tell her about it. I have some decisions to make when it comes to her, because these back-and-forth conflicting feelings are making me crazy and driving her away. She clearly wasn't any safer without me, and she certainly seems happy at my house. Admitting to myself that her happiness might have nothing to do with me is making my chest feel tight. If I felt certain that I could keep her safe right now, then why can't I get over my fears? Kelli deserves more than the broken, guilt-ridden man that I have become, but maybe it's time to step up and try to be the man she needs.

The day I kissed Kelli, everything in my life felt right. I saw my future with her clear as day, and I was so ready for it. I had been her protector, confidant, and friend for most of her life, and that was evolving into something more. We wanted the same things, we knew each other's souls, and there was this undeniable chemistry that wasn't there before. When I got back from leave, I told the guys everything. I carried her picture with me everywhere, wrote to her every day, and we planned out our future together. Josh thought I was crazy, telling me over and over that it was only one week home and just one night with her. He was certain that I was rushing and romanticizing things because I was ready to settle down. He didn't understand that we had spent most of our lives loving each other already; the type of love was just changing now.

The day we lost Ashley is the day that everything changed inside me. A life was lost on my watch, and I lost all confidence in myself. If I couldn't even keep my team safe when it was my one job, how could I be the man that Kelli needed? Caleb blamed me for her death, and he made sure everyone knew it was my mission she had been killed on. I couldn't even be mad at him; it was entirely on my shoulders. I could no longer be the man that Kelli had needed me to be, so I had to let her go. I couldn't face her and tell her of my failures, so I just cut her out of my life. I knew she wouldn't understand, and she would fight for me when I didn't deserve to be fought for. It was easier to just remove myself from her life altogether. From that point on, I only visited my family when I knew she wouldn't be there, and I avoided the majority of her calls and texts.

Danny never knew about what happened between Kelli and me, but Alex did. He called me one night not long after everything happened, telling me that a very drunk Kelli had confessed her feelings for me to him. From then on, he has kept me updated on how she's doing and has been helping to keep an eye on her for me. Kelli doesn't know all this either. I don't think she even remembers talking to Alex that night.

"I think her nightmares are getting worse," Josh said as he finally broke the silence between us. "She asked me to stay with her last night after I woke her up. She doesn't like to be alone. I think it's why she spends so much time with Logan." That made sense. I had been passing off some of my responsibilities so I could spend more time with her, but Josh was right. I was being a pussy and I was still hiding in my office most days anyway. "You aren't the same guy you were after everything went down. You've put in the work to change. Now go get the girl before it's too late."

"Logan is pretty serious about her, huh?" I look over at him, watching his eyes narrow and his hands flex. "You're falling for her, too, aren't you?"

He almost looks ashamed of that. "She's not mine to fall for." He turns to look out the window, then quietly adds, "She's too good for me."

I let loose a laugh at that comment. "She's too good for all of us," I say, though I have to admit Logan and her make sense together. Kelli has parts of her that fit well with all of us. She is so emotionally intelligent with a wild and carefree streak that is so similar to Logan. There is her inner strength and her sassy 'take no shit' attitude that rivals Josh. Her desire and drive to help others, make a difference in the world, and to take care of those she loves fits with me. "I'll talk to her, I promise."

When we pull up to the house thrity minutes later, I grab her bag from the back and head into the house. I put it down at the base of the stairs and look around, not seeing her or Logan. Josh walks out from the kitchen with two beers, but stops mid-step in front of the sliding glass doors, slowly turning toward me.

"Chug this before you go outside," he says, handing a beer over to me. I walk over to grab it and that's when I see what caught his attention. The hot tub is on, and Kelli's back is to us. Her swim suit top is hanging over the edge next to her while Logan sits across from her, head thrown back in laughter. Fire burns through my veins, my pulse racing as my vision tunnels.

Josh's hand pushes into my chest before I can slam the slider open. "Drink that, calm down, and then you can go out there." I take some deep breaths, then move to the kitchen. I am going to need something a lot stronger. I pour out two fingers of whiskey and slam it back, then pour another while Josh watches with an annoying smirk on his face. "What's your plan here?"

I have a few options that I consider while I close my eyes,

trying to get a read on all the emotions flowing through my body at that moment. Anger. Hurt. Jealousy. Desire. My therapist told me to try to only address one emotion at a time to not overwhelm myself. It's the last one I decided to focus on, desire. I slowly look back up at him, "I am going to go join them. You in?"

16

JOSH

This is going to either go really bad or really well. I run to my room and throw on my swim trunks. There's no way I'm letting Brian get out there before me in case he decides he wants to kill Logan. Grabbing another beer on my way through the kitchen, I step out onto the back porch, thankfully beating Brian out. The noise of the hot tub jets block out the sound of me coming outside, but Logan sees me anyway. He winks at me then leans forward to say something to Kelli.

I watch her spine straighten, but she makes no move to grab her swim top still sitting on the edge next to her. Logan and Kelli are in two corners directly across from each other, so I head for one of the others. Today has been tense, and she has been in the forefront of my mind all day. I didn't hear a word that was said in our meeting this morning, too busy replaying Kelli's flirty words from earlier that morning. I told Brian that she isn't mine to like, and I mean it, but damn it if I still don't want her anyway. Being around Kelli quiets the chaos in my mind, and it's something that I am starting to crave when I'm away from her.

I hear Brian come out to the porch right as I'm about to step into the hot tub. Turning, I see his eyes fixed on Kelli's back with a blank expression on his face. "Well look who decided to crash our game," Logan says, leaning back in his spot with his hands thrown over the edge on either side of him.

"What game is that?" Brian asks, moving to the other corner of the hot tub.

"Before either of you get in, you have to know the rules. If you get in, you have to play. And if you choose to not answer the truth or take the dare you are given, you have to leave the game. Are you in?" He looks at Kelli the whole time he talks, never dropping his smirk. Brian and I look at each other, then both climb in across from each other to the two empty corners. Kelli's red cheeks are the first thing I notice, especially as that blush travels down to where her creamy skin meets the water. It could be from the heat, but I doubt it. I really try not to look below her face, but my eyes drop anyway. The bubbles from the jets are making it hard to see much below the surface, and unfortunately, they hide her naked chest pretty well. A very obvious throat clearing gets my attention, causing me to look up and see Brian giving me a death glare. Like he can blame me.

"We got you more things from your house" Brian says, clearly trying to avoid playing this game. "I didn't see a swimsuit though, is there a problem with yours?"

"Not at all, she just lost it to a dare," Logan says cheerfully as he looks entirely too pleased with himself over that. "Speaking of, it's my turn." He looks around at all of us before slowly turning to me. "Truth or dare, Josh?"

I hate this game. I have only played it once and have actively avoided it ever since. For Kelli though, I'll take one for the team, "Truth."

"Good choice, Joshy. How do you feel about Kelli?"

He has me trapped and he knows it. These two can read me like a book, and I haven't exactly been hiding my growing feelings for her. I look at Kelli, her ocean blue eyes meeting my emerald green ones. "I think she is too good for me, yet I want her anyway. She's incredible and I find her on my mind more often than not." A smile spreads across her lips as her cheeks flush. "Truth or dare, Kelli?"

"Truth."

"Which one of us do you find the most attractive?"

"That's not fair, you are all stupidly attractive and you know it." I narrow my gaze at her with one eyebrow raised waiting for her to answer. "Okay, but you can't hate me over this. Face would be Logan, body would be Brian, and sexy dominant broody vibes that I like is all you." Can't say I hate that answer. Anyone with eyes knows that Logan has a model face, and Brian is more cut than I am. Not a lot of women see my attitude and find it attractive, so I like that she does.

Logan's smug face beams at her. "I like your face, too, pretty girl."

She splashes some water towards him, giggling. "Shut it." Her head turns toward Brian, her gaze softening. "Truth or dare, B."

"Truth."

"You guys suck at this game. Where are all the dares?" Logan whines.

Kelli really contemplates her question, finally pushing her shoulders back and looking him in the eye. "How many times have you been in love?"

His brows scrunch as his head tilts to the side, questioning. "Only you, dove. Always you."

Her shoulders immediately sink, her gaze moving down to the water. She has to know that she is the love of his life.

The only one he has ever and probably will ever truly love. He has let things go so wrong for them, the hurt still so fresh at the surface for them both.

"Truth or dare, Logan."

"I'll stick with your boring round of truths."

"Are you falling for my girl?"

Logan's eyes shoot to Brian's. If Brian wants to get his girl, pushing his friends to admit their feelings to her is not the way to do it. "I am falling for OUR girl, yeah." Brian's entire face goes hard as Kelli's face lights up like a Christmas tree. "Back to you, Josh, truth or dare?"

"Truth."

He taps his finger on his chin dramatically. "Ooh I got it! Is the reason you like to share women because you're a voyeur, an exhibitionist, or because you're a control freak?" That's not where I was expecting him to go with that, but I have no problem answering honestly because he and Brian already know the answer. This is clearly for Kelli's benefit and to gauge reactions.

"All of the above," I respond. In high school, I accidentally discovered that I enjoy watching people fuck when I stumbled upon the 'secret' hook up spot behind the gym. Then joining the military, you are often bunked in barracks where you share rooms, and well, I discovered I don't mind having an audience either. Brian happened to share a room with me for a while, and eventually, we just started sharing women. It was easy. I trusted him and he let me control the situation how I liked, so it became our thing. Kelli doesn't look surprised by the question or my answer, which intrigues me. Did Logan give her a heads up about our activities, or is sharing something not foreign to her? Fuck, my dick is getting hard just thinking about it.

"Okay Kel, truth or dare?" I ask, praying she will pick

dare. It's a miracle that Brian hasn't said anything to Logan about the swim top, but the look in his eyes is all lust aimed at Kelli. I really shouldn't poke the bear, but something has to give. We can't all keep getting more attached to this girl without a blow up bound to happen.

"Dare," she replies, looking me in the eye and reading my silent request.

Fuck yes. "I dare you to sit on Brian's lap." She sucks in a breath while looking at the others, then slowly scoots toward him, making sure to keep only her head above water.

"Damn, going in for the kill," Logan mutters under his breath toward me. The feel of Brian's glare aimed at me is doing nothing to take my eyes off the stunning girl in front of me. I would rather have Brian hate me instead of Logan, so here I am testing the waters, so to speak. As Kelli slides herself onto his lap, she leans her back against his chest and lets her head rest on his shoulder. One of his hands is resting over the edge of the hot tub holding a beer, but as his jaw clenches, I know his other is somewhere touching her soft skin.

They look good together, even if Brian is stiff as a board. He said he's ready to be honest with her. What better way to get him there than to make him hold onto the one thing he won't let himself have? Kelli leans to the side and looks up at him with adoration and a little twinkle of mischief when she asks, "Truth or dare, B?"

He keeps his glare on me for another second, grinding his teeth to keep from either yelling at me or thanking me. Either way, I know I'm going to pay for this later, but I'm hoping it pays off. He slowly looks down at her, and the minute their eyes connect, his body starts to relax. "Dare."

"I dare you to sleep in my bed with me tonight." She says it sweetly, but I see the way her eyes cut to the side. She doesn't want to sleep alone, that's clear as day to me, and she's killing three birds with one stone with that dare. Not only would she not be alone tonight, but she's also forcing him to spend time with her, which I can see she desperately wants. What she may not know is the fact that she just hit him where he needs it. He knows about the nightmares and that her asking means she is asking for his comfort when they happen. I look over at Logan, who is looking at her the same way I am, full of wonder and awe. The one thing Brian feels he can't give her, he will be giving her tonight. It was a gift she was giving him and she didn't even know it.

"Any night you want me, I'm there," his voice comes out soft. Love radiates from him as his gaze stays locked on hers, but as soon as he looks away, I see the fear hidden in his eyes. This is going to be so good for them both. Kelli squirms on his lap, drawing a low groan from him. My cock is throbbing now at the thought of her ass rubbing against him. "Alright Logan," Brian continues with a gritty voice, "truth or dare?"

"Dare, duh."

Brian looks down at Kelli as a smile slowly slides over his face. He holds her stare again as he makes his request, "I dare you to turn the jets off." Logan bursts out laughing as Kelli lets out a little squeal. This is going to be fun. At least I won't be the only one with a boner after this. Logan leaps over to the other side of the hot tub and pushes the buttons to turn off the jets. The quiet that settles over us as the jets stop allows the sounds of the night and the critters to be heard, bringing in a sense of calm. That is, until the water settles after Logan gets back in his spot. Simultaneously, everyone's eyes drop down to Kelli's chest.

"This is the best game we have ever played," Logan says, licking his lower lip with his eyes glued to her perky boobs. "Fuck, baby girl, you have been teasing me all night with those bare tits and they are more than worth the wait." Kelli turns her head more into Brian's neck to hide her embarrassment, but really it just gives him a better view of her perfect, round breasts. Her breathing is getting deeper as we watch her chest heave and her legs squeeze together, slowly making eye contact with us all. Brian's hand squeezes her hip, then trails down to rest on her inner thigh.

"He's not wrong," Brian mutters with his eyes not moving from her. "You still take my breath away."

"Okay, my turn," Logan all but shouts, pulling Kelli off Brian's lap and onto his own. "We are pausing the game because I can see that look in your eyes, baby girl. What do you need right now?" We can all see the lust in her hooded eyes, the way her chest is heaving with each heavy breath she takes. She slowly sucks in her bottom lip and chews on it while looking around at us, leaving us all in a trance.

"It's been a while since I've uhhh… No one has looked at me like this in years… I just…" she starts, but clearly doesn't want to say what she's feeling.

"It's okay, baby girl, I know what you need," Logan says right before he gently pulls her face to his and kisses her. It starts out as a gentle kiss, but Kelli quickly turns into him more as he wraps one hand around her waist, the other gently gripping her hair and angling her head until it's all clashing of tongues. I can feel the rest of my blood rushing south as Kelli's nipples harden and a whimper slips from her lips.

She looks like she belongs with Logan as much as she looked like she belonged with Brian. My brain is overwhelmed with thoughts of her being with both of them. With all of us. She looks like ours. She feels like ours. Her body melts into Logans, pushing her ass further into his lap and grabbing hard on to his shoulders. Brian abruptly stands up and gets out of the hot tub, walking into the house without a backwards glance. Kelli pulls back and watches him go with hurt in her eyes. Every part of me hates to see that look on her, leaving me no choice but to fix it. "It's okay, just give him some time. I can go talk to him, if you want?"

"No, don't go," she pleads as she looks back to Logan who gives her a little nod of encouragement, "You like to watch, right?" She looks down at the water and lets her fingers flow through it. "Logan and I talked, he told me he wants me. Do you want me, too?" What the hell happened today when we were gone? Logan must be tired of this waiting around, walking on eggshells game we have all been playing. Her eyes slowly move up and meet mine, and I am stunned. She is too damn sweet, too good, too everything I am not. Watching her eyes fill with a silent plea, longing, and a mix of fear and embarrassment, I decide to give in, just a little.

"Yeah baby, I like to watch. I need control, though. Will you follow my instructions?" I question. She bites her lip, nodding vigorously, her face radiating excitement. "Good girl. Straddle his lap and give him what he wants." She sucks in a sharp breath, climbing fully onto Logan's lap as his hands grip her hips and pull her down snug on his cock. Logan and I haven't shared before, but he knows about my dominant side. He looks up at me waiting for direction, and damn if that doesn't turn me on even more. I move over to put my chest to her back reaching around to roll her nipples between my fingers. "Kiss her," I tell him while I continue to pinch and tease her nipples.

Logan's hands squeeze her hips, encouraging her to grind against his length. She lets out a little gasp as she moves along his hard shaft and pushes further down on him as she rocks her hips. I'm entranced by her movements, her ass moving against my cock every time she rocks back. Moving one of my hands up to grip the hair at the back of her neck, I angle her head so Logan can deepen the kiss. The gravel in my voice is unavoidable as I growl in her ear, "You like the way his cock feels against your needy pussy? How long has it been since someone has given her what she needs?"

"Too long," she gets out in a breathy moan as Logan moves to kiss along her jawline. I bite down the length of her neck on the other side, licking at the sting after each nip. My hand in her hair moves down her back, then slips around to the front, stroking along her hips and teasing along the edge of her bottoms. "Please!" She cries as Logan lifts her breast and bites down on her nipple.

My fingers slide around to the back and down into her bottoms. After grabbing a handful of her juicy ass, I push a finger further down, rubbing a circle around her entrance, then slip it into her wet pussy. Fuck, she is so tight and soft. I curl my finger, stroking her as she continues to grind her clit against Logan. I can't stop my hips from rocking against her ass from behind her as I bite my lip to hold back a groan. I remove my finger, reaching around and up to tease her nipple again as my other hand moves around her throat, squeezing just hard enough. Logan's eyes close as she grinds harder onto him. "Do you see what you do to us, Kelli? Having two men so fucking hard for you, willing to do anything to please you. Be a good girl and ride his cock. Take what you need from him." Her head falls back against me, whimpers escaping her pouty lips.

Sliding two fingers back into her, I stroke at the spot that makes her fingers dig into Logan's shoulders. Her little cries of pleasure have me out of my mind, on the edge of coming. I try to distract myself, so I look over her shoulder at Logan who is still taking turns sucking one nipple into his mouth while playing with the other. Her pussy starts to clench around my fingers and her hips angle more to get her clit right against the tip of his dick. "She's so close, get her there." He moves both hands to her hips dragging her slit over the tip of his dick, sucking one of her peaked nipples hard into his mouth. Kelli tightens around my fingers and screams her release in a mix of 'oh fucks' and whimpering cries. Logan holds her sagging body tight against him while I slowly kiss down her neck while rubbing her arms and shoulders as she comes down.

"Such a good fucking girl for us. You are so beautiful when you come," I say as I can't help but praise her. She is just as sweet as I knew she would be. As she fully slumps into Logan's arms, I step out of the hot tub to grab her a towel, watching Logan continue to whisper into her ear and stroke her back. "Come here," I grab her hand to help her out, but she pulls back and looks down at my erection.

"What about you guys?"

Pulling her out and wrapping her in the towel, I tell her not to worry about us. Logan and I got so much more than we could have asked for tonight, and this night isn't about us. "Go take a shower; we will make sure B is in your bed tonight."

She looks away, the hurt written all over her face once again as her eyes turn glassy. "It's fine, he made his feelings clear tonight," she says as the tears in her eyes start to spill over. I rub my hands over the towel wrapped around her arms. Logan throws the top on the hot tub and comes over to pull Kelli into his arms. He looks over at me and then up to the house. We know each other well enough for me to know he has this, and I need to go knock some fucking sense into Brian. Leaving him to take care of her, I head inside to find my other best friend.

I'm not surprised to find him still in his swim shorts

pacing his room. I lean against his door jamb with my arms crossed, waiting for him to talk. Brian doesn't freak out often; he is one of the most level-headed people I know, except for when it comes to Kelli. I truly believe they could have a once in a lifetime love. Even though it makes jealousy course through my veins, especially after tonight, I want that for him. If anyone deserves it, it's him.

"I fucked up again," he says as he finally sits at the edge of his bed. He looks exhausted. This might be the first time I really notice it, the dark circles under his eyes, the way his whole body sags with each heavy breath. How long has it been since he got a good night of sleep? Kelli's presence here has to be messing with him, and I haven't bothered to check in with him to see where his head is at recently. Logan and I have only criticized him for all he's doing wrong instead of taking the time to ask how he is handling everything.

"Yeah, but you can fix it," I insist. He looks up at me like I'm stupid. "You shouldn't have left, and I don't care why you did. Honestly, I don't even care how you feel about all that right now. I care that you are in her bed tonight and that you get over yourself and your issues in order to be there for the girl that you love when she needs you." The silence stretches between us as he hangs his head and stares at the floor. "She needs you, B, and it looks to me like you might need her just as much. Don't let your past fuck this up."

I turn and walk back down the hall, full of conflicting feelings. He needs to fix things with her, for both their sakes. Whether that looks like them finally acting on their feelings, or just agreeing to being the friends they once were, I don't know. I just know that I want her to be happy, but part of me wants her to find that happiness with me.

17

KELLI

Standing completely under the spray of the shower has always helped me block out the noise in my head, but it isn't doing much tonight. I have no idea where things go from here. Logan held me outside after I came down from the earth shattering orgasm they gave me, all while my emotions came rushing to the surface. The term 'post-nut clarity' has always felt dumb to me, but maybe men were on to something. I was beyond attracted to all of the guys, and the orgasm I got tonight while I was held between two sexy and dominating men was going to be my fodder for years to come. Logan's lips were as soft as they looked, and holy hell, can that man kiss. Gentle, but in control, meeting my tongue stroke for stroke, tasting like citrusy beer. I would have been happy staying attached to his lips all night. The dirty mouth on Josh was unexpected, but honestly, it was every dream come true. What I wouldn't give to be his good girl again.

Logan whispered into my ear how incredible I was and how I could have anything I wanted in this house as he held me together. He said I was in control here and I could have any, or all, of them, in whatever capacity that I want. There's no denying the attraction between myself and all three of them. Not only are they some of the most gorgeous men I have ever seen, but there's also a real connection between all of us.

Logan is quickly becoming one of my best friends. He can read my moods and knows exactly how to distract me and make me smile. He took the time to get to know me and to open himself up to me, as well. That sort of vulnerability is so attractive to me, and I haven't had it since the night Brian and I confessed our souls to each other. Josh is still the quiet one in the group, but even he is letting me see through his tough exterior slowly. He doesn't make me talk about the nightmares, but always shows up to comfort me and ensure I'm okay. He pushes me in the gym when he knows I need to get out my anger and quietly sits with me, taking extra time to stretch when he sees I just need to not feel alone. What we did may have shown that he and Josh are on board for whatever I want to do moving forward, but I can't pursue anything with either of them without having a conversation with Brian. I need to know where he stands. I need to know if he feels even a tiny bit of what he used to feel for me or if there is no hope for us. Hiding in the shower all night to avoid seeing if he will be in my room or not probably isn't my best choice, but I don't think I can face that rejection yet. I put my head back under the spray, reliving that amazing night Brian and I shared long ago.

Brian pulls my feet up into his lap, mindlessly rubbing them while staring at me like he is truly seeing me the same way I see him. Finally. Our buzz from drinks out with Alex and Danny are wearing off, and we are back at my apartment on my couch just enjoying our last bit of time together before he has to go back to finish his deployment.

"You know, I've always seen you as my best friend, too. I didn't say it out loud because I thought it was embarrassing to admit your younger brother's best friend was also yours. But you have been, Kelli. The age difference has never mattered between us. You have always seen me in a way others didn't. You've supported and encouraged me, you've talked with me when I was upset, you broke up so many fights between Danny and me." He laughs and shakes his head while squeezing my feet, continuing, *"When you guys graduated, I truly saw how your beauty was changing from the girl I adored to a woman who took my breath away. I wanted to tell you, but I couldn't do it. I knew you had feelings for me, but I knew my time in the military was not even near being over. I couldn't steal that time away from you. That time to find yourself, enjoy college, meet new people. I thought we were meant to be just best friends, and I could just watch your life unfold from afar."*

I wasn't sure what to say. I had loved this man most my life, and I felt that love shifting from brotherly to more as well, but I always thought it was a one-sided love. Danny was my best friend, yes, but Brian was my best friend in a different way. My love for him has always felt different. Our conversations were always deeper, full of truths we couldn't tell anyone else. Our understanding of each other has always felt beyond its time. Even at six, ten, and fourteen, I knew that. To know that all along he could feel it, too, that I haven't been alone in feeling like we were meant for more, it is everything. Absolutely everything to me.

He sits up further on the couch, letting his hands slide up my calves, gripping under my knees. He pulls me to him so my legs are wrapped over his, and we're face to face. "For the last five years, I have watched you flourish and take the world by storm. Your phone calls and emails have gotten me through so much and been the highlights of my day. I never stopped rooting for you, supporting you, protecting you. You are still my best friend, Kelli, but I don't want to watch your life from afar anymore. Getting glimpses of each other through calls while states or oceans away isn't enough for me anymore. I want to be by your side for the rest of it. Please, baby, tell me I'm not too late. I wanted you to have your time, but time's up. I'm coming home after this tour, and I want to come home to you. Let me come home to you, baby."

The overwhelming steam from the bathroom forces me out from under the water and breaks my reminiscing. I need to get out of this shower and face whatever I will be met with in my room. After braiding my hair, brushing my teeth, and putting on my silk pajama set with starfish this time, I take a deep breath. If he isn't waiting for me in my room, it will be okay. I will have my answer, and I'll get the closure conversation tomorrow. It would hurt. It would hurt so fucking bad, but I would be okay.

The bedroom door is open and Brian is there, laying on my bed looking up at the ceiling with his hands behind his head. He looks up at me, and I don't miss the way his eyes travel down my body before coming back up, snagging on my pajamas. A tiny lift of his mouth tells me he remembers my affinity for animals. "I didn't know what side of the bed you like," he says as if I care that he's in the center.

So, that's how he's going to play this. Still avoiding the serious conversation we desperately need to have. "You can have the left," moving to my side pulling the comforter back, I climb in and cover myself up. "You get to turn out the light."

He gets up to turn off the light, moving to the other side of the bed. I watch with rapt attention as he pulls his shirt off over his head before sliding his shorts down, leaving him only in boxers. The room is too dark to truly see any real detail, which leaves me feeling a little annoyed. When he gets into the bed, he faces me with an arm under his pillow. We lay there not talking, just letting our eyes adjust to the dark while looking at each other, the air growing thicker between us. Eventually, Brian lets out a heavy sigh, "I'm sorry I walked away down there."

"Why did you?"

He's quiet for another moment while searching my face, "I wasn't ready to see you with someone else. I don't know if I ever will be."

"That's not fair to me, Brian. I'm not an object you can keep locked up in case one day you decide to play with it again. You have made it clear I am no longer the one for you. That fucking broke me, by the way. Just cutting me out of your life without a word as to why. You don't get to come in here and tell me that I can't try to move on. That I can't take my taped-up heart and offer it to someone else."

"I know, okay? I know. Fuck," his voice full of frustration as his chest heaved, trying to calm himself back down. "Those are my best friends. They would be great to you, and I know they would be damn lucky to have you. I want that for you. I do. I just fucked up, okay? I will be fine seeing it next time."

I roll over to look up at the ceiling, willing the tears not to fall. That isn't what I wanted to hear. Was there really nothing he wanted with me anymore? The thing that was always different with our friendship was that we could always talk to each other about the hard things. Taking a deep breath to steady myself, I ask the question that has been in my head for four years, "What changed?"

"What do you mean?"

"What changed from you planning a life with me to

ghosting me in a matter of days? What did I do to deserve that?"

He grabs my chin with his fingers, forcing me to look back at him. "You did nothing wrong. I just… I just realized I couldn't be the man you needed. The man you deserved. And I didn't know how to tell you that at the time. You are perfect. You are everything, Kelli, don't you ever think otherwise."

"Who are you to decide that for me? Why don't I get to decide what I need and deserve?" I look around, debating if now is the right time to lay it all on the line or not. "I waited for you the first two years. I waited to hear from you. Some explanation why you suddenly stopped talking to me. Danny told me nothing, and I couldn't ask. He didn't know about us. So, I put my heart on hold. I put up my walls that I thought only you could break down. Then, I found someone to scratch the itch when needed. I told myself that it didn't become more because I was too busy, but really, it was because of you. Always waiting for you. And you gave me nothing, Brian. Nothing. As it turns out though, your friends know how to break down walls, too."

When he didn't say anything, I rolled away from him, letting my tears fall. His muttered 'fuck' is all I hear before I feel the bed move. "Go to sleep, dove, I've got you," he whispers as he pulls my back to his front, stroking a hand over my stomach. It is achingly sweet, making the tears fall faster. How can he be so hot and cold with me all the time? I know he is lying to himself, telling himself he can't have me when really, it would be so easy with us. It has been so long since I felt his body wrapped around mine. It feels entirely too good. It feels right. As hurt as I am, I snuggle in closer to him, letting myself be soothed by him just for one night and let myself drift to sleep.

"Kelliiiiii, where are youuuu?" His voice is deep and so

much closer than I realized, "I like this cat and mouse game, little girl. I will always come after you."

Fuck, I needed to run, but something was holding me back. I was hiding behind a tree in the dark woods, and looking down, I had no shoes on, just my starfish pajamas. His footsteps were getting closer, but I still couldn't run. It was like something was crushing my chest.

"No, goddamnit, Kelli, you need to run. This isn't how we end... RUN!" I tell myself as my legs finally start to move. I hadn't made it but fifteen feet when I'm tackled from behind. "NO!" I scream, "Help me, please, someone help me!" I could feel his hands on my arms shaking me, but Josh has taught me to fight, so I throw my body around trying to land a good hit to get free.

"Wake up, dove, wake up," Brian's worried face comes into view as my eyes flutter open. As soon as he sees my eyes open and the fight leave my body, he wraps me in his arms, nuzzling his face in my hair. "I'm so sorry, Kelli, I've got you now. I'm not going anywhere, I've got you." He wraps me even tighter in his arms, stroking his fingers through my hair, kissing my forehead.

I feel the hot sting of tears as I try to hold them back. Waking to his comforting arms is what I have craved for years. His strength seeping into my tired body should be everything I need, but it's just a cold reminder he doesn't want this. He said earlier that his friends would be good for me, that he would be okay letting me go. The first traitorous tear slides down my cheek, quickly followed by painful, chest achingly hard sobs.

Brian just holds me tighter against him, slowly stroking my back and hair while whispering how I am safe with him and that he has me. It just makes the tears fall harder, because for four years, this is what I wanted to hear from him. My head is a mess. I'm falling for Logan and Josh, but despite everything, Brian still has a vice grip on my heart. My body slowly melts back into the safety and comfort of him as my body tires out and there are no tears left to fall. Before I fall asleep, I remember the term he has been calling me all week, "Why do you call me dove?"

Brian's fingers go still on my back as he lets out a heavy sigh. "I have always felt like our friendship gave me wings. You made me feel like I could do anything, be anything, and you would always be there to lift me up." His fingers slowly start stroking through my hair again as he continues, "I had a stop-over in Yemen a couple months before that visit home. There were turtle doves everywhere, and a local told me about how they mate for life. These birds who could go anywhere and had the wings to do anything choose one mate to be with for life. It made me think of you." He squeezes me a little tighter to him again, gripping my thigh to drape my leg over his. "Go to sleep, dove." Sleep after that comes easy, with my body wrapped around his.

18

KELLI

I wake to an empty bed, and it would have stung, except I felt more rested than I have in weeks. There was still a lot that Brian and I needed to talk about, but last night was a step in the right direction. My phone lights up on the nightstand, reminding me I need to reach out to the hospital again and check in. As I pull it off the charger, the ping of a new email remains on the screen. I click on it, not fully awake yet, but a scream rips from my throat as the email loads. There are two photos staring back at me, the first one is my pillow on my bed back home that looks to be covered in ropes of cum. The second is a gloved hand holding a pair of my underwear wrapped around an erect dick. The subject line says *'one step closer'* and below the photos he wrote, *'Maine is beautiful this time of year.'*

Josh comes barreling into my room right as I jump out of bed. He is at my side looking around the room while holding me before I can blink. When he decides there is no threat in my room, he looks down at me, his murderous expression quickly morphing into something soft as he lifts his hand to wipe a thumb over my cheek. I didn't realize I was crying until it came up wet.

"What happened?" his voice is rough with such a hardened edge that it sends a chill down my spine.

I grab my phone up from the edge of the bed where I tossed it and hand it to him. His jaw clamps down hard as he looks at the email I still have pulled up. "Logan!" he yells as he grabs my hand and pulls me along behind him. We start making our way down to the living room as he yells for Logan and Brian again. Leading me to the couch, he nudges me to sit down, still gripping my phone tight in his other hand. "I think they're in the gym. Don't move, I'm going to get them. It's time we all have a talk." As he rushes down to the basement, I go to make a pot of coffee. I need something to do with my hands so I don't have a full-fledged panic attack. My hands are shaking as I try to pull mugs out from the cupboard. Brian's body crowds me in from behind, grabbing them from my hand and putting them on the counter for me.

I take a second to close my eyes and lean back against him to borrow his strength for just a moment. He smells like sweat and sandalwood again, which has quickly become a favorite of mine. His arms snake around my waist, pulling me tighter to him as my body relaxes into his. "I've got you," his breath tickles my ear. "Go and sit. I will bring in the coffee. I have you, Kelli. We've got you."

My breath feels shaky as I sit on the couch, pulling my legs up into my chest. Logan comes out from the office with his laptop and sits next to me. He feels stiff and won't look at me as he powers up his computer and logs in. My whole body feels jittery, and he must notice because he grabs a blanket that's draped behind him and tucks it around me, all without making eye contact. Josh and Brian come in the room, handing out mugs of coffee before Brian sits on the other side of me and Josh takes the chair across from us.

I get a feeling like I'm in trouble, and they are blocking all sides to keep me from running. Brian's hand snakes under the blanket to grip my thigh that is still firmly pulled into my chest. "We need to talk about the escalations and how we want to proceed from here."

"Escalations, as in multiple? This is the first time he's reached out again," I falter. I was certain I was done crying after last night, but the lump in my throat is getting harder to swallow down. One message in over a week's span isn't that bad in comparison to how often he was reaching out before. My mind is reeling from it all when I recall what exactly the email said.

"He knows I'm in Maine," I mutter. Realistically, he could be bluffing or guessing that I'm in Maine. I'm not all that far from home, and he could be trying to get a reaction from me to confirm or deny that I am here. Plus, Maine is a huge state even if he knows I am here. He didn't specify the town, so maybe he doesn't really know at all.

Logan finally looks up from his laptop, the look in his eyes full of shame. "It's not the first time he's reached out recently, Kelli. It's just the first one I didn't intercept on time."

"What do you mean intercept? What the hell is going on?" I can't keep the panic from my voice. Has my stalker been active this whole time? I was finally starting to feel safe again. The guilt written on all three of their faces tells me enough. They have been hiding things from me when all I asked from them was honesty. I just want to go home, but that place is ruined for me now. I no longer have a home, a place that is mine to be proud of, somewhere where I feel safe. He has taken that from me, and now, I'm stuck here with people who are keeping things from me. Things that are about my life, yet here they are playing puppet masters like I am something for them to control. "Well? Is someone going to answer me?" I fumed.

Josh rests his arms on his thighs, holding his coffee mug between his fingers. "When you first got here, Logan cloned your phone. He never snooped or looked through anything, but he has been keeping tabs on your emails, calls and texts, and any other messages. There were two times prior to this that he has reached out. The first was a message that said, *'You can run, but can you hide?'* and the second one said, *'Keep running, little bitch, because the next time I see you will be the last.'* This email is the third message."

Logan reaches over, removing my coffee from my shaking hands and puts it on the table in front of us. I must have really pissed someone off in a past life to deserve this. The air in my lungs feels like it's choking me, my chest too tight to get in a breath that I desperately need. My body is hauled onto Logan's lap before I have time to fall into full panic, one hand being used to squeeze my hands, the other on my chest as he tells me to breathe. "Breathe with me, nice and deep," he whispers in my ear. His chest is nestled up right behind my back. I try to follow the rise and fall of his chest with my own, focusing only on the feel of him around me. "Good girl, keep focusing on your breathing, you're okay. We've got you."

Feeling my chest finally fully expand with a deep breath, I look back around to see Josh sitting on the coffee table in front of us and Brian in the middle of the couch where I was just a moment ago. I didn't hear either of them move, but being surrounded by them eases some of the fear that was taking hold of my body. Josh reaches forward, taking the hand Logan was holding onto into his and starts lightly rubbing it, easing the tension from my bones. I look at all three of them, letting out a little huff of laughter. As upset as I am, I can't help but see the shield they have unintentionally formed around me. "Have you guys blocked me into this little circle to keep me from running, or is it to keep the outside world from getting to me?"

"Both," Josh replies, always being the one to keep it real. "We didn't do this intentionally. We all feel the same about you and this situation though. It's in our nature and our training to protect the innocent. This is a little different, though, because you feel like ours to protect." His calloused hand gives mine a little squeeze. "Well, mine to protect."

Despite the situation, the walls I had erected around my heart felt like they were crumbling. These men felt like mine, too. Josh and Logan did at least, but after last night, I think Brian might be, too. "We need to go back to the beginning of this conversation. I am going to table the cloning my phone and have a conversation with you about privacy later," I turn back to level Logan with a look. "How did he reach out the other two times? Were there more photos?"

Logan takes a deep breath behind me, then moves me back to the couch between himself and Brian, but Brian scoops me up and puts me in his lap before my butt even hits the cushion. He then spends the next fifteen minutes recapping everything that has happened this week. Showing me the two previous messages, reviewing what all the bricks had on them when they came through my window, which I had not seen yet, as well as going into detail about where he and his team were at with trying to track this guy through his IP address as they tried to follow any cyber trail. Apparently, it was well covered by my stalker. Brian held me in his arms the whole time, and Josh never let go of my hand.

"Why have you guys kept this from me? It's my life. If I

hadn't seen this email this morning, would you have continued to lie to me?" I want to be grateful for all the hard work Logan has been putting in to try and catch this guy, but the fact that he went behind my back really hinders that. I deserve to know what is happening and if my stalker is getting closer to finding me. I know the boys will do everything they can to keep me safe, but I also don't want to put them in danger.

"We should have told you. You were just getting comfortable here. You were happy. We didn't want to take that away. I promise nothing will happen without your knowledge from here on out. I'm sorry. We made a mistake not telling you immediately." Logan doesn't look away from me, letting me see the truth and remorse in his eyes. "We need to discuss next steps and see if we can decipher if he really knows you are in Maine or not. I also need to let Alex know they need to go to your house ASAP and see if they can get that DNA evidence."

"Okay, I need some time to myself. Can you guys talk about it and we can discuss at lunch what you think is best to do from here?" They all nod as I make my way upstairs to get dressed. As I head back down to go sit on the beach for a bit, Logan catches me.

"I'm really sorry, baby girl. We never should have kept this from you. I know Josh puts on this front that he doesn't care about anything, but hurting you is gutting him. He fought us all week telling us you deserved to know. Please, if you shut us out, just don't shut him out, too. This is the most I have seen him care for someone in… well, ever," he explains.

It doesn't surprise me at all that Josh was the one to take my side. He hides himself from everyone, but I have seen glimpses of the man underneath. There is a man that hasn't been given the love he deserves beneath that hard exterior, one that just wants to be seen and loved. It shows in the way he watches me closer the mornings after I have nightmares, the way he takes my hand to show his support, and the way he looks to the others for their reactions when he speaks. "Can you send him out to me when you guys are done talking? I'll be down by the beach."

Squishing the rocky sand between my toes, my mind floats through all the events of the last few weeks. My whole life was essentially uprooted simply because of a quick reaction to a drunk patient. Living in fear isn't something I wanted to get used to, but being a jobless mooch living here isn't sounding too great either. The guys have gone out of their way to help me and make me feel welcome and safe in their home, but this was never their idea. I was someone they felt pity for, that they now feel a sense of responsibility for. If they really wanted me here, they would have respected me enough to be upfront with me about everything.

There are feelings getting involved now, at least on my end. I can't stay here much longer and let myself fall deeper while knowing that I would always be a burden to them and not a choice. I want to be someone's first choice, their priority. I was never my dad's choice, and work was my mom's first priority. I deserve more than that. One more week was plenty of time to give Logan and his team to try and find this guy. If they couldn't do that, I would go home and go back to work. I don't want to spend my life running and hiding. I could sell my house and find an apartment with security until this all blew over and he was caught or he just went away.

Hopefully they were coming up with a plan to get this sorted before then. I know I asked to be in the know, but this is their area of expertise, not mine. I lean back in the chair, trying to enjoy the sun warming my body while my toes play in the sand at the edge of the water, keeping me cool. Nothing

I do now would change anything, so enjoying the peace of my surroundings would have to be enough.

Footsteps behind me isn't enough to convince me to open my eyes and ruin the calm moment I am enjoying. The sound of something being set down next to me however is. Rolling my head to the side, I peek through one eye down at the basket that is next to my chair. Looking up, I see Josh sitting in the chair next to me, watching me, so I decide to sit up and open the basket.

It's filled with grapes, strawberries, some cut up meats and cheeses, and two waters. "You made a picnic charcuterie board?" Surprise oozes from my voice.

"Last time I visited my sisters, they were obsessed with these things. Figured you might like to eat out here since it's your favorite spot and you've had a rough morning." He looks out over the water, looking unsure for the first time since I have met him. "I can go, though, if you want."

"Stay." It's out of my mouth before I can stop it, the relief in his sagging body immediately evident. I have learned so much about Logan this week, and I obviously know the most about Brian, but Josh is still sort of a mystery to me. One that is latching onto me and one I want to discover. "Tell me about your sisters. How many do you have?"

"Two little sisters. Lisa is twenty-seven and married, Hannah is twenty-five and just started a job at the Swedish Cancer Institute working on cancer research. They are the best people I know," he says, his voice evident with the pride he feels toward them, love radiating from the smile on his face as he talks about them. "They have overcome so much, and have really made something of themselves. They may bust my balls a lot, but I would do anything for them." His voice grows quieter as his smile fades. "They would be pissed at me if they found out I didn't tell you what was going on when honesty was all you asked for. It is the least you deserve. I'm sorry, Kelli."

I think that was the most vulnerable Josh has been, and truly, I want more. I wasn't going to lie and tell him it was okay when it wasn't. He knows they all messed up, so instead, I respond, "I know how you can make it up to me."

"Oh yeah?" He says with a smirk as he reaches into the basket between us, plopping a grape into his mouth.

"Tell me more about you. What's the rest of your family like? Why'd you join the Army? Who was your first love? I want to hear all of it." There was about a ninety percent chance he was going to laugh me off and walk away, but to my surprise, he starts talking. He tells me about his home life when he was a kid, the accident that killed one of their teammates when he got injured overseas. He goes into detail about how he mostly worked through the nightmares. I learned about how he started the company, and about where his tech skills came from.

"Why did you join the Army?"

He runs his hand through his hair, "I was an angry kid. I was the boy from the trailer park in dirty clothes with an addict mom, so I wasn't exactly popular in school. I got into numerous fights, but I did my best to be a good influence for my sisters. I didn't want to let the anger rot and fester, and I knew the military would help teach me the discipline I needed. I thought I would just do my four years and get out, but I really thrived in that environment. Plus, it helped me save money to help pay for Hannah and Lisa to go to college."

"Did you get stationed with Logan and Brian right away?"

"Logan first, then Brian got transferred to our base about

a year later. We all clicked pretty quickly, so I always tried to get stationed wherever they were."

"Do you regret getting out when you did?" I ask, pulling a few pieces of meat from the basket.

"No, after everything with my leg and the fact that Brian and Logan were getting out, it was time. I miss it some days, but I'm really proud of what Brian and I have built together and where we all are in life."

Through it all, I find a recurring theme where he has dedicated his life to others, never expecting anything in return. From when he was a little boy to now, he has been this silent force, ensuring everyone else is safe, happy, and loved, all while never ensuring he puts himself in those categories. Josh has never put himself or his needs first, which has led to him completely closing himself off from others. No one met his needs for so long that he stopped expressing them and eventually stopped expressing himself at all. My heart hurts for this selfless man, wanting to be the one thing he takes for himself.

I snatch a strawberry, slipping it in my mouth, as I prod, "You never told me about your first love."

"I've never been in love. Never even been in a relationship."

"What? How is that possible?"

He sits back in the chair, drumming his fingers on the armrest. "I mean, I have dated around, but relationships aren't my thing."

"Is that by choice?"

"I don't know how to be in one, so I've never pursued one. I watched my mother have horrible and toxic relationships one after another, then I joined the Army and was constantly moving around. I don't know if you're aware, but military divorce rates are astronomical. I've never seen a healthy or constant relationship, and I don't want to repeat the cycle by getting into a toxic one. If I ever fall in love, I want it to only be once. I would want a woman I can give myself to wholly and who does the same for me. I don't know how to do that, though. I don't know how I would make someone want to stay. Most women I have been with don't want that from me anyway."

"They just want you for your body?" I tease. "I don't know that I am any better at relationships. I haven't had a serious one either. I feel that when you meet the right person, it will come easy. You will just click and know what to do because you will want the best for them, and you both will work to be the best for each other. At least, that's what I hope."

Josh contemplates that for a while, glancing between me and the lake. Vulnerability written all over his face. "What if I end up with someone who wants kids? I don't know how to be a dad. If my relationship models were bad, my parenting ones were even worse."

"Sometimes knowing what not to do is enough. You know how not to parent, so you can do the opposite of that. No one gets handed a baby and knows exactly what to do. You figure it out as you go, just trying to be better than you were yesterday, all while nurturing the child. It's just like a relationship that way."

"Do you want kids?"

"Someday, I do. I want to be in a place where I can shower them with all the love I have and show up for them every day in whatever way they need."

"You are going to make a great wife and mother one day, you know that? I haven't told you, but I see the little things you do for me. For all of us. It means a lot to me, you caring for me in the quiet. We're really lucky to have you here, Kelli. I'm sorry we took advantage of that."

My chest feels heavy again, my vision blurring. This sweet grumpy man is breaking the walls around my battered heart even more, all without even trying.

After a few hours of talking and finishing off the basket of food, we walk back up to the house as I slip my hand into his. I want him to feel comfort from me, just like he gives to me. I also want more of him than just the glimpse I got in the hot tub. "Will you stay with me tonight? To help keep the nightmares at bay?"

He looks down at our joined hands, then studies my face. "Yeah, my little flame, I will." His lips start to lift before he looks forward with his same stoic expression. My heart picks up its speed, imagining how good it will feel to be wrapped up in his huge arms, snuggled safely against his hard chest.

"Let's go talk to the guys about what their plan is and how we can continue to keep you safe." That shuts down all my stomach flutters. Back to reality we go.

19

Walking back to the house with Kelli's small hand wrapped in mine makes me feel like I am on cloud nine. Since the day we met, she has shown over and over that she is too good for me. Too good for this world. I have never wanted someone so much, no matter how undeserving I am. This incredible woman took a morning where she was overwhelmed, scared, and was told her life is in more danger than she originally thought, and instead of wallowing in that, she questioned me about my life. It might have been a distraction technique, but she was genuinely interested at the same time. She listened quietly, asking questions here and there, all with a kind smile and understanding in her eyes.

I have never opened up to someone the way I did to her. Sitting out on the beach with her, my mind wasn't racing with thoughts of how I wasn't good enough, how she wouldn't be here forever, or any other negative thoughts and insecurities that usually plague me. She brings me a peace like never before, and I don't know how I will ever let her go. When she asked me to stay with her tonight, my chest tightened in a way it never has. She's choosing me. It took focusing on my breathing to get the knot in my chest to loosen so I could answer her with the 'YES' that was screaming in my head. I never stayed any of the other nights I woke her up because I figured she didn't want me there.

Brian's eyes zero in on our connected hands as we walk back into the kitchen where he and Logan are sitting around the island. Kelli makes no effort to let go, so neither do I as she leads us over to the island to join them. She takes the chair between them, and I take the one on the other side of Logan so we can have this conversation. Logan leans over, giving her knee a squeeze and whispers something. Kelli just nods at him with a soft smile. There should be a pang of jealousy, but I don't feel it at all. All I feel is happy that she is so comfortable here with us and that she is taken care of beyond what I can give.

"We talked to Alex for a while, and unfortunately, your pillow was gone from the house when he and his officers got there. They still wiped down everything they could for prints since there is a good chance he took his gloves off to jack off, so he may have touched something. Your back door was picked by him to get in, but everything else seemed in place." Logan clears his throat before continuing. "It seems he may have taken all the contents of your underwear drawer, though, not just the ones in the photo he sent."

Kelli winces and makes a face of disgust before taking a deep breath and sitting taller. "I guess that's as good an excuse as any to go shopping." Logan's hand makes its way back to her thigh as he rubs his thumb over it. We know she is trying to deflect with humor, but she has to feel extremely violated. "Can I call Danny this week and have him find a realtor for me? That place will never feel safe to me again."

Anger flashes over Brian's face, and I know that look is

reflected on mine, as well. He told me how hard she worked to save up to buy that home. Last time Danny and Alex visited us, they raved about all the work she had put into it and how proud she was. The fact that this man was now taking that away from her made me feel murderous. I made eye contact with Brian as we had a silent conversation, swearing we would make this guy pay for everything he has put her through.

"Yeah, baby girl, we can call him together this week and get started on that for you. Whatever you need, we are here for you. We also don't think he knows that you are here. The likely reason he knows you are in Maine is that he could have been hacking cameras to find how you left the hospital and where you went from there. He must have been able to follow my car to Maine, but there is no way he followed it all the way out here. He lost track of you somewhere along the way. I have a coworker tracking your movements from the night you left to see if we can find where your stalker might be looking." Logan looks to me so that I can take over from here.

"I will be adding more cameras around the property line and around our house, as well, for added measure. We are going to continue training in the mornings, but Logan will be joining us to show you how to disarm an attacker with a knife and a gun. Brian will be teaching you to shoot this week, as well. We have guns in a safe downstairs and have decided we will be stashing some smaller ones throughout the house. Of course, we will let you know where they are at." Kelli's eyes start to fill with fear, her knuckles turning white in her lap. "Don't worry. These are all just safety precautions. We don't think they're really necessary, but it's in our nature to be overprepared."

Brian leans into her, stroking a hand down her face, his

thumb skating over her cheek. "We will keep you protected at all costs. We just want you to feel confident in your ability to defend yourself, too. There is no way that we will let anything happen to you."

"Aside from all that, we will also be consulting with Alex and the officers who originally opened your case to talk about how we can try to get this guy to make a mistake or lead him into a trap." This is the first I am hearing about this myself, so they must have been planning this while I was outside with Kelli. "We've got you, baby girl. We will keep you informed of everything, but we don't want you to worry. Now, I was thinking of steak and twice baked potatoes for dinner. Would you want to help me?"

"Mmm, yes, that sounds incredible. Thank you for everything you have done. I know this has not been easy for you all, but I really appreciate it." She hugs Brian and Logan before coming over and giving me a kiss on the cheek. I watch her walk to the pantry while avoiding the stare that I can feel from Logan and Brian.

"Well, that's new," Logan mutters with a smile in his voice before following Kelli to help get dinner started.

Brian slowly gets up, nodding toward the back porch, so I follow him out. "Want to help me chop some wood?" I look over to the covered side of the shed that is filled with more than enough wood to last us the winter months.

"Sure." I move to grab some of the logs that need to be cut while he goes to get our axes. The sun is just starting to move behind the trees, a nice breeze making its way off the water. Perfect weather to keep us from overheating while we work in silence until Brian can work out enough of his frustration and get his thoughts in order. There is something he wants to say to me, definitely in relation to Kelli, but he just needs to figure out how to say it.

Two piles of chopped wood later, he finally puts his ax down, sitting on his stump. "We finally talked last night," he starts.

"About time. Did you tell her everything?"

"No. She still doesn't know fully what happened on that deployment. I told her I can't be with her. I'm not the man she needs." His head hangs low between his shoulders, not looking up.

What the hell? That isn't what I expected at all. "You still love her, why the hell would you tell her that?"

"I broke her, Josh. Those were her words, 'you broke me,' and I won't do that to her again. I can't. I see the way she looks at you and Logan. She would be happy with one of you, hell, maybe even both of you."

"She looks at you the same way. That is not a broken woman, B. That is a damn strong woman who put herself back together and is better for it. Kelli can have anything she wants and I won't lie, I hope one of the things she wants is me. But one of the things she wants is you, too, and I think she wants that more than anything else. Taking your-self out of the equation for her is only going to hurt her more."

I know Logan has told her that she can have all of us if that's what she wants and I am certainly not opposed to it. These guys are my brothers, and it makes sense that we would all fall for the same woman. There's no jealousy there, at least not from Logan and me.

"She deserves the best. You guys better be that for her, but I just can't be," he sighs. I sit down next to him and squeeze his shoulder as I watch the first tear I have seen from him in years fall. "She needs her best friend back, so that is what I will be. She's going through so much. She just needs that boy back that sat with her under the willow tree when life got hard. I love her enough to table my feelings and be what she needs in this moment."

Fuck, he was breaking my heart. "Why can't you be both? Friendship shouldn't stop when you are with someone; it should only get deeper."

"What happens if it doesn't work out? Who does she have then? I abandoned her last time, and I can't do that again. Her friend is who she needs and who can stay in her life for good. That's who I have to be." He wipes his eyes, stands up, and starts walking back toward the house, only to turn around and look me in the eye. "Something changed between you two today. You brought out the man you keep hidden, and that's the man she deserves. Be that man for her, Josh."

How the hell did Brian know that? The four of us had a twenty minute conversation that had nothing to do with us and he could tell that things are different between Kelli and I. He isn't wrong. I poured my heart and soul out to her down by the beach, and she accepted every piece of me. My body craved to be around her, my mind constantly drifting to thoughts of her. She is the sun, and the three of us are happily stuck in her orbit.

Being in her bed tonight is going to be the ultimate test. I want her. Getting the tiny taste last night only made me want her more. The way her body melted into mine, the drag of her hips over Logan's cock, her sweet whimpers as she got close. Her pussy was so tight, squeezing my fingers in a vice grip. I stand up, having to adjust myself before I can pile up the wood we chopped and put our axes away.

Dinner is delicious, if not a little tense. Brian is quiet, only really joining in the conversation to talk with Kelli. I know he isn't mad at Logan or I, but I'm sure it will take time for his heart to follow his head and get on board with the thought that the love of his life might get with his best friends. He wouldn't let this break up our bond, but I could see it putting a strain on it. Logan makes eye contact with me, the question of 'what's wrong' clear in his eyes. I shake my head. That's a conversation we would have later.

After dinner, Brian excuses himself to go straight to bed. He needs sleep and I hope it will actually happen for him. He's worn down and exhausted, and we all need to be at our best in the coming weeks as we deal with the stalker situation on top of everything else going on. Kelli is too wound up from the day to go to bed, so she suggests a movie night. Logan races her to the basement, the winner getting to choose the movie. I stay to clean up the kitchen since they cooked.

Their whispered voices and quiet laughs reach me before I make it all the way downstairs. Logan hasn't been this happy in a long time. He has been lonely for a while, trying to hide it from B and me. We are all different, what with Brian unwilling to move on from Kelli and being okay with that and me never seeing myself as relationship material. Having Kelli around is different, though. Her light shines so bright, it is starting to shine through us and I love seeing my best friends happy.

There's a romcom playing on the screen, but neither are paying much attention to it. They are sitting in the middle of the couch together, playing rock, paper, scissors. I can't hide the unbidden smile on my face, Logan has always loved playing games.

"What do you get if you win, baby?" I ask as I walk around the couch taking a seat at her other side.

"Logan has to rub my feet, but if I lose, he gets to be the little spoon for the whole movie. It's high stakes, so don't distract me."

I lean in close to her, moving her hair to one side. Little bumps erupt along her flesh as I whisper into her ear, "he didn't say who has to be the big spoon. I could take that position for you, but it will cost you." She draws in a deep breath, then straightens her spine.

"I'm ready! Rock, paper, scissors, shoot!" She makes a scissor with her hands while Logan makes paper. "YES!" she squeals, her little shout of glee accompanied by a shimmy dance on the couch, her hands raised above her head. Damn, she is cute. Her body leans up against mine as she kicks her feet out, settling them in Logan's lap.

I can't help but wrap my arm around her and settle her into me while Logan peels off her socks, pushes up her leggings, and starts to rub her feet. Her little sigh of pleasure goes straight to my dick. While my face is no doubt filled with lust, I look over at Logan, his face filled with the softest look of adoration aimed at Kelli. We are so screwed, and I have no idea what it is she wants yet. Does she want me? Logan? Both of us? Hell, maybe neither of us and she's just making the most of her time here. That should set me at ease since I'm not meant to be a forever guy, but the thought of it sits like a heavy rock in the pit of my stomach. I want her to want us. To want to be here and really be something with us, despite the circumstances.

The movie is nearing the end, and I don't think any of us have watched a minute of it. My gaze never strayed from Kelli, who has slowly adjusted her position throughout the movie. She's now laying with her head in my lap while I run my fingers through her hair. Logan never stopped rubbing her, but as time went on his hands wandered. I was enamored as his hands slowly slid up her calves, over her knees, and rubbed small slow circles into her thighs. He knew exactly what he was doing. While Kelli's eyes never strayed from the movie, it was clear she wasn't paying attention. Her hands would squeeze into my leg every time his hands would move, her breath hitching every time he used his nails to add a little extra pressure. The erotic slow dance playing out over the last hour was coming to an end as the credits rolled.

Kelli slowly sat up, stretching her hands over her head, revealing a tantalizing bit of skin below her tank top. Logan and I made no effort to move, a quick glance to the side proving he is in the same predicament as me. How I am supposed to share a bed with her tonight and sleep is beyond me. I need a moment alone in the shower, but I have a feeling even that won't relieve this ache.

Standing and looking us over, Kelli smirks as she goes in search of the remote. "Come on, boys, just stand up. You know how turned on I am, and I felt how hard you both were underneath me already. What's the use in trying to hide it?" Logan barks out a laugh, loving the mouth on her. Calling things as they are is usually my specialty, though I like not being the one to do it this time.

Logan and I make eye contact and we both stand up, making some quick adjustments as we go. Logan grabs the remote, which was under him, clicking off the projector and we all make our way up the stairs. Watching Kelli's hips sway as she walks up both sets of stairs makes things tonight even harder. Literally. At the top of the stairs, before heading toward our wing, she leans into Logan, whispering something in his ear. I watch as he snakes his arms around her, pulling her into a tight hug, then uses one hand to lift her chin to place a soft kiss on her lips.

The green-eyed monster still doesn't rear its ugly head, but I do feel a pang of longing. I want that ease with her. Not wanting to ruin their moment, I make my way to the bath-room to shower and take care of my erection. The steam seeps out of the shower as I step in standing under the spray. Will Kelli still want me in her bed tonight, or would she prefer Logan? I let the water wash away my unease at that thought, and reach for my body wash, squirting a little on my palm.

I let my thoughts drift instead to the sexy little vixen in the next room. She has invaded my dreams this week in the little sleep that I have gotten. Would she be as submissive and dirty as I'm hoping? My hand grips my cock, slowly stroking it as I picture her waiting naked in her bed for me tonight. Her blonde hair spilling over the pillows under her head, knees spread wide as she plays with her dripping pussy. She'd use her other hand to motion me over with her finger, and as I climb onto the end of the bed, she removes the two fingers from her pussy and paints her juices on my lips. Grabbing her wrist, I suck her fingers into my mouth, making sure my tongue gets every last sweet drop of her. Licking my lips, I crawl over her body, taking her plump lips with my own, stroking my tongue against hers, making sure she sees how sweet she tastes. Her name leaves my lips on a moan as I begin to stroke faster.

The noise of the shower pounding on my back and my heavy breathing blocks out the sound of the bathroom door opening. I don't realize I'm not alone until the sound of a metal button hitting the tiles startles me. Peeking over my shoulder, I see Kelli standing naked outside of the shower, eyes glued to where my hand disappears out of her sight.

"You called?" She says, breathless. My heart is pounding in my chest. She chose me tonight, and damn, if it doesn't feel good. I was never the first choice, especially with women. Yet, here Kelli is, choosing me.

"Kelli," is all I can manage to rasp out. She steps into the shower, tracing her hands up my back, around my shoulders, then down my arms. She presses her small, wet body against my back to be able to reach all the way down my arm until she can grip my erection with me. Her small hand can't fully wrap around, but she gives it a good squeeze and strokes from my hand to the tip and back down. "What are you doing to me?" I whisper. It comes out a lot quieter than I was intending, my knees feeling weak as I use my free hand to brace against the shower wall.

Kelli slowly moves around my body until she's standing in front of me, her eyes wide as they rake down my body. "I want to taste you, daddy," she breathes. Before I realize what's happening, she licks her lips and lowers to her knees. I catch her by the throat, pulling her back up to me. My lips a breath away from hers, I stare deep into her eyes, looking for any trace of her being afraid of me. Her pupils are blown wide, but there isn't an ounce of fear.

"You may run this house, but here, I'm in charge. You want to call me daddy, then be a good girl and listen to me. I will never hurt you, but I'm not good at being gentle." I squeeze the sides of her throat just slightly, making myself clear. "Do you still want this?"

"Yes, daddy," she moans, sending a shiver down my spine. I push her up against the wall, molding my body to hers. My mouth crashes against hers in a searing kiss, stealing the breath from my lungs. Her soft lips follow mine, opening on a gasp when I bite her bottom lip. Using that opening, I push my tongue into her mouth, stroking her tongue with my own just as I did in my fantasy. My hands trail down her body, feeling her soft curves melting under my touch. I kiss her until my cock leaks on her stomach, encouraging me to pull back and give it what it wants.

"Get on your fucking knees and suck me like the dirty girl I know you are,"demand. There is no hesitation from her as she drops to her knees, looking up at me as she licks the pre-cum from my tip. A growl rips from my throat as she parts those pouty lips and wraps them around me. Licking the underside as her mouth slides down my dick, she sucks it in until her eyes water, then moves back up and circles the tip with her tongue. I've had good head before, but watching her on her knees while moaning around my cock was going to be my undoing.

I pull her hair into my hand so I can see everything as she continues to slide her lips up and down me. Kelli gags when she takes me in fully, but holds me there before moving back to the tip, still swirling her tongue around it every time. "That's my good girl. Relax your throat for me, and tap my leg if it's too much."

She puts a hand on my thigh, relaxing her mouth and throat as I start to rut into her. Her eyes, so pretty with tears, never leave mine as she lets me thrust into her. Every few hard thrusts, she moans and squeezes my leg but never taps. She feels too good, and it has been too long. I'm not going to last. I feel my balls tighten up as heat races down my spine with my impending orgasm. "Gonna… come.." is all I am able to grit out as I try to pull out from her mouth, but she holds me to her. My cum shoots down her throat in waves as she works to swallow it all down, never breaking eye contact. Letting my spent cock gently fall from her mouth, she wipes the edge of her lips, then licks her fingers clean. Fuuuck, I am gone for this girl.

I grab her hand to help her stand up, moving back to let her under the stream of water. Putting a pump of her shampoo in my hand, I massage it into her scalp. "You are incredible," I breathe. Her pink swollen lips call me to them for a soft kiss before continuing with her hair. I take a deep inhale before rinsing it out, loving the honeysuckle scent and how it calms me.

"I can do this, you know?" Kelli whispers as I move on to washing her body, not making a move to take over for me.

"I know, but I want to." I slowly drag the loofah down her strong legs, imagining them wrapped around my head. Her sweet bare lips beg for me to taste them. The need to lay her down and spend the night with my head between her thighs is enough to hold me back. Quickly scrubbing myself down after I finish with her, I turn off the shower and wrap Kelli in her towel. With a kiss on her head, I tell her I'm going to get dressed and will be in her room in a moment.

Dressed in just my boxers, I make my way to her room where Kelli is wearing the frog themed pajamas from the night I met her. She sees me staring and winks as she climbs into the bed. "I thought it was appropriate to wear these." My lips pull up on their own accord, smiling more around her than I have in the last year. I have never found a woman cute and undeniably sexy at the same time, but she pulls it off constantly. I turn off the light and crawl into the bed with her. Her body immediately scooches over as she presses herself into my side.

Everything I thought I wanted in life was starting to shift. I wanted to be selfish for once, and I wanted more for myself than a life alone. She had me believing that maybe I could be in a relationship, I just haven't met the right person until now. As she shifts to put her head on my chest, her sweet scent wafts up to me again. I wanted to bury my head between her thighs, hearing her scream my name, but I wanted her in my bed every morning, too. These thoughts should scare me, but they don't. Apprehension grips me, keeping me from taking her now. I need to know what she wants first. Sharing her was no problem if that's what she wanted, she just needed to tell me what the expectations were before I got in too deep and she ended up with regrets.

"You are living up to your name again, little flame. Thank you for being my spark today when your world was crumbling down around you." I pull her leg over my body, holding her closer to me. "Can I ask where your head is at with us?"

Looking up, she runs her fingers through my stubble that is turning into a beard. "With you and me, or me and all of you?"

"Both, I suppose."

"Well, for starters, I am wildly attracted to all of you. Brian has made it clear that friendship is all I can expect from him. I'm working on accepting that, but my heart might need some time to catch up to my head." She lays her head back on my chest, lying quietly for a moment. "I have had these impenetrable walls in place for the last few years. You and Logan have been tearing them down brick by brick, making your way into my heart and invading my mind. I don't think I can choose between you two, and if I am completely honest with myself, I don't think I want to choose. Is that okay with you?"

She keeps her head down, absentmindedly drawing designs on my stomach with her finger. With a finger under her chin, I lift her face to mine. "That is more than okay with me. Those boys are my brothers; their happiness is as important as mine. You, Kelli girl, make us all incredibly happy."

My lips land softly on hers, the gentle kiss quickly turning into something more. I push Kelli onto her back, crawling over her body as all my blood rushes south. Our tongues tangle together, my hands pushing up her little shirt to run my fingers over her pebbled nipples. My mouth travels down, licking along her collarbone, nipping a path down her chest, stopping to take a nipple into my mouth. When her whimpers hit my ears, I continue to trail south, pulling her shorts down, thrilled to see nothing under them but her pretty pussy.

My mouth waters at the sight as I push her knees further apart, settling my shoulders between them. I kiss my way up her thigh, blowing along the wet trail dripping from her already. "Is this all for me, pretty girl?" She nods as I lean in, licking every last drop, her hands flying to my short hair holding me to her tightly. I circle her clit with my tongue until she's panting, then spear my tongue deep inside her, repeating this until her body is shaking under me.

"Please, Josh," she murmurs, my name so sweet falling from her lips. I use two fingers to stroke inside her, then wrap my lips around her clit and suck hard. My name on repeat from her as her orgasm barrels through her, walls clenching around my fingers. I would never tire of watching her come. She was absolutely breathtaking.

"You taste like my favorite meal." Staying down, I slowly lick every drop from her as she comes down from her orgasm, groans slipping from my throat. She tastes so damn good, like a dessert I could eat forever and never tire of.

When she becomes fully boneless and sinks into the mattress, I kiss my way back up, pulling her body back into mine. Her leg brushes against my erection as she settles back over me. Kissing the top of her head, I grab her hand that is moving toward it, holding it in mine on my chest. "It's time to sleep now. I've got you, nightmare or not. Goodnight, Kelli."

Her body slowly relaxes into mine and just before her breathing evens out, she whispers, "Goodnight, Josh." For the first time in a long time, we both sleep through the night, not stirring until her alarm goes off the next morning.

20

LOGAN

Light steps patter through my room into my bathroom, followed by my shower turning on. I roll over grabbing my phone off the nightstand to check the time. It's almost eight, which is way later than I normally sleep. I don't think I fell asleep until after two last night. Between the echoes from the shower and her cries of ecstasy floating from her room after, my mind stayed on Kelli. I wasn't proud to admit I jacked off twice last night just picturing what they might have been up to.

When Kelli whispered to me last night that her choice was all of us, my brain short circuited, and I couldn't help myself from kissing her pillowy, soft lips. It took every ounce of strength to not deepen the kiss and haul her to my room like a caveman. Despite wanting to be the one she would be crawling in bed with, I knew she needed this time with Josh. They spent hours down by the beach yesterday just talking, which is an incredibly rare thing for Josh. His smile when they came back inside warmed something inside me.

Kelli stepped out of my bathroom dressed in little cut off

shorts and a slouchy shirt, towel wrapped around her hair. Her cheeks were still flush from the warm shower, making me think of everything she got up to last night and how pretty that flush must have been.

"Sorry if I woke you. I didn't realize you were still in bed," she says as she walks over to the edge of my bed. Before she could move away, I grab her by the wrist and pull her onto the bed with me, wrapping myself around her like a koala. Nuzzling my face in her neck, I get the sweet honeysuckle scent. I ordered her shower stuff to store in my bathroom after the first morning she showered in here, obsessed with walking in and smelling her.

"Did my lumpy body hide under my messy blankets?" I joke. "It was time for me to get up. I needed to talk to you this morning, so this is perfect. I'm really sorry I cloned your phone without your permission or knowledge. I should have asked you about it and explained why I was doing it."

She let out a heavy sigh, "Are you still cloning my phone?"

"Yeah, baby girl. I can stop, but I would prefer it if I didn't. It's easier to do my job without having to take your phone from you constantly. Also, I can warn you if he reaches out again. I won't delete it like I was, but it will be your choice if you want to see it or not. Is that okay?" I push up on my elbows so I can look into her eyes. I don't want her to have to see something like the pictures he sent yesterday if she doesn't have to.

"Okay, I just want to know every time you find something from him, and I don't want it deleted from my phone without my knowledge." Her fingers stroke through my hair, her eyes moving between my lips and my eyes.

"Can I ask what happened last night between you and Josh?" I should let it go, but if she really wants to be with all of us, then open communication is going to be the best moving forward. I've had a threesome, but I have never shared a woman that was more than a one-night thing. I have no idea what the etiquette is or what happens from here. If she wants us separately or together, or if this is even anything more than just some fun for her while she is here.

"We talked and I told him that I didn't want to choose. Couldn't choose." Her flush spreads from her cheeks down to her chest. "I also got another glimpse of daddy dom Josh last night."

I wanted to know every last detail about what happened between them. If I couldn't be the one drawing those noises from her lips, I at least wanted to be able to picture them. "You don't have to tell me details, but we're all in this together. No jealousy, no secrets, just more fun to go around, okay?"

"Brian isn't. He loves me, but refuses to be more than my friend. But I get what you're saying. I thought this was going to be a week away while my stalker was quickly found and arrested. My time here has turned into so much more than just hiding out. Is it awful that a small part of me is glad this happened, simply because it led to me being here with the three of you?"

I lean down, taking her lips in a sensual kiss, letting it linger a little longer than necessary. "I feel the same way." We stayed in bed cuddling and trading kisses for another thirty minutes before I sent her off to dry her hair while I started on a late breakfast.

The next few days blend together. Josh and I train with Kelli in the mornings, focusing more on self-defense and take down techniques along with how to disarm an attacker. She has incredible natural instincts that we truly enjoy watching her hone in on. The pride flows through us for this beautiful woman. Our afternoons are spent together with all of us hiking and exploring the property, playing on the beach, and playing board games. There may also be sneaky make-out sessions any time I can get her alone.

Yesterday, the beach called our name, the weather was perfect to splash around in the cold water. Brian and I blew up some floaties we had bought but never opened while Kelli and Josh hauled a cooler and towels down. Spending time all together brought out a feeling of ease and joy from all of us.

"I want the pizza slice," I say, laying my claim. We have a single tube, a double tube, a flamingo, and a pizza slice float.

Brian side eyes me, chuckling, "Good luck with that; Kelli is going to snatch it immediately."

"Nah, she's more of a flamingo girl. All of her pajamas have animals."

"That's pajamas only. She's claiming that pizza." He sounds confident, but I know I'm right on this.

"I call the pizza slice!" Kelli shrieks the minute she sees the floaties we are carrying. Brian cackles next to me. *Asshole.* We drop them at the water's edge before claiming our chairs. "I brought the sunscreen, anyone need help with their back?" Kelli asks.

I snatch it from her fingers, moving behind her. "I'll do you if you do me, baby girl." Squirting some on my fingers, I rub them together before massaging it into her back. My hands travel from the top of her neck down to the edge of her skimpy red bikini bottoms. She becomes pliable beneath me as I take the extra time to massage her muscles. When I feel her breathing pick up as my fingers trail the edges of her bikini top, I take a step back, giving her ass a light slap. "My turn!"

Her little harumph is adorable as she takes the bottle from me to do my back. I drop a kiss to the top of her head before turning around for her. "I should draw a dick on your back for that," she mutters as Josh snickers behind us. She moves over to do his back after taking her time spreading the lotion on the entirety of my back. "Brian you want me to do yours next?"

"Nah, I'm going to leave my tank top on unless I'm in the water. Thanks, though," he smiles at her, but a small frown settles on her face. Josh looks over at me raising his brow. There's only one reason he would leave his shirt on around her still.

Breaking the tension, Josh grabs Kelli, throwing her over his shoulder and runs for the water. Her delighted squeals echo around us as he runs in to waist height before dunking them both under the water. They come up sputtering and laughing, splashing each other as they swim deeper in.

"Will someone bring me my pizza slice?" Kelli yells to Brian and me. Before I can get up, he pulls his tank over his head and heads into the water with it. I grab the double tube and follow him in.

Brian helps Kelli climb onto the floatie, holding it still as she sprawls out on her stomach on top. He hangs onto the edge of it, keeping her from drifting away. I slip my chest through one side of the double tube as Josh swims over, dropping into the other. Summer days have not looked like this once in the last few years we have been here, but now that we've experienced this, I wanted it all the time.

Kelli's fingers drift over Brian's arms where he is holding onto her float, drawing little patterns on his skin. A small smile plays on her lips. "What are you thinking about, Kel?" Brian asks.

"I'm just remembering that summer day when you, Danny, and I spent hours jumping on your trampoline in the rain. Your mom was pissed because we got water all through the house every time we went inside. We eventually tired out and just laid on our backs, just enjoying the last of our freedom before school started again, not a care in the world that we were drenched. I remember thinking that this is the life I want. Summer days surrounded by friends, just enjoying the beauty of the world around us. I feel that here."

"I remember that day. Opposite weather, but I know what you mean. This is our first time all swimming out here together, and damn if it isn't nice. Even if Logan drowns because he can't swim," Brian sends a spray of water toward Josh and me.

"I can swim, jackass, I just can't swim well," I defend.

"It's why you got the double floatie, huh? So one of us would be with you?" Josh ribs me.

"Poor choice having Josh with you. He'll probably let you drown so he can have Kelli all to himself," Brian chimes in again.

"Ha-ha, laugh it up. See if I make dinner tonight," I huff out.

Kelli laughs so hard, she falls off her pizza float. As her head pops above the surface she is still laughing. "Don't worry, I can swim just fine! I'm also more than happy to cook dinner."

"I'm going back to the shore," I mutter before ducking out of my side of the tube and swimming back. I really can swim, I'm just not very confident in it. Josh swims after me, dragging the floatie with him.

"We're just fucking with you. Don't get mad," Josh tosses out.

"I know," I turn and take the float, throwing it onto the shore next to the others, "I just wanted to give them some more time to reminisce." I nod over my shoulder at Kelli and Brian, who are hiding on either side of the pizza, spitting water at each other.

Josh takes a seat next to me in one of the Adirondacks. "They're so good together when they leave the bullshit behind. When is he going to see that?"

"I don't know, man, but I hope it's soon." Laughter rings out from the lake as Kelli tries to backflip off of Brian's shoulders and fails epically. The thoughts of a future filled with laughter, love, and playful days brings a goofy grin to my face. "I could get used to this."

Josh stays quiet a moment, watching Brian and Kelli play with the ease that best friends should have before he turns to me. "Same."

My workaholic best friends have both cut back to working only four to five hours a day for the time being. The smiles and laughs around our house are flowing more freely than they ever have, and our time spent being present with each other is better than it has been in years. We have Kelli's presence to thank for all of this. She is the sunshine in our home, and in our lives.

Every afternoon, Kelli and Brian go out to the side of our property for target practice and gun safety lessons. Their relationship is getting better, the ease of conversation and casual touches happening more frequently. It hurts watching the look on Brian's face when he is around her, filled with bitter-sweet longing and admiration, yet he's full of pain. He won't back down on the fact that their friendship is what's impor-tant and he won't push it past that. Tuesday afternoon, when they head outside, I pull Josh aside for a long overdue conversation.

Meaningful talks aren't his specialty, but he has been opening up a lot these last three weeks, and I am seeing a whole new side to him. Watching his chemistry with Kelli makes me want this with them, but I am out of my realm here. I've never shared a woman sexually, let alone been in a relationship with a woman who is also with another man. Would this even be a relationship? My heart was captivated by her, and I wanted to be able to call her mine. *Ours*.

We sit in my office looking anywhere but at each other. "I have some questions."

"When a man and a woman love each other.." His voice laced with humor.

"Shut up, man!" My eyes roll to the back of my head. "I've never done this with a woman before. I just want to do this right."

"Basic anatomy, the penis goes in the vagina," Josh jokes.

I take a pen from my desk and chuck it at his head. "Will you take this seriously for a moment? It's the least she deserves."

His eyes soften at the mention of Kelli. "I haven't done this beyond sex really either. Hell, I don't really know how to be good at a normal relationship. We haven't even really shared her yet besides our little hot tub intro."

"Have you been fucking every night?" His smirk answers me before he can. "Okay, nevermind about that. Do you think she wants to be shared? Does she just want to be with us separately?"

"I think this is a conversation we need to have with her. I don't even know if she wants more than sex from us." He avoids eye contact again before straightening his spine. "I want more with her. I don't think I've ever wanted someone the way I want her. Knowing she wants all of us, too, it feels right in a way I didn't think was possible."

He put my thoughts into words. I was the more vulnerable of the group, never having a problem explaining how I feel, but Kelli was making us all better men. "Yeah, I feel the same. So, we just take this one day at a time? Be the best we can for her, keep our jealousy in check, and hope she feels the same?"

"Sounds like the best plan to me. She did hint at you sleeping with her the other night. I was hoping she would ask you, but I think she's still as unsure about all this as we are. If you wanted to take my place tonight, I wouldn't mind."

"Who says I have to take your place?" I raise an eyebrow at him. "Maybe tomorrow night, the three of us can have a conversation. I have to go to the station this evening for a case."

"Mmm, I'm not going to complain about another night alone with her." His eyes linger on the unit picture behind my desk. "You know Roy reached out the other night? He's looking for security for his new hangar. I never thought he would actually do it."

"Damn, good for him. Is he officially open? It's been a minute since we've all gone skydiving; we should make a trip out there."

He gives me a dead stare. "You know Brian won't go. He hasn't talked to anyone since Caleb went around blaming him. Roy even mentioned that he has tried to reach out to let him know the rest of the team doesn't feel the same, but B never got back to him. Apparently, Caleb has been a little extra unhinged lately. He said he saw him like six months ago and he had gone off the deep end with conspiracies and wasn't looking great."

"We will deal with that eventually, one thing at a time. I have to head into work. I'll be back late. I'll reach out to Alex and my team while I'm there and see if they have anything new on the case."

21

LOGAN

I didn't get home until after 2 AM, but it was worth it working on that case. My job has good days and bad days, and nights like last night are sickening, but rewarding, knowing we tracked down everyone involved in the child pornography case. Kelli's case still had no new breakthroughs. One of my coworkers was able to get a ping in Farmington, New Hampshire from one of the Instagram accounts he had created to message her, but that was it. There are no hotels in the town, and he wasn't able to triangulate an exact area. While it is possible that her stalker lives there, it's unlikely since he was in Boston so much the first few weeks he was watching her. My skin crawled with the thought of him possibly looking around for her, but he was still far from us, if that was even where he was at one point.

I rolled around in bed, unable to get much sleep, until I heard Josh and Kelli heading down the stairs for our morning workout. Nothing sounded better than rolling over and closing my eyes again, but I had promised Kelli we would do everything we could to keep her ready for anything. I rolled out of bed, throwing on the closest shorts and shirt I could find on the floor, and made my way downstairs after them. Kelli was wearing the tiniest shorts I have ever seen and a sports bra that gave her ample cleavage, which absolutely made up for being up despite only about two hours of sleep.

"You look like shit, what time did you get in?" Josh points to my reflection in the mirrored wall.

My shirt is inside out and my hair is sticking up in all directions. "Late," I run my hand through my hair and shrug at my shirt. "You want to play attacker today so I can just sit here and give pointers?" I ask Josh as I let myself slide down the wall next to the edge of the mat. Kelli looks up from where she's stretching and begins crawling over to me. My foggy sleep brain zaps to life as I watch her hips sway and tits swell over the top of her sports bra as she makes her way over to me.

Josh bites his knuckle and grunts from behind her, as infatuated with the sight as I am. She plops on her heels as she makes it to me, leaning in for a quick kiss. "I think you look cute as hell, all sleep rumpled," she purred.

I pull her into my lap, nuzzling my face into her neck. "Thank you, but you can't do that again, baby girl. Josh is drooling behind you, and I'm not faring much better." She throws her head back in laughter, exposing her neck which I nip at.

"Maybe I'm feisty this morning. Maybe that's the reaction I wanted from you both." Her breathless voice floats over my skin.

Josh stalks across the mat, pulling her up from my lap. "You can take it out on me, pretty girl," he says before we practice. I coach her through ways to take him down while trying to avoid hurting herself. She was able to escape from a few scenarios, but neither were taking it seriously today.

Kelli crouches into a wrestling stance, eyes narrowed at

Josh. "Come on, big boy, I know how much you like me on my knees. How about you put me there?" she taunts. The wide grin that takes over his face lasts just a moment before his feral side takes over, as he pins her to the mat holding her arms down with his legs. His erection strains through his shorts, inches from her face. They've been laughing and wrestling throughout it all, spending most of the time enjoying their sweaty bodies rolling around together.

"One more, baby girl. You're going to grab Josh from behind, and he'll show you how to get out of it." She doesn't even wait for him to set up, she just runs up and jumps onto his back like a spider monkey. Josh is the best for a reason, though, and he grabs her thigh before dropping his shoulder and flipping her onto the mat. Before I can coach her through how to get out from under him, he drops his hips to hers and brackets her head with his hands. Their mouths crash together in a torrent of passion as they roll their bodies together. "Alright, alright, training is over. Time to cool it down."

Josh takes his sweet time pulling his body off of hers before helping her up. With a kiss to her cheek and a swat on the ass, he sends her off with me to shower while he wipes down the mats. Despite the rearranging of my dick, it was tenting my shorts as we went upstairs. Kelli made her way to my room with me, sneaking into my shower while I climbed right back into bed.

A phone chime wakes me up around 10, the chime being the one I had set for Kelli's cloned phone. The screen lights up with another direct message, this time the screen name was 'Your.Man.W.' When I tapped on it, there was a photo of a map with little red x's on it. It showed the lower parts of Maine and New Hampshire, and the upper parts of Massachusetts. Small towns throughout had red x's on them, including Farmington and our town. He has clearly been busy searching, but we must be doing something right if he deemed her not in our town.

Josh and Brian were going to freak out that he had even gotten that close. The fact that I didn't even know he had been in our area pissed me off beyond words. This was my area of expertise, my career for god sakes, and even I couldn't track him. I was failing Kelli, and I despised that. She was relying on us to not only keep her safe, but to catch this guy so she could live her life and return to work. It was my fault that wasn't happening, I should be better at this. She had to know that finding her stalker was on my shoulders, and I haven't been able to do anything about it yet.

I find Brian in his office and drag him outside with me where Josh and Kelli are throwing a football around. We join in on their little game of pass, and I explain what my team found last night and tell them about the new message that came through this morning. I watch as Kelli's shoulders sink in on themselves the longer I talk, while the guys' spines straighten and their expressions grow dark. My feelings on the matter are reflected on their faces. We were all feeling the pressure of him closing in on where she was, and the failures of not having found him yet were strong.

"So, where do we go from here?" Kelli asks, taking a seat in the grass.

"We keep doing what we have been doing. My team is doing everything they can, and we won't stop until we find him. I won't stop. I'm sorry I don't have more for you, baby girl."

"It's okay, Logan, I know you're doing all you can and I appreciate it."

Brian crouches in front of her, pulling her chin up with his finger. "We will find him, Kel, we will help you get your life back, I promise. We've got you." He drops a kiss to her forehead and squeezes her knee before getting up and nods toward the house, indicating he wants me to follow him.

We walk back into the house together, leaving Josh to cheer up Kelli outside, something we never thought we would say. Brian still looks like he hasn't been sleeping well, but he was more active and engaged with all of us, which was an improvement. "How are you doing?"

"I'm fine, I just hate that we can't do anything to find him. It's killing me to know there is a threat out there, and I feel like we are just sitting on our asses, failing her over and over again."

"I get it. I'm the only one failing her, though. I should be able to track him, and I just haven't been able to. He's too good, and he knows exactly how to hide his tracks. Maybe we need to start stalking him, finding people with criminal histories in the area that have the knowledge and skill to be able to hide from us." I know I'm not the best or anything, but I pride myself on being damn good at my job, and this case is killing me because we have yet to solve it.

He grips my shoulder, giving it a reassuring squeeze. "It's not just on you. You and your team are doing everything you can. We all feel the same way. Whatever we do isn't good enough since he's still out there hunting her down, yet here I am, twiddling my thumbs. This is not falling all on you. If you want to blame someone, blame me for not coming back for her years ago like I promised."

We make our way back to his office, sitting across from each other. He was wrong, though. This isn't on him and Josh, but it's nice to hear they don't blame me for not having found her stalker yet. "Remind me again why you won't let yourself be with Kelli? Josh told me you said it's because she needs her best friend right now, but you know you can be both at the same time. You love her too much to ruin the friendship if things don't work out. And the bullshit of you feeling like you can't keep her safe is not an excuse I'm accepting anymore."

"Am I really keeping her safe here, though? We have been falling back into the easy friendship we used to have and that has to be enough." There's an edge to his tone telling me to drop the subject, but I'm tired of tiptoeing around him. We've all struggled with our PTSD and have made great strides; he just won't accept that he is getting better and healing.

"We both know that's not going to be enough for either of you. So, honestly, what is it?"

His body goes rigid as his eyes darken. "You want honesty? Fucking honesty? Well, here it is. She is my happiness. I will never be as happy as I am when I am with her. She is my EVERYTHING, Logan. For four years, I have let little chunks of my heart and soul break off and die being away from her. Pieces of myself I will never get back." His glassy eyes on me show every inch of pain and truth in that statement. "The thing is, I don't deserve happiness. The possibilities of a future with her, or anyone for that matter. I took away Caleb's future. I robbed him of that happiness when I led our convoy into that trap. This is my consequence from that, something I have to live with for the rest of my life."

Hell, I thought he had made progress in therapy. He shouldn't be punishing himself to a life of solitude for something that was completely out of his control. There was no way for any of us to know we were driving into a trap, and Ashley's death is not on him. "That's a bullshit excuse and you know it. You're scared, so you're taking the easy way out." I didn't get to finish that statement before he jumped out of his chair and yelled.

"There is NOTHING easy about this! About not being with the woman I love. Her friendship is still more than I deserve, but I'm a selfish bastard and I can't be away from her any longer."

"We aren't going to get anywhere with this conversation if you don't get it through your thick skull that you have nothing to atone for. You nailed it on the head admitting you're selfish, though, because you are stealing Kelli's happiness as much as you are stealing your own. Every day that she is here with you, knowing she can't be with you, is killing those same little chunks of her heart. That's the consequence you should be thinking about." I stood and walked toward the door, but stopped before I walked all the way out. "I love you, man. You are the best person that I know, and you deserve the best life has to offer. I'm quickly discovering that, for me, that is Kelli. I know it is for you, too. I hope you get yourself back in therapy or pull your head out of your ass and see that before it's too late."

The rest of the day was glum with all of us in our own heads. Kelli's target practice with Brian lasted twice as long as the previous days. They stayed out there until it started to get dark. This whole situation was rough on Brian, and after our conversation today, I realized he isn't just hurting; he is on the point of breaking. I didn't dare interrupt their time together. That was probably the only time in the last few weeks where he felt in control of his emotions and surroundings. Josh and I had talked about me joining Kelli tonight, and I felt like I really needed the time with her. I needed to be able to hold her in my arms all night and know she was safe, know that she was mine.

When she came in with Brian that evening, I slipped into her room while she went to shower. In nothing but my boxers, I made myself comfortable on her bed and waited. Not knowing how she would respond to me here had my body brimming with anxiety. Kelli's sweet floral scent drifted into the room as she stepped in, relaxing me again. She had her hair in a big bun on her head, a towel wrapped around her with water still dripping down her neck, slowly rolling down her chest in between her beautiful breasts.

Her smile was immediate and bright when she saw me waiting on her bed. "Hello there, handsome, I was beginning to wonder when I was going to find you in here."

"Is this okay?" I ask, my eyes still tracking the water droplets moving down her golden, sun-kissed skin.

She walked to the end of the bed, waiting until our eyes met. Her dainty hands made their way to the small knot holding the towel in place, tugging it until the towel fell down around her. "Beyond okay," she whispered, her gaze trailing down my body. My body's reaction was instant, all the blood rushing to my quickly hardening shaft. My focus was pulled from her tantalizing hips, down to her strong legs, back up to her perfect pink, hard nipples and stunning, ocean blue eyes that were fixed on mine. She got on the edge of the bed, crawling over me until she sat, straddling my hips, lining us up perfectly with only my boxers in between.

"I want to take care of you tonight." My hands reached for her scrunchie, pulling it from her hair as the wild curls flowed down around her shoulders. My hands itched to pull her to me, so I did exactly that. Letting my hands weave through her hair, I tugged her down to me, taking her lips in a scorching kiss. Feeling her melt into the kiss, I moved one of my hands to grip her hip while grinding up into her. I had to bite her bottom lip to stop a groan from passing my lips at the feel of her naked body on top of me.

Her hands reached for both of mine, grabbing them and holding them above my head as she laced our fingers together. "What if I want to take care of you?" She breathes onto my lips. I don't think I have ever had a woman take charge in the bedroom, but I liked it. Her hips rolled over mine in a slow, tormenting rhythm, her lips gliding down my neck until she nipped at my ear. Blonde curls curtained around our faces as she kissed her way back to my lips, my hands squeezing hers to keep from taking control.

Her soft lips molded into mine, full of hunger as she swept her tongue along the seam of my lips. I opened up, letting her take what she needed, loving the feel of her tongue against mine. My hips ground up to meet hers, giving us more of the friction we were both craving. Our bodies flushed together, focused only on the pleasure we could draw from each other. We were so focused that neither of us noticed when Josh slipped into the room, taking a seat on the chair in the corner.

I slowly pulled back from our kiss, looking at the flushed beauty on top of me. "I came in here with the intention of making sure you were okay after today, and to ask if I could hold you all night, but this is just as good."

Her eyes widened in mock horror, letting her nails trail down my chest. "You came here in only your boxers, knowing I was coming from the shower and would probably be naked, but you only wanted to talk and cuddle?"

"I'm with Kelli on this one, you wanted to fuck," Josh piped in from his spot in the corner, scaring the shit out of us both. Kelli jumped and I tucked her behind me to keep her from falling off the bed while hiding her from view. Josh's laugh was sinister, "Too late to hide her, buddy. I got the full, incredible view of her perfect ass grinding on you when I came in."

I threw the pillow next to me at him, but he swatted it down. "How long have you been in here?"

"A few minutes, but don't stop on my account. I'll stay quiet over here."

Kelli peeked from around me, giving Josh a saccharine smile. She climbed back on top of me, letting her fingers trace my lips. "I'm okay. Honestly, those messages to me all feel the same at this point. He is hunting me, and he will continue until he finds me or he is caught. I have accepted that." Her gaze trails down me then moves to Josh. "While I would love to have you hold me all night, I really want to fuck you first. I don't mind if Josh stays since it's his thing to watch."

The strength and resilience that she has continues to blow me away. I would give this woman anything that she asked for, and the fact that she was asking for me? Yeah, I would absolutely give her that. I grab her hips, flipping us over with her beneath me. "You've consumed my heart and soul. If you let me inside of you, there is no turning back for me. I will share with my brothers, but no one else. You are mine, baby girl, do you understand that?"

She blinked up at me, then leaned up for a kiss, but I pulled my head back. "Say it, Kelli. Say you understand that this changes things for me, and no matter what the future holds, you are mine now. Ours now."

"I'm yours," comes her soft voice before she reaches up to grab the back of my neck to give me a heated kiss. Her hips start rocking up into mine again, but I am not ready for that.

"Need to taste you, it's all I have been able to think about," I pleaded as I trailed kisses down her body, then settled in between her beautifully spread legs. Lavishing her soft thighs with kisses, I suck her skin into my mouth, leaving my mark at the apex of her thighs. I heard Josh's chuckle and his muttered 'caveman' from beside us. Her floral scent fills my nose as I lick from ass to clit in one go, delighted in hearing her low moan. Circling her clit with my tongue until her legs squeezed against my shoulders, I then moved to spear her pussy. "You taste so fucking good, baby. You taste like mine." I continue to lavish her pussy with my mouth. Taking my time, I licked every perfect inch of her pussy, trailing kisses on her thighs to rile her up as she pulled my head back to her slit where she wanted it most. With more slow licks I devoured every drop of her, winding her body tighter. My tongue flicked her swollen little bud before I sucked it into my mouth.

I feel her body start to tense around me, her breathing becoming more erratic. Inserting two fingers, I stroke her sweet spot as I suck her clit into my mouth, flicking it with the tip of my tongue. Kelli explodes around me, crying out my name as her orgasm crests.

With a satisfied smile, I sit up, licking my fingers clean. "She's so pretty when she comes, I could watch it forever," Josh's gravelly voice sounds from the chair. I can't hide my smirk as I look over at him, seeing him palming his hard cock through his pants as I slide off my boxers.

"Want to see it again?" His smile is down right feral as he finally pulls his eyes from Kelli to nod at me. He gets up to pull out a condom from her nightstand, handing it to me before sitting back in his corner to watch. I don't think Kelli would mind if he joined, but the fact that he was staying there while we did this the first time shows how much he cares for us both. Maybe this sharing a girl thing wouldn't be so hard to figure out.

Kelli's eyes are locked on where I'm rolling the condom on. Her tongue slips out to lick her bottom lip before biting down on it. "Logan, I need you now," she pleads.

My cock twitches as a growl leaves my throat, making me beg her to say it again.

"Please fuck me, Logan, I need you so badly." I take a steadying breath so I don't embarrass myself and come without her even touching me. Hearing those words leave her pouty lips while looking like an angel spread out in this bed under me was more than I could have ever asked for.

Gripping my cock at the base, I swipe it through her folds a few times before slowly pushing myself in. She is so tight, her pussy is like a vice grip around me, pulling me in further. My eyes squeeze shut as I focus on my breathing again, still sinking into her. Kelli's whimper stops me, my eyes finding her focused on where our bodies are connected. "You like watching me take what's mine, baby girl?"

She bites her lip again, nodding at me. My hips rock forward more, seating me to the hilt. Her stunning blue eyes met mine and stayed locked there while I slid out of her and thrusted back in. She felt incredible, this moment felt incredible. Finally being connected to her in this way was what I needed. I continued my slow, torturous pace of sliding out and slamming back in. One hand played with her pebbled nipple while the other rubbed her clit.

My body was begging me to really take her and claim her as mine, but I needed this to be as good for her as it was for me. I needed her to truly feel that this was more than just a first fuck. My hips picked up their pace, hers continuing to meet mine, thrust for thrust. I bent down to take her other nipple in my mouth, lavishing it with the attention it deserved before moving to the other. My hands moved to grip her hips as I angled her better and pounded into her faster, feeling her body start to tighten around me.

"Don't... stop..." Kelli cried out beneath me.

"Are you going to come again for me, baby? Claim my

cock like I am going to claim you," I grit out. I could feel her holding back, so I sat back up, never slowing my pace and smacked three quick slaps down on her clit. Kelli came around me crying out her release, her pussy trying to suck me dry. I lightly rubbed her clit, drawing out her orgasm. Josh's grunts pulled our attention, both of us watching as he stroked himself to completion, spurts of cum coating his hand. "You see what you do to us, pretty girl?" I whispered against her lips, picking up the pace of my thrusts, "Now it's my turn to claim you."

I pushed Kelli's knees out, spreading her more fully for me. Looking down at her glistening pussy, I saw the hickey I left on her inner thigh. My need to mark her as mine again took over and I pounded into her, as her tits bounced in front of me, begging me to mark them. As the heat of my impending orgasm traveled down my spine, I pulled out of Kelli, ripped the condom off, and exploded onto her body. Ropes of my cum coated her breasts, stomach, and pussy until she was covered and my dick was spent.

I carefully leaned down, taking her lips with my own, as I uttered, "Mine."

Josh groaned from beside me. "Yeah, yeah, you beat your chest and claimed her as yours. Can you get off her now so I can clean her up?"

Kelli's giggle from below me sounded so sweet as I rolled over into bed next to her while Josh wiped her off with a warm towel. "Thank you," she said, as she crawled out of bed and headed toward the door. "You make a good team," she called over her shoulder as she walked out and headed to the bathroom.

I crawled under the blankets and waited until she made her way back to the room. Josh lifted up the comforter on the other side of the bed for her to get in, and she scooted over to my side while he climbed in after her. I reached out, pulling her body backwards into mine, kissing the mess of hair in my face. "You are incredible, baby girl. It's my turn to take care of you now, though. Go to sleep; I'll keep you safe and keep the nightmares away."

She leaned forward to give Josh a kiss before snuggling back into me. "Thank you both for tonight. Goodnight, my guys." We laid there until her breathing evened out and soft snores were coming from her.

Josh made eye contact with me over her head, whispering, "I liked the way that sounded. Being her guys."

"Me too, buddy, me too. Night, Josh." I was quick to follow Kelli into dreamland, where the three of us slept night-mare free all night.

22

BRIAN

"**Y**ou look like you slept like shit again," Logan observed.

I narrow my eyes at him over the edge of my coffee mug as he pours one of his own from the carafe, then joins me at the island. His grin is undeterred by my glare. "Thanks, asshole, you look like you slept well."

"Oh, I did. I haven't slept that good in years. I'll have to repeat that night time routine every night from now on." His smile is so wide now, knowing that this is killing me. I know exactly what he got up to last night. I mean, he and Kelli weren't exactly quiet. I'm pretty sure I heard Josh in there as well. I might have let a muttered 'asshole' slip again before we were no longer alone in the kitchen.

"Good morning," Kelli's cheery voice pipes in as she heads straight for the carafe, as well. The coffee churns in my stomach. I want to be happy for everyone in this house, as they are clearly finding happiness together, but knowing Kelli is sleeping in someone else's arms every night and that it's my own doing cuts like a thousand little knives. I had her in my arms for one night, and for that one night, everything in my world felt right. Now I lay awake listening to her come at the hands of my best friends. 'This is how it has to be' is the mantra playing on repeat in my head, as I then watch Josh walk in and kiss her forehead on his way to get coffee.

"Are there any plans today?" I ask to try and distract myself. If only it worked.

"I have been having issues with one of the new cameras I've been working on. The motion sensor isn't syncing up with the rotating base. I really need to put in some hours this week to get it figured out," Josh grumbles over his coffee mug.

"I need to go into the precinct for a few hours, too. I have a new case that came in last night that they need me to work on." Logan looks between Kelli and I with mischief in his eyes. "Maybe you two can have a movie marathon on this gloomy day."

It was downright nasty outside. A storm rolled in late last night and was sticking around, low thunder rolling with scattered downpours. Movies while cuddled on the couch with my favorite girl sounded exactly like what I wanted to do today. "Rock, paper, scissors for who gets to pick the first movie?" That was always how things were decided between us and Danny when we were kids, and Kelli always found a way to win. Logan snickers from beside me and winks over at Kelli. "What am I missing?"

"I conned Logan into foot rubs with that game last week," she smirks. I can't help the huff of laughter at Kelli's remark.

"I don't doubt that. This girl has a knack for winning that stupid game, but I refuse to give up trying." Really, Danny and I knew she almost always picked scissors, and we would have done anything for her, so we were constantly letting her win. Still will.

"I don't have to go in for another hour. I'll make pancakes to fuel everyone up for their wild days." I swear, it's like living with a personal chef with Logan around and I will never complain about it. We all eat together, that hour being spent arguing if games like rock, paper, scissors are chance, luck, or strategy. At the end of it, no one's opinion has changed, but my stomach hurts from so much laughter.

I saw Logan's hand slip under the table to give Kelli's knee a squeeze at one point, but the anger and jealousy over it didn't feel deep. It felt more like jealousy that I couldn't do it, as well, and anger that I had made so many mistakes in life that I would never be able to have that. If I was bound to only have little moments with her for the rest of my life, I would relish in those moments.

Before we went downstairs, Kelli used Josh's phone to call both Danny and her nurse friend, Natalie. I had no idea that he had been helping her keep in touch with them. The smile on her face as she caught up with Danny and they gossiped like schoolgirls warmed me from within. I knew my best friends would be good to her, but I never expected to see such a huge change in them so quickly when it came to her. Especially from Josh, who was sitting in the corner, just watching her with a small smile on his face. I have a front row seat to my best friends falling in love with the love of my life. It was the sweetest form of torture.

Kelli won our game by choosing her beloved scissors and chose a Fast and Furious movie, a favorite from when we were kids. I claimed the middle of the large couch, hoping to sit as close to her as possible. She sat next to me, but was careful not to touch me or invade my space, which felt like another stab to the chest. The first half of the movie, my gaze ping ponged between the screen and her beautiful face until I couldn't take it anymore. A fuzzy blanket was draped over the edge of the couch, so I pulled it down and spread it over us, pulling her into my side in the process.

One arm draped over her, while the other held her hand in mine on top of the blanket. She let her body soften into mine, her head leaning against my chest, her fingers playing with mine. I spent the second half of the movie just watching her head move slightly up and down with every breath. My fingers made small circles on her palm and the inside of her wrist, loving the feel of her soft skin in my rough hands.

How many times in our childhood did I have her sitting next to me on the couch, under our willow tree, in the car when we drove her home from her soccer games that I took for granted? Her sweet floral scent surrounding me. Her wild blonde hair curled around her face. Her pink, pouty lips parting on a big inhale. I would never take this for granted again. This feeling of utter contentment.

Happiness.

Peace.

Home.

The end credits pulled me out of my thoughts, as Kelli started feeling around for the remote, asking, "Want to watch the next one?"

"Sure, the storm isn't going anywhere, so we might as well enjoy a lazy day."

"I want to stretch out, though. Can I lay in your lap?" she asked with a small amount of hesitation.

My breath caught in my throat. I was already pushing the best friend limits by holding her hand, yet I already felt too deep, and I couldn't keep the words from falling out. "Stretching out sounds good. Do you want to be the little spoon?"

Her soft smile radiated through me, making my heart rate pick up. "Always," she beamed.

We snuggled back onto the couch together, her small body cradled by mine, my arm wrapped tight around her. My past, present, and future all should have been wrapped in with her. Even now, she saw me in a way no one else did. Yesterday, at our target practice, she knew I was on edge. She knew I was struggling with my fears of not being able to keep her safe. So, she stayed out there with me until my anxiety felt manageable. I didn't have to talk about it, I just got to be present with her. I got to watch her make shot after shot onto our makeshift targets until the knots in my body started to release. She waited for that change in me, never once complaining that we were out there for hours.

There was something about being able to be seen without having to be heard. My desire to be with Kelli would never diminish. The ebbs and flows of the sea would never relate to my feelings for her. My love didn't wane. It didn't falter. It hid in the depths of my soul where I couldn't let it out. Couldn't let it float to the surface for fear it would drown her and drag her down into the darkest depths of me. Kelli was all things bright, I couldn't risk dimming her with my damaged soul.

"Thank you for spending the day with me," my voice came out gritty.

She turned around to face me, our legs tangled together. "I love spending time with you." Tender hands reached up to lightly scratch along the stubble on my neck and jaw, stunning me into a trance. "I wish we had a willow tree here. Maybe then you would finally let me in."

My eyes closed, relishing the feel of her warm hands on me. "That always was my favorite spot. Something about sitting beneath its long branches, hidden from the world, made it feel safe."

"I'm going to close my eyes with you, and we are going

to picture ourselves sitting beneath that tree. Safe from the world." Her fingers moved from my face to clasp our hands together between us. "Let me in, Brian. Please."

"Promise to keep your eyes closed?" Her head nodded against mine. "When I went back overseas after that week home with you, I was on cloud nine, and I was sure I was never coming down. I wouldn't shut up about you and our plans. Those next few weeks of us talking every day, I put so many plans into motion that I never got to tell you about. There was a down payment put on a house that Danny and Alex later bought from me. There were emails to a custom jeweler. Kelli, I saw our future so clearly, and it was a sight to behold. I meant every word when I told you that I was coming home to you.

"Then the incident happened. It was all my fault. I was in charge. I planned out the route. It was my responsibility to keep my team safe, and I didn't. I know you've heard bits and pieces of the story and have seen Josh's scar on his thigh. That day broke me. As a man, as a soldier, you are not supposed to show emotion, to let things break you down. Josh, Logan, and I have been fighting against that stigma since. Josh had his nightmares, I have faced some PTSD and carry the guilt around with me like baggage. Logan took online classes to learn about healing with trauma to help us and those in our squad. I thought that I would heal like everyone else. But I learned that I didn't deserve to heal. Caleb lost the love of his life that day because of me. I deserved to be half the man I was, to never find true happiness, to never be solely responsible for someone's safety again, to remain broken.

"Immediately after, I couldn't reach out to you with everything going on. As the days and weeks passed, I couldn't reach out because I didn't know how I would explain it to you. How you were planning your life with a failure of a man. You are so good, dove. I knew you would stick it out with me, no matter how unworthy I was. You deserved more then, and you deserve more now. Eventually, avoidance just became easier than facing you and telling you the truth. That I could never be the man that you thought I was. That I was undeserving of your love, and that you were better off without me."

Tears were streaming down Kelli's face when I opened my eyes. She sat up and looked at me with pain and anger radiating in her watery, blue eyes. "You don't see it, do you? You stupid, stupid man. Of course I would have stuck it out with you, I still would. I'd still choose you now, a hundred times over. The reason you aren't the man you were before, the reason that you can't give me all of you, or half of you as you think, it's all on you. You are the one holding yourself back. You are the one not letting yourself heal. You are to blame, but not for the ambush, because that is what it was. That is not something you are responsible for, it's something that only one hurt man blames you for. But you are to blame for not having happiness. Don't you see the only thing holding you back… is you?" Her chest was heaving as the words spilled from her mouth.

"I am right here, Brian. Right. Here." Her words are accentuated with slaps to her chest. "We could still build that beautiful life together. The four of us. But, you won't let it happen. Yes, you were right the other night. I do need my best friend right now. So, be my best friend, Brian. Be the best for me. Don't I deserve that?"

The knot in my throat is so tight, the sting in my eyes turning to a burn as the first hot tear slips free. "I'm so sorry,

Kel. You do deserve the best, but that's never going to be me." Why couldn't she see that she needed protection? Protection that I couldn't be trusted to give? She needed an all-consuming, all-encompassing love that my blackened heart wasn't capable of anymore. I would give her everything, but it would never be enough. I laid my soul bare to her, and for the first time, she didn't see me the way I did. "I am here for you. For everything else. I just can't love you the way you deserve." The tears flowed freely from my eyes now as my heart shattered its last few pieces.

"I'm sorry, too, B," she rasped through her sobs as she walked away from me to a place I knew I couldn't follow. I know letting her go is the right thing for her, so why did it hurt so damn bad?

***

Kelli didn't come out of her room for the rest of the afternoon, and wouldn't open her door when I knocked on it with lunch. I was considering leaving it at her door when Josh stepped out of his room and nodded for me to follow him in. His desk was littered with wires and small camera parts, so I sat on his bed not willing to risk bumping something. "What's up, man?" I asked, putting the plate onto his nightstand.

Shutting his bedroom door, he turned to me and gestured for me to stand up. I had a feeling I knew where this was going, but I did it anyway, a glutton for punishment. I was doubled over before I could even take a step toward him. I slunk back onto the bed, clutching the side of my gut where he had landed a hard blow. "I guess I deserved that," I rasped out.

He stood there in front of me, arms crossed over his chest,

while I tried to fully recover my breath. "I don't want to get in between the two of you, but I won't allow you to hurt her, either. You said you were going to be her best friend. Friends don't cause pain like you caused her today. She sobbed on my bed for an hour before I could calm her down. I didn't ask what happened, and I won't, but you need to do better," he gritted through clenched teeth.

The pain in my gut was throbbing; I forgot how hard he could punch when he wanted. "I told her everything. She called me stupid." My laugh lacked humor, but his didn't. I hated the fact that I was the reason she was upset. Josh's punch was the least of what I deserved. "How do I fix it? You guys told me I needed to be honest with her and I was."

"Well, first, you accept that you are stupid. In her jumbled cries, I heard 'bought a house,' 'ring,' and 'selfish, stubborn idiot'. You thought that was the right time to tell her you bought her a house and were designing a ring?" He shakes his head at me, and my shoulders slump, knowing he's right. "You have to give her time. You essentially told her she wasn't worth the effort from you to get over your issues. I know you don't see it as that, and you think you have to be alone to pay your penance or whatever, but be real, man. She is worth every damn thing in the world, including you getting over yourself and loving her the way she deserves. Hell, that means one more man I would have to share her with, so you know I am not telling you this for my benefit."

"It's because she's worth everything that I can't darken her soul with mine," I mutter.

"Her light can't be darkened, it shines at every depth." He shook his head at me again. "You'll figure it out one day, I just hope it's not too late. I'll make sure she gets her lunch." With his back to me, he sat at his desk and got back to work, dismissing me. I left the plate with him and went down to the gym to punish myself some more.

I didn't join them for dinner that evening. I wasn't sure how much time Kelli would need from me, but I was sure their dinner would be better without me there. My home was becoming her home, too, which was all I ever wanted. My best friends were becoming her best friends, and she was being fiercely protected by them, even if it was from me. They were falling in love with her, and it had only been a few weeks. Her warmth, her selfless heart, her beauty, her humor, her vast knowledge. She was a different caliber of woman than either were used to, and they were quick to fall under her blinding light. Not that I blamed them, I had been struck by that same light my whole life.

Lying in bed, I tried to force myself to sleep, so I didn't have to hear her cries of ecstasy tonight. I wasn't proud of it, but I had gotten myself off to those sweet cries every night since she started sleeping with Josh. There was no world in which I could let myself have that small piece of her tonight after the cries of heartbreak I had put her through this morning. Just my luck, though, their sleepover seems to have moved to Logan's room just across the hall. I know it wasn't intentional to torture me with; it was probably because he had the biggest bed. It hadn't slipped past my notice that the sleepovers had gone from two to three participants last night, though. The moans floating through the walls were much closer and louder now.

Rolling over to the other side of the bed, I tried to block out the noise and not picture what was happening across the hall. Kelli's whimpers still managed to drift into my room, turning my cock to stone.

Josh's deep voice followed, "Open your eyes, pretty girl, watch as he devours you". My mind immediately pictured

Kelli spread out on the bed for them, Logan eating her like a man starved while Josh watched. Her pretty rosy nipples hard and waiting to be sucked. I still haven't seen her fully naked, but I already know she has the prettiest pussy. She comes on a cry, shouting Logan's name and my dick throbs with the need for relief.

A cold shower is definitely needed after that, but before I can get out of bed, they start all over again.

"Did he get you ready for me? Be my good girl and get on your hands and knees," comes Josh's voice, full of gravel. Fuck, I can't leave now. My hand doesn't listen to my head and pulls down my boxers to grip my hard length. "Open up for him, Kelli," Josh continues with a low groan, which I know means he has sunk into her tight heat. I really try not to picture it, Kelli on her hands and knees with Josh fucking her from behind while she sucks Logan. Precum drips from my tip as I make slow strokes along my length.

"This mouth, baby girl, god damn," Logan grunts. Her pouty lips would look so perfect wrapped around him, and I suddenly want nothing more than to walk in there and watch. "Fuck, fuck, fuck, I'm going to come," Logan sputters out quickly, followed by a loud groan. Imagining it's her lips around my cock now, I pick up the pace of my strokes as I visualize her blue eyes watching me while swallowing me down.

"Hands down," Josh continues, as I hear a loud crack where he must have spanked her ass. Kelli's moans come out muffled now, where she must be face down in the mattress. Her juicy ass in the air with a handprint on it is all I can see now as my balls start to draw up. "Come for me, Kelli," Josh calls out with another smack as Kelli shatters, her muffled cries setting me off. Josh's grunts follow my own as I spill onto my stomach.

Shame beats down on me quickly, embarrassed to have listened and gotten off to them without their knowledge. I was weak, my desperation for crumbs of their relationship just pathetic. I cleaned up, crawling back into bed with a pillow over my head in case they went again. This was my future as long as Kelli was here. I needed to get over it, stat.

23

BRIAN

The storm was still sticking around a little the next morning, so we all ate breakfast together, then got ready to play our version of Jenga in the living room. While Josh and Logan got the game set up, I pulled Kelli to the side. "I'm sorry. I didn't do a good job of expressing myself yesterday. I never want to hurt you. Seeing you cry breaks something in me."

"I think you were really clear in expressing yourself and I'm allowed to be hurt by that. We are allowed to feel the way that we feel, B." Her watery eyes pinning me in place.

"I know, but I still went about it all wrong. I live with a lot of regrets in this life, but walking away from you that way will always be my biggest." I clench my hands at my sides to keep my arms from scooping her into my chest.

Her sharp inhale is the only reply I get before she nods and sits on the couch with the guys. I know she's thinking the same thing I am. That a life was lost on my watch, but even that doesn't compare to the loss of her from the life we were planning. Part of hating myself is hating that I was such a selfish bastard to feel that way.

When I sit in the chair across from the couch, Josh hands me a pen and points to the pile of cut up paper on the table. "Every paper needs a question. It can be dumb, inquisitive, funny, sexual, or whatever, nothing is off limits. Put them all in the bowl and every time you successfully pull a block, you have to pick out a paper and answer the question." We all started filling up the bowl with whatever we could come up with. Logan was going through the papers twice as fast as us with a ridiculous grin, so I knew all his questions would end up being sexual in nature. When all the papers were placed in the bowl, Josh offered to go first.

He pulled out a block and put it on top. His first question pulled, he read, "If you could do the Amazing Race, who would you choose for a partner?"

"Oooh, good question," Kelli winked at him.

"Oh, shut it, I know it was you who put it in. I would go with Brian. He has the strength, running stamina, and he speaks some Spanish and German."

Logan looks at him totally offended. "I'm better at puzzles and cultural knowledge. Plus I can drive a stick and he can't. Enjoy losing." Josh and I laugh as he crosses his arms, scowling.

"My turn," Kelli pulls out another block and question. "How many sexual partners have you had? Why do I feel like this bowl is three quarters full of questions like this?" She raises her eyebrows at all of us then starts putting up her fingers like she's counting through them in her head. As her fingers get to ten she puts them down then continues counting as we all stare wide eyed. "Four!" She exclaims, clearly proud of her joke as three grumbles go around the room.

Logan pulls a block successfully, reading his question out loud. "What is your favorite sexual experience? Well, that's an easy one. My first time with Kelli where she let me go all caveman on her. Literally."

I try to hold in the rumble in my chest, but his smug little wink tells me I am not successful. I grab another block, then pull out a scrap of paper. "What three items would you save in a house fire? Hmm, that's a tough one. I would go for the photo albums, since my mom gave me some and I don't think she has copies. My hard drive so we don't lose all our work information."

"Boring," Logan coughs into his fist.

I cut him a glare. "I want to say your favorite apron just so I can burn it myself in front of you. But, I would have to say my blue and white plaid shirt." My eyes drift to Kelli, her soft blues meeting mine with a shy smile. It's the shirt I was wearing the night everything changed with us. It also happened to be the one I was wearing in the photo I stole from her dresser that was now hidden in my nightstand.

Josh pulls a block successfully, drawing a question from the bowl. "Marry, fuck, kill with the others in the room." He deadpans toward Logan. "Kill Logan, fuck Brian, marry Kelli."

"What?! You would fuck Brian?!" Logan screeches.

"If it means I'd get to marry Kelli, sure."

"I'd be honored," Kelli's quiet voice cuts in, all of us turning wide eyes on her.

Logan's smile is so wide as Josh's face flushes beet red. "Your turn, baby girl." Kelli plops her piece up top before picking out a question.

"What would you tell your childhood self? I would have so much to say to her, but I think I would tell her it's okay to pursue your career and passions, but don't let life pass you by while doing it. From the minute I started nursing school until now, that has been my sole focus in life. I haven't taken a fun vacation or traveled like I always wanted; I just worked."

"There is no time like the present to change that. We can all take a trip together when your stalker is caught, if you want. We can decide the destination the same way, by putting ideas in a bowl and randomly picking."

She smiles sweetly at me. "I love the sound of that, B."

"I'm filling that bowl with only tropical locations, and if you guys pick something stupid like California, I will punch you," Logan quips before picking next. "What is your love language? Easy, quality time is what I prefer and acts of service are how I best express my love." That seems extremely accurate for him, as he goes above and beyond for Josh and I everyday.

My block starts teetering the tower as I pull it out and set it on top. "When was the last time you got off? Seriously Josh, I expect this from Logan." He just shrugs at me like it's no big deal. Do I lie, or admit it was last night and let them wonder if it was due to them next door? I can't lie, I don't live like that. "Last night." The three of them exchange a glance, but don't say anything as we continue to play. The tension between us all leaving the longer the game goes on. They may not have forgiven me for upsetting Kelli last night, but things were getting better, at least.

A little after lunch, there is finally a break in the rain, so I convince Kelli to come shoot with me while we have the chance. She has been doing surprisingly well with her aim after a week of practice, so I wanted to make things a little harder, and remind her of the joys of our childhood. As we walk out to the spot where our targets are usually set up, Kelli spots the bottles and cans that I snuck out to hang up in random trees. Her laughter flows through me when she real-izes what I'm up to.

"Do you remember doing this for me when we were younger?"

"You were so annoying with that stupid slingshot." Her tone is teasing as she bumps her shoulder into mine. "My humble best friend suddenly got a big head, with his 'I can shoot anything anywhere with this thing' attitude," she says, mimicking me from when we were kids.

I had gotten that slingshot for my birthday and practiced in the backyard with it every day for weeks. I was convinced I was far superior than anyone, and that it made me cool as shit. Danny and Kelli apparently got annoyed with my constant bragging and showboating, so they set up what they deemed 'impossible targets.' Soda cans had been strung up on trees in the park down the street on what I swear was the windiest day of the year. They were swinging like crazy, and I could hardly hit a single one.

Of course, they thought it was hilarious and wouldn't let me have a re-do when the wind died down. I never picked up that stupid slingshot again, but those two heckled me about it for years. Well, payback came today in the form of lingering wind from the storm.

"You were getting too big for your britches, hitting all of my targets, so I figured we could have a little fun today. If you happen to not be able to hit any, I won't even bring it up again every chance I get." The smile on our faces wide as we laughed and walked down memory lane. This was exactly what I knew I could give her that the others couldn't and why I knew she needed her best friend back while her life fell apart around her.

"Alright, B, you're on. But, if I hit more than five, you have to tell everyone how amazing of a shot I am every chance you get, and how I'm better than you." Her confidence was so sexy, and her little smirk adorable. She put her hand out for me to shake. "Deal?"

"Deal." I shook her hand, then handed her the handgun we had been working with all week. She didn't know, but we all had gotten it for her specifically, the size perfect for her with minimal kickback. I watched as she walked around the woods looking for a good spot before setting up in a comfortable stance and taking aim. Her first shot just barely missed, the wind definitely aiding in that. Her second missed by a lot, lodging into a branch behind one of the cans. She let out a huff, readjusted her shoulders, and let off the next shot that was followed by a ping on the can she hit.

I expected a little celebration, or a smug look over her shoulder at me. Instead, she took aim at the next, hitting that as well. I had five cans and five water bottles strung up in total, and after about twenty shots, she had eight hits. My head shook as I watched in amazement. Moving targets in the trees and she still had better aim than some of the men I served with, proving once again, this woman was so far out of everyone's league, it wasn't even funny.

She finally turned back to me with that smug look on her face as light rain started falling. "You want me to keep going in the rain, or is that good enough for you?"

I took the gun from her, emptied the magazine, and put it in its case. "We can go in, smart ass. You are an amazing shot and better than me," I mocked. Her laughter rang out again, the tightness in my chest expanding. A low roll of thunder sounded overhead as the rain started to pick up. "Let's go, dove."

I grabbed her hand to help maneuver through the soggy ground. The wind picked up, pelting the rain in our faces. We raced back, but we were already soaked, our legs covered in mud by the time we reached the house. I pulled open the door to the back of the garage, letting Kelli in before slamming it shut behind us. "Well, that came out of nowhere."

I slipped off my boots as Kelli did the same. "Let's strip out here and throw our things in the wash so we don't track it through the house."

"You trying to get me naked, Brian?" She giggled as she pulled her sweater over her head.

"Trying to get you clean and dry, but naked is a nice bonus." I stripped off my jeans, followed by my sweater, leaving me in only my boxers. I reached out to take Kelli's socks and sweater from her, just waiting for her to take off her pants, when her eyes suddenly locked on my side.

Shit.

"Where the hell did you get that bruise from?" She asks as she lifts my arm to examine the purple bruise that's forming where Josh punched me yesterday. Her wet fingers traced over it, then tracked higher to the tattoo on my side. "Brian. What is this?"

Avoiding the second question, I laughed off the bruise, but it sounded as forced as it was. "Oh, uh, Josh didn't take too kindly to me making you cry yesterday. We've always dealt best with our fists for things like that." Her eyes shot up to mine, but quickly dropped back down to the willow tree tattoo that was on my side. At the base of the tree, figures of two kids could be seen between the branches.

"We will circle back to that later. When did you get this?" Her fingers tentatively traced the outline of the willow.

"Three and a half years ago," I respond as her fingers slide down my side before she finally lets my arm drop. She turns around to strip off her pants, adding them to the pile, before heading inside.

She looked back over her shoulder, eyes sliding down my side, giving her head a small shake as a tear slipped down her cheek. "It's beautiful." I hate seeing the agony in her eyes, but the glimmer of the tears make her blue eyes shine. Her eyes have always been able to draw me in. I could see straight through to her soul through them. She never closed them off to me, not until this moment. Watching that light in her eyes shutter and dim struck me right through to my damaged heart.

I threw the clothes down, grabbed her wrist, and turned her to fully face me. I didn't want to be the reason for her tears anymore. For years, I dreamed of being the guy to easily hold her in my arms, kiss her until we were both breathless. For just one moment, I wanted to be that guy for her. "You're beautiful."

Her lips pop open on a sharp inhale, so I take advantage of that. In one quick motion, I scoop her up under her thighs, pressing her against Josh's truck behind her. My lips meet hers in a hungry kiss. Her supple lips, finally back on mine after all this time, is enough to make me weak in the knees. I pour my heart into the kiss, letting my hips hold her in place so I could run my hand up her side with one hand while the other tips her head back, allowing me to deepen the kiss. Our tongues danced, our hips starting to rock against each other. I was hard as steel, lined right up against her hot center. Pulling back from our kiss, I peppered kisses over her face, across her lips, and down her neck. Nuzzling my head into her neck, I breathe in my favorite honeysuckle scent.

I left my head there, both of us breathing heavy, reeling in the feel of being in each other's arms this way again. I shouldn't have done this, but every part of it felt so right. I felt complete in a way I hadn't in so long. Her dainty hands threaded through my hair, pulling at it to make me look at her. Her bright eyes saw everything in mine, my love and desire for her, but also that closed off part that wouldn't allow me to be with her. I watched that light in her slowly dim again as she slid down my body, her head hung low. She left and went upstairs to shower, and when she came back downstairs later, we didn't talk about it again.

24

KELLI

ogan crawled onto his bed next to me, pulling the comforter down from over my head. "Why are you hiding in here, baby girl?"

"My brain is melted, so I decided I would melt with it in bed all day."

His goofy smile and piercing blue eyes read me like a book. "We give you one day off of workouts and you become a slug. I like it, but unfortunately, your pajamas today have seahorses, so they aren't fitting the vibe. It means you have to get out of bed; you should have worn the chubby mermaids. Come on, get up!"

"Chubby mermaids?"

"Yeah, you know, manatees. I mean it, pretty girl, we are getting up."

My legs kick under the sheets, but then Josh strides in and lays on my other side, trapping me tight under the blankets. "He got a tattoo of us, in our favorite spot. Why can't he let me love him?" The traitorous wobble in my lips gave away my hurt.

"You can still love him, just in a different way. He will

pull his head out of the sand eventually and see that his pain is self-inflicted, but it is going to take a while. Did you know he started a college fund for my future nieces and nephews?" Logan shakes his head as Josh continues on. "He feels guilty over everything that happened to my leg during the ambush. I will never take anything from him, and he knows that. I don't blame him, I never have. But to ease his guilt, Logan and I discovered he set up accounts in both my sister's names and has been putting money in it every month with a note that it's to be used for their children when they come."

Logan's fingers trail along my face, tucking an unruly curl behind my ear. "He doesn't know that we know. He will never be able to heal until he can learn to either drop the guilt or learn to live with it. He's made progress, and he will get there. He just needs a big push. Until then, we all love him the best that we can in a way that he allows."

"He loves you so much, Kelli. I was there the day he got that tattoo. He said he got it on his right side because that's where you always sat. Where you were always meant to be, right by his side. So that's where you can stay, okay?" Josh's soft lips press lightly to mine.

The blankets are ripped off me the minute Josh pulls away. "Alright, time to get up! I know exactly what will cheer you up." Josh scoops me into his arms, carrying me downstairs to plop me on the couch.

"I think I kind of like princess treatment, can you carry me everywhere?"

"Happily, Kel." He drops a lingering kiss to my forehead before heading to the office.

Logan starts on French toast on the brioche bread we made earlier in the week while Josh comes back to set me up with his tablet to call Danny. I have never been taken care of in the way these two have been doing for me. They always know exactly what I need and go out of their way to make sure I feel safe, happy, and seen. My heart is healing with their presence every day, where they are building back the pieces that were broken.

I still feel like something is missing though, and I know that something is Brian. I don't know that I will ever feel complete without him loving me as more than a friend, but I have to try. Never did I think I would have two amazing men in my life, both of which I am falling hard for, harder than I thought was possible. My battered heart has the capacity for so much love, and I want to give it to them.

Last night, as we all laid in bed, we talked about what the future could look like for us. This last week, I have been thinking more and more about how Boston didn't feel like home anymore. The fact that they were also thinking about a future with me almost brought me to tears. I want to be in their life beyond just being their forced roommate, and they felt the same. Life doesn't always play out how you imagine, and in this instance, I am beyond grateful.

Danny didn't answer my call, but texted Josh to say we could Facetime tonight. I decided to try and call Natalie to catch up. I haven't told the boys, but I reached out to the hospital through Alex and put in my resignation. I couldn't make them hold a position for me when I didn't want to return there. My work wife was not going to be happy, but she deserved to know. Mercy was the only hospital I have known; I have spent the majority of my days and nights there for the last five years. Writing that resignation email was easier than I thought, though, a sense of peace flowing through me when Alex confirmed it had been sent when we talked two days ago.

Natalie answered on the fourth ring, her tired face filling

the screen. "Please tell me you are coming back now. My new work wife sucks."

Chuckling at her desperate voice, I shook my head. "Sorry, love, I am not coming back now." I peek behind the couch to make sure no one is nearby. "In fact, I am not coming back at all."

"You what?!" She shrieked through the tablet at me.

"I put in my resignation. It might have been a little rushed, but I felt such a sense of calm when I made the decision. Boston doesn't feel like the place for me anymore. My house there will never feel safe again, and something about out here just feels like home."

"I can understand that. I wouldn't be able to go back to that home either. What are you going to do now?"

"I have Danny working on moving my things into storage. There is a smaller hospital in the area that has some open nursing positions. It would definitely be a change of pace, a slower one, but it could be a good thing. I would have more of a work-life balance for the first time. I think I might finally have something to be home for that makes me crave that balance."

"Please tell me it's the hotties you're shacking up. Let me live vicariously through you; tell me every juicy detail." Her eyebrows wiggle at me. "Which one is it? Josh? Your bestie? The sweet funny one?"

I roll my eyes at her. "The sweet funny one's name is Logan, and it's actually Josh and Logan. My bestie is still just my bestie." It hurt saying that out loud, but it was so nice to finally tell someone about my budding relationships. I was going to tell Danny tonight, too, though I think he has an idea since I mentioned looking for a new home in this area. "I am really falling for them, Nat. I have never been cared for the way they care for me. They encourage me, support me, quite literally at the moment, they are open with me, and my god, they are incredible in bed. I'm having the best sex of my life, times two. I have always been a firm believer that you need at least six months with someone before the word love can come into play, but they make me question that. I don't think love has a timeline anymore. A month with them 24/7 and I can confidently say I am falling in love with them both."

Natalie stares at me, open mouthed, until a tear slips down her cheek. "My little cynic fell in love. I am so happy for you, Kelli. No one deserves this more than you."

We spend another twenty minutes talking until Logan comes in to tell me breakfast is ready. I said goodbye to Natalie with promises to call again next week with more details on my sex life because she didn't get enough this time. Logan's chuckle behind me told me he heard that part of our goodbyes. I follow him to the kitchen, where he has breakfast spread out on the island. All the guys are sitting there waiting for me, which is really sweet.

"This looks incredible, handsome. Thank you." I kiss Logan's cheek before settling into the last open barstool. All three sets of eyes turn to me. "What?"

"That's the first time you've used anything besides our names. Or daddy." Logan winks, while Brian chokes on a sip of his coffee. "I liked it."

"Why is he handsome, though? What if I want to be called handsome?" Josh pipes in from next to me.

"Well, you are all handsome, but you can be 'bear.' You have this growly demeanor with gigantic muscles, but you are the best cuddler. I'm still calling you daddy in the bedroom, though."

"HA! She called you fat. We all know I'm the best cuddler," Brian chimes in.

"False. Josh might not have that trimmed and cut build

like you two, but damn, he gives off big boy vibes and he fits it… everywhere," I say with a wink as I take a bite of my French toast and let out a happy moan. Damn, Logan is such a good cook. "I mean it in the best way; he's bear and I am sticking to it."

Josh's lips brush my ear as he whispers, "I love it, little flame. I'll be your big boy any day." He kisses the side of my head and makes sure the guys can hear. "Plus, this big boy can kick your asses, and you both know it."

"Fine, he can claim best cuddler, and I'll claim best with my mouth and the title of handsome. Can we all move on now?" Logan, who is on my other side, gives my leg a squeeze. "We didn't mean to, but we might have overheard part of your conversation with your friend out there." I could feel the blood drain from my face. Were they going to be upset? I should have told them that I quit. Did they even want me living in the area right away? Had they heard me say that I loved them? *Shit.*

Logan's hands cup my face, turning me to face him. "Breathe, baby girl. Breathe with me." He takes several big breaths with me until the ringing in my ears stops and I feel the color return to my face. "That's my good girl. Now, erase whatever is going through your pretty head right now and just let us talk, okay?" I nod, not yet trusting my voice to not shake. "Good, now don't freak out, but I am pretty sure Josh heard the entire conversation."

Josh has the decency to look guilty about it, but his earnest eyes keep me from getting upset. "I wasn't intentionally listening. I was sitting at the dining room table, but I don't think you saw me. When I overheard that you had resigned, I was going to sneak away because I figured this was something you didn't want me hearing yet, but then you started talking about how you felt at home here, and you were going to look at the local hospital for work. I was rooted to the spot."

"We want you to know we are really proud of you for following your heart and quitting that job. Whatever we can do to help with getting your stuff sent here, too, we will do it. There was no time for us to talk it over, but I can tell you with one hundred percent certainty that we all agree that we want you to stay here. Not just until this stalker business gets sorted either. You don't need to rush to find a new place. Stay here, in our home, with us." Brian's last words were soft, and they shocked the hell out of me. I didn't think he would want my relationship with his friends continuously shoved in his face.

"He's right. I know you can't apply for a job until we find your stalker, but we will help you find something when you can. Move in with us, Kelli. Not just temporarily. It may be fast, and it may be crazy, but you make our house a home." Josh says as he threads his fingers through mine, brushing my knuckles along his lips.

"We can move some of your stuff up here this weekend to help you feel like this place is yours, too. It could definitely use a woman's touch. Some color probably wouldn't hurt either. Make our house your home, too." Logan's thumb swipes under my eyes to catch the tears I hadn't realized I had been letting flow.

They all looked so earnest and eager, like this was the best idea they had ever had. I really don't know if I'm ready to live with them forever. It has only been a month, and while things are great now, they aren't guaranteed to stay that way. Would Brian get resentful? Would I be okay if he brought another woman home? Despite my reservations, I wanted to stay. They are right, I feel at home when I'm here with them.

"I will stay, but I want you to know I might still look for

my own place once I get a job. This is all so new, and I don't want you to regret this rash decision. Can we take it a day at a time?"

Josh pipes up, "Yes, absolutely. Brian and I will get as much of your stuff from storage as we can this weekend. You are welcome to put whatever you want in the house. We have a large storage room in the garage you can use, too. We want you here. Today, tomorrow, and every day after." My lips find his, tender with a hint of salt from my tears. This shy, grumpy man is turning out to be the softest underneath it all.

"It's settled then! We have a new roomie. We can go shopping next week for any new things you need, too. I know you've been getting restless being stuck here. I think a shopping trip in town would be okay. Now, everyone eat, the breakfast I worked hard on is getting cold," whines Logan.

The rest of the breakfast was spent talking about what things they should grab first from storage, what things we could upgrade for the house, and what positions were open at the local hospital. Not once did they mention anything else from my call with Natalie, specifically the fact that I told her I was falling in love. My breakfast sat like a rock in my stomach the rest of the day. Did Josh not hear that part? If he did, did he tell Logan? Do they not feel the same and don't want to embarrass me by bringing it up? The questions ran through my head all day, making it hard to focus on anything else.

By the evening, I was a mess of feelings. They didn't feel the same, and I was okay with that. Logan said that Josh had heard the entire conversation, so he had to have heard me say that I was falling in love. They would have said something if their feelings matched mine. It was really soon; there was no reason for them to feel the same, honestly. Like I told Natalie earlier, I could see now that there was no timeline for love.

Yet, my stupid heart hurts. I wanted them to feel the same all-consuming feelings I felt. Their touches left my skin buzzing, their kisses quieted my mind. I could feel their presence when they were near, and felt an ache when we were apart. I spent my days with them, and as if that weren't enough, they were almost always in my dreams. I didn't want to be alone in these feelings. I didn't want to be alone in anything anymore.

I showered in mine and Josh's bathroom to give myself some space to think. Maybe it was best if I slept in my own bed tonight, alone. Whether they were meant to hear it or not, I had dropped heavy feelings on the guys today. If I was brave enough, I would ask Brian to sleep with me again. I didn't want to push him; he said he couldn't do more than friendship with me and it really wouldn't be fair to ask this of him. But since the guys have started sleeping with me, I have only had two nightmares, and I didn't want to go back to having them again. Getting fucked to sleep and the all-night cuddles weren't things I was going to complain about either.

When I got out of the shower, I took my time drying my hair and doing my nightly skin care routine. In my room, I put on my favorite pajama set, the ones with butterflies, and crawled into bed. One night was all I would give myself to wallow in my feelings, and then tomorrow, I would just be grateful that I had two amazing guys that cared for me deeply and a best friend that loved me.

Tucking the blankets up to my face, I let the tears fall. Not even ten minutes passed before my bedroom door swung open with Josh barging in. He tossed my blankets off me, picked me up bridal style, and carried me to Logan's room. He crawled into the bed with me in his lap and kissed every tear that slid down my cheeks.

"Please don't cry, you're killing me." His arms wrapped tighter around me, as Logan tucked my hair behind my ear.

"Why are you hiding from us, baby girl?"

I was too mortified to answer, but his question just made the tears fall faster. It was such an embarrassing thing to cry over, and I certainly couldn't admit it to them, so I just shook my head and tucked it in closer to Josh's chest.

"Well, if you won't tell us, we have something to tell you. I need you to stop crying, though. You're breaking my heart here." I took some deep breaths trying to compose myself while they dried my tears. "That's better," Logan said when I got myself together. "We had something special planned for you tonight. Well, it's actually something for all of us, really." He looked around the room then, my eyes following. There were candles lit on every available surface in the room. He had even cleaned, not leaving a single sock on the floor or junk on the dresser.

"Last night, we talked about what our future might look like if we pursue this relationship. When you fell asleep, Logan and I talked about how deep we were in this with you. The future we want with you. I love you, Kelli. I am so stupidly in love with you. I have never felt the way I do when I am with you, and the thought of you leaving makes me physically ill. When I heard you tell your friend you were falling in love with us today, I thought my heart was going to beat right out of my chest. I felt a joy beyond anything I've ever fathomed. I love you," Josh proclaimed.

Before I could respond, Logan pulled me onto his lap. "I love you, too, baby girl. I thought I knew what love was before you. I thought I knew what my dream woman would be like. Yet, here you are, being so much more. Making me feel so much more. You are just more, Kelli girl. More than I dreamed of. More than I deserve. More beautiful than the best sunset on the lake after the perfect day. I know it's only been a month of you in our lives, but damn if you haven't just stamped yourself onto my soul, onto my heart too. I love you."

The tears were flowing freely again, and there was no hope of stopping them now. "I love you both, too," I rasped out before Logan's mouth crashed down on mine. His kiss bled into my soul, stamping him there to forever be a piece of me. Our salty kiss turned sweet as he pulled back and kissed down my tear-stained cheeks and neck.

"We wanted to try something new tonight, if you are up for it," Josh murmured in my ear, rubbing his hand down my back.

"Are you finally going to fuck me together?" I ask with an excitement I've never experienced. Logan snickers against my skin, still kissing down my neck. I have been asking to try it, but they insisted on taking things slow when it came to taking them both at once. Last night, they took turns fucking me while I had a plug in my ass, and it only intensified my desire to take them both.

"No, Kelli, we are going to make love to you together." A shiver wracked through me at Logan's words. Josh pulled off my tank top, freeing my breasts for Logan to lavish. Lifting my hips he pulled my shorts and panties off, one leg at a time, before lying next to us in bed.

"Undress me, Kelli," Josh said in his deep voice, hooded eyes trailing down my body. I climbed off Logan to slowly pull Josh's shorts and boxers down his legs. His hard cock sprung free, slapping his stomach. I meant it when I said he was a big boy this morning. He was hard and large everywhere. Thick and long, his purple head already dripping precum was just begging to be sucked. Settling myself between his legs, I leaned down and sucked one ball into my mouth, then the other, letting them pop before licking him from base to tip. My tongue swirled around his head, lapping up his salty release before swallowing him down.

"I love watching your eyes water when my cock hits the back of your throat." Josh grabs my hair into a makeshift ponytail so he can watch every inch of him sink into my mouth. His green eyes darkened as I gagged every time I reached the base. I might not be a deep throat queen when it came to his large size, but he never seemed to mind. In fact, he seemed to love the fact that he was almost too big to take. "You make such pretty sounds when choking on my fat cock. I told you I would happily be your big boy, Kelli girl."

I gasp as Logan's hand slaps my butt, lifting me to my knees. His hot mouth licks me from clit to ass and back again before lavishing my pussy. He happily defended his self-proclaimed title of being the best with his mouth. The way he could fuck me with his tongue was unmatched. Josh's hips buck, fucking into my mouth while Logan continues his assault on my wet pussy before moving two fingers to my tight hole. He sinks in to stroke my inner walls, never removing his mouth from me.

I could feel my orgasm coming on like a train barreling down the tracks with no brakes. Lights flashed behind my eyes as my body exploded into little pieces. Logan's fingers stroked me through it as Josh pulled my mouth off him, laying me on his chest. When every last drop of pleasure has been wrung from my body, Logan removed his fingers, licking them clean.

Josh pulls me up further until I am lined up perfectly on him. His hand strokes up and down my back, his piercing green eyes filled with lust. The flickering light from the candles enhances his strong features, drowning me in his raw beauty. "There's something else we wanted to talk to you about. We both got tested last week when we went out for groceries, and we're clean. I know you said you are on birth control the first time we were together. Could we…" Josh trails off.

"Yes! I want to feel you inside me with no barrier."

"Then be our good girl and sit on my dick," Josh demands as we both let out a collective breath as I slide down his erection, taking him to the hilt.

"Fuck, why is that so hot?" Logan groans from behind me. "Ride him, baby."

I hold onto Josh's barrel chest, grinding myself up and down him. He lets me find my rhythm for a few minutes before his hands grip my ass, pulling my cheeks apart. A lid pops open behind me, giving away what Logan is about to do. He gently pushes my back down towards Josh's chest. His lubed fingers circle around my ass before one slowly pushes in past the tight barrier. He circles that finger around some more before easing a second one in.

The burning sensation is still new to me, and I try to breathe through it. Josh grips my chin, forcing me to look at him. "Relax, baby, let him in." I suck in another unsteady breath, letting it out slowly while forcing my body to relax. As soon as his finger slips further in, I feel more pressure and less pain.

Josh pulls my chin down for a kiss, his warm lips stroking against mine. He nips my bottom lip, then sucks it into his mouth as I melt further into him. His tongue caresses mine, his hand holding the back of my head, the embrace radiating the passion he is pouring into it. His hips slowly rock into mine. Logan's fingers slide in and out, scissoring me open in preparation for him. Goosebumps spread across my arms and down my legs at the feel of them working me over.

"You ready, baby?" Logan asks, pulling his fingers from me and lubing up his cock. I nod, incapable of voicing how ready I am for this. Josh's fingers reach down between us to circle my clit, keeping me relaxed for Logan.

His cock presses into me, stealing the breath from my lungs. "That's our good girl, taking us both. You're doing so well." Josh puts more pressure on my clit as he praises me through it. Logan keeps sliding in until I feel him bottom out against me.

"Holy fuck ,you feel so good, Kelli. So perfect for us." His hands rub up and down my back, loosening my muscles further. "I'm going to move now, pretty girl." He slowly pulls out, and as he pushes back in, Josh pulls out. They seesaw back and forth in an agonizingly slow rhythm until the pain is gone and all I can feel is pure bliss.

"More," I manage to moan out. I feel so full, every nerve on edge as tingles spread throughout my body. They pick up the pace, continuing to drive into me in alternating thrusts, all while praising me. Our sweat slicked skin grinds together, sweet moans being drawn from all of us. I can feel my body moving closer to release, but I want more. I need more.

"Please, I need more," I grind out. Josh grips my throat, as Logan leans back to give my ass a hard slap.

"Is this more, baby? You like when we are a little rough with you?" Josh's fingers squeeze at the sides of my neck, adding just enough pressure. Logan's hips pound into me from behind, another slap cracking down onto my ass. "Your perfect body is squeezing us so tight, that greedy pussy is so wet, sucking me in." Their rhythm picks up again as heat blazes through my body, the first signs of my impending orgasm flooding my body.

"That's our good girl, come all over our cocks." Josh's raspy voice sends me over the edge. His mouth covers mine, stealing the scream of pleasure as I crash around them. Logan is the first to follow me over that edge, shouting my name as he fills my ass with hot spurts of his cum. My body slowly comes down from my earth-shattering orgasm as he pulls out of me slowly.

Josh flips me over, shoving my knees to the side as he continues to thrust into me. "Look at me, Kelli. Give me one more."

I shake my head, my body spent. "I can't."

"Yes, you can. Come with me, pretty girl." His fingers find my clit again, driving my body right back to that edge, his hips never faltering. "I can feel you fluttering around me. Come for me."

Lights flare behind my eyes, my body shattering right over the edge again. Josh's name finds its way to my lips as he growls out his release, coming with me. My body floats back slowly to reality, and I have become utter mush. My heavy eyelids finally open to Logan's fingers trailing down my face and neck.

"How are you feeling?"

"So good. So tired." His soft laugh floats around me before he presses his lips to mine in a delicate kiss. Hands grasp under my knees and shoulders, lifting me from the bed. Logan carries me into the bathroom and straight into the shower where Josh is already waiting. They take turns gently washing every inch of me, trailing kisses along my body the whole time, rubbing out all my sore muscles. I feel cherished by them, loved in every sense of the word. Logan turns off the shower, drying me off gingerly before carrying me back to bed, setting me in the middle.

They blow out all the candles before sliding into bed on either side of me. I turn to Josh first, kissing his kiss-swollen lips. "I love you. You have so much to give, and you have given it all to me. Thank you for trusting me, talking with me, being so patient with me, and being my strength when mine was gone."

Rolling over, I am met with Logan's soft gaze and sweet smile. "I love you. I have never smiled as much as I do with you. You light me up from the inside, you're the joy I have been missing in my life. You cherish me, encourage me, push me. I love who I am with you." His kiss is feather light, yet holds so much emotion.

Josh pulls me back into him, wrapping his body around mine. "Goodnight, our perfect girl. We love you," he whispers in my ear before my drained body gives in to sleep.

25

KELLI

That Sunday, Josh and Brian drove down to Boston to clear out as much of my stuff from storage as they could fit in Josh's truck. Alex and Danny had moved about half of my house into the storage unit, leaving just enough for the house to look staged for the realtor they hired. Logan and I had entirely too much fun on Sunday evening and Monday going through all the boxes and seeing what goodies they had brought back. We found a box of my kitchen gadgets that have found new homes in the cupboards, and tons of boxes of my clothing, shoes, and accessories. There were a few boxes with knick-knacks that we distributed through the house, and some books and random photo albums that would need to find a home, too.

"I declare that it's time for a dinner break." Logan flops onto the floor next to me.

"I like that plan, but I don't think I can move from this spot. The fun has worn off and now, I'm just tired." I lay back, joining him sprawled out on the living room floor.

"That's not a problem. We can lay here while Josh hauls the unopened boxes into the garage storage and the ones with books and photo albums to the basement. Brian will cook us dinner."

"I heard that," Brian hollers from his office down the hall.

"You were meant to!" Logan yells back. "Go get Josh for us and tell him we need his big boy muscles."

I erupt into over-exhausted giggles. "Stop teasing him about that."

He rolls to his side, tucking a rogue curl behind my ear. "It's all out of love and a little jealousy. We can't all be blessed with cocks as thick as an arm."

Josh's head pops over the railing from upstairs, staring down at us. "I don't know how to feel right now."

"Proud, buddy. Now get down here and help, I can't move another box," Logan whines.

Josh moves the rest of the boxes to where we ask for them to go, then enjoys a beer with Logan and I on the outdoor sofa. Surprisingly, Brian grills chicken and veggies for us. He even sets the outdoor table for dinner so Logan and I can continue to be lazy.

Brian sets the last plate of food onto the center of the table before calling us over. "Do you feel more settled with more of your stuff here?" He asks, putting a chicken breast on my plate.

"Yeah, I do. I feel bad taking over your storage room though."

"Don't. We were thinking of going shopping tomorrow. I know you love cozy pillows and blankets and colorful curtains. We can pick some out tomorrow for the couches and chairs." Brian adds some of the grilled vegetables on my plate before passing them to Logan.

"We also want you to pick out new sheets and décor for your room." Josh squeezes my knee under the table, looking a little uncomfortable. "We thought you might not want to use the ones you already had."

"Because he jacked off on my bed? Yeah, that's a good assumption." I don't mean for it to sound harsh, but that photo still pops in my head sometimes unbidden. "I love the ones you have in there, can't I just use those?"

"Of course you can. We just want you to feel like that room is yours. Like this home is yours." Logan looks lovingly at me from across the table.

"I do. I just don't need anything else for it. The rest of my décor will make it up here eventually. Though, I will never complain about fuzzy pillows and blankets."

"Will you complain about new lingerie? Because we are getting you that, too." Logan winks.

"Why would I need that? I thought you liked me naked." I wink back while Brian groans from the head of the table next to me.

"We do," Josh answers quickly. "We know the rest of your lingerie was taken, and we would like to do that for you. There's also the bonus of getting to see you in them."

"I guess I can accept that." I certainly wasn't going to fight him on that. What girl doesn't love new undies? "I can't believe I have three guys willing to spend the day shopping with me. This is every girl's fantasy."

After dinner is cleaned up, we all head to the basement to organize my books and photos into the bookshelves. It would have been quick work, but Brian opened the first photo album and soon we were all sprawled on the couch looking through my old photos.

"Look at Brian!" Logan's loud laugh echoes through the room as he holds up a picture of Brian, Danny, and I. Brian's new braces are on full display in a wide smile, a puka shell necklace around his neck, with a terrible bowl cut on the top of his head.

"Fuck you." Brian snatches the photo from him, putting it back on the page.

"I thought he was cute, and the puka shells were all the rage," I say, nudging Brian with my shoulder.

"Speaking of cute, look at little Kelli." Josh pulls out my soccer photo from when I was nine. My curls were actually pretty tame for the photo, a large gap-toothed grin on my face. "You're going to make the most adorable babies."

Brian looks down at me, his brown eyes boring into mine. "Yeah, she really will." His large hand slips into mine, his thumb stroking over mine. We all flip through more childhood photos, Brian and I telling embarrassing stories about each other as we go. Josh pulls out a photo, slipping it to Brian and I without saying anything. It's a photo of Brian and I sitting below his willow tree, my head resting on his shoulder. He sets it aside, then leans toward me when I raise an eyebrow at him. "I'll give it back. I just want to get it blown up and framed." These were the moments that I understood his resolve to focus on our friendship. If things didn't end up with a happy ever after, we would lose all this, a lifetime of memories and friendship. Not that it made it any easier to not pursue the future we dreamed of together.

I was utterly exhausted by the end of the night. Josh pulled me into his bed with him after my shower, snuggling me into his hard body. His cedar and vanilla scent enveloped me. "You really think I'll make pretty babies?"

He nuzzles his head into my neck, "Yeah, I really do."

"I think you would make pretty babies, too." My voice gets quieter as sleep beckons to me.

"If I made them with the right person, they might be."

"Mmm," I coo as I snuggle further into him, "could you see me being that right person?"

His chest rumbles behind me as his arms tighten around me. "Yeah, love, I could. Go to sleep now, we have a busy day tomorrow. If you're trying to stay awake for Logan, don't. It's just you and I tonight. He got called into work while you were in the shower and will most likely be gone most of the night."

"He is going to be so tired. He helped me run all over this house all day. His back was killing him, especially after our sparring this morning."

"He'll be okay; he's used to an unpredictable schedule." His fingers lightly scratch up and down my arm, melting me into the mattress. His soft lips kiss the side of my head. "Go to sleep, baby, we have a busy day of spoiling you ahead."

The events of the last five weeks replayed in my head as I tried to drift to sleep. I knew that something was missing from my life before, but I found those missing pieces here. These boys have taken me in, no questions asked, despite knowing that having me here would potentially put them in danger. They have gone above and beyond to make sure I feel safe, cherished, and at home with them. My life has taken this unexpected and unpredictable turn, but I can't even be mad about it. It was crazy this all started with one unruly patient, and here I am falling in love while hiding out.

My stalker has been suspiciously quiet this week; the guys swore they weren't hiding things from me and he just hasn't reached out, minus that map. Maybe he was finally giving up, which was my hope. If I came out of hiding, started applying for jobs and visited Boston, would he come back after me again? I wasn't sure if I was ready to face that possibility, but it kind of seemed like the only choice. Josh said I would have to wear a hat tomorrow to try to block my face from any security cameras. It seemed like too much and not enough at the same time. For the first time in almost two weeks, my stalker chased me through my dreams.

The morning workout with Josh was brutal. The sleep I got after Josh was able to pull me from my nightmare was fitful at best. Logan was still at work by the time we had showered and eaten breakfast. He called Brian to tell him he might finally have a lead on a big case, so he wouldn't be home for a while and we should head to the stores when we were ready, that he would meet us there later.

This was my first time out of this house since I got here over five weeks ago, and I was beyond ready for it. I missed civilization, and an ice-cold coffee while shopping felt like the perfect outing with the guys. I pulled on some cut off shorts, a loose crop top, and my Chucks before pulling my hair into a bun under one of Brian's baseball caps. We filed into Brian's jeep and headed into town.

26

STALKER

Four fucking years. Four years without the love of my life. Four years of going through the grieving process. Four years of trying and failing to move on. Four years of hating the man who was supposed to keep our unit safe, but he didn't. Four years of feeling like Brian needed to pay for Ashley's death.

Then, there was Kelli. Her viral video crossed my screen one afternoon and the lightbulb went off. I recognized her immediately from the photos Brian had posted all over his bunk. For weeks before Ashley's death, he wouldn't shut up about her. Seeing her on my screen felt like life was shining a light on what I was supposed to do next. Karma was dropping a pretty package in my lap in the form of the love of Brian's life. Finding out that she was also living in Boston at the time was the ultimate cherry on top.

I had only been in Boston for a year, working cyber security for a financial firm. It was soul-sucking work, but turns out everything happens for a reason. Making Kelli pay for Brian's actions was better karma than I could have ever dreamed up. An eye for an eye and all that.

Brian had a lot to make up for. Not only was he responsible for me losing my future wife, he is also the reason I was honorably discharged. The unit could never look at him the same after the ambush, and it was my responsibility to ensure he was aware of that. It's his fault they wouldn't mentally clear me and the hostility everyone felt was a result of his actions.

When I first started messaging and following Kelli, I didn't have a clear plan. She was oblivious to the world around her, which made it almost boring. I started leaving notes for her to heighten her paranoia, which worked like a charm. I would spend some nights after work studying her and looking up everything that I could on her. It was a little disheartening to discover she wasn't in a relationship with Brian anymore, but I knew him. We had served together for years. He was not a guy that jumped into things lightly, so there was no way that he wasn't still pining over her.

The most surprising thing that happened, though, was I started to like the girl. She made smart moves like buying knives to hide throughout her home and installing a security system. She even had security walk her to her car after work and started paying attention to her surroundings whenever she was out. The thought of her on the lookout for me, preparing for me… it made my dick hard.

Everything was going well until she went on a date with that douche nozzle. Kelli was mine to play with. He had no right putting his hands on what was mine, and I made sure both of them were aware of that fact. Unfortunately, things went downhill from there. I had plans to scare Kelli back into submission, and then I was going to take her. I even bought a home just over the border into Maine that would be perfect to keep her in. Nice enough that she might want to stay, but with lots of land and no neighbors in case I decided it would be the best revenge to kill her.

Really it was a 50/50 shot. Either we would fall in love and that would kill Brian, or it wouldn't work out and her death would be on his hands. That would kill him, too. Seemed like an easy win-win in my book. It was going well until she disappeared from the hospital after I sent the messages through her windows. She was either taken from the hospital through the only halls that didn't have cameras, or they were wiped. I combed through them for hours and found nothing.

It took a few days to realize she had to have help since I was tracking her credit cards and she wasn't in her house, any hotels nearby, or at her friend Danny's house. I watched some of her nurse friends, but she didn't seem to be staying at their houses either. My first clue to her location was seeing Brian and Josh at her house. They cleared the camera feeds of her driveway and front door, so I couldn't see what they drove or what they were doing there, but I saw them in the backyard camera feeds. I thought that maybe they were looking for her, too. I tried looking up their addresses, but I couldn't find anything on them. No homes or cars were registered in their names. I knew then that she had to be with them and they must have wiped all traces of themselves from places that I could find them.

That led to my next step, which was to find guys from our unit and see if they knew where they lived. After talking to a few, I was pointed to the area of lower Maine and New Hampshire. No one could remember exactly where, but they knew it was in that area. I searched and searched, but couldn't find proof of her anywhere. It wasn't until Josh and Brian went to the storage unit that her stuff was being stored in. When I saw Danny moving her stuff there, I paid the owner to notify if and when someone stopped by her locker, and finally, it had paid off.

He called me on Sunday and sent me the video footage of Josh and Brian driving up and filling a truck with her boxes. I was able to hack enough cameras to keep up with their whereabouts to the point that I was able to follow them back to their home. I was surprised to find that they lived together and with Logan. I drove past the entrance to their house and immediately noticed all the cameras they had.

Lucky for me, there was a house down the road for sale that was empty. I made it available to myself in order to keep an eye on them. It made sense now why I wasn't able to find any information on them. Logan and I were the hackers of the unit, and while he was good, I was better. My best computer systems were at home, but I had my laptop with me at least. After watching their home for the night, I decided the best course of action was to try and hack their cameras to see if there were blind spots for a way in.

I had to hand it to them; their systems were good and their firewall was near impenetrable. Despite trying for hours, I couldn't get into their system. The best I could get was live feed from two houses down that had a camera on the road to monitor their comings and goings. Five weeks of trying to find Kelli after she disappeared from the hospital, and it had finally come down to this moment.

The emergency bag I kept in my car had everything I should need to grab her. I had a sedative, rope, zip ties, a few knives, a gun, a mask, and some gloves. In between tries to access their cameras, I thought of all the ways I could get her out of the house. Logan left Monday evening but had no passengers in his car, which meant she was there with Brian and Josh alone. By Tuesday morning, he still hadn't returned home. If there was a time to get Kelli, it would be when at least one of the guys was gone.

As I was getting ready to sneak through their neighbor's property to get a better visual of their house, I saw a Jeep on the live feed of the road. Wouldn't you know it? Brian was behind the wheel with Kelli in the front seat and Josh in the back. Their pathetic attempt of disguising her made me laugh. Even under a hat, those curls would stand out anywhere with her lithe, little body. They obviously had no idea who they were up against, which worked in my favor. I closed up my laptop, grabbed my bag of clothing, and jogged out the door.

My car was hidden in the driveway when they drove past. I waited a few car lengths before pulling out behind them. The downfall of them living out in the middle of nowhere was there was very little traffic, but I made it work. Being the whipped pussy he always was, Brian stopped to get her coffee. His love for Kelli was obvious in the way he looked at her coming out of the coffee shop. This day was going to be glorious. I just needed to get into their cameras so I could watch Brian's life fall apart around him.

Their next stop was a large department store with home supplies. I couldn't help but chuckle as I put on my own hat and glasses. This disguise was working in my favor. I kept the sedative in my pocket and gun in the back of my jeans in case I got the opportunity here. I discreetly followed them around the store, all of them oblivious to anything around them. They were love-sick fools, only focused on each other. Kelli sucked down her coffee in no time, giving me the perfect opportunity to grab her. She would have to use the bathroom eventually, separating her enough for me to intervene.

Less than an hour later, she told Josh and Brian she had to pee, and headed to the front of the store. She was less than five steps from them when Brian nudged Josh, telling him to go with her while he stayed with their stuff. Josh came up from behind her and grabbed her hand, walking to the front with her. His lips skated over her knuckles as she went into the women's restroom and he went into the men's. This was my chance, but I would have to take down Josh first. He was a big fucker, scrappier than any of us ever were. I made a rash decision, untucking my gun and following him into the restroom. The butt of my gun hit him on the side of his head, making him drop before he even had the chance to look over his shoulder. I took a second to enjoy the view of him sprawled out on the dirty floor, the big guy that no one wanted to take on crumpled before me. It felt good making him feel an ounce of the pain I did. He wasn't to blame for Ashley's death, but he never sided with me on blaming Brian either.

I slipped from the bathroom, moving straight into the women's, making sure to keep my head low the whole time. As luck would have it, Kelli was alone in there, washing her hands at the sink. My arm was around her throat by the time she looked up, but she surprised me with an elbow to the gut. My hand moved to cover her mouth before she could scream, but she knocked me on my ass with a foot placed behind mine. Her body landed on mine, knocking the breath from my lungs. We grappled on the floor, her tiny fists landing some good shots on me.

I lunged for her again, pinning her with my legs, which gave me just a moment to get out the syringe and plunge it into her neck. She fought the sedative, her hands scratching at me, her feet still trying to kick me off. The whole thing made me hard as a rock, this wild girl fighting me as she was drug under. When her body went fully still, I took a moment to compose myself, fixing my shirt and hat. The taste of copper filled my mouth where she had landed a good hit, splitting my lip. I was going to have so much fun with her.

Cradling her in my arms, I made a hasty exit from the store, appreciative of the fact that we were near the entrance. Rushing to my car, I laid her in the backseat, securing her wrists with zip ties. I had a few options here, but decided the hour or so drive to my house in lower Maine was worth the risk. It was where I had everything set up for her arrival, and where I felt the safest.

The drive was quiet, the sedative keeping her under the whole time. I would have to wipe the cameras at the store when I got home and hope that I got to it before Brian and Josh. I could have risked doing it in the car with my laptop, but distance seemed like the smarter choice here. My driveway was long and far from the main road. Such a wonderful feeling to finally be here with Kelli in tow after all those weeks of work. This next week with her would show what my future would hold. I am hoping for a future with her, or at least a few good fucks out of her. That fire in her was such a damn turn on, I bet she would fight me in bed, too.

Carrying her into the house felt like a new start. I may have lost the love of my life, but I had another shot at love now. I had the windows boarded in the master and locks on the outside of the door to keep Kelli safe. I decorated the room with the colors she had in her room at her house. I even left her pillow in there that I had taken from her home. The only clothing in the closet were my shirts and her underwear that I also took since she wouldn't need to wear anything other than that. A photo of Ashley and I stayed on the night-stand; she deserved to see that I was finally getting revenge for her death.

There is a poetic justice in Kelli suffering for the sins of Brian. Watching the life drain from Ashley haunted me for a long time. Lately, it seems to bring a sense of peace knowing I can see that same light leave the eyes of his girl. It was where my head was leaning, taking her life. Brian had always been a stubborn bastard; there's no way he would allow her and I to live a happy life together. It might kill him inside, but he would ensure that he got her back. The only way to prevent that was not leaving him anyone to come back for.

I left her on the bed for the sedative to wear off, heading to the office to cover my tracks and ensure our safety here. I couldn't risk being found, but part of me really wanted Brian to know it was me who took his precious Kelli. Maybe I would give it a few days of enjoying her company in my bed, then I could let him know he brought this on himself. A tape of us fucking would be top tier to send, but I needed to see his reaction. Otherwise, what was the point? With the store cameras cleared, I went to check on my new guest who should be up by now.

27

KELLI

My eyes felt heavy, my mouth dry and gritty, and my side was throbbing. I groaned at the discomfort, peeling my eyes open, one at a time. Yellow walls met my blurry vision, as I tried to roll myself over. I felt as if I was moving through putty, every movement sluggish. Finally splayed on my back, I tried to remember what happened. I remembered shopping with the guys. We had found some rugs and pillows that would bring a little color and fun into the cabin. Then, I went to the bathroom with Josh, and that's when it all started to come back to me. I fought with someone in the restroom before he injected me with something. My bets are on propofol, which means that my body should start working with me pretty quickly as it wears off.

Despite using what I've learned with Josh and Logan, I wasn't able to fight him off. They always say never let someone get you to a secondary location because you're unlikely to live or be found. This definitely wasn't the store, and I definitely was going to get murdered. This is it. I finally found love again, just to be killed. What the fuck had I done in my past life to deserve this? The longer I laid here, the more I started to feel the beginnings of a panic attack. I cannot let myself spiral, I need to find a way to live.

Wiggling my arms brings on a tingling sensation, which is good. My head rolls easy from one side to the other, then snags on a photo on the nightstand next to me.

Holy.

Shit.

The couple in a sweet embrace smiling at the camera are wearing military uniforms. They are two of the people from the unit photo in Logan's office. If I remember correctly, the woman is the one who died when they were ambushed. The room spins around me as I try to wrap my head around this. I wasn't targeted because of my video, I was targeted because of Brian. He is never going to forgive himself if I die.

A creaking of the floor sounds somewhere in the hall before a jingle of keys and turning locks sounds. The man that steps into the room hones in on me, a disturbing smile at odds with his emotionless eyes. He has the eyes of a killer, someone who feels nothing. He looks a little shorter than the guys, and he's definitely skinnier. His hair is long and unkempt, a scraggly beard covering his face. His dead eyes meet mine as a tremor rolls through my body. I focus on my breathing, trying not to panic.

"Nice to see you awake, Kelli." His voice was rough, an edge of arrogance coming through. "Welcome to our home."

Prickles move through my legs as I wiggle my toes. "Our home? Who all lives here?" My voice is hoarse, but at least it doesn't quake.

"Us, of course. You and me. I made this room especially for you, so I hope you like it."

My eyes roam the room, taking in the boards over the two windows that are lined with the same curtains I had at my house. A door to my left seems to lead into a bathroom, so at least there's that for when he inevitably locks me in here again. I have a few ways to play this out. I can play nice while the guys look for me, because I know they won't stop until they find me. I can try to play dumb and find a way to get myself out when he underestimates me. Or, I can start guns blazing with my disdain and knowledge of who he is and fight him every step of the way until I am free.

His eyes don't hold an ounce of remorse for terrorizing me, which rules out option number three. My self-preservation is screaming at me that death at his hands is a real possibility if I don't play my cards right. "I like the colors you chose. Do you mind telling me your name since you know mine?"

He eyes me warily. "Those fuckwads didn't tell you about me? You were hiding out with them for weeks. I don't know if I believe that."

"I saw you in one of their unit photos in the office, but they didn't tell me any names. You did serve with them though, right?" I really couldn't remember his name, but I also don't know how much he knows about the guys currently, and I can't risk giving up any information that could harm them or turn his wrath toward them.

"It's Caleb. We served together before Brian fucked up everyone's lives and walked away scot-free. I don't want to talk about that, though. I've waited a long time to have you, Kelli."

Sensations were now floating through the rest of my body, so I slowly sat up on the bed, testing out my strength. My head was still spinning a bit, but my movements were decently coordinated. "You are the one that was following me and leaving me notes?"

"Ashley used to love when I left notes hidden for her to find, so I thought you might feel the same."

God, this was feeling like a case of transference now. Was he trying to get revenge on Brian, or was he misplacing his feelings for his dead girlfriend onto me? It's possible it was a little of both. The room was still spinning around me, but I was keeping my cool as best as I could. "Notes can be nice. Where are we, Caleb?"

He moved from the entrance of the room to sit on the edge of the bed, his hand reaching out to toy with the comforter. "I already told you, at our house. You really are a beautiful woman. I see why Brian is so in love with you. Hell, you've put me under your spell. I've always loved a woman with a little fire." His tongue slips out to lick over a cut on his lip he must have gotten in our scuffle. "You definitely have fire."

My mind shoots to Josh and his nickname for me. He must be as scared as I am. God, I hope they can find me. I scoot my body further up the bed and away from him, but he grabs onto my ankle before I can make it too far. "I'm going to make us some food. Don't get any ideas, or I will tie you up. Or maybe do, I think we could have a lot of fun that way." He is up and locking me back in the room in no time, the sound of clicking behind him as he goes.

I curl my body up by the headboard, reeling from his touch. I don't know what I thought would happen if my stalker ever found me, but raping and killing me wasn't it. My arms shake as they wrap tighter around my legs, trying to hold myself together. This can't be happening, this can't be real. We should have never left the house. Josh is going to blame himself for being so close when I was taken. I might never see him again. I might never see any of them again. My breaths started coming faster, and my whole body was trembling now.

I let myself give into the panic for just a moment before pulling on my big girl panties. I can't just roll over and accept this. I have to fight. The guys would expect me to fight, especially since they trained me for this. There is no doubt in my mind that Caleb is not exactly right in the head. I quietly and slowly move around the room on shaky legs, trying to find anything that can potentially be a weapon or way to get out. The guys have been trying to find him for weeks now with no luck, and I don't think I stand a chance if they take that long to find me. I just need to be careful and do exactly what they taught me. It's a real possibility that the only way I am leaving this house alive is by getting myself out.

I check the boards over the window first, which have at least forty nails in each. The nightstands are empty, and there is nothing under the bed, so I move to the dresser. I'm horrified to find MY underwear in the top drawer. I knew he had taken them, but seeing them here makes my stomach roll. Worst of all, the pair on top is the one he had in the photo he sent. Quickly closing it, I find the rest of the drawers empty. The closet has some men's tees hung up and not much else.

Moving to the bathroom next, I am horrified to find it stocked with some more items from my home. Clearly he took the liberty of stealing my extra bulk buys of my soaps and lotions. Rifling through the drawers, I found some hair pins which could come in handy. Other than that, it is also pretty bare bones with nothing I can think of to use to my advantage. It will all come down to my ability to undermine and escape from him.

Hiding the hairpins I snagged under the edge of the mattress, I sit back on the bed, trying to come up with any sort of exit plan. Caleb comes back, those keys jingling again to bring us some sandwiches. He has decent muscle tone and has at least eight inches on me, but I have been training for this. Unfortunately, he sets my plate and a water bottle on the bed before sitting on the chair by the door to eat his, making it impossible for me to strike at this moment.

"I didn't poison it or anything, you should eat. I already told you, I like a woman who fights. Keeping you unconscious would take all the fun away." His smirk is downright savage. Eyeing the sandwich, I decide to eat it. I'll need my strength.

"What's your plan here, Caleb? We just live here forever, me locked away in this room?"

"Of course not. I'll keep you here until I decide how to best torture Brian with your stay here. Maybe enjoy the fact that I have a woman in my bed. It's been a long time." His gaze chills me to the bone as it rakes down my body. "Once I have my fill and I ensure he feels every ounce of pain I did, I'll get rid of you," he says nonchalantly. He takes a bite of his sandwich, his eyes getting a faraway look before focusing on the picture of him and Ashley. "I thought about keeping you, ya know. Then I remembered, you only get one great love and I already had mine. It's only fair Brian loses his love, too."

Bile rises in my throat and I try to swallow it down. He is beyond unhinged and I am going to die here. There's a good chance he is going to kill me before I can escape, but there is no way in hell he is getting a piece of me first. I will die before this man defiles me. The guys would never recover if Caleb raped me. Taking slow sips of water and focusing on my breathing, I think of my guys. I can do this. I can get out for them, for the future we talked about. I will be fine, I will survive this. My love for the three of them, Josh and Logan's love for me. It is enough. I will get through this. This time, love will be enough.

28

LOGAN

Sipping my coffee that has long since turned cold, I look over the files on my desk and then at my computer screen again. Things have been non-stop since I got called in last night, but I think I might finally have a breakthrough on Kelli's case. When Josh set up our security system at the house, I put a failsafe program on it that would alert me and my team if anyone tried to break through the firewall and access it. At the time, I never dreamed it would be needed, but that was my home so I did it anyway.

It was triggered last night, and the only reasonable explanation why someone would try to get access to our security cameras is that Kelli's stalker had finally found her. That thought both terrified and thrilled me. We were finally getting closer to catching this creep. I made an executive decision to not tell Brian and Josh about it yet because my team and I were still trying to trace where and how this person was trying to get access. Until I had something to bring to them, my ass was not leaving this office.

I felt like I was missing something, though. It didn't make

sense that she was suddenly found at our house when she hadn't left it once. There was more going on, and I was determined to figure it out. My fingers flipped through the photos in the file of every note and threat Kelli had gotten when the edge of one slipped, making a small slice through my finger. Seemed to be par for the course, since I got a nasty cardboard cut on my thumb yesterday moving those boxes around with Kelli.

Fuck. That was it.

Brian and Josh went to her storage unit Sunday, then suddenly her stalker found her. Coincidences like that don't just happen. I yelled for Barry, my colleague who called me in last night, to join me as I pulled up her storage unit name online. Barry was your average cybersecurity nerd but with a deep voice, and he didn't take shit from anyone. "Call this place for me and see what you can find out about Kelli's storage unit. If anyone was hanging around there, if anyone rented one next to hers, if they have cameras, whatever you can find out. Threaten them if you have to, but I know this is how she was found. It has to be."

He left my office right as my phone rang, Brian's face popping up on my screen. "Hey man, I might not make it shopping. I think I have a lead on—"

"Kelli's gone. He took her. I need you to hack into the security cameras for this store RIGHT. FUCKING. NOW." His voice was full of panic, voices yelling in the background. My heart started to pound, my hands shaking before I took a deep breath, pulling myself together. This is not the time to freak out. This is the time to save my girl.

"What store?" Brian tells me the store and location as my hands start to move. "Find the manager immediately. See if the cameras are real and are on, and find out if they are externally saved or not." His heavy steps transfer through the phone as he runs for help. I hear him talking to someone as I try to also see what I can do on my end, but he will be able to get to them faster in person if they have cameras there.

"They have a security room with live cameras, but they are just saved to their cloud system. They're taking me back there to look through them now."

"Good, you are going to get in there way faster than me. Where's Josh? Tell me exactly what happened." He runs through the past ten minutes; how he let Josh and Kelli go to the bathroom while he stayed in the rug aisle with their stuff. When they didn't come back after a few minutes, he started to worry ,so he went to check on them. He found Josh passed out in the bathroom, bleeding from a gash on the side of his head, and when he went to the women's bathroom, Kelli was nowhere to be seen, but there was a needle cap on the ground.

Panic laces my bones as I try to tamp it down and stay level-headed. We need to keep our wits about us to find her quickly and get her back to us safely. We are going to need all three of us to do that. "How's Josh now?"

"Major headache, possible concussion. He's getting bandaged in an ambulance now. They guy clocked him good; he knew exactly where to hit."

"Fuck." My hand scrapes down my face as the agony of this whole situation floods through me. "Anything on the cameras yet?" I can hear muttering in the background, but can't make it all out.

"There!" Brian shouts. "He has a hat pulled low, and he definitely drugged her. He is carrying her out of the bathroom. How the fuck did you guys not see that? How did he get out of the store with no one saying anything?" He yells at the man he is talking to. "Do you have cameras in the parking lot? Pull them up!"

More muttering makes its way through the phone before

Brian yells again. "They don't have cameras outside of the store, but he said the store next-door does. I'm running over there now." His breathing comes through hard and fast, his feet pounding on pavement. "She's been gone for twenty minutes at least now. He could be doing anything to her," he says quietly.

The knot tightening in my throat is hard to talk around. "We are going to find her. She's strong, she'll be okay." Josh's low voice sounds not too far off, explaining what the medics said as Brian fills him in on where we are at in our plan to get her back.

I am trying to listen to them talk to the next store's security when Barry makes his way back into my office. "I got something."

Putting my phone on speaker to still hear the guys, I nod to the chair across from my desk. "What did you get?"

"Owner said someone paid him a couple hundred to inform him of anyone coming or going to her unit. Said he sent the guy video footage on Sunday afternoon. His description was vague at best. Tallish, slight beard, unkempt, brown eyes, and brown hair. Could be just about anyone. He did give me the guy's number that he left though. I guess your guy is getting sloppy because the phone is actually registered. Know a guy named Caleb Black?"

My vision tunnels, ears ringing as that name ping pongs through my head.

"What the fuck did he just say?!" Brian shouts through the phone.

Barry leans further forward, eyeing me to ensure it's okay to repeat that before speaking into the phone. "The number belongs to a Caleb Black."

You can hear a pin drop, both in my office and through the line. "B, focus. Go check those cameras right now. I will do everything to find him on my end. Make sure this is right. Verify it's him on those cameras. Now." Josh's voice is soft and I know he is talking him through this, too. The good news is we know Caleb. We know where he excels and where his weaknesses are. The bad news is the same - we know Caleb. He's always been a little more likely to make questionable decisions, the first one to use fists instead of words.

Turning to Barry, I start making a plan. "I'm going to try to ping his phone, get me that number. I need you to look up everything you can on him. Where he lives, what he drives, places he frequents. Anything at all, and I need it now."

He is gone and back in thirty seconds, dropping the number on my desk. "I'm on it." When he heads back to his desk, I take thirty seconds to breathe. Caleb took our girl. She's gone. Red starts creeping into my vision, my hands wrap around my coffee mug and throw it against the wall, causing coffee and ceramic to shatter onto the wall and floor.

We promised her we would keep her safe. We told her we loved her and promised the possibility of a future if she wanted it. She was ours, and we let him take her. I needed her back. We taught her how to protect herself, she was smart, she was a fighter. She would stay safe until we got to her. Brian never gave her enough credit, never seeing the strength in her. She would be okay; she had to be.

I started the search on tracing Caleb's phone, praying it was quick and really his phone. "How's it going? Was it him?" I ask into the phone on my desk.

"They are rewinding the cameras now." Josh's voice is just as strained as mine. "There!" Brian shouts from next to him.

"Fuck," I hear Josh mutter followed by silence. "It's him."

"Are you sure?"

Brian must take the phone back as he comes through again. "Yes, after he dumped her into the back of his car, he took his hat off for a moment to fix his hair. He looks like shit, but I would know his face anywhere. Red Toyota Camry license plate 3593MM."

I still can't believe this whole time it was Caleb and we had no idea, though it makes sense. His ability to remain untraceable, his knowledge of how to remain hidden in plain sight, how not to get caught. "His phone was last used in our neighborhood last night, motherfucker. It was in the house for sale down the road. He has it turned off now, so I can't trace it again until it's used. Barry is looking up everything we can get on him. What's our next move?"

"We're going home to load up. We packed those kits with this nightmare in mind. Find out what you can. We will be there in about an hour." Brian takes a shaky breath, his voice cracking. "We're getting her back, right? We have to."

"Yeah, B. We're getting her back." Hanging up, I go to see what Barry has found so far.

"I've got a truck, a home, and an apartment all in his name so far. Still looking," Barry says over his computer before I could even drop into the chair beside him. "Wrote down the addresses and license plate number."

"I need you to look up another license plate. He was driving a red Toyota Camry when he took Kelli." I hand over the license plate number while looking through the information Barry has written down. "How far away are his house and apartment from here?"

"His house is about an hour from here. I looked at the map; it's a pretty secluded location. If I were to take someone that I was hiding, it would be there." He was still busy typing as I typed out that address to the guys. "The Camry is registered to an Ashley Hanson."

"Bastard, of course he has her old car. Any possibility you can track it?"

"No, it's a pretty old car, there's no lo-jack on it. I'm going to keep looking up everything I can." I squeezed his shoulder in thanks and went back to my desk to look up his house. It had to be the place. There was no way that he would risk taking her back to his apartment in Boston. I felt it in my gut; my girl was there at his house.

I couldn't wait for the guys, he already had an hour head start on us. I grabbed my keys, wallet, and gun from the small safe in my office. Brian never let us forget how alone Kelli has been most of her life. How alone she felt in the world most of the time. How much she insisted that she could take care of herself regardless. She wasn't alone anymore; she had us. I let Barry know I was leaving and rushed to my car, calling the guys again.

"Is that his house?" Josh asks by way of answering.

"Yeah, I am heading there now. It's a secluded location about an hour from here. I will check it out. You guys can meet me there."

"Fuck no! You are not going without us. If you think she's there, we're all going. Brian, turn around," Josh demands.

"What if she's not there? We shouldn't all go. It would be better to have our gear, too, since we don't know what we're up against," I argue.

"Again, fuck that. We can take him on, hands behind our backs. Call Barry and have him send some guys out to the house in our neighborhood where you last pinged his phone just to make sure he didn't go back there. We are already turned around and heading towards you. We are only ten minutes behind. Do not do anything stupid and wait for us."

"No promises. He has our girl."

Josh lets out a heavy sigh. "Yeah, okay. Be careful, I'll

keep you updated on our location." He hung up right as I reached the highway heading south, flooring it. *We're coming, baby girl, just hang on.*

29

CALEB

Watching people never used to be my thing. I mean, we watched terrorist groups overseas, but that wasn't just watching one person. I also found it ridiculously boring; I preferred the action. Watching Kelli, though, I really liked that. She had this conflicting mix of fear and grit that I found intoxicating.

I wanted her fear. Her tears. I wanted to taste them as I tasted her. I wanted it as much as I wanted to see that fire come out again. Her body was small, but toned to perfection. Her long legs exposed, muscles flexing with every movement. She put up a hell of a fight in the bathroom, and I know she will again when I take her as my own. I could feel the blood coursing through my veins at the thought of her thrashing beneath me.

That never used to be my thing either. Ashley was docile, sweet down to her core. It never made sense to me why she was serving, but she said she felt it was where she could do the most good. Some good it did for her.

Yet, here I was watching Kelli through the hidden camera in the vent. Hard as a steel pipe thinking about going back in there and finally discovering what is beneath those little jean shorts. She ate most of the sandwich I gave her, acting sweet and scared. I saw her shoulders set after her mini meltdown, determination written all over her face. This was going to be so damn fun.

I changed the setting on my computers to make sure the camera was recording, not just watching. What a show we would put on for Brian. I still haven't figured out how to see his reaction when I send the video, but I will find a way to break through their security systems eventually.

Finally, everything was falling into place for me. Ashley's photo on my desk stared back at me, so I put it facedown. She didn't have to see this part. She was all about the 'sisterhood' or whatever bullshit she believed in. This was all for her, though. I watched as Kelli paced the room some more. I wanted her on edge. Restless. Then, I would strike.

Twenty minutes later she had a sheen of sweat on her face, her pacing not having stopped. I made my way back up the stairs to her room. Part of me was surprised she hadn't tried the strength of the door yet. With two padlocks outside, she wasn't getting through anyway, and maybe she knew that. Unlocking them both, I carefully stepped into the room, closing the door behind me. She was standing at the other side of the room, watching my every move.

"You look a little flushed, Kelli. Is something wrong?"

Her laugh was humorless, a little deranged. "You tell me, Caleb. You kidnapped me, locked me in this room, and told me you are going to try to fuck me then kill me. Do you see anything wrong with that?"

"Going to. Not try. I'm going to fuck you, Kelli. Brian needs to feel the level of pain I do. He won't be around to watch you die, but he can watch this." Adrenaline was flowing through me, my blood all rushing to my throbbing dick. I could see it written all over her, she was going to fight to the bitter end. It would make submission that much sweeter.

Her fists opened and closed, begging for the fight. Part of me wanted to walk back out, make her wait longer. The fear of the unknown drowning her. But, I couldn't wait any longer. I needed to have her, needed to have this. Four years of pain would be erased with this. It had to be.

Striding across the room to her, I watched her body clam up. She stood stock still as I traced a finger down the side of her face, down her neck. "It won't be so bad, baby," I whisper in her ear. "I'm a good lover, I won't even make it hurt that bad." I felt her body slowly relax against me. Maybe I was wrong and she really wanted this. It took away the thrill of the chase, but I still would have the thrill of sinking into her, taking something that wasn't mine.

My finger began moving back up her neck as I wrapped my hand around her throat, squeezing tight as her eyes went wide. "You're mine now, baby."

Two things happened at once. Her knee rammed into my dick, as her arms came around, fisted hands slamming onto my forearm. My arm dropped as I doubled over in pain. "You bitch!" I spat out, trying not to hurl.

She tried to run around me toward the door, but I hooked her leg, tripping her before she got too far. Her face hit the ground hard, blood already dripping out of her nose. Pushing past the pain, I jumped onto her, pinning her down. The smile on my face felt feral. "There you are, baby, I knew that fire would come out."

"I'm not your baby," She growled at me, blood dripping down her cheeks and into her mouth now.

Rolling my hips down onto her, I leaned down to lick up a trail of blood. Kelli's hips bucked, pushing me forward and as

I tried to catch myself, she got her thighs around me, flipping me over. We grappled on the ground, both fighting for control. Hits landed from both of us. I could tell the guys had trained her. Kelli's heel of her hand connected with my nose, the crunch audible. Blood began to pour from it as my eyes watered. My retaliation hit didn't make solid contact as Kelli got up and ran out the bedroom door. Spitting out a mouthful of blood, I wiped under my nose, stalking after her. There was nothing out here for her, no help she could find before I caught up to her. Hello, little mouse, I am here to hunt.

30

BRIAN

Logan's car was parked down the road from the house, hidden behind a patch of trees. I pulled the Jeep up behind him as Josh and I hopped out and jogged over to him. "What do we know?"

"There are cameras on the outside of the house, but I snuck around it getting as close as I could. There are two windows boarded up from the inside in the back on the second floor. This has to be the place. I couldn't get close enough to see if the car was in the garage, but I feel it. She's here."

"Do you have any weapons?" I ask as Josh tucks the glock he pulled from my Jeep into the back of his pants.

"I have my service weapon, but that's it. Are you going in unarmed?"

"I have the switchblade from Kelli's purse. It's not much, but better than nothing." A dry chuckle leaves my lips. She insisted she bring her purse shopping even though we told her she couldn't pay for anything. We compromised that she could leave it in the Jeep, which just saved my ass from going in with absolutely nothing. "What's our plan?"

"There are three entrances: front, back and garage. My guess is she's in the room upstairs in the back that has the boarded windows. Figured we could each take an entrance. What do you think, Brian?"

I didn't want to be in charge. The last time I led a team, my life imploded. But Kelli was worth taking charge for again. "You two take the home since you have the guns, and I'll take the garage. We move as one, stay out of sight until the last possible second. Move through quietly until you find one of them." My heart was in my throat, but they needed to know this now. Anything could happen in there. "Kelli is your priority. You get her out and you keep her safe at all costs. She's here because of me. I've got Caleb. Love you, brothers."

They will get her out safely. Their love for her was felt in their every action. There's a chance one of us won't make it out of here. We all met with psychologists to go over PTSD signs, symptoms, and outcomes. Caleb has nothing left to live for; he has proven that by taking Kelli, knowing we would come for her. He will fight to the death, and I will take his life without remorse, but not at the risk of Kelli losing hers. I wouldn't survive it. I just need her to be okay, and I will handle the rest.

Josh's hand wraps around the back of my neck, pulling my forehead to his. "We are all leaving this house together. All of us. This isn't the same, Brian. Now let's get our girl." He lets go with a squeeze. "Love you, brothers." We separate, making our way towards the house so we can save our girl.

I'm the only one who can view both the front and back of the home, so I motion Logan and Josh forward when we are all in place. Crouching low, we make our way up and into the house. The garage side door is unlocked, not surprising in this secluded location. Sure as shit, the red Camry is parked in here, but Kelli is nowhere to be seen. We have it right. We are getting her back. As I look through the car and garage, a high pitch scream comes from somewhere in the house.

Everything goes black as I rush into the house, yelling for Kelli. So much for going in quietly. She needs to know we're here for her. We came for her like I promised her I always would. The garage opens up to an empty hall that I follow to the back of the house. Josh is there in the kitchen, gun out, aiming it up the stairs. Logan comes from another doorway as I look down at what Josh is staring at.

"The front of the house is clear. They have to be upstairs," Logan says as he zeroes in on what we are staring at. The bottom step has a bloody kitchen knife with a trail of blood and red smeared handprints leading up the stairs.

We rush for the stairs together, all three of us yelling for Kelli now. All the doors up here are shut, but one with padlocks on it has a bloody handprint in the center. Too large to be Kelli's, so it has to be Caleb's. That doesn't tell us whose blood it is, though. I step in front of Josh and Logan. I have to be the first through the door; if someone is going to get hurt, it is going to be me. Kelli can't lose the men she loves. She deserves the happiness she has found with them.

Logan and Josh hold up their guns behind me as I kick open the door. My eyes immediately find Kelli, crumpled in a ball in the opposite corner. Caleb is standing in front of her, the front of his shirt covered in blood, with blood dripping from his face, his nose clearly broken. He is holding his stomach right over the growing red stain, his other hand holding a gun pointed at me.

"Drop the gun, Caleb," Logan calls from beside me now, slowly stepping toward Kelli's unmoving body.

Caleb's eyes stay locked on mine. "Stop moving, or I shoot." His face is pale, hand shaking slightly. My strong girl must have stabbed him, but I can't focus on anything other than if she is okay.

Not removing my eyes from Caleb, I ask Logan, "Is she breathing?"

"I think so. Caleb, let me help her," Logan pleads.

"This is between you and me, Caleb. Let her go. Let Logan help her." Logan took another small step toward Kelli.

"Caleb," Josh says as he steps forward to my other side, "It's three against one. Come on, man, drop the gun and let her go."

"STOP moving!" he shouts, still not moving his gun from being pointed at me. "You guys can shoot me, but I doubt you can do it before I also shoot him. Want your golden leader to die?" I glance at Logan, then Josh, begging them with my eyes. My life isn't worth hers. Risk it.

Neither one moves.

If Logan is wrong and Kelli isn't breathing, we are wasting precious time. She needs help. I can't risk her life; she is the only thing that matters to me. I love her, and if I have to die to save her, it would be my honor. I lunge forward, grabbing for the gun in Caleb's hand as two shots ring out. Heat spreads through my shoulder as I tackle him to the ground. Josh is at my side grabbing the gun in an instant, Logan crouching down to Kelli.

Caleb sputters below me as I try to get hold of his hands, but my left arm won't cooperate. "Is Kelli okay?" I yell. No one answers me, Caleb's body now unmoving under me. "LOGAN! Is Kelli okay?" I shout again, my vision going hazy.

"She's okay man. You're both going to be okay," Josh says, his face swimming in front of mine, "Just stay with me brother." It's the last thing I hear before it all goes black.

31

JOSH

I roll Brian's body off of Caleb's, placing him on his back on the floor. I search the floor for the switchblade he had to cut his shirt off to see where he's shot. "Tell me she's okay," I yell over my shoulder to Logan. I know he's only a few feet away, but I am crumbling inside at the thought of her being hurt.

"She has a nasty lump on the back of her head, but she's breathing. Focus on Brian, help should be here soon. I called when you guys pulled up. How is he?"

I pull his slit shirt to the sides watching blood pump out of his shoulder with each heartbeat. Pulling my shirt off, I press it to his wound. Gently lifting him, I look at his back. "Left shoulder shot, no exit wound. He's losing blood too fast." I put more pressure on his shoulder, reaching over to put my fingers to Caleb's neck. "Caleb's gone."

Logan grunts in acknowledgement. He's gently shaking Kelli's shoulders, pushing her hair off her face, trying to wake her up. "She fought so damn hard. Did you see him? He had one foot in the grave before we even got here. She did so good."

I look back over at her again, but have to look away. "Seeing her like that makes me want to shoot him again." Her face is bloody and swollen, scratches and the red of bruises forming on her arms and legs.

"Come on, baby girl. Wake up for me. Show me those stunning blue eyes," Logan's voice is rough behind me. Her soft whimpers break through the silence as she slowly comes to. I take in my first full breath in over three hours. Three hours. That's all he had her for, and my entire life felt like it was ending. The far-off sound of sirens reaches the room as Kelli's soft voice asks, "What happened?"

Turning to see her ocean blue eyes awake, I break. The tears that had been threatening to fall begin streaming down my face onto the shirt I am holding to Brian. She's really okay. We have her. Help is here for Brian. Caleb's gone.

I look at Logan, his wet face mirroring mine. He's still stroking her face, whispering that we will all be okay into her ear. Voices downstairs come resounding through the house as we shout at them to help us up here. They get Brian onto a stretcher, which is when Kelli realizes he's been shot. The medics checking her over try to get her on a stretcher, too, but our girl is not to be messed with. She is by Brian's side in an instant, breaking apart.

I send Logan in the ambulance with them, promising to meet them at the hospital after I get things taken care of here. I need a moment to get myself together. Today was so much. Too much. I almost lost the love of my life and my best friend. I killed a prior team member today. I can't process all that in front of them. Caleb fucked up; he did horrible, inexcusable things to my girl and Brian, but he was sick. He hasn't been mentally well in over four years. We all knew it, and yet, we didn't ensure he was getting the help he desperately needed. I would have to live with that knowledge for the rest of my life. Ashley would be so disappointed in me, and that hurt. Yet, I would do it all over again in an instant if it meant saving my girl. Fuck, I'd kill anyone to keep her safe.

Brian is going to need help after this, and he won't be getting that help alone. His martyr bullshit is ending now. His guilt needs to be dealt with because he will try to put Kelli's kidnapping on his shoulders alone. I won't let his pain hurt those around him anymore. Brian is going back to therapy whether he likes it or not. I think all of us going, separately or together, is going to be something I make mandatory.

Today would haunt all of us in different ways, and there is no way I will let it tear us apart the way Brian let it do with him and Kelli. He is so in love with her that he was happily going to trade his life for hers today. He owes it to himself and to her to heal and fight for her. She deserves to have all three of us. He has a lot of groveling to do, but we'll help him do it. Our girl deserves everything she desires in the world, and my brothers deserve to stand in the light of her love.

There would be a long talk happening with Brian at the hospital, but first, I needed to make sure everyone is okay.

I watch as the coroners put Caleb in a black bag, carrying him from the house. I told the officers everything I knew, telling them to make sure that all of this evidence was given to the Boston PD for Kelli's case. Then, I got in Brian's Jeep, going straight to check on my family.

32

KELLI

I hated being on this side of medicine. They won't let me out of this stupid bed as a concussion protocol, but at least I have Josh and Logan with me. Josh has been lying in bed with me, and at first my nurse was pissed, until she discovered he had been knocked out earlier today and never fully examined. She redressed his head and cleaned up the horrible skin glue job the EMT's had done. She griped about their work, but I knew it was probably Josh's fault for telling them to do it quickly and to let him go.

Brian was still unconscious when we got to the hospital, where they immediately rushed him off to surgery. We are still waiting to hear how surgery went and if he's going to be okay. I was patched up and examined with Logan at my side through it all. Minus some small scrapes and bruises, I have a concussion and some bruised ribs. I'm pretty sure Josh also has a concussion, but he refuses to acknowledge that.

Logan hasn't said anything this whole time. He just paces my room when the nurses come check on me and sits by my side, holding my hand when they are gone. I have so many questions, and I know they have them for me, but I can't talk until I know Brian will be okay. Logan's fingers draw circles on my wrist, while Josh's gently stroke my stomach under my hospital gown. We stay like that for another hour in utter silence. A knock at the door draws our attention as a doctor walks in.

"Good evening, I am Dr. Peterson. Is one of you Logan Pierce?" he asks.

"That's me. Do you know anything about Brian Stirling?" Logan's hand squeezes mine.

His laugh is deep. "Yes, that's why I'm here. I was one of his surgeons. You're his emergency contact. Is it okay if I speak freely, or would you like to move to the hall?"

"Here," all three of us say in unison.

"Okay, well he is in the recovery wing. You should be able to see him in an hour or two. It was really touch and go there for a while. His heart arrested twice, but we were able to get him back quickly. He lost a lot of blood and the bullet did a lot of damage to his shoulder. He will need months of physical therapy. This was a tricky surgery, and it's a real possibility he won't ever get back to full strength and range of motion with that arm. Overall though, he's a lucky guy. An inch over and we would be having a very different conversation."

There is a collective sigh of relief between us. "Thank you, doctor," Logan breathes out from beside me.

He's okay.

He's okay.

That's when it hits. The pain, the anger, the fear, every emotion that I shoved down today in order to keep a level head and make it through. Uncontrollable sobs wrack my body as every emotion imaginable rolls through me. I cry out the anger and the fear, letting it wash away until all that is left is relief and safety in the arms of the men that I love. Logan climbs up next to my other side, and the three of us hold on to each other. A tangle of limbs and tears and connected hands between us. We lay together until we have nothing left but love.

When I finally gather myself, I start my story in a whisper. Exactly what happened and what I remember from the moment Caleb entered that store bathroom to waking up seeing Logan's worried face hovering over mine. They hold me through every word, anger and pain emanating from them while I tell them about his threats, his hits. Their pride shines through when I tell them how hard I fought, the moves I used. I told them I got all the way to the kitchen before he caught up to me, but not before I grabbed a knife from the block and stabbed him. That's when he took the knife out of his stomach and used the handle to knock me out, carrying me back upstairs. I got the courage to ask the question I wasn't sure I wanted the answer to.

"Did I kill him?"

"No baby, I did. I shot him when he shot Brian. You did so good, little flame, so damn good. We are so proud of you."

"And we're so sorry, baby girl. We promised to keep you safe, and we didn't." Logan squeezes my hand in his.

"Stop. No one is carrying guilt that isn't theirs. He was mentally unstable and the only person who should have guilt is Caleb. You guys knew him for years, and I'm sorry you lost him. I'm not sorry for finally feeling free though. I just want to heal and move on, together."

Logan pulls me closer against him, his cinnamon and juniper scent relaxing my muscles as it flows through me. "Together, baby, always together," he whispers.

Josh's lips linger on my head before getting up. "I love you. I'm going to see about getting us set up in Brian's room.

You aren't getting discharged until the morning, so maybe one of us can stay in each room."

I watch Josh slip from the room, then turn to Logan. "Is he okay?"

"He will be. Josh was close with Ashley; he always has had a soft spot for protecting women, you know? I think he feels responsible for not getting Caleb help after her death. I'm sure being the one to pull the trigger today just hit that home a little harder for him. I know he would do it a thousand times over though, to save you."

I nod, understanding that from my bear. Taking a life, even to save one, could not be easy on anyone. "Are you okay?"

"I thought we were too late. Seeing you crumpled on the ground like that, it broke something in me. It may take a while of me not leaving your side to put that part back together."

I love this man so deeply. He could never leave my side again and you wouldn't hear me complain. He has been awake for almost two days straight now. He looks utterly exhausted and wrecked, yet here he is, holding me like I'm the most precious jewel and staying awake since it's not safe for me to sleep. "Can you kiss me, handsome?"

He carefully pulls me over top of him, his hands running through my hair at the side of my head. Soft lips meet mine in a salty, sweet kiss that's filled with so many words we are too tired to say. I lie on his chest, kissing him with every ounce of love in my body. We lie together, tongues tangling, hands absently gliding over each other, until Josh returns with a wheelchair in tow.

"They said we could go see him, but that this has to be your chariot of choice, baby." He chuckles at my horrified look. "Let's get a move on. Get your sweet ass in here."

Logan helps me from the bed, making sure I am covered in my scratchy hospital gown before putting a blanket on my lap.

We make our way through the hospital to the recovery wing. It's a smaller hospital, so he is only upstairs a few halls over. I halt Josh outside the door, not ready to see him yet.

"What's wrong?" Josh asks behind me.

"He's never going to love me back after this, is he?" I hate how small my voice sounds, but I know he is going to make this the end for us. If he wouldn't let us be together before, how could he look at me after this? I know he's going to put everything on his shoulders, blaming himself.

Josh crouches down in front of me, lifting my chin with his finger. "He needs therapy. We probably all do, but that's a conversation for later. He has never stopped loving you, not for one second. We won't let him get away with his bullshit baggage anymore, okay?"

His earnest green eyes pierce my soul. "Okay," I whisper as he kisses me quickly. I reach for his neck, trying to get more, but he leans back laughing, trying to move around me to push my wheelchair in the room. I grab his wrist, pulling him back to me.

Josh leans back down, keeping his lips just inches from mine. "Behave, Kelli girl. The doctor said you have to take it easy, and I have been dying to spank that juicy ass peeking out of that gown."

My body turns molten, my panties incinerated. He might have just been trying to get me out of my head, but damn, it worked. Brian looks over as we enter, his face falling when he looks down at me. Pain is written all over it as his eyes catalog every bruise he can see. My face probably looks the worst, a bruise forming around my nose and eyes where I bashed my face onto the floor. Miraculously, I didn't knock out any teeth or break my nose, but that doesn't mean it looks nice.

Josh rolls me up to his right side, and the minute I reach for his hand, his façade cracks. His lip trembles as he tries to hold his emotions in check. Stroking his hand, I reach up to touch his cheek. "It's okay. You're okay, I'm okay. We are all going to be okay." My thumb brushes away the rogue tear that falls as we sit there reveling in the fact we are alive and together.

"I'm so sorry," he whispers, sounding every bit the broken man he claims to be.

"None of that. You don't feel sorry for a damn thing. We are alive, and we are moving on." I look at the guys, standing on his other side. They both nod in agreement down at us, hands in their pockets. We stay in the room for another hour, taking it all in, feeling the heavy weight of the day slowly lifting.

Eventually, a nurse comes in saying Brian needs to rest and I need to get back to my room. Logan and I go back, Josh staying with B for the night so he won't be alone. The look in his eye tells me it is more than that, but that's something to get into another day. Logan spends the night in my bed, despite the nurses bringing him a cot. I get woken up every few hours for checks, and he doesn't complain once, just holds me tighter after each one.

JOSH

Logan pushes Kelli back to her room where he is going to stay with her tonight. It's hard letting her out of my sight, but it's time Brian and I hash this out. I should feel bad that he just got out of surgery a few hours ago, but I don't.

"How are you feeling?"

He grumbles, trying to adjust himself in the bed and wincing every time his shoulder moves. "Like I got shot in the shoulder. Thanks for saving my life."

"Yeah, well, you better not make me regret it." I kick my feet up onto his bed, relaxing into the chair.

"What the fuck dude? That's fucked up."

"Yeah, well so are the bullshit life choices you've been making. I'm tired of it. We all are. That shit stops now."

"What are you talking about? The doctor said I need to rest, and you need to get your feet off my bed." He tries to shove them off, but I plant them right back in place.

"Logan and I have allowed you to be a martyr for too long. We watched you shut down when you pushed Kelli from your life the first time and we won't let it happen. That's on us as much as it is on you, and I'm sorry for that. But now that we know her, love her, we aren't letting you do that again." Brian looks more upset than pissed, so I take my feet off his bed and lean forward. "You're going back to therapy. You're going to pinpoint the exact reason you feel you can't be with Kelli, and then you're going to fix it."

"I don't know how to do that. To fix it. I have made so many mistakes, Josh, too many for her to forgive."

"That's the thing about our girl. She will forgive you anyway and not hold it against you. You wax poetic about how she sees the real you, the parts you don't always show. It's time you do the same for her. See the big heart that is so full of love to give. The strength in every ounce of her. The forgiveness she gives so freely."

He looks distraught still, like he really doesn't know how to move forward from here. "Can you help me get set up with Krystal again?"

"Of course. I was going to see if she will see Kelli, too; I know she specializes in trauma. Look, B, you're going to mess up again. We all are. Well, maybe not Logan, but I know I will piss Kelli off again eventually. That's okay, though. We are in this together, and Logan and I will help you along the way. This is new, and we are figuring it out together. We will help with anything you need. The one thing we won't take is you shutting her out or hurting her again." I cross my arms, ensuring he understands that I'm serious.

"You think she can really love me after all of this? After I made mistake after mistake, including getting her kidnapped?"

"Yeah, B, she hasn't stopped loving you for a second," I promised.

He nods his head, then leans back against the pillows, looking up at the ceiling. "Thank you," he whispers.

I lean forward to grip his leg, giving it a reassuring squeeze. "We're a unit. We always have been. That unit just includes Kelli now, and we aren't complete without you. It hurts us to watch you hold yourself back and not be part of the family we are creating with her."

"I'll do better. For her. For all of you, I promise."

"Good. Now, do you want to hear what happened to Kelli, or are you going to lose it?" I don't want to make Kelli talk through it all again, and I can't have Brian shutting down again.

"Can you tell me in the morning? I need some time, and I need to sleep."

"Okay man. I'll be here with you if you need anything." We sit in silence for a moment before soft snores drift from him. I take the quiet time to reach out to Danny and let him know what happened and where we are. He promises he and Alex will be here the moment visiting hours start and they will get Logan's care for us on the way. I then reach out to Brian's old therapist Krystal and get a plan set into motion with her. Trauma can either bond you or break you, and I wasn't going to let it break us. With everything taken care of, I slip down to Kelli's room to check on her one more time, happy to see her and Logan asleep in bed together. Then I head back to Brian's room and crash on the cot a nurse brought in for me.

KELLI

Alex waltzes into my room the minute they allow visitors. He takes one look at Logan's large body wrapped around mine and snorts a laugh while I hold a finger to my lips, telling him to hush.

"He has had maybe four hours of sleep in the last three days; let him sleep," I whisper as he walks over to my other side, giving me a kiss on the head.

"I have so many questions, but first, you look like shit, and Danny is going to lose it when he sees you. He's up seeing his brother first." I flip him off, attempting to stick my tongue out at him, but my nose screams at me. That's going to be tender for a while. He grabs my free hand, giving it a squeeze. "I'm so glad you're okay."

"Thanks, Alex. Thank you for everything you have done. For me, for my case, for keeping Danny sane. You have been a port in this storm, and I am so grateful for you."

"You know we'd do anything for you. It's just nice to know you are finally safe." His eyes land on Logan again. "Well, your body is, not so sure about your heart."

I run my hands through Logan's soft messy hair. "They're keeping that safe, too." Alex's eyebrow raise in question, a snort leaving me in response, but I wince at the pain in my ribs. "Oh come on, you and Danny send me off to live with three amazing and delicious men, and don't expect something to happen?"

"Fair. Can I ask… how are things going with Brian?" He looks down at the bed, his hands, anything but my face.

"What do you know, Alex?"

"You don't remember, obviously, but you spilled your guts to me in a drunken word vomit a few months after Brian ghosted you. He also happened to share his feelings with me and asked me to keep an eye on you. I've been filling him in on your life monthly for years. Half your birthday and Christmas gifts from me have really been from him. Your secret love has never been a secret to me." My mouth drops open. The whole time I felt abandoned by Brian, he was still trying to be in my life in the only way he felt he could. My mind was reeling with this new information.

"Does Danny know?"

"No, it's the only secret I have ever kept from him. I don't want to keep it anymore, Kelli. Please."

I can understand the burden that's been on his shoulders because of this. "Things are complicated, Alex. My heart has always beat for Brian, he just has to figure out how to allow that love in. He feels undeserving, and that's not something I can fix for him. He has to love himself first, and he just isn't there right now. I'll tell Danny everything, promise."

Danny showed up soon after, ensuring Logan woke up with his screeching over the state of my face. It looked better than I expected, but my body felt like I had gone a few rounds in the ring with an ogre. The doctor came in, signing off on my release with the orders to come back with any confusion, nausea, or headaches. Alex won the game of rock, paper, scissors for who would stay behind with Brian for another night until he could be released.

Logan still refused to leave my side, but was still too tired to drive home, so Josh drove his car home. Danny drove me in the Jeep, while Logan slept in the back. I came clean to him about everything on the drive. The past between Brian and I, my relationship with Josh and Logan, and everything that happened with Caleb. He cried with me at the hard parts, and laughed with me over Josh's secret dom side. He had always suspected there was more with B and me, and said he was hoping something would happen.

At the house, Danny and Josh pampered me while Logan napped. They treated me like I was on the brink of death, not dealing with a concussion and bruising, but it was nice anyway. Danny painted my nails for me like when we were kids, and we caught up on everything that has been happening with him.

After cleaning up from dinner, Josh declared I needed rest and carried me upstairs to bed. He walked straight to Logan's room, where the scent of lavender drifted from the bathroom. Logan was sitting on the edge of the tub, lighting candles as the tub filled with bubbles. It was a sight to behold, the muscles in his back rippling with each movement. The doctor said I had to take it easy, but I was only human, and I was craving their touch.

Logan finally looked back at me, his smile soft. "Hi baby, I got you a bath ready. I put some Epsom salt in it to help." Josh's hands ran up and down my arms, setting off goose-bumps along my skin. From behind me, he gently lifted my shirt, pulling it over my head before dropping to his knees to pull down my shorts and undies. Logan sucked in a breath, watching Josh's every movement. He lowered himself to his knees in front of me, allowing his hands to trail up my legs. They both started at my ankles, trailing their hands up my body, kissing every scrape and bruise on their way.

I melted into their touch, overwhelmed by the sensations.

They made their way up my body until I was pressed between them. They helped me slip into the tub, my muscles instantly relaxing into the heat. Logan carefully wet and washed my hair, while Josh softly washed my body with a cloth.

"I hate every mark on your body, but I am so damn proud of you. You are so beautiful. Your strength. Your resilience. Your light that leads the way for us. You are everything, Kelli girl." Logan's soft voice trails out between light kisses to my face.

"Let us take care of you tonight, baby, please," Josh begs, his fingers gliding through my core under the water.

"Yes," I breathe out. Their hands on my body is driving me wild. I need this closeness with them again. Need them to know I'm safe and I'm theirs. They help me from the bath, toweling me off before leading me to the bedroom. I lay out in the middle of the bed while they stare down at me.

"Show us." Logan speaks first, rubbing a hand over his erection in his shorts. I let my knees fall apart, spreading my legs out wide. "So fucking pretty."

Josh climbs up the bed, his head dipping between my legs, licking my center that is already dripping for them. "And so damn sweet." He dives in then, tonguing me with fervor. This is a reclaiming. They knew I didn't let Caleb touch me, but they still needed to erase his touch from my skin and replace it with their own.

Logan strips out of his shorts, stroking his hard cock, eyes roaming my body. He moves to climb on the side of the bed, tweaking my nipples. "Make her come." Josh doubles his efforts, adding two fingers to stroke inside me, licking circles around my clit. I need more. Leaning my head to the side, I try to take Logan's dick in my mouth.

"I don't think so, love." He pulls away from me, "Tonight is about you."

Josh groans into me, the vibrations coursing through me. His fingers rubbing over my inner walls, his mouth never letting up, licking me like a man starved. My orgasm builds, tingles traveling through my body. "Don't stop, please don't stop, daddy," I moan out, hands stroking through his hair. The growl in his chest is feral as he sucks my clit hard, right as Logan sucks my nipple into his mouth. Pleasure radiates through me, my body floating around me as they stroke me through my climax.

Josh gently climbs over me, taking my mouth in a searing kiss. "Fucking love when you call me that," he says with a gravelly voice that's contrasted by his tender movements. He rolls to the side as Logan takes his place between my legs. Hovering over me, his lips meet with mine as he gently cups my face. His moan sends shock waves to my oversensitive clit.

"You taste like your pussy, baby. I don't want to go a day without that taste on my tongue." He kisses me again, deeper this time, still gentle against my face. His hips rock into mine, his hard cock gliding through my wet lips, hitting my clit with every glide. After a few glides, I feel a hand grab his dick and notch it at my entrance. He pushes into me in one hard thrust, both of us moaning at the sensation.

"You were taking too long," Josh mutters from beside us, making me realize Logan's hands never left my face. God damn, why is it so hot that he helped his best friend fuck me? Logan sits up on his elbows, locking his blue eyes to my own. His thrusts are long and soft, afraid he's going to hurt me.

"I need more. Give me more." He moves up onto his hands, thrusting his hips harder into mine. His cock rubs my inner walls just right with every thrust. "Fuck, right there, baby." He picks up the pace, grinding into me in perfect rhythm. His hands reach out, holding onto both of mine above my head, his eyes filled with lust.

"I love you so much, baby girl. You're mine. Ours. Forever. Say it."

"Yours forever," I repeat to him, feeling the truth of it in my soul. His hips piston into mine, my second orgasm building. Arching my back, my eyes close as my muscles tighten.

"Open, pretty girl," he growls at me. "Look at me when you come on my cock." My pussy flutters around his cock, strangling it as I come, screaming out his name. His hips pump three more times before he is spilling into me, hips pulsing out every last drop. Careful not to crush me, he rolls us both to our sides as he pulls out, letting his cum leak onto the sheets. "I don't know what I love more, watching you come, or watching my cum drip out of your puffy, pink pussy."

I whimper at his words. These two always know what to say to make me savage for them. Before I get too comfortable, Josh sits on the other side of me stroking his hand down my back, giving my ass a light slap.

"My turn." He sits up against the headrest. "I want you to ride my cock while I hold you." I sit up, giving him a sweet smile. My bear, tough and strong, but so soft in the center. Climbing up the bed, I drop a leg to either side of him. He lines up his erection with my center so I can sink down onto him. "Goddamn, you feel so good. Ours forever."

"Yours forever." I hold onto his shoulders as I rock my hips, grinding them down over him. It feels so deep in this position, his cock seated to the hilt. My clit rubs against his pelvis with every roll of my hips. He grips my hips gently, rolling me faster over him. This might be the fastest three orgasms I've ever had. Emotions heightened, my body is responding to their every touch.

Josh leans forward, nipping my kiss-swollen lips before kissing me deeply. My mouth opens for him, our tongues stroking before he sucks my tongue into his mouth, all while never stopping the roll of my hips. "I love you, Kelli Winters," he whispers against my lips. His tender heart threatens to push me over the edge for the third time. He must feel my pussy squeezing him because he groans, gently dropping his forehead to mine.

"I love you, too, Josh Baker," I whisper back, letting my nails reach around his head and scratch through his hair.

"Come with me," his rough voice demands, "Now, baby." His demanding voice sets me off, shattering around him for the third and final time tonight. My pussy milks his cock, each spurt of cum painting my inner walls. His arms wrap around me, holding me through our orgasms as we come down. His hands rub up and down my back as he kisses my shoulder and neck.

When my body fully relaxes into him, Logan appears from the bathroom with a warm, wet cloth. He helps me off Josh's lap and cleans me up despite my protests that I can do it. They settle me into the center of the bed, wrapped between them. Things almost feel complete, like the pieces of my life are falling together. Almost.

33

An hour after Kelli was discharged yesterday and the guys left with her, I was ambushed. Alex handed me a tablet that was on a video call with my old therapist and walked out of the room saying to let him know when I was done.

"What have you gotten yourself into now?" Krystal jokes. She has been my therapist for the last four years, but I haven't had a session with her in about eight months. I felt like things were fine and I didn't need to see her anymore.

"Got shot saving my girl. You know, your average Tuesday," I quip back. I have always been honest with her, but I left it a little surface level, never willing to dive into the depths of my thoughts with her. She knows all about Kelli and my feelings for her though, as it was half of what we talked about in the past.

"I love that you can find the humor in your situation, but I'm sure that was terrifying. I cleared my schedule and I am not getting off this call until we work through every deep, dark thought in that head of yours. It's time we wade through and unpack your baggage. You have a busted shoulder; you can't afford to carry it around anymore."

She isn't wrong. If I want a shot at fighting for Kelli, I can't do it with a mile of baggage and broken feelings dragging behind me. "I'm still in love with her. If I need to let it all go to be with her, then here we go. I feel guilty for leading my team into an ambush. I feel guilty for Ashley getting killed and Josh getting injured when I walked away without a scratch. Despite that, my biggest regret is walking away from Kelli. I feel guilty for the way I left her. I am scared that I'm not enough for her. I'm scared that I will tarnish her with my darkness. I'm scared I can't keep her safe. Most of all, I'm scared that if I lose her again, I will never recover."

Krystal's infamous pink pen pops out with her folder. "That's a good start, Brian. You better set this tablet up somewhere comfortable, we are going to be here for a while. We have talked circles around your guilt with the ambush in the past, and nothing changed your feelings on it. I'm going to try a different approach this time, okay? Do you think Kelli should feel guilty that you got shot?"

"Hell no!" I practically shout. "Why would I think that?"

"She's the reason you were there. You wouldn't have been in that house if it weren't for her." Krystal's face is blank, like this is a normal line of thinking. It's not. "If you don't think she should carry the guilt, then you should feel the same toward yourself. Everyone in your convoy signed up to join the Army. They did that knowing they would deploy and be put in life threatening situations, and yet, they did it anyway. You made decisions based on the information made available to you. There is no blame in that situation. Just like with Kelli. You walked into that house knowing you would probably be in a life threatening situation, yet you went. In both cases, someone out of your control made a choice to incite violence. That is on them and them alone."

Holy shit. I understood the comparison. "Okay, doc, I see what you're saying. That doesn't mean all that guilt and baggage is gone, though."

"No, Brian, it doesn't. But it does mean you have people to share the load with. Give some of that guilt to Caleb. Give some of it to the terrorist group that ambushed you. And everyday, try to give them a little more to carry, because it should be on their shoulders, not yours," she explains.

"So, I just need to share the load. It's really that simple?" This feels like a literal head scratch moment. How did I not understand this during my first three years of therapy?

"Essentially, yes. I'm not going to ask you to completely get rid of all guilt because I know you won't. Now with Kelli, maybe you can work on atoning for your guilt on how you left her by owning up to it and trying to move forward. You sit in your feelings too much, not allowing them to evolve. It's a trauma response, but one you need to let go of. I get it, you left Kelli to live her life and you feel terrible. Great. You told her, so now it's time to move on and fix things. Tell me about what happened with her when you got shot."

"We found Caleb holding her hostage in his home. Seeing her crumpled on the ground, unsure if she was dead or alive, is an image that will haunt me for the rest of my life. I couldn't breathe, couldn't do anything but pray we weren't too late. A part of me welcomed the thought of death when I lunged at Caleb, because living in a world she wasn't in would be a pain far worse than death. Seeing her in my hospital room yesterday woke something up inside of me. I saw the strength radiating from her. Because of Caleb's anger toward me, she was stalked, kidnapped and beaten, and she was sitting there with fire in her eyes without an ounce of anger towards me. She didn't need me to protect her, she is fierce enough on her own."

Krystal's face lights up through the tablet. "Now we are getting somewhere!" Krystal and I talked for four hours, diving into every thought and feeling that I had. She asked me why I was taking my therapy more seriously now. It took a moment of thinking, and I was thrilled to say it was for Kelli and the guys, but at the same time, it was equally for me.

When Alex came back to the room that afternoon, we talked for hours as well. He called me an idiot, which isn't surprising. He has been calling me one for years. He opened up to me about how his first year on the job, his actions got his partner shot. He made a full recovery, but he felt a lot of guilt over it before he came to the realization that people will always make mistakes. We will all mess up, but it's about what we do with those mistakes that matter, and that I was being a pussy about it. Leave it to him to always call things as they were.

I thought Josh and Krystal's talks had been a lot, but Alex's made the biggest impact on me. "I have an opinion on the relationship between you and Kelli that I need to get out."

This should be good. "Spit it out then."

"You have this habit of looking through things with only one view, and it hinders you in a lot of ways. You felt a need to protect Kelli, which I don't fault you for, but it was the wrong kind of protection."

"The hell does that mean? There's only one way to protect someone." My voice comes out a little angrier than it should but Alex isn't bothered by it.

"Kelli has been fighting for herself for years. She fights to be the best in her career. she fights for what she wants out of life, hell, I've watched her knee a guy in the balls at the bar because he put his hand on her waist when it wasn't wanted. She has the strength to protect herself from anything that comes her way. She needs a safe place to land after being the bad bitch she is with everyone else, day in and day out. That's what she needs from you."

He is insinuating that I have let her down in the way she really needed this whole time. She loved me and wanted me anyway, even though I was too bullheaded to see that she was a force on her own. Alex pulls out his phone and shows me a photo of the medical examiner's report for Caleb to really drive the point home. The note at the bottom essentially said that he would have bled out from the stab wound and that the bullet just got him there quicker. Kelli had already saved herself before we even got there, she never needed us to save her. She just needed our love.

"I see it now, I see her."

He takes his phone back and fixes me with a 'duh' stare. I didn't want to go one more day without being able to call her mine. I had been a selfish prick for years, breaking her heart little by little. I have a lot of work to do in order to mend those pieces and show her that the boy she loved can be the man she deserves. I have always loved her enough, I just thought that meant I should let her go. Now I could see that loving her enough meant also respecting her enough to make the decision for what she wanted. All I could do now was work every day to be a man good enough for her.

Alex makes a call to Danny that evening to check on everyone at home before making himself as comfortable as he can on the cot Josh slept on last night. I am surrounded by people that love and support me, and for once, I feel like I am opening myself up to it. After adjusting the pillows around my shoulder, I drift off to sleep, dreaming of getting out of here and seeing my girl tomorrow.

"Hey, jackass, wake up. I got us breakfast," Alex says as he walks back into the room.

My eyes feel heavy, but the smell of bacon and coffee can always get me out of bed. I try to lean up as pain shoots through my chest and down my arm. I wince, grunting through the pain as I lean back against the bed. Kind of forgot that I was still in the hospital. Alex is standing at the end of the bed, shaking his head at me, coffee tray and a bag of food in his hands. "Thanks, asshole, what'd you get?"

"Breakfast burritos from a café down the road. Hospital food is shit. Kind of don't want to give it to you, though; you kept me up all damn night with your grunting and groaning."

"He wouldn't be groaning if he didn't refuse the right pain meds." My doctor walks into the room at that moment, interjecting in our conversation. "How are you doing today, Brian?"

"Ready to get out of here, doc."

He pulls on some gloves, checking my shoulder and pursing his lips at my scrunched face. "I really think you should stay another day. You lost a lot of blood, and you should be taking the medication we give you."

"Look, doc, I've got a nurse girlfriend at home that will take great care of me. Tylenol is plenty fine for the pain, and I'll continue to take the antibiotics. Please, just let me go home. Any issues or concerns and my girlfriend will drive me straight to the ER. Promise."

"Okay, I will go get your paperwork started. You better take it easy, I don't want to see you back here." As he strides out of the room, I look to the bag of food, avoiding Alex's knowing stare.

"Girlfriend, eh? Does she know that?" He asks, putting

our coffees on the table next to my bed before pulling out two wrapped burritos and handing me one. I don't have to answer that, he already knows the truth. It's him and Josh I have to blame and thank for this anxiety pulsing through me over the thought of getting home to Kelli.

"She will," I finally reply around a mouthful of amazing burrito. "Can we make a stop on the way to the house?"

Three hours later, we are pulling up to the house as Danny comes out to help. "Hey brother, how are you doing?" He wraps me in a careful hug before opening the trunk. His loud whistle tells me I might have bought enough. "How much did your dumb ass spend?"

"Almost a grand," Alex unhelpfully tattles as he starts filling his arms with flower vases. Danny chuckles, shaking his head as he grabs some more, following Alex into the house. I can only grab one because of the sling on my left arm so I'll have to send them back out to grab the rest. This might be cliché, but Kelli has always loved fresh flowers. She used to go through the neighborhood with scissors when we were kids, cutting flowers from people's houses and making bouquets for my mom's kitchen.

She was out on the deck, wrapped in Logan's arms when I walked into the house setting the vase on the dining table. They were wrapped in their own little bubble out there, oblivious to the world. Josh was sitting on the couch, grinning at me like an idiot.

"So, the conversation went well with Krystal?" He smirks.

"Was it the twenty vases of apology flowers that gave it away?" I snark back. He walks over, clasping my good shoulder and giving it a squeeze.

"About damn time, brother. Now, go get the girl." He

nods to the patio. "Take her out to the beach, I'll get this all set up for you."

I slide the glass door open, Kelli and Logan turning at the sound. Her bruised face lights up with her stunning heart stopping smile as she takes me in. She is up in seconds, rushing over to me, wrapping her arms around me as I breathe her in, my right arm holding her tight.

"I'm so glad you're home."

Home.

With her, I am home. She has always been home to me, I just have been too stupid to see it. "Take a walk with me?" I ask, slipping my right hand into hers as I lead her out toward the water.

"Good luck!" Logan shouts after us like the dickhole that he is, knowing smirk on his face. We walk in silence until we get to the water's edge and sit in the Adirondacks that Kelli moved out here for us. She was always doing little things for us, fixing things to make our lives easier and better.

She tries to pull her hand from mine as she sits, but I just move the chairs closer together so I can grab her hand again. Her nails have a pretty pink polish that I'm pretty sure my brother painted on last night. He has been painting her nails for her since they were ten. She stays quiet, looking out at the lake, waiting for me to say what I need to say.

"I'm so fucking sorry, dove," I blurt out. "I have so much to apologize for, but I want to start at the beginning. I don't know if you remember, but when you were nine, I found you sitting under our tree, spitting mad. You told me that a boy in your class made fun of you for not having a dad around and pushed you down. You said that you got up and socked him in the gut before storming off and crying in the bathroom. I was furious, wanting to make him pay. I vowed to myself that from then on you were mine to protect and I was going to do a damn good job at it. I always thought that was what you needed, someone by your side to protect you.

"I was so wrong though. You protected yourself then, and you've been doing it since. You need someone to be there for the after. To hold you when you cry, someone to just be by your side through it all,only stepping in when you ask for it. You needed a safe harbor. A soft place to land. It took me way too long to see that. If I would have just listened to you from the beginning, I would have known that. I'm so sorry."

Her blue eyes glittered in the sun, shining so softly on me. "You have always been my safe harbor. You were the one I went to when I needed to sit in my feelings. The one I could express everything to and you listened with no judgment. That tattoo on your side killed me because the evidence was right there for you to see, you just never looked hard enough. You have always been by my side. You have always been what I needed, until you weren't."

"You have spent your life fixing people. You are so self-less, holding everyone's hand through their hurdles, both in your private life and at work. I didn't want you to have to be that for me. I didn't want to be one more thing for you to have to fix." Emotion lays thick in my throat, admitting that to her.

Her small hand reaches up, fingers brushing over my chin. "Oh, Brian, you were never broken. You were hurt, but again, you looked at it wrong. It is my job to help people through their hard times, but I do it because I love it. It's what I'm good at and how I show my love. Can't you see that? That I wanted to help you because I love you, and that's what you do for those that you love."

"I love you so much, Kelli. I am so completely and wholly in love with you. You are the sun that my heart orbits. The tree roots that keep me grounded and steady through the storms. The other half of my soul. My turtle dove. I know I have caused you years of pain and heartache that I can never make up for, but I promise I will spend every day of the rest of my life trying. If you'll let me." She is off her chair and in my lap in a flash, her soft lips pressing to mine.

"I love you, B. I have loved you in some way most of my life. I won't lie and say that the way you have treated me is okay. You've hurt me, but I want to move forward. You've carried so much pain and anger for so long, it's time to share that load. I want to be with you. With all of you. I'm a package deal now."

I held her close, feathering kisses on her lips. "I know, baby. They have been my brothers for years, but you have been mine for longer. It feels right to be together, all of us. Our own family. I still have a lot of guilt to work through; the kidnapping made it worse. But, I am working on it and I will continue to. You deserve the best, and we want to give it to you." She snuggles into my chest, my fingers grazing over her shoulder and arms. It hurts to see the marks on her skin, but fuck if it doesn't also amaze me. Kelli personifies strength. She brought men to their knees, literally and emotionally. Spending the rest of my days worshiping at her feet with my two best friends was a better future than her and I had originally planned.

I had years of groveling and heartache to make up for, but I would happily do it. Sitting here with her in my arms, knowing she is ours to love is the most at peace I have felt since that night in her apartment four years ago. Knowing the guys are inside rooting for us and setting up flowers for me is the cherry on top.

Dropping a kiss on her head, I mutter into her hair, "I have something to show you inside." We walk back toward the house, where I can already see they have gone above and beyond. Rose petals begin at the steps of the deck leading into the house.

"What are you guys up to?" She giggles next to me. Fuck, I love that sound.

"I got a few apology flowers. They clearly decided some were better on the ground than in vases," We walk up to the house where she slides the door open, stepping inside. Vases cover every possible surface that we can see. The dining table, coffee table, side tables, even the mantle above the fireplace is covered in flowers. Standing in the middle of it all is a smug looking Josh and Logan with Danny and Alex sitting on the couch holding ridiculous grins.

Kelli stands there stunned, taking it all in before slowly turning around to face me. "This is a few flowers?" I can't help my own stupid grin as I nod down at her. Her bottom lip starts to quiver, tears gathering in her eyes. "I love you," she leans on her toes to press her soft lips to mine.

"Fucking finally!" Logan shouts.

"Get a room!" Danny hollers.

"Only if I get to watch," Josh adds.

"Gross, that's my brother and best friend. I don't need the details," Danny chokes out.

All the while, Kelli melts against me, her lips smiling against mine. I push her hair to the side leaning down to whisper in her ear. "I can't wait until we're both healed. If you think Josh and Logan make you scream, just wait until you have all three of us." A soft whimper leaves her lips as goosebumps spread over her skin. Now I am thinking of all the other ways to make her whimper. There is no way we are making it the two weeks my doctor suggested. I look over her shoulder to Josh and Logan, their hooded eyes telling me they are thinking the same thing.

"Okay, enough sexy stuff. Can we play a game or something? Alex and I leave in the morning." Danny gets up from the couch, heading for the basement in search of a game to play. "Also, I want pizza for dinner!"

My shoulder is killing me, and I consider that I might have overdone it a little today. I follow Kelli up the stairs, trying not to let her see the pain written on my face. "Sleep with me tonight?"

"Oh, hell no, you don't get to come in here and steal her night one. If you want to sleep with her, you sleep with all of us," Logan whines from behind me.

"We won't all fit on one bed. Plus, I have to be careful with my shoulder, I can't risk one of you trying to snuggle up on me," I say as an excuse.

"Can we get an Alaskan king bed? I bet we could all fit on one of those!" Kelli's excited voice asks as we get to the landing.

"Not tonight." Josh kisses her head, walking straight to Logan's room. "Kelli's with us, you know, since you can't risk snuggles."

Kelli looks between us, a small smile on her lips before her eyes land on mine. "Are you hoping for sleep, or are you trying to get me in bed?"

"Both." Might as well be honest. They've had her for weeks while I had to listen, and it's been torture, even if it was my own fault. I can't go one more night without knowing what she feels like wrapped around me.

Josh backs out of Logan's room, eyebrows raised. "Alright, everyone in," he grins as he points at Logan's room. It's like the air is sucked from the room when we cross the threshold. "Strip. Brian, you're on the bed," his deep voice commands the room. It has been too long since Josh and I shared a woman. I have a dominant side, but there is something about being told what to do by him that turns me on.

Kelli is the first to get naked, helping me take off my sling and clothes. I sit there completely useless, trying not to swallow my tongue at the sight of her. She is fucking stunning from head to toe, with perfect perky breasts and dusty pink nipples that beg to be sucked. Her bare pussy makes my mouth water at the thought of tasting it. Unaware of my inner freak out, she carefully pushes me back onto the bed to wait for Josh's next instructions.

"Logan, lay next to Brian, Kelli's going to ride your face. Show our boy what he's been missing."

"Oh, fuck yeah." Logan hops on the center of the bed. "Have a seat, baby girl." Kelli climbs up over his body, seating her thighs on either side of his face before fully sitting on him. The groan that leaves him as he gets his first taste is thunderous. Kelli gyrates over his mouth, rocking her hips on his tongue. Her hands cup her breasts, pinching her nipples, head thrown back in ecstasy, as Logan swaps between piercing her core and flicking her clit with his tongue.

Josh stands at the end of the bed, watching. "Kelli, how about you give Brian a taste? He's waiting so patiently." She looks down at me as she reaches between her thighs, swiping her fingers through her glistening pussy. I thought she was going to feed them to me, but instead, I watch with rapt attention as she paints those fingers across her own lips. She leans down, pressing her slick lips against mine. My tongue darts out, licking her honey off her lips.

"Fuck, you're so sweet, baby." I pull her head down further against me, plundering her mouth with my own. The wet sounds of Logan devouring her spurs me on as Kelli turns to putty between us. I can feel her body shaking as she nears her climax. She sits up suddenly, screaming out in ecstasy as she floods Logan's mouth with her release. Watching Kelli come might be the most beautiful sight I have ever seen. I want to watch her break apart between us every day for the rest of my life.

Josh helps her off of Logan's grinning face, his stubble wet with her release. "She's ready for you now, B. Are you clean?"

"What?" I ask, confused.

His eyes bore into mine. "We've been taking her bare, are you clean?"

I can't get my answer out fast enough. "Yes, I'm clean." I'm finally going to feel Kelli's tight pussy squeezing my cock, and with nothing in between us. There is no way in hell I am going to be able to make this last. Kelli's lithe little body crawls over the bed to me as her eyes go wide. I guess she didn't pay attention to my cock when she helped me undress earlier. I use my good hand to stroke my shaft, "Like what you see, baby?"

I don't consider myself massive but I know I have a big dick, as thick as Josh and longer than them both. Kelli nods, her eyes never leaving my cock as she moves between my legs to take me in her mouth. Her tongue swirls around the tip, licking the precum from the slit. "Holy fuck, Kel, you gotta stop or you'll make me come. Sit on my fat cock."

"She's got such a filthy, hot mouth, doesn't she? I swear she sucks my soul out through my dick every time," Logan laughs.

Kelli's coy smile tells me she knows exactly what she does to us. With her legs on either side of me, she lines herself up, impaling herself on my hard-on, stopping a few inches in. "Shit, you're tight. Relax, baby, you can take me." She takes a deep breath, circling her hips until she starts sliding down the rest of my erection, finally seated to the hilt. I hold her hips in place, needing to breathe for a moment before she moves. Her pussy has a death grip on my cock already, so I start a grocery list in my head just to distract myself.

"I need to move, B. Please." Kelli grinds her hips into me, unable to stop herself.

"I love when you beg. Lean forward, love." Josh smacks her ass as she carefully leans over me, her tits rubbing against my chest, her arms holding her up on either side of my head. I watch as he hands Logan a bottle of lube. Kelli continues grinding herself over my cock, dripping onto me. A cap pops open, followed by her pussy squeezing tighter around me as Logan begins fingering her ass.

Kelli moans out his name, sweat starting to slick over our skin. "She loves being shared, doesn't she? Every time you add another finger, she squeezes me so tight." Her pussy flutters around me, and clearly, she loves when we talk about her like she isn't here, too. I feel Logan remove his fingers, and notch himself at her back hole. I move my hand up to stroke her face, coaxing her through, "Breathe, baby, let him in."

Kelli whimpers, her body quivering as Logan slowly pushes himself into her. "Fuck, it's so tight. Your fat dick fills her so well." He grunts out. Once he is fully in, he slowly starts to move, fucking into her ass.

"You okay, baby?" Josh asks from the other side of the bed. She looks at him with lust filled eyes, nodding. "Such a good girl, taking them both. Rock yourself between them, Brian can't help you this time. Fuck yourself on their cocks."

She preens at the praise, starting a gentle rock between us. Logan and I both groan as she fucks us together. "I'm not going to last long, baby," I pant out.

Josh crawls up to my side, sitting on his knees. He taps

Kelli's cheek with his crown. "Open." She turns her head to the side, sucking him down eagerly. "Fuck, that's my good girl." He grabs her hair at the nape of her neck holding her head in place. "You keep grinding those hips, driving them wild. I'm going to fuck your face. I'll be gentle this time."

She smiles around his dick, picking up the pace of her hips. Watching Josh's cock disappear into her mouth, spit dripping down her chin while Logan fucks her ass is enough to set me off. My orgasm barrels down my spine, my seed coating her pussy in hot ropes. My orgasm sets off Kelli's as she screams around Josh's dick, strangling our cocks. Logan follows quickly behind, spilling his cum in her ass. As her body shakes between us, Josh's hips sputter, grunting out his release into her mouth. Before she can move, he grabs her by the throat pulling his spent cock out.

"Open," he growls at her. She does, showing him her mouth full of his cum. "Good girl, let me feel you swallow every drop." He squeezes her neck tighter as she swallows all of him. My own spent cock stirs at the sight.

Logan slowly slips out of her, then helps lift her off of me. They all fall onto the bed, tangled limbs and sweaty bodies. We lay there catching our breath, enjoying the post orgasm haze still flowing through all of us. Eventually, Josh gets up to start the shower before coming back into the room.

"I'll make sure she's in your bed tonight," he says as he picks her up, carrying her to the bathroom with Logan not far behind. I roll off the bed heading to my room not even bothering to get dressed or grab my clothes. I slide into my bed, setting up pillows to keep my shoulder still through the night. Kelli's soft footsteps cross the hall as she enters my room and crawls into bed next to me, snuggling into my side.

"Thank you for tonight. I can't express how I'm feeling,

just that I am utterly consumed by you. I love you so much." She kisses my chin before snuggling back down into me.

"I love you too, B. Thank you for making me feel complete."

Her soft breathing echoes around me just a few short minutes later. I still can't believe I allowed myself to think that staying away from her was the best decision for us. I will never be able to forgive myself for all the pain I have caused her, but for her, I will do my best to move on. She is my beginning, middle, and end; I just wrote the extended version of our lives. Having her in my arms, in my bed, loving her out loud would now be my greatest joy. I kiss her wild curls, pulling her tighter into me, following her to sleep. I get the first full night of sleep since the night she moved in.

34

The next few days were filled with movies, snuggles, and a lot of shared love. Brian tried putting on a brave face through his pain, but was still in a lot of it. Kelli hired a physical therapist to come to the house for the first month to jumpstart his recovery. We were all worried about his healing and how much function he would recover. Josh had to put in a bit of extra time working since Brian was laid up, but he still joined us for every meal and checked in with Kelli multiple times a day, even if it was just to give her a drive-by kiss. Our big bear was so in love, and he turned into putty around her. It was beyond adorable to see.

I took over dealing with the case for everyone. I was never as close with Ashley or Caleb as the others were, so things were a little easier on me. Alex and I worked together to ensure everything was handled correctly and that the case would be closed out with no loose ends.

I was so damn grateful that our girl was safe, and she still wanted us. A week later we decided to lay everything out on the table for her. We had a discussion last night while she was distracted on her phone call with Danny and agreed this was what we all felt would be best moving forward.

"Hey, baby girl, we wanted to talk to you about something." I take a sip of my beer.

She sets down her fork, eyeing us. "Okay, is something wrong?" she asked warily.

"Absolutely not," Brian grabbed her hand on the table. "We just talked last night and we want you to know that now that things are settled and your options are open, we want to support you in whatever you would like to do moving forward."

"What do you mean?"

Brian looked toward Josh as he took over, "We mean that you mentioned wanting to stay here and we want nothing more than that. But, if you changed your mind because you made that decision thinking you would be stuck here anyways, that's okay, too."

"We don't want you to go, but we will understand if you want to," I cut in. "We want you to know that you have your power back. You get to make the choices here and we will stand by your side no matter what you choose. If you want to work, we will help update your resume. If you want to continue just being here with us, we will gladly support you. If you want to get a place in town, we will paint the walls. We don't care what your next steps are, we just want to be here with you as you make them."

The three of us sat with bated breath, waiting for her to answer. Josh anxiously picked at his beer label while Brian played with her fingers. After a moment of her staring at us, she burst out laughing.

"You are all idiots," she wheezed out around her laughter. "I really love all the support, but I told you before and I'll tell you again, I love you all. I want a future here with all of us, together, in our home. I just want to be here where you guys are." Thank God because I loved it here, but I would have followed her anywhere, if that's what she wanted. "I do want to go back to work, though; it has been hard for me not to work. I will gladly take your resume help for my application to the local hospital. Before I do that, though, I need to go back to Boston and clear out the rest of my house and get it sold. Having that house still is a weight I don't want to carry anymore."

"I'll go with you." Brian volunteers and we all stare at him, deadpan.

"You would be utterly useless to her. You can't lift anything and you still have physical therapy three times a week. I really can't take the time off work since I've been covering for you. Logan, you're up."

"Hell yeah, I was going to fight you guys on it anyway. Ready to spend some alone time with me, baby girl?" Kelli's eyes light up as she nods emphatically.

"Fuck, this sucks. Baby, will you sleep with Josh and I tonight and not let Logan participate? He's going to be insufferable while you guys are gone." Brian gives her his best puppy dog eyes.

"I think I can think of a few things we can do to make sure you guys know I'll miss you." She winks at him, and I know I am in for a sweet form of torture tonight.

When we make our way upstairs for bed, Josh leads Kelli into Brian's room and I head to mine like the good boy that I am. Before my bedroom door can close, Brian stops it with his foot.

"Where are you going?" He asks, his voice gruff.

"You said I can't participate, so this is me, not participating." His saccharine smile hits me with force.

"Not participating doesn't mean you can't watch. There's

a chair by the window." Watching is more of their thing, but I am starting to see the allure. Watching Kelli get worked over does it for me every time. I follow him into his room taking a seat in his oversized chair. Josh already has Kelli splayed out on the bed in only her underwear as he and Brian slowly undress.

"What were your ideas for tonight, pretty girl?" Josh asks, climbing onto the bed.

"Why don't you sit at the head of the bed and I'll show you?" Her sultry voice exudes innocence when we know she is anything but. Josh moves to sit against the headboard, anyway, as she says.

"You want to run the show tonight? Be our good girl and tell Brian what to do." Kelli crawls in between Josh's spread thighs sucking his balls into her mouth. His groan matches mine as my dick stirs to life in my sweats. She pops her mouth off, looking back at Brian, standing naked at the end of the bed.

"Josh is going to fuck my mouth while I fuck yours. Get to work, B." Her hips lift up giving Brian and I the perfect view of her little thong barely covering her pussy. My hand slips into my pants to grip my throbbing cock as Brian leans down on the bed. He slips her panties to the side and dives right in, his tongue going deep in her pussy.

Kelli's mumbled moan comes from around Josh's cock as her head bobs up and down. Josh's grip on her hair squeezes tighter, my hand on my raging erection doing the same. I push my pants down, freeing myself to really enjoy the show they are putting on. Kelli's mouth is working over his cock, gagging as she reaches his balls. Such a pretty sight. Brian's still kneeling behind her, two fingers in her pussy as he works over her clit with his tongue. I watch as chills rake down Kelli's body, her signal that she is getting close. Brian doubles his efforts, and as he nips at her clit, she explodes between them. Her mouth pulls off Josh to cry out her release, a string of drool connecting from her mouth to the tip of his dick. I have to squeeze myself at the base to keep from blowing my load at the sight.

As Kelli comes down from her orgasm she sits back on her heels, hooded eyes raking over the three of us. "Switch, I need you to fuck me now, daddy."

Josh grabs the back of her head, taking her mouth in a punishing kiss before moving to get behind her. He peels her soaked panties off as Brian sits against the headboard. Kelli's mouth is on him in an instant as she licks the precum dripping down his shaft. My eyes can't be pulled from the sight of her tongue swirling around his head, then licking up and down his shaft before finally she takes him in fully.

"Fuck, that hot mouth of yours is incredible," Brian grunts out. My dick is leaking down my hands as I start pumping slowly, trying to hold off on my release until she comes again. Josh pulls apart her ass cheeks and spits in between them letting it drip down onto her swollen lips. He sinks into her, taking her hard and fast. My attention moves back to Kelli's face, her eyes rolling back as she's being worked over. Brian holds her head in place with a handful of her hair as he ruts up into her mouth. My hand works over my shaft in tandem with their thrusts.

"Such a good girl, letting them use your pretty holes." My gaze trails between the three of them chasing their pleasure. The heat is barreling down my spine as my balls draw up, my orgasm on the brink of being released. "Come with me, baby girl. Come for us."

Her body shudders as she screams out, her mouth shoved deep on Brian's cock as he spills down her throat. Josh grips her hips tighter as he pours himself into her, my own cum spilling over my hands and covering my stomach. Chest heaving, I use my discarded shirt to wipe up and slip from the room, leaving them to calm down and have the night together before I whisk her away in the morning.

Before I went to bed, I snuck back downstairs to bake muffins for the road tomorrow. Acts of service have always been my love language for others; it's why I like to clean and cook for the guys so much. Being able to show Kelli my love that way is a dream for me.

No one in my family cared much for love languages, so seeing Kelli's face light up this morning when she saw her bag packed and in the car with a coffee and muffins waiting for her was enough to make me melt. She understands that's how I best show my love, and she is grateful for it. She wraps her body around mine, inhaling against my shirt. "Thank you, Logan. You always take such good care of me."

I couldn't keep the smile off my face the entire three-hour drive to Boston. This woman owned my heart, body and soul. I wouldn't have it any other way. We went to the hotel I booked to drop off our bags before heading to her house to start. "You know Danny and Alex offered to let us stay with them, right?" She asks as we head back to Josh's truck he's letting us use.

"Baby, I have you all to myself for the next couple days. If you think I am not going to take full advantage of that, you are mistaken. Those poor guys already had to endure our fuckfest when they stayed with us, I think they deserve some peace." Her cheeks flush as her teeth sink down on her plump bottom lip. We haven't all been together since that first night. Brian woke up with a lot of pain, so we decided to wait until he was more healed before doing that again. She has been rotating beds every night since, until last night. I knew she was thinking about it, though, how she felt between us all, being filled in every hole. Fuck, now I had a semi.

"Let's go before I take you back to the room and spend the next hour with my head between your legs." She squealed and smacked my chest.

I pull into her driveway and shut off the truck, but Kelli doesn't get out. Her body is rigid as she sits staring at the house. "Are you okay?"

"I haven't been back here since the night he broke my windows." She still hasn't turned to look at me.

"What do you need? I can take you back to the hotel, bring you to Danny's, go back home. Tell me and I'll do it."

She finally turned to look at me, those blue eyes softening. "I like when you call it home. I like that it's my home now, too. I'll be fine, let's go do this." We unbuckle and pull bags and boxes out of the bed of the truck. I let her lead me into the house so she can take all the time she needs. Unsurprisingly, my strong girl barges right in, reclaiming what was hers. She shows me around and then we go to work. Half her belongings are in storage already so we started sorting what was left into keep, trash and donate piles. She mentioned wanting to donate most of her furniture since she decided to make her move in with us a permanent thing. While she was sorting through her bedroom, I called and scheduled a local women's shelter to send a truck to grab it all.

Kelli filled up bags with clothes, shoes, and unused products that they could also take. She was so selfless in everything she did, so different from the way I was raised. I admired her for going through the unimaginable and still looking for the good in life and finding ways to help others. We got through the two bedrooms and bathrooms by the time the truck showed up to take her couch, beds, and other random furniture she didn't want to keep.

We decided on a taco truck for dinner and to finish up the rest of the house tomorrow. The one downside of living in a smaller town was that there weren't incredible food choices around every corner. We sat on the benches by the truck, demolishing our food. "How are you feeling about everything now?"

"Better. We should easily be able to finish the rest of the house tomorrow, then maybe knock out the storage unit the next day? Alex and Danny just packed everything, so there is probably a lot in there that can be donated, as well."

"Sounds good to me. I booked a moving company to bring your car and whatever you want to keep to our home."

Her eyes narrowed, brows scrunching. "Isn't that why we brought the truck? Between that and my car, we can drive it all back."

"Sorry, baby girl, but you're driving with me." Was I being a caveman? Absolutely. Was I really sorry about it? Nope. I still don't love the idea of being away from her, even for a three-hour drive. I know it's not necessary anymore, but I don't care. She stares at me for a while, seeing the determination in my eyes before she gives in.

"Thank you. For everything. Today would have been tough without you."

My arms wrap around her waist, pulling her closer to me. "I loved spending the day with you. I know you'll have tough days, but that's why you have us. Lean on us when life gets too heavy."

Her soft body melts into mine as she looks up at me through her lashes. "Take me to the hotel now, Logan." I have never moved so fast, practically dragging her to the truck. Thankfully, the hotel isn't far because her hand rubbed up and down my leg the entire drive there. I opened her door, leading her out by the hand. I booked us a nice hotel to make the most of my time alone with her. We crossed the marble floor of the entrance to the elevators stepping onto the first available one. The doors closed behind us, trapping us alone.

I couldn't wait another second, I was so keyed up for her. Grabbing her face, I pinned her to the back of the elevator with my hips, taking her lips in a searing kiss. I rolled my hips into her, making sure she felt just how badly I wanted her. Her arms wrapped around my neck, her nails scratching up into my hair, weaving her fingers through it. My lips explored hers, kissing until the doors opened on our floor. Bending down, I threw her over my shoulder, giving her ass a slap as we walked to our room, her giggles flowing behind me the whole way.

I let us into the room and threw her onto the bed, her body bouncing, curly, blonde hair feathering around her face. She looked like an angel, cheeks flushed, blue eyes shining, lips sucked in as she stared at me. Reaching behind my head, I stripped off my shirt, quickly followed by my shoes and socks. Her eyes tracked my every move, searching over each inch of my chest. Undoing my belt, I threw it onto the bed before shucking down my pants and boxers.

I climbed onto the bed, hooking my fingers beneath her leggings, pulling them down her legs, throwing them behind me. Kissing my way up her leg, I let my fingers trail lightly in their wake. When I got to her lace covered mound with a wet spot already in the center, I buried my nose in it, taking a deep inhale. "You smell so good, baby girl." Hooking my finger in the edge of her lace panties, I move them to the side, burying my tongue in her wet center. "Mmm, you taste even better."

My thumbs spread her lips, giving me better access. Licking up both sides of her, I move to flick her clit with the tip of my tongue before giving it a tender bite. Her breathy moans are becoming my new favorite sound. I slide two fingers into her tight, wet heat, continuing to lash at her clit with my tongue. In minutes, she is screaming out my name, her release soaking my face. I lick her through her orgasm until her body stops trembling around me.

Sitting up with a cocky smile, her cum on my chin, I strip her out of her shirt. "Sit up, love." She does immediately. I reach around to unclasp her bra, trailing my fingers up her back and over her shoulders, taking the straps down with me. With her fully nude, I grab her hips and flip her onto her stomach. "On your knees."

She sits up on her knees facing the headboard. Plastering my front to her back, I run my fingers down her arms again clasping her hands together in front of her. I reach behind me to grab my belt, bringing her clasped hands to the top of the headboard where there are several, small cutout designs. I loop the belt through a cutout, securing her hands through the loop.

Leaning on my heels, I admire her stretched out before me. Josh may be the heavy handed one in the bedroom, but that doesn't mean he's the only one. With her hands looped at the top of the headboard, her ass pushed out deliciously. "Such a beautiful view. Your fine ass begging for my hand, that pretty pussy weeping for me."

My hand lands hard across her backside, the delicious skin pinking up. She whimpers, leaning her shoulders down more to stick her ass up further. "You like that, Kelli girl? You like a little pain with your pleasure?"

"Yes. Please, Logan," she purrs, the sound going straight to my already painfully hard dick.

"That's my good girl, begging me so sweetly." Her other cheek jiggles with the next smack as I soothe the sting with open mouthed kisses. Gripping my cock, I slide it through her slick folds, pushing in. She was made for me, the way her pussy grips me every time.

My fingers tighten around her as I slowly pull out and slam back in, loving the feel of her juicy ass slapping against me. I do it again, ramming into her as she cries out. "God, yes, harder!" I smack her ass again, continuing to pound into her. Thrust, thrust. Smack. Thrust, thrust. Smack.

Her cries echo around the room, driving me wild. I can feel her inner walls start to flutter around me, my balls drawing up, our orgasms barreling through us. "Come," I growl at her, reaching around to land a hard slap right on her clit. She shatters around me, her orgasm setting off my own. My vision goes fuzzy, sweat dripping down my chest as I pour my spend into her, her greedy pussy squeezing out every last drop.

My body stretches over hers to undo my belt from her hands. Kelli crashes down on her stomach on the bed as I roll next to her so I don't crush her.

"You're amazing," she mutters with her face in the pillows. A snort escapes from me, my fingers running through her hair. That was some of the best sex of my life, but I always think that when it's with Kelli. Every time is better than the last. I have learned her body, her likes and dislikes, what makes her whimper, what makes her scream, and I love all of it.

This girl is it for me. Her stamp on my soul is permanent, etched in so deep I could never dig it out, not that I'd want to. I've never felt this way about someone before. I have found my home in her, and I don't even care that she's also in love with my best friends. When we first moved in together, we joked that our wives would just move in there with us as one, big, happy family. That was the dream. Keeping our friendship tight, raising our kids together, being together in the one place that felt like home for us all. We have a real chance to do that, just all with the same amazing woman. I want that so damn bad, I just need to make sure everyone is as all in on this as I am.

Kelli finally picks her head up from the pillow, turning to give me a sleepy smile. I pick her up, carrying her to the shower with me, showing her my love in the best way I know how. I hold her against me while I take my time washing her hair, scrubbing her body, and massaging her muscles. She takes the cloth from me when I'm done, washing me with just as much care and attention. When she's done she drops the cloth, wrapping her arms around me, pressing her lips to mine.

She rocks her hips against my hard-on, nails digging into my back, so I pick her up and make love to her against the shower wall. Our bodies move slower, savoring every moment of being together, pouring our hearts out with every touch. Her orgasm builds slowly as we take our time, both groaning out our release to the steam around us. I dry her off and carry her back to bed, curling her body against me. This right here, with her safe in my arms, I feel complete.

Brian: How's our girl doing?

Logan: It took her a minute to walk in the house yesterday, but she did good. She had a bad nightmare last night though.

Brian: What can we do?

Logan: Well I fucked her back to sleep. Third time's the charm and all. *winky face*

Brian: Told you he'd be insufferable.

Josh: He shouldn't be bragging, the first two
clearly didn't do the trick.

Logan: Asshole. I don't know what to do to
help. She's donating almost all her furniture
to a local women's shelter, along with
almost everything else left here. I don't think
she wants the memories that will come
with it.

Logan: She did find a box of fall decor and
asked if she could decorate the house
for us.

Josh: That's our selfless girl. I will order
some stuff today.

Brian: What stuff?

Josh: Fall decor stuff she can decorate with.

Logan: Her eyes lit up talking about
decorating. Christmas is going to be wild
this year.

Brian: This might be the first time I'm looking
forward to the holiday.

Logan: I think we need to double up at night
for a bit until the nightmares go away again.

Josh: I will talk to her when she gets home,
see what I can do to help.

Brian: Never thought I would be grateful to
be part of a harem. Nice to have back up to
make my girl happy.

Josh: Our girl

Logan: OUR girl, jackass.

Brian: Jeez, touchy subject. She was mine
first.

The drive back home is a quiet one. Kelli is exhausted, mentally and physically, and I would be lying if I said I wasn't worried. I know she wanted to be rid of the house and the baggage that it came with, but it might have been too soon to have her open up those wounds. I grip her thigh, giving it a light squeeze as we pull off the highway. "How are you doing, baby girl?"

"I'm okay. Ready to be home again. I just need the house to sell quickly so I can stop thinking about it and have money again. I really would love to get the house all decorated for fall with it."

The headlights shine in the inky woods around us as I pull onto our road. "You don't need to worry about money. Whatever you want for the house, I'll get. Whatever you want in general, I am happy to provide."

Her head rolls along the headrest to look at me. "I'm not taking all your money. I like having my own."

"Fine, you can have your own, but you can and will also use mine. The guys and I do well for ourselves and we want to take care of you. Also, I might have a trust fund with some extra spending money."

Her eyes blink slowly, roving over my face. "I don't even want to know how much you guys have, I like that none of us live in excess."

I click the remote to open our front gate as I pull into our driveway. "Keep that in mind when you see what Josh ordered." Before she can ask about it, I pull into the garage and see the bags and boxes stacked up out here. Josh and Brian come out from the laundry room to pull Kelli out of the car and wrap her in hugs.

"What's all this?" She points at the piles of supplies.

Josh sheepishly looks at the ground. "Logan said you mentioned decorating for fall. I got some things we can put on the porches and mantle and whatever. Whatever you hate, we can return."

Kelli's eyes turn to saucers as she peeks through everything. Over her shoulder, I see blankets and pillows, pumpkins of all sizes, wreaths, bales of hay, even coffee mugs with pumpkins on them. Behind it all are a few barrels of beautiful mums. Kelli looks to Brian, already knowing that was him.

"I thought we could put them on the front steps," he says as he rubs the back of his neck with a small smile.

"Thank you. Thank you all, this is amazing." Her voice breaks as she takes us all in.

"We would do anything for you. Spending the weekend decorating our home together as a family is certainly no hardship." I pull her into a tight embrace, my lips meeting hers for a soft kiss.

Brian pulls her into him next, his kiss much deeper than mine. "Welcome home, baby."

EPILOGUE 1

JOSH

Four Months Later

My phone pings from the desk beside me with the video footage of Kelli driving through the front gate. She's been working at the hospital in town for just over three months now and she loves it. She works three ten hour shifts a week, which is a dream. Brian and I have hired more staff, so we never work more than forty hours a week anymore either. It has been a nice change for all of us. We have kind of been waiting for that honeymoon-phase feeling to end, but it hasn't, and I'm not sure it ever will. We all just enjoy each other's company too much.

Brian's physical therapy is going better than expected; he is already back to eighty-five percent mobility and they are hopeful it will continue improving. He spent thirty minutes yesterday chopping wood with no complaints of pain or issues. It's been a huge weight off of all of our shoulders. Kelli's house was also sold over asking price and her case has been closed for two months now. Everything has kind of been falling into place for us.

Brian and Kelli are both still seeing Krystal for therapy, and it has been amazing for them. Kelli hasn't had a nightmare in two months, and Brian has been lighter than he has been in years. He's been open and honest with all of us, and the guilt that he used to carry around is almost invisible . Laughter rings through our house daily now, and there are no unhappy tears from anyone. Brian has been groveling for months, even though Kelli forgave him immediately.

Preparing our home for Christmas might have been the most over the top I have seen him go. We currently have five trees spread throughout the house that we decorated together, thanks to his sucking up. I wanted to bitch about it, but Kelli's delighted squeals when we took her to the tree farm and he told her how many trees she could get were totally worth it. We all pretend like we run the house, but Kelli's the one who is really in charge.

I head out of the office to find Logan and Brian in the living room. "She's pulling in now. What should we surprise her with first?"

"I want to say the upstairs because it's the least exciting, but I'm not sure we can hide this one." Logan looks over at the puppy sprawled out on the floor.

"She's sleeping, so as long as she doesn't wake up, we can do the other surprises first."

Brian disagrees. "Nothing is going to top the dog, so might as well start with the smaller things."

Christmas is next week, but we did a few things early. Mostly because she is off of work next week and we needed her to be gone to work on one of the surprises, and the puppy was ready to be picked up so we are doing some celebrations early. The front door opens as Kelli strides in and we all rush to the entrance to greet her.

"Hey, baby girl, how was work today?" Logan wraps her in a hug.

"Long. I am so glad I have the next week off to be a bum with you guys." She puts her purse on the entry table and kicks off her winter boots. "I'm going to shower then we can make dinner."

"Actually, we have something we want to show you." I take her hand in mine, leading her up the staircase. Luckily, Brian and Logan have been wearing out the puppy all day so she stays asleep, sprawled out on her new bed. As we get to the top of the landing I pause and look at the guys. "I know Christmas isn't until next week, but we did a few small things early."

I head toward Logan and Brian's rooms first. Both of their doors are open, showing the new Alaskan king beds they have. Kelli stops in her tracks, looking from one room to the other before turning around. Her glassy eyes travel between ours. "You did this for me?"

Brian steps into her, wiping his thumb over her cheek to catch the rogue tear falling. "Yeah, baby, we did. All the rooms have these beds now, so you can be the center of a snuggle sandwich any night you want with no complaints of the beds being too small."

There may have been some complaints these last few months. We aren't small guys and spreading out with three or four people in a bed is not easy. I know our backs will thank us as much as Kelli will. Brian drops a chaste kiss to her lips before I lead her down toward my room. I have been slowly moving all of my computers and work equipment down to the office over the last few weeks to make space in my room. Kelli has been using the closet in her room for all of her clothes and things, but she never sleeps in there. She's been mentioning turning that room into solely a guest room since we have had family come visit more with the holidays.

Over the last three days while she was at work, Logan, Brian, and I have built a walk-in closet in my room where my office stuff used to be. We even moved all of her things over since we have Brian's parents coming to visit in a few days. As she steps into my room, her eyes go wide as she takes in the double doors along the side wall.

"What's this?" Her voice is quiet as she tentatively steps forward. Logan steps around her, opening the doors so she can see in. The outside of the drywall still needs to be painted, but the inside is done to perfection, complete with a small chandelier hanging in the center. Kelli steps in and spins to take in every inch of the space we crafted for her. "It's beautiful," she croaks, the tears spilling down her cheeks now. She turns and leaps into my arms as I bury my head in her neck. "Thank you," she whispers to me.

When I set her down, Logan grabs her hand. "That's not all, pretty girl. We have one more thing downstairs."

"I don't know if I can take any more surprises."

"You'll want this one, trust me," Brian says from in front of them, leading the group downstairs. "We know you said you aren't ready for babies yet, and that a dog is the logical next step. So, we got you a new addition to the family." We all stop in front of the empty dog bed in the center of the living room.

"Shit, we left her right here," Logan says scratching his stubble.

"It's a her? What's her name?" Kelli squeals looking around.

"She doesn't have one yet. We thought we would name her together." I start walking around the room trying to find her. She's a fluffy chocolate lab, she couldn't have gotten that far. We all start searching the house when a small yip comes from the kitchen. We rush in to find her pulling a bag of chips out from the pantry. Kelli rushes in, scooping her into her arms. The puppy lavishes her face in sloppy kisses as Kelli's laughter rings out.

"Nala. I think we should name her Nala." She brings her back to the living room with all of us in tow as we circle around her, giving her the pets and attention she demands.

"It's perfect," Logan declares as Nala climbs all over us on the couch.

"Thank you for her. For everything, this is the best Christmas ever." Kelli takes turns giving each of us a kiss.

"Christmas hasn't even started, baby, this is only the beginning." I wink at her, letting her see all the dirty promises in my eyes.

Brian leans over, putting his lips to her ear. "We got you the puppy, baby, you know what we want next." His hand trails down over her stomach, "We can practice anytime you want."

Logan strides over, throwing Kelli over his shoulder. "I think I'm going to start that practice right now."

EPILOGUE 2

KELLI

Eight Months Later

I pull up to the garage, pulling my car in. Logan had an addition put on, so now we have a massive four car garage. I didn't complain, I would never have to shovel my car out of the snow again. Not that I did it this last winter. One of the guys always had the driveway shoveled and my car warmed up by the time I needed to leave for work. Grabbing my bag from the back seat, I head into the house, dropping my bag and shoes in the mud room as Nala bombards me with kisses. At only ten months old, she is already a massive ball of energy and clumsy limbs. Last night was my first night away from all three of the guys and I could easily say I didn't love it.

Danny and Alex took a last-minute mini vacation to Bar Harbor and convinced me to join them for one night. The guys all had to work and couldn't go with me, but they encouraged me to go. I don't get to see Danny nearly enough anymore, so I took advantage of the best friend time. We did some hiking, drank too much wine, and he painted my nails like always. It was nice, despite being away from home.

Leaning forward, I give Nala the love she demands. "Where are your daddies, baby?" She rushes into the living room where I follow and promptly stop short.

Logan, Brian, and Josh are all standing in a row, dressed in full suits, smiling at me. The dog runs circles around their legs as I stand there stunned. "What's going on?" My voice sounds small in the large room.

Brian steps forward, taking my hand in his. "We have some things we want to show you." His lips land on my cheek before he leads me to the back door. Logan opens it, giving me a wink as I walk through. He and Josh follow close behind us as we walk down the patio and into the yard. The sun was just beginning to set, pinks and oranges streaking through the trees, lighting up the lake.

There, in front of us, in the center of the yard, is a small tree that wasn't there before. A willow tree. The tears are already falling down my cheeks as we walk to it. Brian stops right next to it, taking both my hands in his.

"You are my best friend, and the love of my life. Every day you push me to be a better man, and I will never stop trying to be the best for you. If there is one thing I have done right in this life, it's loving you. The guys helped me plant this willow for us all to have a safe place from the world. When things get too heavy or we need to talk, we will meet under the willow just like we used to. Our kids will grow up swinging from its branches, knowing they are surrounded by love. I love you so much, dove." His kiss is soft, lips pressing against mine before he steps back giving my hands to Josh.

Josh wipes at my tears before leading me further down to the water, stopping about halfway between the willow and the water's edge. He turns to me then, clasping my hands in his. "My little flame. You are the one thing I never saw coming in my life. I love everything about you, and every day, I fall more in love than the last. You have given me a peace I have never known and a family I have always wanted. There is nothing I wouldn't do for you. You tattooed your name on my heart, so I put it there permanently." He unbuttons the top of his shirt, pulling it to the side to show me his chest. My name is tattooed in a beautiful scrawl right over his heart. "I love you so much, Kelli." He kisses away the tears that won't stop falling before taking my lips in a searing kiss. Pulling back, he gives my hand to Logan who has the biggest smile I have ever seen.

Logan leads me down to the water where our chairs are set out. There are string lights glowing in the trees around us that weren't there before, with white rose petals covering the ground and in the center of it all, a heart made of red rose petals. He stops me in the center of the heart, taking my hands. Brian and Josh are on either side of him, while Nala is still running around, sniffing all the petals.

"My sweet Kelli girl. You stole my heart from the moment you came downstairs and demolished your breakfast burrito. Never did I think I would find a woman who would care for me in the ways that you do and that would love my found family the way that I do. I have had a missing piece all my life, and that piece is you. You complete me and are more than I could ever deserve. I am so in love with you."

The three of them lower to a knee as one, as the ugly sobs start wracking through my body.

"Kelli," Logan continues, grabbing my hand while pulling a little square box from his pocket. "We want to love you for the rest of our days."

"Will you marry us?" They say as one, as Logan pulls the

box open, showing the most beautiful round diamond surrounded by blue stones.

"Yes!" I manage to get out between sobs. Josh lunges forward, picking me up, and swinging me around in his arms.

"She said yes!" He yells out, planting kisses all down my face.

"We have to put the ring on, put her down," Brian laughs from behind us. I slide down Josh's body as Brian takes the ring from the box, slipping it onto my finger. "We wanted the stones to match your eyes," his voice soft, a quiet I hardly hear from him.

Wrapping my arms around him, I kiss him with every ounce of love I am feeling. "It's beautiful. I love it." He dips my hips, deepening the kiss. "I love you, B." I whisper against his lips. Logan snags me as we stand back up.

"Can I tell them now?" He asks, a smug look on his face as I nod. The guys have been asking for months if I think I will want kids soon. They all want a family and want to start as soon as I am ready. I wanted to get settled into my job and have some time with just them first, but I'm ready now.

"I told them I didn't need the grand gesture because I had something up my sleeve," he winks before turning to the guys. "Kelli took her IUD out last week. And she's ovulating."

Josh and Brian's mouths drop open, a tear dropping down Brian's cheek. "You're ready?" I nod again, not trusting my voice at this point.

"Rock, paper, scissors to see who gets to fuck her first?" Logan asks with a serious face.

Before anyone can respond, Josh picks me up, throwing me over his shoulder and heads for the house. He looks back at Brian and Logan. "You guys coming?"

They race after him, getting us back into the house and

into Logan's room as quickly as possible. Josh lays me on the bed before stepping back to pull his suit jacket off. "Undress her."

Logan sits me up, pulling my shirt over my head as Brian starts undoing my jeans. After Logan gets my bra unclipped and pulled off, he leans me back down so Brian can undress me the rest of the way. I lay there splayed out, completely naked for them, as they stand around me in their suits just drinking their fill. If this isn't every woman's fantasy, I don't know what is.

Josh is the first to speak, putting his fist out in front of him. I can't help but laugh as the others follow suit and they count out rock, paper, scissors, shoot. Logan and Brian both pick paper, Josh choosing scissors.

"That's not fair, best two out of three," Logan whines.

Josh is stripping the rest of the way before there are any more protests. "Turn around and get on your knees, love." I do immediately, putting my ass in the air for him. His hand comes down in a hard smack before rubbing the sting. That hand smooths up my back before pushing my shoulders down to rest on the bed.

He moves back enjoying the view of my ass up in the air, pussy in full view for all of them as they stand at the end of the bed. "Get her ready for me." Brian is there in an instant, burying his face in my pussy. He licks me from clit to ass and back before he starts fucking me with his tongue. He works me until I am dripping down my thighs, my hands gripping the sheets.

"She's ready," He proclaims proudly, mouth glistening with my juices.

Josh kneels on the bed behind me, lining himself up. He sinks into me groaning out in pleasure, "I love the feel of your pussy squeezing me." He grips my hips tight, rutting into me with passion. "Fuck, I'm not going to last long, just thinking about getting you pregnant is going to make me come."

I whimper, loving the thought of that as my pussy gushes around him, making him groan out again. "Logan, get up here." Josh grabs a fistful of my hair and pulls slightly so I follow him up until I'm on my hands and knees.

Logan climbs up on the bed next to me, his proud length bobbing in my face. "Suck him deep baby. Get him ready to take you next." My mouth opens, eager to take him. He paints my lips with his precum before feeding me his length. I moan around his dick, loving pleasing my men. Logan and Josh follow the same rhythm, fucking my face and pussy in tandem. Brian climbs on the other side, his hands roaming over my body, toying with my nipples.

Overwhelmed by the sensations of it all, heat travels down my spine, my orgasm imminent. I pull off Logan's dick, "Yes, Josh," I cry out as I shatter around him. My body is in complete euphoria, as Josh's hips falter and he spills his cum into me in hot ropes. He stays in me, hands rubbing up and down my back before slowly pulling out. I can feel his cum start to drip down my thigh before he uses a finger to wipe it up and push it back into my pussy. Fuck, I've read about that in books, but it's even hotter in person.

"You ready for Logan, baby?" He asks, voice soft like he's in awe.

"Yes, please."

They swap positions as Logan lines himself up behind me, sliding in in one smooth movement. His hips immediately set a ruthless pace. "Seeing that ring on your finger is making me feral," he growls out at me.

Josh grabs my hair, angling my face to Brian. "You want his fat cock in your mouth?" I nod my head before leaning forward to lick the drop of precum from his slit. Josh pushes my head onto Brian's dick, controlling the rhythm and depth. He knows I love to choke on Brian's cock until I have tears streaming down my face.

Logan eases one hand around me to rub circles on my nub. "I need to feel you come on my cock before I come. Come for me, Kelli girl." His unrelenting hips pound into me as he rubs faster.

With Brian's dick down my throat, I come again, my pussy trembling around Logan's cock, my toes curling at the earth-shattering feelings. He pumps his hips a few more times before yelling out my name, coating my pussy in his seed. As he pulls out, my body falls to the bed feeling utterly spent. Fingers and hands run through my hair and down my body.

Brian gently rolls me over, planting a sweet kiss on my lips. "One more, pretty girl, you can take it." He gently lifts my legs, and pushes his hard cock into me. With all the cum in me, it glides in easily. Josh and Logan kneel on either side of my chest, both hard again already.

Brian looks me in the eyes, his warm brown ones meeting mine. I know I must look utterly wrecked by this point, but he still looks at me like I am the most beautiful thing he has ever seen. He keeps his pace even and slow, reaching up to hold my hand at my side. He's making love to me in every sense of the word. His eyes turn glassy as he uses his other hand to slowly rub circles on my clit.

Josh and Logan stroke themselves on either side of me. "Always such a good girl for us, Kelli. Letting us fill you with our cum. We can't wait to see your belly swollen with our children," Josh's gravelly voice grits out.

"We love you so fucking much. Can't wait to call you our wife," Brian's voice is thick. They all look down at me with so much love, it sets me off for a third and final time, the longest of my orgasms. My body trembles as Brain fucks me through it, then follows me over the cliff calling my name as his dick swells and soaks my pussy with his spend. Josh and Logan are right behind, spilling themselves a second time onto my chest in hot ropes of cum.

This is where I was always meant to be. Surrounded by my men, loved, and safe with them.

ACKNOWLEDGMENTS

Holy cow, I did it! My debut novel is in your hands, and I can't thank you enough for taking the time to read it. I have so many people to thank, but I am going to selfishly start with myself. Stepping outside of my comfort zone has never been an easy thing. Taking this leap of faith and pursuing this wild dream is not something I thought I would have the guts to do, but I am so damn proud of myself for doing it anyway. Take the leap, friends.

To my girls, Jausta, Maggie, Arianne and Sara, THANK YOU for reading through my drafts, giving me feedback and encouragement, and for believing in me and pushing me. You are my book tribe that I am so grateful for. This one is for you, ladies.

To my husband and daughter, thank you for giving me the time and support to do this. Mr. Lane, you are the greatest man and your belief in me is all I could have dreamed of. My baby B, the number of times you have cheered me on and celebrated me without really knowing what you were celebrating has given me so much joy and encouragement. I love you both so much.

Bri, my developmental editor, thank you for the honesty and encouragement. Thank you for taking my neuroticism in stride and hopping on a call and going a little off script for me when I am dying for more feedback. You have helped take this book from bare bones to a story unfolding. Thank you!

Sara, my editor, thank you for catching the 3,000 commas

that I missed. While that's kind of an exaggeration, it's also not at all. Your fixes and edits were so needed. You're the best!

To my ARC readers, you are the real MVPs. As an indie author self-publishing her debut novel, I have been in way over my head. Your support and reviews make such a substantial difference for me and I can't thank you all enough!

This is just the beginning; the best is yet to come.

Wanderland Series: Coming Next!
First up, Thoren and Lily in Wandering Closer

ABOUT THE AUTHOR

Etta Lane is a married mother who loves to read spicy romance as much as she loves to write it. She loves the outdoors, adventures, and game nights with friends. When she isn't reading or writing, you can find her spending time with her family or Facetiming her sister.

CONNECT WITH ETTA

Instagram: @ettalane.author
Facebook: Etta Lane
Facebook Reader Group: Etta Lane's Reader Group
Email: ettalanewrites@gmail.com

* 9 7 9 8 9 9 1 3 8 9 5 1 8 *